THE GALLOWAY COLLECTION

Volume 8

THE DARK O' THE MOON

By S.R.CROCKETT

Edited by Cally Phillips

Ayton

Republishing the past

First Published by MacMillan in 1902.

This edition © Ayton Publishing Ltd 2014.

This book is available in both digital and print formats:
ISBN: Print edition 978-1-908933-11-9
ISBN: Kindle edition 978-1-908933-50-8
ISBN: epub edition 978-1-908933-51-5

INTRODUCTION

Mr Crockett has found again in this sequel to 'The Raiders' the inspiration which grey Galloway gives him with its hills and woods and floods. His descriptions of sky and landscape are always in harmony with the action of the story.

This sequel to 'The Raiders,' first published some eight years after the original, moves the story on a generation. Maxwell, or to give him his full title John Faa Maxwell Heron, is the son of Patrick Heron and May Maxwell, whose relationship is told in 'The Raiders.' It stretches the imagination that Maxwell has grown up in quite the time frame allowed between the two narratives but this is not important. You will boggle your brain if you try to apply accurate time frames to either the stories of Patrick and Maxwell Heron or indeed Marion Tamson and Silver Sand. The reader does best to suspend disbelief, and accept that in Crockett's fiction we are reading historical adventure romance, not straight history.

We can safely assume, however, that the main action is set in the year 1724 since the story focuses round the Levellers Rebellion which took place in that year.

Maxwell inherits both his father's unheroic nature and his need for adventure. At the opening of the novel he is captured by the smuggler gypsy Hector Faa who is intent on marrying Maxwell to his daughter Joyce. It seems that this is an act of personal revenge for Patrick marrying May. Though he loves Joyce, Maxwell refuses to marry her on demand and from this action the narrative springs. After four 'introductory' chapters the narrative voice shifts and Maxwell tells his own story, in a tone familiar to his father's in 'The Raiders,' and favoured by Crockett in many of his works.

Whereas in 'The Raiders' the adventure part of the story centres around free-trading, the core of this adventure is the Levellers Revolt. The historical event is fictionalised bringing in several characters we are already familiar with from 'The Raiders.' Marion (Sammle Tamson's daughter who was abducted in 'The Raiders') has grown up to be quite a woman. In disguise as 'Dick of the Isles' she leads the Levellers until there is conflict with Harry Polwart (one of Hector Faa's gypsy men). The woman in disguise (as Shakespeare frequently showed) offers a rich vein for adventure and social commentary. And of course for love. In this story, Marion falls in love with the King's man Austin Tredennis which adds further complexity to the fast moving plot.

While you have to keep your wits about you to keep up with the disguises and movement throughout 'The Dark o' the Moon,' it is in no way hard going. Indeed Crockett frequently plays with a light ironic tone. When her disguise is revealed Marion says, *'I am as ready as any to die but oh! I hate to be laughed at.'*

There is also humour as Eppie Tamson deals with the Levellers. Crockett revels in showing his strong but ordinary female characters standing up against both state and rebels. Throughout, most great characters are subject to irony. We might remember the disdain with which the Hanoverian dynasty is held in 'The Raiders'. In 'The Dark o'the Moon' nothing has changed. The Hanoverian Princes are seen as little more than rogues and philanderers. It is dealt with humorously but there is substance underneath as Crockett suggests: *'that was happening in the Lowlands which happened a quarter of a century later in the Highlands'* – the Clearances. This is particularly interesting because the Galloway Levellers have been largely overlooked in Scottish History. Rising under the banner *'A free land and a free folk,'* the Galloway Levellers discover that real freedom is harder to achieve in their everyday lives. Squabbling between factions seems to be the order of the day, whether that be against the oppressors (the Hanoverians) or between the locals (especially the gypsy factions). One thing is certain, everyone has to take their fair share of lampooning in this novel. *'The highly descended Fitzgeorge has certainly caught the*

4

Hanoverian manner of speech, and was possessed of about the average quantity of Georgian brains,' provides one of many examples.

Crockett has little time for those in power who abuse it, and his stories frequently illustrate how the ordinary people become caught up in the middle of such actions and affected by them, usually to their detriment. By doing so he seeks to remind us that history affects everyone, it is not just a thing of nations and monarchs, it is an everyday reality for the ordinary people too. They just have little power to control the history that goes on around them. This is perhaps one reason Crockett adopts his own particular style of appropriating big historical events and placing them firmly into the stories of fictional ordinary people.

In the 'Dark o' the Moon,' the character of Silver Sand is once more central to the action and it is a welcome return. Maxwell finds him hard to fathom, and is not sure whether he can trust the old man. To him (and sometimes us) Silver Sand seems to stand on both sides of the argument at once, but finally he is part of the resolution. His views of honour and justice are contrasted with the slackness and pragmatism of the Hanoverian monarchy.

Crockett takes other characters both historical and fictional and introduces them to the story to good effect. The minister of Balmaghie, John MacMillan (fictionalised by Crockett in 'The Standard Bearer') makes a significant appearance. He intervenes when the gypsy Harry and Joyce are due to marry and Maxwell begs for a delay. In the character of Harry Polwart, Crockett creates a new version of 'Blind Harry', but this one is no poet of the people. Perhaps in ironic parallel to the Hanoverian dynasty, the Faa dynasty are central to the story and Hector Faa is finally brought to acknowledge Silver Sand as the leader of the Gypsies. It is not an unexpected plot twist when it transpires that Hector's daughter Joyce is not what she seems either. But this is no weakness of construction. The twists and turns of the plot are all carefully woven together and humour is at the

5

core, especially the 'war' of the sexes and the reversal of roles.

This story presents as a gloved hand but there is an iron fist inside it. The reader can choose to simply go with the light romance adventure, or explore the deeper socio-political comments contained therein. For the modern reader it is an interesting book not least because one can see a nineteenth century perspective on eighteenth century events.

If you read a number of Crockett's novels, as I hope you will, what is especially enjoyable is the way that the characters flow and move around from one story to another. And it is fascinating to have the ability to view a specific place; remaining a kind of constant, through the historical periods Crockett visits; from the medieval through to the nineteenth century. Crockett offers the reader the chance to explore five hundred years of life (and history) in a barely known part of rural Scotland. If you know Galloway it is like a love story to the land, which you will appreciate. And if you don't know Galloway it might well make you fall in love with the land, its people and its history.

Cally Phillips
(editor, The Galloway Collection.)

CHAPTER ONE
THE SHIEL OF THE DUNGEON

At the Shiel of the Dungeon of Buchan—a strange place half natural cavern, the rest a rickle of rude masonry plastered like a swallow's nest on the face of the cliff among the wildest of southern hills—this story begins. The Shiel of the Dungeon was indeed a fitting dwelling-place for Hector Faa and his folk.

Ever since the first days of the Great Riding and the death of so many of that wild confederacy in the Pit of Sheep beneath Craignaimy, the Faas and other malefactors had been scattered north, east, and south. And now of them all only the chief, Hector, remained, daily risking death to abide among his native fastnesses, where, save for a few faithful tatterdemalions, he dwelt lonely as Cain in the Land of Nod, in the days ere yet he gat him a wife.

Thither we must go that we may begin to tell the strange history of these latter days, as strange and memorable as any that went before—the sad yet laughable rebellion of our poor cotter folk, which, few outside the bounds of Galloway have even heard of; the freaks of Freetraders in the Solway passage, the deeds of outlaw Hector and his kin among the cave dwellings of the Dungeon of Buchan, together with the marvellous end made by my father's friend, commonly called Silver Sand, but of right and title 'Lord and Earl of Little Egypt,' and King of all the wild folk called Gypsies in this realm of Scotland.

There was a lass looking out of the four-square aperture which served the Shiel of the Dungeon for a window. In bad weather this was closed with a painted board, and in times of danger a green bough or a sod from the hill-side screened it. But now it stood open, and, as the light of the evening sun slanted along the precipice front, the head of a young girl was set in it as a picture is set in a dark frame.

It was the face of Joyce Faa, watching from her rock fortress for her father's return—the eaglet spying for the eagle's homecoming with the lamb in his talons. This is the picture of the outlaw's daughter as she looked in the gloaming of that summer day, framed in yonder little square of blackness high up on the 'gairy' side.

Hair raven-black, but light as hill-mist, swept back from a broad, low brow. Her face, full oval, yet clearly cut, eyes a wonder of blackness, with sparks of passionate fire shifting and passing in them, angers, defiances, relentings, passionate April weepings, all to be dried up in the quick sunshine of her smile.

So at least the matter is reported. The writer of this chronicle cannot compass this vein continuously, being now somewhat too old and having also a kindly consideration for the good-will of his reader. But in so far as it describes Joyce Faa, the outlaw's maid, it is doubtless accurate enough, being the words of a young man in love, set down upon paper many years ago when these things happened. For love, being the great revealer, no woman should be described save by the man who loves her.

Joyce Faa sat, therefore, by the window, the house-place all a-dusk behind her, the smoky walls flickering with the little leaping flames from the hearth, where an old woman crouched, chunnering to herself and feeding the fire with rosin knots and roots of heather. Before the girl's eyes the sunset ran from slaty gray overhead to smoky orange, where it lingered along the purpling hill ledges westward beyond Loch Moan.

But a voice broke harshly upon the girl's reverie.

'On the Rig o' the Jarkness three times the tod has cried!' it said. 'Ha, ha! Hark to Auld Hoodie up amang the clints o' the Dungeon. Ken ye what he says, lass? 'Bluid! bluid! bluid!' What else should Hoodie Craw say when he dichts his neb on a lamb's innocent briest bane, an' looks ayont the hills for mair and better?'

'Hush, Meggat, hush!' cried the girl, shuddering and shrugging one round shoulder petulantly. 'Peace to your croakings! 'Tis worse than all the hoodie craws that ever were nested betwixt Buchan's

Dungeon and Ben Gairn! Do not trouble me. I am watching for my father, do you hear?'

The withered and many-wrinkled crone emitted a strange chuckling laugh, not a whit like honest human mirth, but rather resembling the rumblings of water prisoned in caverns underground.

'Your faither. Ay, ay—ye watch for your faither?' such was the burden of her muttering and mumbling. 'Faither,' quo' she. 'Nae faither hae ye, my bonnie, this side o' the Black Flood that shall ae day rise ice-cauld aboot ye frae feet to chin. Faither, indeed Neither Hector Faa, nor ony Faa that ever was born to streek hangman's tow ere begat the like o' you, my dearie. And auld wicked Meggat shall see ye richtit yet, ere the corbies pyke her banes. (Little will they get for their pains—an it werena marrowless auld shanks and saddle-leather!)'

A fit of coughing shook the crone as the smoke of the green wood curling down from the low roof tickled her throat. The girl moved hastily as if the sound somehow annoyed her.

'Meggat' she cried, with a peevish impatience, 'I wish you would be quiet! I cannot hear my father's signal for your din.'

Then quickly, even as she spoke, she lifted up her hand, and a change came into her voice.

'There—I hear them—they are coming,' she cried, and slipping down from the window-seat, she ran and opened the low door of the Shieling, to which (on the outward side) heather and bog-myrtle had been nailed in sweet-scented sheaves to hide the outlaw's retreat.

With a well-accustomed bend of her graceful head beneath the lintel, the girl found herself without. She stood on a path perilous. Immediately below was the wide gulf of space, sinking away so sharply as to turn a stranger giddy; but Joyce Faa straightened herself and stood erect, with the grace and strength of a young birk-tree rooted in the clefts of the rock. She was, indeed, no stranger here. For three years she had stood and watched at this spot every night at this hour of sunset. Down the long valley of the three

9

lochs she looked, and as she leaned eagerly forward the dark masses of her hair broke tempestuously from the single strand of ribbon that confined them, and fell over her shoulders, outlining them smoothly and largely as water does a rock in the linn.

Behind her, almost from her heels, fell away the great cauldron of the Dungeon of Buchan, wherein white ground-mists crawled and swelled, now hiding from sight and now revealing the three lakelets, the Round Inch, the Long Loch, and the Dry. There were also in the Dungeon gulf tonight certain eery cloud-swirls, that seemed to bubble and circle upward like the boiling of a pot. Yet all was still and silent at the Shiel, so that the faint streak of wood smoke from old Meggat's fire on the hearth rose straight up the cliff front, and was lost among the heather and rigged brushwood above. Down in the caldron itself, however, there was a veering, unequal wind, or, rather, strife of winds, teasing the mist into wisps white as lambs' wool and light as blown gossamer.

'Ay, ye are richt, they are coming,' said old Meggat Faa, who now came to the door and leaned out, a strange huddle of patched cloaks and ancient rags. For Meggat's clothes ever hung about her like hiplocks about a sheep's hurdies before shearing time.

'Would to God that they would bring back nothing that does not belong to them!' said the girl, wistfully. 'Meggat, I am sick of this thieving, underhand work. Why can we not set out our rigs of potatoes, and plant our bear and oats on the sunny holms of the Dee like other folk?'

'Hear till her,' croaked the old woman, lifting up her hands as to ancient Eastern gods of thieves and reivers; 'certes, lass, ye are nae richt Faa ava. Whatna gypsy o' the richt stock ever wished the like. And there is nae talk o' thievery in the matter. 'Tis but the payment of lawfu' skaith-mail. Wha dare meddle wi' honest John Macmillan o' the Bongill or auld Raif Wabster at Craigencallie sae lang as they pay Hector Faa his just and honourable dues?'

'It is taking what is not our own to take,

whatever you may say,' said the girl, scornfully, pulling out a sprig of white heather by the root; 'all the words in the world will not alter that!'

'And what for should it?' cried Meggat, with sudden heat, striking her palms angrily together. 'What signifies a bit sheep at an orra time aff the hills? Or a side o' beef in the Martinmas brine-tub? God feeds the ravens and gies the young lions their prey, says the Guid Buik. Surely He owes as muckle to us that dwell in thae uncanny clefts o' the rocks. And do thae gutsy farmer bodies doon in the straths owe us ony less? Meat to oor bellies, cleading to oor backs, they may weel pay for the priviledge o' wakenin' in their naked beds wi' hale banes and an unslitten hals.

To this diatribe the girl seemed to pay but little heed, her eyes, grown great and vague, being bent towards a certain point in the gloom beneath. The old woman went on:

'Guid richt, indeed!' she cried, fiercely; 'let them that drave us like wolves to the mountain-taps keep us when we are there. Them that dwell beneath the gled's nest maun pay the gled's cess! Forbye, when a' is said and dune. Hector Faa does his traffic mair up by Carrick and Colmonel than wi' his ain kindly country o' Gallawa'. And what the waur is ony fleabitten Ayrshireman's coo o' a bit lossin', I wad like to ken?'

CHAPTER TWO
HECTOR FAA'S CURSE

'Fetch the loon this road, Mort! Hark ye, man, be some deal mair tender wi' him, or Hector Faa will thraw your neck like a scraichin' chuckie's. There— lay him on the daice (dais). Fairly and saftly, Mort Faa— hear ye me? The laddie is no a barn-door ye are dingin' doon to win at a miser's gimel!'

'Ay, ay, Meggat, we hear ye weel enench. Ye needna scraich there like a swine at the pig-killin',' returned the shorter and stouter of the two men. They were carrying a young man between them.

'Gin ye had wrestled a' the nicht till the sun-risin' to keep hand o' this laddie, as ye caa' him, and gotten your hams nearly dung oot by his wastrel o' a companion, and tired their beasts wi' bringin' him up thae weary glens, ye wadna be sae nice wi' ony low-country calf!'

While the two men were placing their prisoner on the couch of heather and brushwood in the corner, and, in obedience to Meggat's shrill commands, withdrawing sullenly to their own wattled abodes on the hill-side, Joyce was walking homeward with her hand on her father's arm. Hector Faa loomed up tall against the gray shining of the mist, and answered shortly as the girl plied him with questions.

'What ails ye, faither?' she said, turning easily to the country speech, which far-wandering gypsies of good blood do not often use. 'What ails ye, that your answers are so few and short to the bairn that has waited for you hour after hour wi' a dim e'e and a beating heart?'

'Hush thee, Joyce' said Hector Faa, patting her hand not unkindly; 'I have muckle on my mind this nicht. Your faither's life hangs now by a single thread, and, I fear me, that thread is o' the hemp! But what matter? It would only be the last singing of an old song.'

The girl gave a little stricken cry and then was silent, waiting, as a nestling with eyes aloft may see and yet be unable to avoid the pounce of the kite.

'What is it now, faither?' she said, and her voice was low and the words seemed to choke in her throat. 'Ye surely havena slain a man to his hurt—there is no blood on your hands, faither? Tell me—tell your ain Joyce.'

'And what if there were?' answered Hector Faa, scornfully. 'What were one more or less to the daughter of the outlaw?'

'Faither,' said the girl, earnestly, 'tell me truly. I know that you have slain your enemies at the cave of Isle Rathan and elsewhere, but that was in fair fighting. Oh, faither, tell me that this day you have done no murder!'

And she clasped him about the neck so tightly that, being near the verge of the precipice on the narrows of the path up to the Shiel, he had perforce to clutch at the rock in order to sustain them both.

'Joyce Faa,' he said, 'hearken to me. I have slain no man to his hurt, though God knows I have had provocation enough. Will not the baited bull turn and gore his tormentors? Will not the hunted quarry be allowed to stand at bay? I have shed no blood today unjustly. Joyce, I have only executed justice for two ancient wrongs. I have paid a score in full that has long been on the slate. A proud, scorning woman, a boastful vaporer, a false friend, and a fine landed gentleman—these are bitter at the heart this night! Ay, and they shall yet sup sorrow with a deep ladle, or Hector Faa be done with them! Ah, Mary Maxwell— Beauty May, that refused to share the gypsy's heather bed, you shall rest somewhat less easily on down and feathers this night, for the thought of that which I have reft from you! And you, my laird of Isle Rathan.'

'What of him—what of Mr. Patrick Heron?' cried the girl, breaking in upon him; 'you have not harmed him, surely! Is he not a friend of Silver Sand's—of my uncle's?'

Hector Faa laughed a short, defiant laugh.

'Maybe,' he said, bitterly. 'John Faa's friends are mostly the enemies of his own kin. What good hath Silver Sand ever done to the Faas? He has taken our groats and silver pennies, indeed—and for what?

Plainly, for naught—for less than naught! That he might betray us, Joyce—that he might exile and outlaw us, while he lies soft on a lord's linen, and dines off plate of silver in the company of the King's Justicer that condemns us to the halter!'

'But did he not warn you on the night of Craignaimy, father?'

'Warn us—truth, that did he sickerly!' cried the man, with bitterest scorn on his face; 'but to what purpose, save to make our poor lives more outcast than before? But I, his brother, who alone of the Gitano have been faithful to the laws of Egypt—I, that am neither renegade nor favoursomer, have this night evened matters rarely—ay, with my ancient enemies and with mine own fause kin!'

He stopped and laughed aloud, as he saw the Shiel of the Dungeon before him.

'Master John Faa Maxwell Heron! Indeed, a bonny name! The lion and the lamb lie down together—'

'What do you mean, father?' said the girl, wonderingly.

Hector Faa turned about and pointed to where a faint streak of light marked the heather door of the Shiel. 'Get in there, and you will learn,' he said, sternly.

Then after his daughter had left him alone the outlaw turned to the south and stretched out his right hand in one of those gestures of defiance such as in these days, only the wild folk of the hill use.

'A black curse on Rathan—the curse of Deva on the Isle of Rathan! The scorns and the shaming of a woman —the hatred of a man! These shall return tenfold upon hall and acre, upon hearth-stone and roof-tree! A thousand times have I cursed Patrick Heron and his wife—in winter and summer, in bed, board, and estate! In bride-time and bairn-time, in flock and herd have I cursed them! May the day dawn, and that right early, when there shall not be a reeking chimney on their broad lands, and when of their great house of Rathan there remains not so much as one stone upon another—because of the

14

dead that are as coral in the Cave of Blood this day, and the evil despite they and theirs have done the seed of Egypt!'

When at her father's bidding Joyce Faa entered the little square living-room of the Shiel she found it brightly lighted by a fire of green birk twigs which Meggat had bidden Mort Faa and Grice Baillie to bring her from an adjoining cave, where a stock of these things was kept. The old woman was bending over a young lad, as it seemed to her, scantly on the border of manhood. 'Pale and slender, and with fair curls clustering round a broad forehead' —that is the description of him as he appeared at that time. As in a former case, it is communicated to the writer by an interested person for the purposes of this chronicle.

'A bonny lad! certes, a bonny lad,' murmured the crone, her palsied head nodding and jerking at every word. 'Joyce, come ye here, lass, and help me to lay him better at his ease than thae muckle cowts left him, that kenned nae better than to throw him doon wi' a clash on the floor like a bag; o' saut!'

The young man had not yet opened his eyes. The excitements of his capture, the weary journey, jolting on a wretched saddle up perilous hill-tracks, the unkindly and awkward handling of rude captors, had so told on the wounded youth, that for several hours he had been in the hands of Mort and his associates even as the bag of salt to which Meggat compared him. And without doubt these rough catherans were glad enough to be rid of their burden, and slink off to their roast of spareribs and their cups of smuggled brandy.

Sleeping accommodations were scant at the best in the Shiel of the Dungeon, but within Hector Faa had arranged a number of cubicles, screened off from one another by hanging curtains of coarse stuff. Joyce came and stood a moment silent over the youth as he lay on the heather roots spread upon a broad bench of beaten earth. She had never seen (so she owned to herself) any one so delicately featured, and in a moment more she had raised the young man in her strong arms. A surprising feeling of motherhood

15

stirred in her heart, some strange grace of natural pity warring with the inherited hatreds she had learned from her father.

With one hand she swept the middle curtain aside, and, entering a small recess where the rough rocky walls were half concealed by hangings and pitiful little attempts at ornament—rough slabs of colored stone from the hills and scraps of carpet and hangings, she laid him down on her own bed.

As she did so Joyce discovered a slow ooze of dark blood among the lad's curls, and, bidding Meggat hold aloft the rosin faggot, she examined the wound with a light hand and practised eye.

'Who has done this?' she cried. 'Surely they need not so have mishandled a laddie—one that is little more than a bairn!'

And at the words, as if he resented the imputation of childhood the young man opened his eyes. He looked in bewilderment at the girl who stood bending over him. Then his eyes fell with more comprehension on the wild, decrepit figure of old Meggat, as she stood at the bedfoot holding aloft the torch.

'Who are you, laddie?'

The words came from Joyce Faa's lips almost without any will of her own, and with a shrewd, bright smile (his mother's, so they say) the young man answered, 'The child's name is John.'

Poor Joyce had had small opportunity of becoming familiar with the letter of Scripture. She took the information seriously, and continued, 'You do not wish us to know your other name?'

'I will tell you gladly, if you will help me to sit up and inform me where I am!'

'You are in the Shiel of the Dungeon,' said the girl, 'and I am—'

'Hush!' said the old woman, sharply. 'There are names and places which are none the better of being bandied about in the hearing of every chance-comer!'

'I fear me, good lady,' said the youth, 'that I am no chance-comer. Well do I know who brought me here, and for what purpose. Not by chance is my sconce ringing as if a million bees had hived in it. You are, I take it. Hector Faa's daughter, and I can bear witness that your father is rightly named 'Hector of the Strong Arm'!'

The girl turned and muttered something in a low tone to the old woman. Then, as the youth strove to raise himself on his elbow, she took him by the shoulders and laid him softly back again upon the pillow.

'Rest ye there, young lad,' she said. 'We will first foment and cleanse the wound, and then we will talk concerning names, places, and such like, an you will.'

'A prisoner may not make conditions—especially with so fair a jailer!' smiled the youth, (Where thus early he got the assurance I know not.)

Then the girl, finding an obstruction in the way of her surgical operations, with the most natural grace in the world set her hand to the edge of her kirtle, and, bending down, drew a knife from a sheath held in place by her garter. This she applied with the most matter-of-fact air to the back of the youth's stock, to which his long, fair curls had become matted. Lightly and deftly she did her work, the knife, an exceedingly workmanlike weapon, flashing to and fro before the eyes of the young man as he lay watching her with a soft, amused smile on his face.

Joyce Faa was thus engaged when the door of the Shiel opened, and Hector Faa stood on the threshold. He paused in a kind of amazed wonder at what he saw. Then he stepped into his house with a grim air.

'Well, Master John Faa Maxwell Heron,' he said, addressing his prisoner, 'you are being better done to here, in the wolf's lair, than I was when your father and kin hunted me in the days of the Great Killing, when I lay, perforce, in dens and caves of the earth, and for provend gnawed my own wrist-bones!'

'I thank you,' said the youth thus addressed; 'I am indeed being tended far above my deserts. And, sir, since you have brought me so far without any will of mine, perhaps you will indulge me with this young lady's name, that I may thank her for her kindness to a wounded man and a prisoner.'

'Joyce Faa is my daughter,' said Hector Faa; and, as if to stop any further catechism, he added, sharply: 'Joyce, stand aside! You have done enough! The young man and I will now have some conference.'

The girl turned about with the knife still in her hand, and for the least part of a moment young Maxwell Heron saw the dark blood mantle her cheek, and a certain look of kinship to the outlaw glitter from her eye like a knife thrust. Then, all sudden, the softer light came back into her eyes. She let the knife drop upon the table, and with a blush she moved away to the fireside without speaking. There she began to busy herself with the earthen pipkins on the embers. The youth continued to watch the girl languidly, in spite of the formidable presence of Hector Faa, who did not at once begin to speak.

Suddenly the young man called out: 'Well done! I could not have managed that!'

For with a large, easy movement, simple and natural as breathing, the girl had unhooked the great pot which bubbled and boiled over the fire, and hung it three or four links higher up.

The action naturally attracted no notice in the Shiel of the Dungeon. Hector barely turned his eyes in his daughter's direction, while the girl herself sat down on a stool and gazed pensively into the fire.

'Now, young man,' said Hector, grimly, 'you and I will begin to cast up our accounts!'

'I am not aware that there have been any intromissions between us,' said Maxwell Heron, dryly; 'I never set eyes on you before today.'

The gypsy outlaw showed his teeth in a very ugly grin.

'I have heard say,' he went on, letting the words drip slowly from him, 'that it is the way of the God you Christians worship to visit the iniquities of the fathers upon the children unto the third and fourth generation. Well, I am going to let a godly second generation know how the arrangement feels when it is called on to pay for the sins of the first!'

CHAPTER THREE
JOYCE FAA

Prisoner and captor faced each other silently in the Shiel of the Dungeon. Hector Faa loomed up strong and dark by the hearth, the firelight playing on his dark beard and flecked hair. One hand gripped a knife in his girdle—not the honest smuggler's 'jockteleg' but the Spanish navajo, brought from Albacete by some far-travelled Romany. The youth, on the other hand, lay on the bed in the alcove, the curtain drawn partially aside. He raised himself a little on his elbow. He had always been delicate since his birth, and in some things his ways were not the ways of those about him, as during all his life he had found out to his cost. Doubtless the gypsy held the opinion that young Maxwell Heron would be easily frightened.

But cowardice is not a Heron vice, though mayhap they have other and bigger ones.

'There will be a hard man brought low, a proud woman on her knees this night in the House of Rathan!' said the outlaw. The young man moved slightly on his pillow, and a smile flickered faintly about his mouth. This seemed somehow to irritate his captor.

'Ay, smile!' he said, with sudden black fury; 'but let me tell you your mirth is strangely ill-timed, as I shall show you! You are in the hands of your house's sworn enemy—of Hector Faa, who dwells at the Dungeon Shiel! What find ye matter of mirth in that?'

The young man did not reply. He had been thinking that he could have made a better guess at the occupation of his father and mother on that the first night of the son's trepanning. He knew that his father would be busy planning and organizing a campaign, and his mother out on her beast, riding fast from house to house to raise the country upon the reivers' trail.

Hector Faa, however, took the youth's easy manners as a kind of personal defiance and it was with a still a sullen glitter of his sombre eye that he continued. 'Thirty of the Calore, the best blood of the Romany—these have I seen shot down one by one by the men of your house in the Cave of Death. And among these hills thirty womenfolk waited for them in vain, even as tonight the woman who bore you runs to the door and back again crying, 'He will not come!'

'Do you mean to kill me?' said Maxwell Heron, in a quiet manner—the way of a child that knows no reason be afraid.

'Kill you!' cried Hector Faa; 'that were over eager an exit! Somewhat slower shall be the gypsy's revenge! First we will drain your father's money-bags. He shall pay for your body—ear by ear, tooth by too finger by finger. He shall sell his land to raise ransom. For your sake he shall die landless—fiefless; stripped even as the gypsy outlaw of the hill stripped!'

'There is a proverb,' said Maxwell Heron, called 'Mickle land—little wit!' If you strip me of my land perhaps in time I shall get some wit—which, indeed my mother says I greatly lack.'

It was now the gypsy's turn to be disconcerted by the youth's assured calm.

'Have you no fear to be where you are? Has no father told you—have ye never heard tell of the House of Craignaimy, of the Murder Hole in Lochricken, of the Brig, over the Black Water, where the outlaws broke their way through, and sent your coward kin whirling down to the Airds pool?'

'I have heard of these things,' said the young man; 'but I never yet heard either a Heron or a Maxwell called a coward kin."

'Well, you hear it now,' said Hector Faa. 'Was it not a coward act to outlaw the man they could not fight— to set the dogs of the law on the wild deer of the hills they could not catch with their own hounds? I tell you Hector Faa and his folk dwell like corbies in the clefts of a rock because of these two—Patrick Heron of Rathan, your father, and William Maxwell of Craigdarroch, your mother's brother. Since I cannot reach them, on your head it shall be! As they have dealt with me, so will I deal with you!'

'Well,' returned the youth, dropping his head

back on the pillow a little wearily, 'if you can put off this discussion till the morning I shall be much obliged to you. One of your lads gave me a most unkindly clout on the crown, and your saddle-bags are none so soft as the couch which, I fear me, I have caused this fair maiden to give up to me.'

At the youth's first soft-spoken words the outlaw started forward, his terrible Spanish knife half-drawn from its sheath. But out of the gloom on the other side of the fireplace his daughter darted still more quickly. She caught the threatening arm, and set her other hand to her father's breast.

'No, no, father! no!' she cried; 'he is a brave lad and young. Hold him to ransom, if you will. But let there be no bloodshed on the gypsy's hearth-stone. Let me be his keeper. I will answer for his safety with my life. You can surely find a more profitable revenge than murder in cold blood!'

For a moment Hector Faa paused irresolute. Then he let the half-drawn knife slip back into its sheath with a click.

He nodded grimly and turned on his heel, saying only: 'Then on your head be it, Joyce Faa, if you let him escape from the Shiel of the Dungeon!'

As soon as the two were left alone (for old Meggat had vanished at the entrance of Hector), the young man said: 'I would that you had not said that. You have tied me faster by your words than the varlet who gave me the crack on my brain-pan.'

'I do not know what you mean,' said the girl, moving uneasily.

'I mean,' said Maxwell Heron, smiling, 'you have made yourself responsible for my safe-keeping. How can I escape, knowing that the blame will fall on you?'

She looked at him to see whether or not he jested. Then, her eyes reassuring her on that point, she answered: 'My father has captured you—that is his risk. I have undertaken to keep you—that is mine. Why should you care?'

And he had nothing better to say in reply than just this: 'Because your eyelashes are long and black!'

But he had quite miscalculated the effect of his

21

words.

'You look like a woman, and talk like a fool,' cried the girl, flashing up in sudden anger. 'I am no silly ninny that you should offer me the mockery of vain compliment!'

The youth started up again on his elbow eagerly.

'I ask your forgiveness,' he said; 'it is I who am the ninny. Your words rebuke me. But how did you learn such things up in the folds of the hills?'

With a slight motion of her hand Joyce Faa sent the youth back to his pillow. Then she said, simply: 'I was born in France, and lived there till I was sixteen with my mother, and after her death with the good Sisters. Then I went six months to school in Annan. That was when my father was a drover on the English border—'

Maxwell Heron was on the point of saying: 'Yes, I have heard of that!' But his good angel stopped his mouth in time. For, indeed, it was currently reported that the details of Hector Faa's droving, had they been fully condescended upon, would justly have brought him to the gallows. So with wisdom and discretion beyond his years the youth only nodded.

'The rest my uncle Silver Sand taught me—and these!'

She opened a little door, and revealed a score or so of books in a small square 'aumry' let into the wall of the Shiel. 'And now you will drink this draught, and get you to sleep!'

She poured out of a leathern bottle of pitched goatskin a cupful of a pale yellow liquid, and brought it to the bedside. Maxwell Heron protested (like his father's own son) that he had no intention of going to sleep, 'in such agreeable society,' he meant to add, but something in the girl's eyes prevented him.

'Take it!' she said, firmly.

'An it were mandragora I would drink it!' he said, smiling up at her.

'It is herb tea,' she answered, gravely. But whether with the intent to prick the wind-bag of his fine phrase the youth could not at that time make up his mind.

At any rate, he drank the draught down with a single movement of his arm, and lay back. Joyce Faa came towards him, and with one strong arm lifted up his head while she adjusted his pillows with the other. He tried to protest, but a certain sweet lassitude took him by the throat, and it came to him that he was smiling broadly and foolishly, at he knew not what. A perfume of wild hill plants was in his nostrils, thyme and bog-myrtle newly trodden upon, and the tall rushes in the meadow-lands where the springs are thickest. He heard the bees hum among the heather bloom, the cries of many nesting birds. The winds blew caller and thin about the highest hill-tops, at which he breathed more largely, and a great blue shadow seemed to sweep over the landscape swift as the flight of a bird. Then for a long moment he saw everything as it were through running water. And Maxwell Heron fell on sleep.

CHAPTER FOUR
SILVER SAND—THE MATTER OF THE WAGER

It all arose out of a wager I had with Jasper—young Jasper Jamieson, that is; Big Jasper, so-called to distinguish him from his father, Jasper the Elder—Little Jasper, yet not old. It was a curious wager, to begin with, and turned out yet more curiously. We rode out together on a May morning. I had upon me a suit of new clothes just come from the town of Edinburgh, where I had gotten such learning as I possessed, and my father, Patrick Heron, of Isle Rathan, in Galloway, had given me five golden guineas to be my summer store, laying on me the injunction not to spend them in change-houses and promiscuous folly, but to pay my legal debts with them, if any such I had.

Well, there were one of two small commissions—to Robert Faulds, of the Plainstones at Dumfries, for ribbons of a new puce colour, very becoming to clear complexions, like mine, which I desired to bring home to make rosettes for the knee gathers of my breeches—where it was the fashion to wear them, together with other matters. But since Robert Faulds (decent man, now a Baillie of the burgh) was a much richer man than I, and also well aware that I, Maxwell Heron, was my father's son, I judged that Robert could better afford to wait than I afford to break into my five good gold pieces at once.

But to the wager.

Jasper Jamie was my bosom friend. And when did twenty years lack a friend of the heart, being a healthy youth and fond of ploys jointly engineered between the gloaming and the mirk? Mine was merry of heart and eke of countenance—the 'moral of his own father in his youth,' said my mother. For the rest, Jasper Jamieson was tall, large-boned, strong of limb, a little reckless, perilously willing with his fists, equally ready to fight and to forgive, ever getting into scrapes, and anon elbowing himself out of them by dint of sheer good-humour and graciousness of disposition.

His father was of the first who painted landscapes upon canvas, which were sold in Edinburgh and London to folk who desired such. But more often he drew the likenesses of country gentlefolks to hang on their own walls in order that their descendants might see whence they got their noses. Sometimes he drew the nose in first and added the ancestor after—which, by all accounts, is a paying trade.

As for me, I was the scion of fighting houses on both sides. Father and mother both had taken their part in those bitter strifes of the past, which they loved to speak of by the fireside on the winter nights. Yet the son of the 'drawer-wi'-pent,' as old Jasper Jamie was called in our parts, had all the fighting qualities. While, on the other hand, I had—well, it is not easy to tell what I possessed in their place; but, at any rate, I was not made for the rough-and-tumble of life as I found it in my native province, as this faithful narrative will too abundantly prove.

At school they used to call me 'lassie-boy,' because of a certain delicacy of feature unusual among boys, and also because my mother, ill-advised and ignorant of such matters, had ordained that I should keep my hair long. She also forbade me to fight with my fists, for which, indeed, I was very ill-fitted. So in consequence of these disabilities I suffered for a while the pains of very purgatory, till at last, in one desperate moment, after suffering tormentings innumerable, I drew my knife and nicked my two leading tormentors as they ran from me, one in the calf of the leg and the other somewhat higher up, in that part of his body where the wound would do the least permanent harm, yet (for the present) cause a maximum of inconvenience.

For this I received my first thrashing from Henry Gowanlock in the Grammar School of Dumfries. I endured the hardness of the 'taws,' not, I fear, without tears or as became a hero. But at any rate after that I was at least left alone in the playing-grounds. A boy who keeps his father's jockteleg (which is to say smuggler's sheath-knife) in his pocket for emergencies, and is known to be ready to use it, cannot be wholly disrespected in the most democratic of seminaries.

So I had gained something by my shedding of blood and tears, though, indeed, it was done out of sheer desperation, and not from courage, as some thought. And, chiefly, I gained for all time my friend Jasper, the boy who carried on his person a little triangular scar, which one only saw when he went swimming. He it was who had twisted my love-locks at school—though by the time we were twenty I surmise that he would have given a great deal for that same hair. For his own was but very hog's bristles, while I could wear mine combed out to the length and likeness of a wig, and tie it with a plain black ribbon at the back, as was the fashion. Also by that time Jasper cared most of all to take the eyes of the ladies, as all such ruddy young lumps of manhood do—as I judge, because the very awkwardness of their own beef and bone constrains them to admiration of that which is frail and fair and delicate. And now, when I think of it, mayhap that was the bond which bound Jasper to myself, even more than the jag I gave him with my father's jockteleg.

But I—being, as I say, equipped with features wellnigh feminine, as well as with a marked fairness of the skin and blueness of eyes, not to mention my unfortunate love-locks—was late in beginning to think of maidens and their charms.

So our wager (will I never get to it?) did not concern the sex, as most young men's bets do, not always to their honour.

After all it amounted to no more than this. Jasper also had gotten him five pounds from his father, and was storming to be rid of it. So, his heart being enlarged within him because he was going to see Toinette Gowdenlocks, the daughter of Henry of that ilk, our Dumfries schoolmaster (whose 'taws' in past days had so often caused us to 'loup when there was nae ditch and claw where we werena yeuky') he must needs make me a bet that I would not name the most common bird in the woody country-side through which we were passing.

I asked him how we should settle it.

'Settle it, Maxwell Heron,' he cried, making his pony passage and champ the bit as it was his pride to do. (He was practising to show off before Toinette, as tricksome a minx as ever flirted a Spanish fan.) 'Maxwell Heron, you never had the instinct of a right gentleman in ye, man. Here's five silver shillings— cover them wi' other five. There ye are! Now, what bird that flies the air, think ye, will we see the oftenest between here and Barnbarroch Mill Wood? 'The shilfy' (chaffinch), says you. Then, to counter you, and bring the wager to the touch, I'm great wi' the black coats. I'll e'en risk my siller on the craw. He's Mess John amang a' the birds o' the air!'

So on we rode in keen emulation, and as we went I made a list of the birds we encountered. When there was no doubt, and we were both agreed, I pricked a mark after the name of each we saw. At the Faulds of the Nitwood the mavis led by a neck from my friend the 'shilfy.' But there, as ill-luck would have it, we encountered a cloud of rooks making merry about a 'crawbogle' that had been set up to scare them off some newly sown land. Jasper shouted loud and long. The siller, he maintained, was already his. I had as lief hand it over. I told him to bide a wee—all was not over yet.

Now I began to remark, that while the chaffinch and the sparrow, the robin and his swarthy rookship occurred in packs and knots and clusters, there was one bird which had to be pricked off regularly and frequently This was the swift (or large, black swallow). Whether it was that his long, elastic wings and smooth swoopings brought the same bird more than once across our vision, or simply because every barn and out-house sheltered a couple, it was not long before it was evident that both Jasper and I had small chance of heading the poll with our favourites. By the time we had gotten to the Moss of Little Cloak, and left the woodlands behind us for that time, the prickings of my pencil had totalled as follows:—The swift (or black swallow), 74 ticks; the chaffinch or 'shilfy,' 46 ticks; the 'cushy doo' or wood pigeon, 38 ticks; the 'craw' or field rook, 37 ticks; the magpie, 23 ticks; the mavis, 19 ticks. And this, though mightily uninteresting to most folk that read or hear tales, is yet of value. For it tells what birds were most plentiful in our Galloway woodlands on a certain May morning in the year of grace 17—. Also, when this history comes to deal with the matters to which it led, this boys frolic of ours is worth noting. Also, in a long, weary travel, it is none such an ill way of passing time.

Now at this lame and impotent conclusion of our wager, right fretful was our large-boned Jasper.

'Since neither of us hath won,' he cried, petulantly, 'come, my brisk lad—come, I'll toss you for it!'

Now this spinning of a king's effigy in the air hath ever seemed to me a yet more foolish affair than the laying of a plain wager. So I made a demur, alleging (though, as I knew, quite uselessly) that though neither of our birds had come out first, yet since my shilfy had beaten his crow, the stakes were therefore mine.

'Arrant cowcake,' cried he, after his natural rude manner of speech, 'the fellow who bet on the black swallow— he won or nobody did. You, my friend, wagered on the shilfy. Therefore, whoever won, you certainly lost, and so the money is forfeit to the pool. Now then, Mr. Maxwell, let us spin a coin as to whose the two good crown pieces shall be.'

And he paused with a lucky groat on his thumb-nail, of which coin he was greatly enamored.

'See here, Jasper,' I said, making a final remonstrance, 'this is still greater folly. For if I win, I must treat you at the nearest public-house. And so, in like manner, if you are in luck. 'Tis an inn-keeper's dodge, this daft coin-spinning, depend on't! Better keep that crown of yours to buy a fairing for pretty Mistress Toinette!'

But of course he would hear no reason, being filled with the glory of the May morning, like a young colt ramping with good feeding and lack of exercise.

So 'his Majesty!' I cried at last, to quiet him, since no other might be. And lo! there on the green turf was King George, his image and superscription uppermost, as if he had sprung up with the daisies.

'Hand over!' quoth I, with intent to provoke; whereat Jasper said something pretty round, and clinked the coins most reluctantly into my palm.'

'This wagering is none so dusty a business, after all,' said I; 'faith, this will buy me the Ben Jonson, his plays in folio, that I so much desire. 'Tis indeed a great game, the wagering!'

But for the moment Jasper was sulky, though the gambler's never-failing resource came upon him.

'Double or quits!' he cried, pulling out half a guinea from his fob.

'Nay,' said I, suavely, 'I promised my mother never to gamble. 'Tis wicked,' says she, and, more than that, you might lose!' So I'll stick to my promise to my mother, thanks to you all the same, Jasper Jamie!'

'You are a great coward,' he cried, very angrily; 'you win, and then you will neither give a man his revenge nor yet a pint stoup of ale to wash down his ill-nature withal!'

So, knowing that he would not be content otherwise, I bade him lead the way to the nearest change-house. For, though I had no pleasure in liquor (which, indeed, is for great-boned, well-stomached folk), I had never intended aught else, either by the way or in the good burgh town of Dumfries, where excellent excisable stuff has been vendible ever since the first inhabitant set up a shebeen on the easterly shore to corrupt the honest travellers from the adjacent free and temperate province of Galloway.

And so by the wild, benty hill-side of Barclosh, and over the trembling green bogs of the Knock Burn, we made straight as a die for Tarkirra, that remarkable place of public entertainment among the muirlands, where the gray granite boulders lie thickest, and the reek of the unlicensed 'kiln' steals most frequently up the face of the precipice.

CHAPTER FIVE
THE INN OF TARKIRRA

It was no ordinary change-house; so much is certain. Nor yet were they common muirland folk that made assignation there, as well I saw so soon as I lifted the latch to enter. And right sorry was I that we had two such good beasts with us, as Jasper and I had perforce to leave tied up to the rings let into the wall of unwhitewashed masonry which surrounded the little steading of Tarkirra.

'Ye are welcome, kind sirs!' So a voice, harsh as a frog's croak, greeted us as we set our noses within, and a strange-looking being moved out from the dusky glow of the foul fireplace into the clearer light that streamed from the glassless window. The speaker was a dwarf, with long arms that wambled from side to side as he hirpled about the house or sat crouching like a beast in the corner. His gnarled thighs and outjointed knees prevented quick movement, but he rocked himself to and fro as he went on concocting his messes over the red peat fire upon the unraked hearth.

'Ow ay,' this fearsome carl chuckled, without taking any further notice of us; ' ye'll no ken me, but ony o' thae decent men by the fireside will tell ye wha' I am. Grisly Tam o' Tarkirra, they caa' me in their daffin'. But when they wad hae puir auld Tam to fill the pint stoup, when they hae sma' siller to pay for it, it's nae less than Laird Tarkirra that they will set their tongues to, the vaigabonds!'

As the darkness of the evil-smelling little cothouse gradually melted down before our eyes, through the reek of a score of pipes and the downblow of a narrow chimney, we could see that the place was occupied by wellnigh a dozen men. Some were lying stretched out on settles and bard benches, others sat about on chests and empty kegs, while others again, of temperament less exacting, reclined on the earthen floor with no better protection than a ragged cloak. And for a long minute no man said a word to us, but their eyes followed our every movement as if we had been not only intruders, but spies as well.

'A good day to you, gentlemen all!' I said, trying a genial tone in order to pacify them; ' 'tis a sultry morning without, and the promise of a hot day for the time of year. Will you do us the honour of taking a glass with us of the best our host can provide?'

'Ay,' cried Jasper, incautiously, 'come all of you and drink. 'Tis my friend and no other that has the siller to pay for it. He has just rooked me of a wager, and stands committed to baptize his gains with a tankard of mountain dew.'

Then, from the farthest corner of the room, someone spoke out sharp and sudden:

'And who may you be, my fine young gallants, who flutter it so bravely thus early in the morning? Put names to your head-pieces ere ye ask gentlemen to drink with you. Think ye that in asking us to pledge you, ye are flinging bones to a score of tinkler's messans?'

'Tinklers ye are,' chuckled the dwarf landlord; 'and what better could ye wish to be when twa young lords come to veesit ye, mounted on sic beasts as yon that are flappin' the flees wi' their tails at the dyke-end o' Tarkirra?'

Then I answered first, having, in the absence of qualities more heroic, some readiness of the tongue.

'I am Maxwell Heron by name the son of the Laird of Rathan. Over there is my friend Jasper Jamieson, the painter's son, out of Edinburgh town.'

The man who had spoken took a stride nearer to me, and I could see his face now—a dark and many-scarred physiognomy, crowned with a thick thatch of hair, blue-black brindled freely with streaks of purest white, like sheep ribs scattered over the heather of a hill-side.

'Ah!' he said, smiling sardonically, 'Patrick Heron's son, is it? It sticks in my mind that you had John Faa' tacked to the front of your name when you were christened. What has become of that? Are ye ashamed of the name of Faa that now ye say no word of it?'

'Nay,' answered I, readily, 'neither shamed nor

forgetful. 'Tis an older name than any in Galloway—
ay, older even than MacCulloch and MacDouall,
which are our oldest. But, thanks to a friendly
heaven, my friend John Faa, Lord and Earl of Little
Egypt, is not dead yet. He comes oft about our house
of Rathan, and for that reason I do not use every day
a name that belongs to another.'

'Ah, Silver Sand! he is the great man ever!'
croaked the dwarf, with a glance of covert provocation
towards his principal guest

The darkish-visaged man with the brindled hair
uncovered a set of glittering teeth in a sneer.

'Ah, John Faa is indeed ever the great man,' he
said, as though every word were a bite. 'You say right,
Grisly Tam, there is nothing he will not do for them
that have no claim on him, that are never one drop's
blood to him! But to us—bone of his bone—'

'The glasses, landlord!' cried jovial Jasper,
interrupting; ''tis dry work argufying. We were better
employed melting these crowns of young Laird
Rathan's.'

In another moment the dwarf was chuckling
and tinkling glasses and pint stoups about the table,
but not a man stirred till he of the brindled locks,
with a wave at his band, gave them his permission to
partake. And then they came readily enough, all
swank, sunburned fellows, lathy and tall, and, as I
could see, well armed with pistols and whingers.

I understood it at once. We had put our heads
into a regular smugglers' nest, and no mere 'white
smugglers' either—that is, small farmers and cottiers
sons, taken to the free traffic for a few dollars and the
fun of it These men were 'black' smugglers of the most
determined sort, outlawed hill gypsies mostly, the
scourings and out-sweepings of the narrow seas, to
whom sticking a knife into a man came as easy as a
whiff of East India tobacco to a Dutch skipper—
though, indeed, weakling as I was, I had no right to
speak on that last account, with Jasper Jamie sitting
opposite to me upon a certain triangular scar.

But I stood up to our fate as well as I could; and
as for Jasper, whose perception of affairs was by no

means in proportion to his size, he rattled on, as usual, with a world of nonsense, touching glasses with this one, hobnobbing with that other, all the while making a mighty jest of the squandering of my gains, and telling over about the 'shilfies' and the black crows as if it had been the wittiest jest that ever was heard tell of. But that was also of a constancy the way with Jasper, and is so, I think, with most big-bodied men, who bite so hard upon one end of a jest that they never get time to consider the other.

So it fell out, at least, on this occasion. For I could see the wink and nod that went on all about us, the jerked thumbs, the secret finger play, the questioning arch of the eyebrows, the backward nod of the head. And I judged that even if our throats were not in danger (and of that I was by no means sure) of a certainty, Selim and Moma, my father's two good beasts, haltered out there by the wall, stood a warm chance of having their marks doctored before the next 'Jeddart fair.'

Yet I said nothing, but stood up to the evil-tasting liquor and pledged the crowled little equintard of a host, and also, when I could get near him, my fellow of the brindled hair—pledged and better pledged till my eyes stelled in my head. For being by nature no great fighter, I had all my days the instinct of the weak as to whom it is well to keep in with.

After the first glass or two this man seemed to mellow, asking me as to my mother and her health, with other questions which showed no small knowledge of our concerns at Isle Rathan.

'How came yon to be acquaint with my mother, sir?' I said. 'Did you know her before she married my father?'

For, indeed, I was very sure I had never seen the man about the house of Rathan in my life, and I considered it unlikely that my good mother had any acquaintance of whom I had not heard. For she was very free-spoken by nature and fond of telling tales of her scapegrace youth, sometimes to the no small confusion of my father, who of late had begun to set up for a grave man of years and affairs.

33

'Ay, some time before her marriage it was that I knew Mistress May Maxwell.'

'At her father's house of Craigdarroch, was it?'

At my question his smile grew yet more grim.

'I had once the pleasure of your mother's company upon a journey,' he said, tartly enough, which saying dumfounded me still more, for I had all my mother's journeyings by heart, having had them retailed to me a thousand times in the days of my youth.

'I think, sir,' said I, looking directly up at him, 'if you will have the goodness to tell me your name I may chance to know you, for my mother's friends are mine.'

'My name you shall know in good time,' he answered.

'At present it would serve no purpose, and is best given the go-by.'

Whilst Jasper Jamieson and I were thus misspending the clear-aired, high-roofed summer day amid the foul reek of a hovel, there came from without a sound that by its effect upon our companions was evidently a signal. It was the lowing of a cow, growing louder and more insistent, like one that has waited too long for the milker's hand.

Instantly the men gathered about their leader, and he of the Brindled Locks spoke in whispers to them. Then he went cautiously to the door to find out where lay the danger. But on the threshold he met the dwarf coming in.

'It is Robin Trevor, the Dumfries ganger, with one companion — a better - looking man than himself,' he panted, his tongue hanging out of his mouth like that of a dog on a hot trail. 'They are coming this way! What shall we do? I shall be ruined!'

'Do?' answered Brindled Locks. 'There is but one thing to do, man, and we must do it.'

'No in my hoose!' cried the dwarf, jerking his hands and arms outward from the elbows in such spasms that the joints cracked. 'Kill gin ye like, but shed no man's blood on my doorstep, and before witnesses. For though ye can gang where ye will and naething said, puir Tam o' Tarkirra maun stay here and bear the brunt o' your misdeeds!'

'Peace, you crippled fool!' said the other. 'What need to shed blood? I know a place among the sands of Barnhourie that will do the business of a whole regiment of gangers, and never a mound or a burial hillock to tell the tale!'

During this colloquy I was stepping to the other door, having touched Jasper on the elbow to follow me, when I was suddenly called back.

'Stand where you are, young Rathan,' cried he of the Brindles. 'Ye have heard overly much for your skints safety, my good lad. To the door, Grice! Your pistols, gentlemen.'

And with a certain grave courtesy he disarmed us.

CHAPTER SIX
THE DOOM OF THE GAUGERS

Within the change-house of Tarkirra there was silence—the breathing silence of many men all listening and waiting. I do not know what was in Jasper's mind, but I was minded to cry a warning through the closed door as I heard the King's officers ride up. But beside me stood the man with the brindled hair, a knife in his hand. He laid the palm of his left on my shoulder. By that I knew that if I did cry out I should merely throw away my own life without benefiting those without. So, in the circumstances, I held my peace.

Then there came the noise of heavily shod heels upon the cobbles without. The butt of a riding-whip clanged sharply on the door.

'Open there, in the King's name!'

The command came in strong, masterful tones. A sickness welled up in my heart when I thought of the quicksands of Barnhourie, and would so soon close those bold, imperious lips.

'Open, I say, Tam the Dwarf! It will be the worse for you, if you do not! I come to search the house. I have been watching you for months!'

'Then I fear ye havena watched sharp eneuch this mornin', whatever!' chuckled the dwarf, below his breath. He was leaning forward with a grin of anticipation on his face. The thought of men dying was meat and drink to him, so be that the blood was not shed on his doorstep.

The man with the brindled hair motioned him to open the door, and he moved sluggishly to obey, trailing one foot over the other audibly as he went.

'Comin', sirs, comin', as fast as a puir auld cripple can hoteh!' he cried, so that the excisemen could hear.

'Faster! Faster!' the voice came from without, fortified with an impatient kicking and rapping on the old door which made the iron stanchions shake in their sockets. 'You were none so lame when you were carrying the kegs of good French brandy into your thieves holes, I warrant! But I have you this time, Grisly Tam! The cargo of the Harkaway was landed on Wednesday. I have traced it here, and it has never gone over the hill of Tarkirra.'

The dwarf opened the door.

'Will ye please to step ben, an' see for yourself, Mr Supervisor?' he said, very humbly standing aside.

'You need not deny it, Tam. I know you of old. There never was a cargo brought to the Dutchman's Hole but you had your finger in the pie. And this time you have, as I judge, got the whole pie—and the dish, too. What filthy pigs have been here?' He paused on the threshold, sniffing disgustedly at the tobacco reek which was pouring out from the kitchen, and I thought that perchance he might take warning even then.

'Only twa-three decent herd lads aff the hill,' said the landlord. 'Will ye please to enter, sir?'

'Then whose horses are those at the gate out there?' he inquired, abruptly.

'Juist the young laird o' Rathan's an' a friend o' his. They lookit in at auld Tam's for their mornin' and a word o' daffin'.'

'What? Patrick Heron's son! I must have a look at him! This is no place for the boy!'

Then I could contain myself no longer. In spite of the knife-point so near my ear I shouted a warning to the bold ganger without.

'Keep away,' I cried; 'run for your life! There's death here.'

'What's this—what's this? Stand out of my way, sirrah! In the King's name!' And I heard the rattle of the dwarf's bones as he was whirled back against the wall.

A very tall man pushed open the inner door and strode recklessly within, his spurs clicking, and his hand on his sword-hilt. He stood against the light, trying to distinguish objects in the gloomy house-place of the Tarkirra Inn, as easily and boldly as though he had been making his promenade of the plain-stones of Dumfries upon a market day. I admired him vastly. For though I made no sort of

37

manly figure myself, all the more did I admire those who do.

But on this occasion there was not much time for admiration or anything else. All passed as swiftly as a swallow flashes athwart the window, swooping after a gnat in the summer twilight.

'Whom have we here—whom have we here? Ah! Would you? Treachery! Out of this, Trevor! Ride and warn—'

But further speech was shut within him, as the two men became the centre of a swarm of men, who sprang upon them simultaneously from every side. At the same time I heard the dwarf close the outer door, and the sound of yet another struggle in the narrow, earth-floored passage-way which led to the kitchen. That was Jasper trying to make his way to the horses.

'So, Sir Supervisor,' said Brindled Locks, stooping over him, as he lay helpless, 'you are a bigger fish than I thought to see in the nets this day! But now I will show you what it is to put your black spite on Hector Faa!'

'Hector Faa!'

The name came upon me like a thunder-clap. The twenty-years' outlaw, the daring smuggler, the buccaneer, the almost pirate! He it was who in the days of the Great Hill fighting had carried off my mother from the great cave on Isle Rathan. He it was who, escaping all perils of snow and storm, had found his way to France, and from thence had made shift to avenge himself upon the country which had outcasted him.

For a while the trapped exciseman said nothing, staring upward into the eyes of his enemy from the floor, where he lay bound and helpless.

'Now,' said the gypsy, truculently, 'you have come to the far end of your man-hunting, my brisk lad!'

He stooped down and set his hand on the gold lace upon his captive's shoulder. For Mr. Supervisor Craig was a handsome man, and dressed accordingly. Hector Faa tore the epaulet off by sheer strength. For in those days the higher excisemen were King's

38

officers, and wore such badges of rank.

'Was it not enough for you to chase me on the high seas when you were in King George's navy, without hunting me with dogs after you got your own snug berth ashore? Better for you, my lad, had you stuck to the salt junk and cask-water yet awhile, than have fallen into Hector Faa's clutches!'

'I have a wife!' said the officer of excise, almost meditatively. It was his sole appeal for life.

Hector Faa drew back his hand, and I could see the fingers firm and close, as if to strike.

'Ay, and so had I!' he cried, his voice filling the house.

'Eighteen years ago so had I! But from yon shore I saw the brig in which she sailed sink into blue Solway, and not a soul within her saved! And who commanded on the King's ship that sank her? By whose orders were the guns shotted and the lanyards pulled? Answer me that, good Mr. Supervisor Craig.'

'Not by mine,' answered the officer, calmly. 'I was no more than a lad of ten at that time.'

'No!' the gypsy thundered in reply, making the very rafters shake with his vehemence. 'No, not you, but your father, Captain Elihu Craig, of the Waterwitch! In the bay of Bough Isle, between Castle Point and the White Horses, there, with his bow-chasers, he sank the Bonne Fortune, of Bordeaux. That was a bad day's work for the house of Craig. But since with the Fortune went down Elise, the wife of Hector the gypsy, it became disastrous! And now you, Mr. Supervisor, are to draw up the net that your father let down. Ye will find it a bonny fishing.'

'My father did but his duty, sir,' answered the bold exciseman, 'even as in spite of your threats I shall do mine. That your wife was on board a smuggling craft— thrice summoned to surrender before being fired upon— could be no fault of my father's, any more than it was mine!'

'Enough!' said Hector. 'Since the auld cock hath flown over the wa' o' the kirkyaird, we will e'en thraw the neck of the young bird! To the sands of Barnhourie with them—the ganger and his mate! And as for these pleasant young gentlemen'—he turned to us as he spoke— 'pack them on their horses, and we will show them that Buchan's Dungeon is a safer hold than the gaol o' Dumfries, and that where the writ of King Geordie, that gracious Dutchman, never ran, there are yet men who obey the finger-wag of Hector Faa!'

CHAPTER SEVEN
THE HEAD OF THE HOUSE

Down in the low country of Rathan the preparations for my rescue were rendered more difficult by an unforeseen occurrence. Ordinarily, if one of my standing, with a father so well known, and a mother so—well, a mother like my mother—had been taken by the outlaws and sequestered for ransom, the whole countryside would have risen to our aid as one man. But in the hurly-burly of a little Servile Rebellion, I came near hand to being forgotten.

It may be that the reader has heard of one Sammle Tamson and his wife Eppie, sometime indwellers of the white cot-house of Mossdale on the flowe of Bennan.

If not, I will say no more than that Sammle was a long man, loosely built of frame, sane and kindly as to his heart, but with his upper works somewhat damaged, and with a memory altogether wool-gathering and unreliable. His wife Eppie was the opposite of her goodman on all these counts. In person she was a short, well-to-see, rosy-cheeked, buxom, of great precision and readiness of tongue, and of unparalleled instancy and vigor in action. In short, she could bite, though generally she only barked.

These two had followed for long the fortunes of the house of Heron, in good repute and in ill. Sammle, with his long limbs and his unshaken belief in the infallibility of his wife Eppie, proved himself no mean instrument, having in that hard matrimonial school learned to obey orders at the run and without the asking of many questions.

Eppie and Sammle Tamson now dwelt in the old Tower of Rathan Isle, for our new dwelling-place was built upon the mainland to the left of the village of Orraland, on a pleasant brae with a far-extending view of the sea and of the blowing sails of ships coming up the Firth with the tide. It was a somewhat less romantical, but an infinitely more convenient and amenable place of residence than the little sea-girt tower in which I had first seen the light of day and tried (no doubt) to outscream the sea-mews.

The long man was my father's general factotum—or, in the language of the country-side (and also of Scots law), his 'doer.' But Eppie was generally looked upon as the constructive and compulsive brain, and Sammle only as the very imperfect instrument. So it came about that it was the general will and desire of all our tenants to 'keep far ben wi' Eppie'—or, in other words, to be assured that Eppie's word and interest was theirs in asking any favour of my father, and specially such as concerned steading roofs to be thatched or rights of grazing over adjacent moorland commonties.

It was over these last that all the pother began between the lairds and the better-class of farmers with their well-wishers on the one hand, and the cottiers and poor folk generally on the other. Doubtless there were rights on both sides—ignorance and prejudice also. The landlords were all for turning out the small tenantry to make room for large farms, and shutting off villagers from ancient grazing rights, in order to fence enclosures for the rearing of black cattle. Hence, for a year or two past, the ill-feeling had been growing, and the cottiers, angry and suspicious, were full of threatenings and unbalanced humours.

We find Sammle Tamson, of the tower of Rathan, preparing to go out upon his rounds. He had been more than ordinarily aggravating that morning, and the temper of his wife had in consequence veered gradually more and more to the east, from which snell direction it threatened to blow a hurricane of some duration. Marion, Sammle's daughter, was from home, but then Marion was a privileged person, coming and going without even Eppie saying 'whither goest thou?'

'Did I ever see siccan a man in my born days?' the latter cried, coming to the door of the little 'chaumer' (the same in which I was born); 'did I no tell ye to put on a clean sark this mornin', when ye will hae to appear afore your betters. And what do I find? I gang to the basket for the dirty claes, and there

42

amang dishclouts and floorcloots—ay, an' the fyled blankets o' the last sax months, even there ye hae gane and stuffit the bonny frilled sark o' seventeen hunder linen, that I goffered and ruffled wi' my ain hands in the sweat o' my broo! Talk o' man earning his bread, an' Aidam haein' the curse o' labour laid on him in the gairden o' Eden—fegs, it's Eppie Tamson's thocht o't that women hae their ain burden to bear and Aidam's, too. And I'm sure gin he was as useless an' tormentatious a hound in paradise itsel' as his kind are unto this day, he gat aff far ower cheap. Mair like the thing if he had gotten share and share aboot wi' the auld serpent. Dust should he hae eaten, and on his belly should he hae gane a' the days o' his life. And, by my certes, it's little better ye wad hae been this day, Sammle Tamson, had ye no a weel-handed, thorough-gaun wife to ready your meat and keep your nakedness decently clad. And after a' her pains this is her reward. Ye gang and stuff a new clean sark (that wad weel hae becomed a lord o' Parliament) amang fyled claiths and tarry hiplocks! Get oot o' my sicht, man! Ye are no a man ava Sammle Tamson. Ye are nae better than a string o' puddens and haggises that I hae to fill at the tae end wi' a spune—and at the ither— What's that ye are mutterin' to yourself Let me hear it!'

'But, Eppie,' said Sammle, meekly, 'ye ken that was because I had this Levellers business on my mind, sae that I had nae heart to be deckin' myself in purple and fine linen, as ye micht say.'

'The Levellers, sorrow faa' them!' cried Eppie, diverted, as her goodman probably intended that she should be, to a subject fitted to give less personal scope to her linguistic faculties; ' Levellers, indeed— kinless, feckless loons, that can neither till their grund nor yet be at the trouble to keep the craws frae their pickle seed corn. And when the laird does put his hand to, and tries to improve the face o' the country, they are juist like the man that sowed tares in the Bible. They come not but for to steal, and for to ding doon an' to destroy! Fegs, gin I thocht that ye had ony trokin' and come-hithering wi' siccan loons o'

Satan— Sammle Tamson, ye wadna gang forth this day wi' uncloured ham-pan, I can tell ye that, my lad!'

Sammle was engaged in pulling on a sock when this fell threat reached him. He generally did his personal needs, as it were, piecemeal, adding another article to his toilette according as he kicked against it on the floor, or had it flung at his head by his justly indignant spouse.

'What for dinna ye keep your socks thegither on a chair like ony ither decent man?' she cried. 'I declare to peace if I wasna a langsufferin' woman ye wad anger me ane o' thae days!'

'Weel, weel, wife, ye see I wad never ken whatna chair it was I had laid them on, and as it is, its easy to mind!'

'How's that, ye seefer?' Eppie shot the question out of her mouth as peas leave the school pea-shooter when the master's back is turned.

'Oh,' said Sammle, settling himself down to an explanation, 'as lang as my stockings are on the floor, I aye ken whaar to find them. For there's only yae floor, ye ken. But as for chairs—'

'But answer me aboot thae Levellers, Sammle,' she said, abandoning the stocking question, not in despair, but only putting it off till a more convenient season, as it were.

'Dinna tell me that ye hae ony sympathy wi' a parcel o' run-the-road ne'er-do-wells?'

Sammle Tamson scratched his head. He had, indeed, gone rather more deeply into the rebellion than became the husband of a wife like Eppie and the servant of a well-considered country gentleman like my father, Patrick Heron of Isle Rathan and Orraland.

So it was with considerable natural embarrassment that he answered his wife.

'There's something to be said for the puir craiturs, too, Eppie, ye maun alloo!'

'What's to be said for them or the like o' them, it wad pleasure me to hear ye lay your tongue till't, Sammle Tamson? And you, a man o' some poseetion (whilk ye owe to me), o' some siller (and that also ye owe to me), and a decently brushed Sabbath-coat to

44

your back, to gang colloguin' wi' a set o' penniless loons, sae lazy that they wad never get five meenites exercise were it no for the trouble they hae in scartin' themsel's! Think shame o' yoursel', man! And ye hae never pitten on the ither sock after a', though ye hae on baith boots! Do ye mean to shame me afore gentle and simple alike? Faith, my man, I'll e'en gang ower by to the minister's and get him to debar ye frae ordinance. For your ongangin's and heart-breakin' contrariness cause me daily to fa' frae grace—me that hae been a communicant for thirty odd years, and a decent woman forbye. Yesterday, on the sma'est computation, I used nae less than six minced oaths till ye, ye lang-leggit, spavie-jointed contriver o' ineequities that ye are!'

With both stockings on, Sammle Tamson went out. It was a blowy morning.

CHAPTER EIGHT
THE LEVELLERS IN COUNCIL

Sammle went about the gable of the house with something of the gait of a dog that has been kicked off a doorstep. It always took him about half a mile before he could recover his self-respect after one of his marital dressings-down—that is, unless he met his daughter Marion. Then he recovered instantly.

For at the very sight of her white apron glinting through the birk copses and up by the hawthorn hedges, he would begin to smile. On this occasion he came upon her by the landing-place, where one or two boats were hauled up on the beach in shelter of a little pier.

Almost at any time Marion was, as the country saying goes, 'a sicht for sair e'en.' She and I had always been the best of friends, all the more that though I admired her greatly—ay, and told her of it—I never made love to her. But even disinterested admiration does not go without its reward. Marion took one glance at her father's woe-begone expression and then she burst into a merry laugh, which showed teeth like milk—small and even.

'What was it this morning, father?' she cried, as she came up to him with a hop-skip-and-jump. 'Are your boots not mates? Did you forget to take your breakfast, or give it to the dog without noticing, as you did last Sunday?'

'It was the socks,' said Sammle, sadly. 'I had yin aff and yin on when she catched me at it. I canna keep track o' them, ava! I maun hae them tackit thegither, and then I'll surely mind!'

'And where gang ye noo, faither?' She turned as she asked the question, and accompanied him down to the landing-place to help him into his boat. For it was as likely as not that Sammle Tamson would push off without a single oar and have to row himself back with a thwart, or, if that did not occur to him, drift out to sea helplessly till some one put off in pursuit.

'Where am I gangin?' said Sammle, looking away in some embarrassment. 'On Maister Heron's business— what else?'

His daughter stood directly in front of him and laid her hands on his shoulders. Then she pecked upward at his ear, exactly like a bird that gives thanks after taking a drink.

She whispered a single word, dropped down again on her heels, and pointed up at him with her finger poised, and an exceedingly arch expression on her face.

'Ah!' she said, triumphantly, 'you see, I know!'

'Guid's mercy save us!' gasped Sammle Tamson. 'Ye will surely never say a word o' this to your mither, lassie?'

'Dinna ye fear, faither. Lassie I may be—I canna help that; but gin ye are deep in this business, I ken them that are deeper!'

And with that Marion Tamson, having seen her father settled in his boat, with the requisite number of rowlocks and oars, and with his face towards the stem, so that there was a reasonable probability of his reaching the Orraland shore (without turning more than half a dozen circles and catching an equal number of crabs), walked slowly and thoughtfully up to the old Tower of Isle Rathan.

But as for Sammle Tamson, the mind of that philosopher dwelt vaguely on the troubles of the times—villages left without inhabitants, cruel taskmasters, men who would wrest away ancient rights of tilth and pasturage, remove the ancient landmarks, enclose, exclude, give up to black cattle bred for English markets, the scanty garths and green gussets hardly won from the encompassing heather by dint of the plough and spade of untold peasant generations.

Among such oppressors of God's heritage he was far from including my father Patrick Heron, who was a just man, stirring no man from that which had been his forbear's, and asking no more than an easy quit-rent, often merely nominal (and that frequently remitted), from the poor cottier folk who had squatted on the hillward verges of his lands.

Now Sammle Tamson had in him some of the

qualities of a reformer. His strange exterior concealed a keen and eager spirit. His wife had trained him to self-repression. He had among his neighbours a high repute for probity, though his absent-mindedness clouded his capacity for action. It was characteristic of the man that, though on an errand of great importance and with his heart full of the oppression and injustice which he saw around him, he should stand half an hour staring at the pebbles on the Orraland shore before he drew up his boat.

Finally, recalled to himself by a dash of rain in his face from a passing shower and the tide washing simultaneously about his feet, he strode away up the tangle of woodland which fringes the bay, and in ten minutes was breasting the brae towards the dark, heathery fastnesses of Screel.

The path led him to the left, in the direction of the narrow gulley called at that time Tudor's Caldron. It is a strange, deep gash riven in the mountain's side, secluded from every haunt of man, and visited by none save by the wild goat that springs from rock to rock along the steeply shelving sides.

As he made his way westward, with surprising craft Sammle took advantage of every cover. He followed the dark purple lip of a peat moss from which the fuel had been cut away for a hundred yards. He crouched behind a boulder till a wandering herd with a couple of scouring dogs passed off the sky-line. Nevertheless, it was swiftly, though with the utmost circumspection, that he approached the tangle of six-foot-long heather which conceals the descent into the Caldron of Ben Tudor.

The afternoon had early broken down into a thronging procession of white cirrus cloudlets, varied occasionally by one of haughtier build, as some towering cumulus overrode the lift with his bulk crenellated like a feudal keep. Shining glints of thunder-shower shot down occasionally from these, and once Sammle felt on his face the sting of hail. Having arrived at the shaggy verge of the Caldron, from which through the interstices of whin, broom, and rock-climbing ivy, he could look into the untracked and untravelled wilderness, Sammle lay down on his breast and studied the landscape. Far out to sea, towards the open water of the firth, a schooner hung off and on, waiting for night or tide. But Sammle was at this time no smuggler, though possibly he might have been indicted for conspiracy.

'Wee-wee-wee! Wurley-wurley-wee-wee!'

Thus Sammle Tamson cried to the upland silences, and up from the pit-bottom, from this clump of birch and that thicket of broom the voices of a score of lambs replied, crying as though they had lost their mothers—brisk yet pitiful.

Then, without further pretence of concealment, the warden of Isle Rathan descended into Tudor's Caldron.

'Sammle, ye are welcome. Come your ways, man. Hoo did ye get aff withoot Eppie seeing ye? What's your news?'

These were some of the greetings which reached the long man's ears as he stumbled and slipped down the last precipitous slopes of heather, and found himself suddenly in the full parliament of the Levellers. Twenty or thirty men of all ages were seated about; young men scant of years and beard yet already brown-faced and eagle-eyed. Old men bent and worn were there also. But the most part were men of middle-age, grey-haired, a little bent about the shoulders, and all clad as uniformly as a king's regiment in broad blue Kilmarnock bonnets, rig-and-fur stockings, coat and knee-breeches of a saffron-tinted grey homespun, while about every left shoulder a plaid checked of black and white was swung with martial precision.

These elders were the representatives of the crofters and cottiers of Galloway, some of them already dispossessed, others under warning to remove at the next term, while a few of the younger men, being without immediate stake in the conflict, had joined the movement simply for what of excitement could be extracted from it.

'Weel, sirs,' said Sammle, taking his seat on a convenient boulder whose mossy upper surface,

49

shaped like a square gravestone, formed a kind of natural Speaker's chair to the assembly, 'I hae grave tidings. I heard an that I'll no name (but that ye can guess at), mention it as bein' intended by the lairds o' Duchrae and Grenoch to shift all and hale o' the inhabitants o' Whinnyliggate and Crae Brig at the term. It was mentioned at the lairds' meetin' on Wednesday in Dumfries toon—'

An old man rose from a tussock of heather.

'Deed, then, Sammle Tamson, an' ye say richt. This will be sair news for us to carry to the head end o' Balmaghie. But surely a' hope is no yet by wi't! We will gang and speak them fair. We will offer to pay ony reasonable sum for the pasturage o' oor kye on the green slopes o' the Bennan, and tell the laird that gin he winna steer us frae the bit plots o' grund that were oor faithers' afore us we will be his faithfu' servants, as in former times—'

'It is ower late, I misdoot,' began Sammle. But from the further side of the Caldron of Counsel rose another voice.

'Ower late! Ower late, indeed!' It was a swart, fierce-eyed, gypsy-looking youth who spoke. 'We have borne over-long with oppression. Never yet was the law o' tyranny and wrong enforced in Gallowa'. Surely we are the sons of our fathers this day. Shall a thousand men stand craven before them that are but a score in number? For the lairds are little more than that, and from the sea-edge crofts and the hill-side sheep-folds men will rise by the hundred to ding doon their dykes, and pu' up their spindling plantations by the roots.'

Then all the young men cried out together, 'Weel spoken, Harry Polwart! So say we a'! Your health, Gypsy Harry!'

Nevertheless a few greybeards murmured, men who remembered the sore times that came upon the land when the troopers of Claverhouse and the levies of Lag rode hither and thither, and when the very face of the moorland was quartered as with hunting dogs. In especial, Sammle Tamson shook his head.

'Na, na, brave lads!' he said, 'let us avoid the

shedding o' bluid! Ye maun mind that in that case it is no the lairds wad hae to fecht, but a' the poo'er o' the King! And if it comes to open war the sodjers will ride us doon like meadow-hay, even as they did at Bothwell Brig and the Rig o' Pentland. Them that flee to the sword shall perish by the sword—'

'Better to perish by the sword than perish of cold and starvation on the hillside!' cried Harry Polwart, vehemently. 'If Hector Faa has lived for forty years an outlaw against the King, think ye that the lairds can put down a thousand men that are men?'

'And that is the very reason that Hector Faa has been spared,' said a grey-bearded man, to whom the others paid great respect. 'Hector is but one, and the powers that be are busy. So long as he does no more than slip an orra sheep aff the hill betimes, or drives awa' an Ayrshireman's coo in the gloaming sma' notice is ta'en o' him. But had he a thoosand men at his back—a' rank plunderers like himsel'—the government wad send a thoosand troopers, and ten to the back o' that—ay, mair and mair, till Hector Faa wad swing by the neck for the robber and catheran that he is! We are decent men, and want neither comparison nor likening to that robber!'

'Talk, talk, talk!' retorted Harry Polwart, fiercely; 'that is all ye do or have done this twelvemonth past! Prating is gone clean out of date. Those that are ready to do, let them put points to their pikes and look to their priming! For I have a leader ready, and I will name a place of meeting! Who will follow us? This very night we will begin our work, and if by the morrow's morn there remains a stone upon a stone in all the enclosure dykes of Merrick, may I Harry Polwart be hanged for a thief in front o' the Castle o' Kirkcudbright!'

'And a right lively chance of that same you will have, Master Harry, if ye do as ye say,' answered the grey-haired man who had spoken before. 'But this leader of yours, who is he? Surely he has a name that can be named in the council of the Levellers o' Gallowa'—that is, if he be indeed a leal man and no traitor!'

'He is no traitor—I will risk my head upon it, as, indeed, his deeds shall this night prove! There are reasons why I cannot speak his name. But this I will say. He who will lead us to fame this night is not, indeed, of our degree, but his heart is with us in the struggle. Who will join? Up with your right hands!'

At least half of those present held up their hands, including all the younger men.

'At the cross-roads of Rascarrel, then!' cried the gypsy; 'the time, ten of the night! And our watchword, 'A free land and a free folk!'

Meanwhile in my father's new house of Orraland there was much gathering of forces and counting of war-gear. First in the intended fray there was, of course, my uncle Fighting Will, otherwise William Maxwell, of Craigdarroch. Never yet did any trouble come to a head but Will Maxwell sooner or later found his way to the post of danger. And generally sooner than later. Indeed, his bull-neck and the tussock of grey bristles which covered his head generally bore up from nowhere in particular, with the first mutterings of strife, as surely as gulls drive up on the front of a Solway storm to whiten the new-ploughed lands.

With him came half a dozen Maxwells, mostly nephews and cousins, all young storm-petrels, scenting any bold adventure, and uncommonly active meantime with their knives and forks. For my father liked the repute of keeping a generous table, though he never permitted any kind of excess, either in himself or in his guests.

'I canna think what has gotten into the countryside lads,' cried Will from one end of the hall to the other (Will generally had to get half a furlong away in order to get the speaking distance which suited his voice, his utterance, when excited, being so volcanic that it seemed as if the first gust would blow his interlocutor oflf his feet). 'I have been down at the village recruiting, and feint a pretty lad can I find that will button on his jack and follow after to rescue our Maxwell. Such faint hearts as they are become all of a sudden! They are away on one pretext or another— one hath taken a turn at sea and is gone to Maryport—another is visiting his friends in the country —for his health says his mother, when I know to my cost that only last Monday as ever was he reached me at single-stick with as sound a clout on the head as ever I gat in my life!'

'That is not like our Orraland lads,' said my father; 'they are not usually backward when there is the chance of hard knocks—and' (here he sighed a little) 'I did think they were better affected to me and my son. But these are troublous times, and while they last every man must fend for himself.'

'They are all rogues,' cried Will, 'and, I warrant, are up to their necks in this Leveller business, with intent to burn what they cannot build and uproot what they cannot plant. A little judicious hanging would benefit some of them greatly. That long-shanked rascal of yours over on the island is as great a rogue as any.'

'Ay,' cried our cousin Andrew Agnew from the Shire-side, as blithe and swank a young blade as ever lifted his leg across saddle-leather, 'we have them in our parts, too; but my father is, as ye know, King's Justicer, and I hardly think they will meddle with him. But I am sorry you should be troubled with the vermin hereaway. Laird Rathan.'

For my father was still known by the name of his ancient possession, though his recently acquired lands were both larger and richer.

'Well,' said Patrick Heron, 'my wife May is somewhere in the saddle twixt here and Kirkcudbright, and if she bring not word—ay, and also recruits a-plenty— then indeed I will say that there is neither virtue nor spirit in the young men any more—'

'Better send me to wil' them in, father,' cried a bright and flower-faced girl, entering the long hall of Orraland from a door at the side, and making the circle of men turn about with her voice, which was indeed always sweet-sounding and memorable. My sister Grisel she was, and of her anon. 'Her mother over again, the minx!' was my father's constant verdict about Grisel. And that of others will appear in the course of the narrative.

'Better let me be your recruiting sergeant, father, and I will cost you never a shilling for binding arles. Faith, an I could not enlist a triple regiment, never call me Grisel Heron again. I should be unworthy of my name!'

'Ay, and what bounty would ye offer as so powerful an inducement. Mistress Flibberty-gibbet?'

said my father. For of course she was his favourite, as I was equally my mother's.

At this our Grisel pouted, and nodded her head first at one of the company and then at another. For she was, as I say, ever a tricksome minx.

'Would you dare to list, Andrew Agnew, and leave the arles to me?' she challenged him.

'Ay, blithely that would I!' cried the bold son of the hereditary Justicer.

'And you, Colin lad?' She turned to Colin Gilmour of Nine Mile Burn.

'Indeed I am with you now, and always, pretty Mistress Griselda,' added that somewhat more formal youth, getting up and bowing to her.

And you, my cousin Grant?'

That I wull, Girzy, though Guid kens ye are a besom and wull no gie a man a kiss—no, though ye promise him twenty times!' cried a youthful muirland kinsman from the wilds of Urr. His frank utterance of his experiences caused a laugh—which, however, in no wise disconcerted the young lady.

'Give you a kiss? I wonder to hear ye, Grant,' she said, with a show of indignation. 'And you scarce running by yourself yet.' Then she explained to the company. 'At home they feed him out of a coffee-pot, ye ken, with a bag over the spout, like a pet lamb!'

She put her head to the side, consideringly.

'Does he not look a pet—no long frae his mammy?' she cried, clasping her hands in affected admiration. And the like o' him to be speaking about kissing—fie, for shame, Grant! Wha has been learnin' ye sic words? Shame on ye, bairn! Gin your mither hears ye, she will hae ye weel skelpit!'

'Hush, Grisel,' interrupted her father, 'this is serious enough, though I do not believe they will do Maxwell any bodily harm. His captors will think more of ransom than of revenge, being that sort of rascal. And as for you. Mistress Minx, it is easy to engage already enlisted men. But you are welcome to try your hand on the Orraland callants, who, says brother Will here, cannot be made to budge for any manly arguments.'

'Faith, an I were,' she said, confidently; 'methinks I could put my colours on every mother's son—from Tam Kinstry, the meal-miller's son, to Camsteerie Cormack, that they engage for craw-bogle on odd days when the craws get overly well acquaint wi' the ordinary ones!'

But into the great hall of the house of Orraland there came one who in a moment changed the current of all men's thoughts, even staying the daffing of that our spirited maid, Grisel, and, as it were, by his mere countenance lifting a weight off the general heart.

'Silver Sand!' cried my father, hastening forward with both hands outstretched. 'Oh, I am glad—so glad!' cried Grisel, throwing herself without ceremony on the newcomer's neck and kissing him heartily.

'Is that what you mean by enlisting a recruit?' said young Agnew, slyly; 'then my turn next, if you please.'

And yet, unless you had known his name and story, there was nothing in the man's appearance to warrant a reception so distinguished in the house of Orraland. But though my father was a man of counsel, and Will Maxwell a deacon with the sword-blade and pistol-butt, yet nevertheless with the advent of Silver Sand it was felt by every man that the only natural counsellor had appeared for any, enterprise of danger and uncertain issue.

A grey, thin-faced man, with a mouth about which played a lurking smile, his countenance lined and weather-beaten, curious arms hung very low by his sides, his appearance at a distance not striking, but when seen nearer of an indescribable dignity of composure—a man who (as one knew instinctively) had often looked on death and danger with the same quietly humourous regard. That was Silver Sand, the good angel of the house of Rathan, and the friend of all within its bounds.

Yet in spite of his ordinarily iron quiet, he seemed affected by the warmth of his welcome.

'What's this —what's this that I hear?' he said. 'Patrick, I am heart-sorry. Lassie, be not feared. We will find your brother of a surety!'

56

'But, Silver Sand, how came you to know of the capture of my son Maxwell?' my father inquired.

Silver Sand glanced quickly up at him.

'Ye ken my ways of old,' he said; 'though simple enough, yet they are not common folks' ways of obtaining knowledge. But if I told them, they would be of little more use to me—or to my friends, either. But in this case the explanation is a simple one. I will bring in one who will tell you more and better all that I know.'

And with these words he opened the hall door, and who should come in, limping, with both hands on a stick, his lips compressed with pain, a bloody bandage about his head—who but young Jasper Jamieson, that had been my companion when we rode so blithely away from Rathan in the spring morning.

'This lad has the master-key,' said Silver Sand; 'after we have heard his tale we can concert our plans.'

'What brocht ye here like this, Jasper?' 'Whatna lass were ye seekin' when ye gat that clour frae her faither's shillelah?' 'What hae ye dune wi' Maxwell?' 'Where have you left my brother, Jasper Jamie?'

These were some of the cries that greeted the young man, as he stood blinking and dazed in the warm dusk of the chamber.

But the master of the house held up his hand.

'Sit ye down, Jasper,' he said, kindly; 'take a cup of wine before you tell your story. I see it in your eyes that my son is not dead.'

So kind and courteous was my father on all occasions, even when his heart was troubled and sore within him.

CHAPTER TEN
A CAPTAIN OF REBELS

Jasper Jamie told his tale in the hall of the house of Orraland, and in the midst of the telling my mother came in, still young and comely, and the most spirited woman in the Stewartry.

'With Hector Faa!' cried she, when she heard all, and then at a certain thought of the things and times that were bygone, she suddenly paled. But, recovering herself, she added, 'Yet I do not think that he will dare to shed my laddie's blood—no, not even Hector Faa dare do that! He has a daughter, they say?'

'One that passes for such, at any rate,' said Silver Sand, gravely; 'and a fine lass, whatever be her kin.'

'Then I am none feared for my boy,' said she that had been called in her youth May Mischief, tossing her head with something of her ancient manner (Grisel hath it also); 'there lives no woman born of woman that has the heart to stand by and see Maxwell Heron mishandled!'

And by this she meant, as I presume, that I had been delicate of body from my birth, and hard to rear through the bitter Solway winters and cold easterly winds that come to us across the snows of Cheviot and the waves of the North Sea. I know of no other reason why my mother should so have spoken, for at that time my experience of women in the way of making love to them had been just none at all.

Now, when they were listening open-mouthed in the hall of Orraland to the tale of Jasper Jamie, all about our bird wager and the inn of Tarkirra, my sister Grisel slipped out, not, of course, wholly unobserved. For at her departure the young men, as it were, disengaged themselves, sat less erect, and ceased from emulous glances across to the place where she stood. Yet none ventured to follow, well knowing that such a movement would have called out the whole flock.

But Grisel, as soon as she was well assured of my safety, flew to a point of rock which overlooked the bay. The tide was now full, and Isle Rathan, our ancient principality, lay (as I can see it lie even as I write) anchored among a broad, surprising glitter of wavelets, silver-sheened and changeful in colour as a dove's breast.

Having arrived at this point, which lies not far from the place that is called Balcairy, Grisel waved a white kerchief thrice to the left and as often to the right, in that order, looking all the while over to the island in the shining fairway, as if for an answering signal. Four times she did this in vain. The old grey tower of Rathan stood up still and lonely in the sunshine, a thin pew of peat reek from the chimney of the kitchen-place alone giving token of habitation. The rocks near the landing-place seemed fairly to blink with the heat, but it was only the wet sands sending up a wavering haze about the isle.

Suddenly in the great blue day an answering fleck of white, no larger than a sea-bird's wing, was waved frantically to the right, and again as often to the left.

A figure ran down the beach, pushed off a skiff, and rowed swiftly towards Grisel. That young maid, apparently satisfied with the success of her signal, sat down on the cliff-edge upon a spot at once well secured from observation, and yet from which a view of the isle could be had down a kind of gully as through a telescope. She sat nursing one knee between her clasped hands, and humming an air under her breath. She kept smiling also all the while, like one who waits for a love-trysting. (Now Grisel is my sister, and perhaps it is wrong to tell all her doings and misdoings; but all these things are long past and become a matter for smiling gossip and forenight reminiscence. Besides which, I have her permission—laughingly given, it is true, and with the request that I should keep the book from the hands of her daughter Bell. But from what I hear, anything I may have to write will neither harm nor yet inform that young woman.)

Well, as I say, there sat Grisel on her rock smiling at the little black dot, with the line of sparkles on either hand, which was the flashing of the oars as the boat came nearer across the water.

No sooner had the bow grated on the shingle than Grisel fairly broke and ran from her covert. A tall young man, dressed in sailor clothes, sprang out lightly, and Grisel (sad I am to write it down!), forsaking all maidenly modesty, rushed laughingly down to him, and caught him in her arms with impulsive abandonment. The stranger responded as fervently, but with a certain careless equality of affection strange in a youth thus highly favoured by a maid so courted and coveted as the eldest (and only) daughter of Patrick Heron of Isle Rathan, and May his wife.

'Come—come quick—to our place! I have so much to tell you, dearest heart!' said Grisel, with her arms about the young man's waist.

'Help me with my boat, then I' he replied, still tugging the skiff higher up the shingle. Presently they came up the beach, walking together with linked and woven arms, the tall youth leaning over till his cheek was resting on Grisel's fair hair.

They were clearly very fond of each other, yet the equality of regard between them was clearer than ever. Indeed, if anything, the balance of demonstrative admiration was on Grisel Heron's side—which was not as it should have been. When they were a hundred yards from the beachy and the spurs of rock had shut them off from observation Grisel thrust her companion off at arm's length from her.

'Oh, you look like a painted picture—I wish I could wear them! But I suppose they would be too large—'

'Oh, far too large—beside, two of us would spoil the game!'

'Oh, Marion, dear—I mean Dick—dear Dick, they have found my brother!'

'What!—has he come home?'

The youth in the blue suit with silver buttons and the broad bonnet on his head turned about quickly.

'Nay, not home,' said Grisel; 'but they know where he is—he is held for ransom by Hector Faa!'

'You take the matter pretty coolly. Mistress Grisel,' said the youth, who was, of course, no other than Marion of Isle Rathan, the adventurous daughter of Sammle; 'had I a brother like yours, methinks I should be more concerned. To say that he is safe in Hector Faa's cave is like the old woman of Dumfries, who, being asked of her son's welfare, answered, 'Oh, oor Jock's weel. He was hangit for sheep stealin' at Dumfries on Wednesday week. But the Lord be thankit, Jock's gane to a better place!'

'Marion—Dick, I mean, I never can remember— it will be splendid; you are captain, so we will get the band to deliver him—'

'The band has other purposes than to rescue a laird's son held to ransom,' said the apparent Dick of the Isle. 'More like that they should catch him and hold him to ransom themselves!'

'That would be excellent, too. Mar—Dick, I mean; we could keep Maxwell in the Great Cave on Rathan, and hold him to ransom till he married you!'

'We have talked quite enough nonsense, Grisel,' said her companion, sharply; 'you remember the tryst tonight by the cross-roads of Rascarrel. If you are true to your oath you will be there, and you know the costume!

Grisel looked a little mournful. There is no girl of any pretension to beauty who has not at one time or another had a certain curious ambition to know how she would look in boy's attire. And the costume which Marion of the Isle wore was certainly most becoming.

'No, that is for the captain alone—the post of danger!'

'I don't care about the danger. You could have that, and welcome, but the knee-breeks are certainly monstrous fine!'

'Grisel, I bid you remember your oath—this is a hanging matter if we are caught, and what is very well for Sammle Tamson's daughter to risk will not do at all for Mistress Grisel Heron of Orraland and Isle

Rathan.'

'Oh, I wish I were just a common person, so that I could wear the things you have!'

'Ah,' laughed the youth; 'but then, you see, I wear them because a great number of people think that I am not at all a common person!'

'What are you, then?' said Grisel, who, being denied and disappointed, was inclined to be a little bitter.

'I am the new leader of the Levellers of Galloway,' said Marion, with some pride; 'soon to be in rebellion for their rights and privileges! And you are no more than a soldier in the ranks, so you have to obey me. And, mind, not a stitch of difference—the roughest material, and put on over your ordinary clothes.'

'A bit of trimming—or at least strings to the—' pleaded Grisel.

The other stamped her foot with a gesture not at all masculine.

'Not a stitch—not a single bow of ribbon under penalty of—'

'Death? Oh!'

Grisel clasped her hands in mock terror. 'No; of being sent home!'

Mistress Grisel stood a moment, frowning and making prettyish pouting months (I have caught her practising them before the glass. A vain piece was our Grisel, all the days of her!) I think she meditated paying off some of the disappointment about the captain's dress upon her dearest friend.

'And so you will do nothing about rescuing my brother from Hector Faa?' she said.

'Gladly; I will do what I can to release him; but not with the band of the Levellers. I have sworn an oath to think of nothing and care for nothing till these poor cottiers and crofters are restored to their ancient privileges!'

'I thought you liked Maxwell?' Grisel suggested, plaintively- (I hear her, the minx, and not an inch of earnest intent in her, but only guile and a pretty maliciousness.)

'I like him well enough,' answered the maiden of the island; 'but what is it to save one man and betray a cause? Besides which, I do not believe that the Levellers would follow me into the wild hills where Hector Faa has his stronghold.'

'No, the Levellers might not; but I know the young fellows would follow you to the gallows foot!'

'I sometimes think,' said Marion, a little pensively, 'that that is indeed whither I am leading them!'

'Come,' cried Grisel, 'that, at least, is not spoken like Captain Dick of the Isle. But you need not spend overmuch pity on Maxwell. Hector Faa's daughter Joyce is beautiful, they say, and—well—she has never seen a man like our Maxwell, I'll wager!'

'She has seen men who are men,' said Marion, a little sharply. 'I have lived among these outlaw folk and know!'

(A saying which bore some deal heavily upon me.)

Grisel let the information sink in, going on to enlarge upon the reputed beauty of Joyce Faa, and the wild and savage scenery with which the outlaw's haunts was surrounded.

'I warrant' she said, 'Max is by this time fathoms deep in love, and hath made a score of drafts of Joyce Faa's head with a burnt stick on a planed board, if he can get no other material. For that is our Maxwell to the life.'

In this again, as was her wont, most shamefully belying me.

And all the time my sister kept watching Marion from beneath her eyelashes, as she sat gazing to the north and strumming on her knee with her fingers in a kind of dreamy abstraction.

At last the young Captain of the Levellers spoke.

'I would not like your brother to be in any real danger. I will speak with Silver Sand. Tonight, after our work is done, I will tell you what he says.'

She paused and sighed.

'Now must I hasten back to Isle Rathan, or Davie Veitch will be tired of keeping the company of

63

my petticoats so long in the Cave.'

'Why does he wait there—for his Sunday clothes?' asked Grisel, looking at the well-ordered blue suit which Marion wore.

'No; but that I may have liberty to come and go freely. When I am spied from the cliffs men say, 'There, I declare to peace, is that Davie Veitch rowing over to see his lass again. None but Sammle Tamson would put up with such a runnagate!'

'So, to save your own character, you make ducks and drakes of poor Davie's?'

'Oh,' said Marion, lightly, 'it is so long since poor Davie had any character to speak of, that a bit of my ill-doing will rather cover his nakedness than otherwise!'

Then she mused a little, and, suddenly pushing off, set to the oars without the masculine preliminary of spitting on her hands. She was quite half over before she rested.

Then she leaned a moment on her oars letting the water drip from the blades. She watched the distant blue mountains very faint on the horizon. There was the Merrick, yonder more tenderly blue, soft-bosomed Cairnsmuir, and though she could not see it for the lowering mass of the Black Craig of Dee, somewhere to the right lay the Dungeon of Buchan, of which she was thinking.

'I should like to see that Joyce Faa—just once! I do not believe she is so very beautiful!' said the Captain of the Levellers, while the little ripples of the tide ran away from under the boat's counter, laughing derisively.

CHAPTER ELEVEN
PATHS PERILOUS

Meanwhile I remained with Joyce Faa in the Shiel of the Dungeon, and regarded none of these things. It was a lot in itself not unenviable. The fine clear mountain air, the wild birds swinging all about upon their varied necessities, the romantic Shiel itself, all the eagles'-nest business of watching this one's flocks and that one's byre— touched the side of my nature which rejoices in being different from ordinary work-a-day folk about me.

I knew vaguely that my father had once on a time been seized by such-like longings, as for example, when he looked out of Rathan Tower and saw Silver Sand's camp-fire down in the birken glade of Rathan Isle. But, then, Patrick Heron was early left an orphan and could do as he chose, whereas I, with the best mother in the world, had been so watched and checked, so cossetted and debarred, that, being none of the wild birkies who make it their business to dare everything, I had chiefly grown as I was trained, and filled very much the room in the world that my good and dear mother intended I should.

But in this excursus, whatever might be the issue, I was free from blame—or, at least, I held myself so. For it was not my fault that I was held for ransom by Hector Faa, or that his daughter had a head like the cutting on an ancient Greek gem and the colouring of a ripening pomegranate, eyes purple-dark, lips scarlet, and, what was more to me than all, a swift wilful kindness in her glance, a charm even in a certain tumultuous way she had of heaping her hair together swiftly when the hill-winds from the Dungeon depths fretted it.

Yet I was not in love—or, at least, I did not know it. And even now, when I come to look back on all calmly, and everything that came out of it, I do not think that I was in love.

I was so easy to be understood myself, specially to a woman, with my girlishness of feature and the ways of a delicate boy, that ordinary women did not greatly move me. But rather I loved the society of those of them who were apart from the ruck—of my mother, for instance, she that had been called May Mischief (who would have thought now, to see how careful she was that I should keep out of that same?), of sonsy Eppie Tamson upon the Island, and—yes, though her age and beauty might cause others to smile, of Marion also, that young palm-tree by the rivers of waters, as a poetic and deeply smitten Cameronian had once called her.

But with none of them all, save with my mother, was I in love, a thing which, when I recalled what other young fellows of my age and station had confided to me concerning my own sister Grisel and a score of others, proved conclusively to myself that there was a want somewhere about me—a something that kept me from being or at last behaving quite as other men.

All the same, it was undeniably pleasant in the Shiel of the Dungeon. If Joyce Faa and I were not lovers, there were few boundaries to our friendship for each other. Having once accepted my parole, she and I wandered freely upon the tops of the wild mountains of slate and granite. Joyce it was who showed me how to climb the face of the great Craiglee precipice by paths that seemed no more deeply cut on the granite than if they had been scored with a slate-pencil.

Often we went hand in hand. For in necessary places she would give me hers, with none of the silly young maidish coquetry I had seen my sister and other pretty girls practise—ay, even upon each other, as it were, to keep their hands in.

But though I sometimes saw the corner of Joyce's mouth draw meditatively down, and surprised a deep and passionate glance in her eyes, I knew well that these were by no means love tokens. Nor did I presume at all upon the state of her heart with regard to myself. I had the instinct to let well alone, and I was not going to break off the first poet's song of my life before the primal stanza had been sung.

I knew that Joyce Faa pitied me because I had been mishandled, and that by her own kinsfolk.

Certainly, a marvellous kindliness looked forth from the deep places of her eyes, the which were indeed very deep. And when a beauteous maid looks so upon a young man—why, things begin to happen, even if their hearts are as free of any intent of love-making as hers or mine.

It came about after this fashion. Hector Faa was often away from the Dungeon, and when he returned it was his habit to bring with him certain of his dependants or spies, who would sit about the fire in the Shieling for hours, chattering and drinking, before going off to their couches in the lateral caves darkly inhabited by Grice Faa and his kind.

It was not my custom to pay much heed to these. They well knew who I was, and as I sat at my evening meal glanced often in my direction, evidently measuring with a grumbling envy the amount of ransom their host might he able to extract from the well-to-do laird of Isle Rathan and Orraland on my account. About this time, I take it, Joyce and I were completely 'fey.' We paid no heed to the days as they went, she happy with the first real companion she had ever had, since she left her mother's land of red roofs, white houses, and broad blue rivers placid in the sunshine while I, having once given my word, tried no ways of escape, but, excellently well content, played the play out, sucking the orange of the present, careless as to whether in the future it would agree with me or no.

I think we were both a little bewildered by the pleasure we found, each in the other. Yet, as to this, to escape misconstruction, I must hasten to make myself clear. It was not the ordinary pleasures of wandering lovers—not stolen reluctant glances, woven responsive hands, shy kisses sought, refused, yielded. Not these; no, nor any of them! ('Then the more fool you!' my father would have said.) Rather, be it understood, it was a relationship of the frankest and sanest comradeship, of happy young feet that loved to wander along the selfsame paths, of health and mutual liking and kindred vigours of blood, of silences that were never awkward, and of speech that never grew tiresome.

I found Joyce Faa grave beyond her years, often content to be silent with me for half a day, with nothing all about us but God's high airs, the wide swooping courses and clanging choruses of the birds, and our two hearts that beat as one (in no mere lovers' sense) plunging and loud as we mounted upward, anon flagging deliciously as we flung ourselves down side by side on the heather. This was our comradeship day by day, and afterwards we slept soundly in our several curtained bunks in the Shieling as snugly as in the several cabins of a ship, with our heads within a foot of each other, and the steady snoring of old Meggat in our ears as a lullaby.

Yet I do firmly avouch and record it, that we thought not of love—at least, I did not—till one night I had a somewhat startling proof that others did it for us.

Joyce and I had been out all day on the hills, as was our wont at that time. To say that we thought no evil is a statement far within the bounds of our innocency.

The sweet and gracious time was good enough for us. From horizon to horizon the heather glowed red as wine on the lees. And over this, league beyond imperial league, the honey-bees trilled their low falsetto, while the orange-buttocked bumble-bees boomed a vigorous bass.

I do not remember what we had said to each other. I cannot report these day-long talks of ours. Indeed, it was not so much what we said as the pleasure we had in saying it—or still better, that of being silent at pleasure. For often our silences would explode into bursts of gay confidential talk—yet talk such as the whole world might have listened to, so purged was it of the ordinary common-places of love-making. I have often been told that I am a fool. It may be. I deny it not. Another in my place, and with Joyce Faa for a companion, might have done other and better. No matter. This is what I did.

And, more than that, the other man would have been dead long ago with a cairn over him for all

68

memorial— that is, if he were fortunate. Otherwise the old Murder Hole of the Raider folk has not been fathomed yet, and lies but a mile or two, as the crow flies, westward from the Shiel of the Dungeon.

But to the story of how I found out that others had been busy with thoughts and intents that were alien to my own heart or at least, had not broken in upon me in their power.

I cannot tell what had come over us that night. But Joyce and I had to be called three times by Meggat Faa before we came in to the supper of sheep's kidneys and newly dug potatoes which she had prepared for us. Yet I can charge my memory with nothing that should have made us so forgetful - exactly the same turn of the path where on the night of my coming Joyce had met her father. The moon was rising red over Curlywee. The mist streamed like a snow-white, torrent down the mountain slopes, we could just see the silver gleam of the Middle burn in its birchen hollow, peeping here and there through the ground mist as through a bridal veil. And the hoarse roar of its headlong progress from loch to loch came to us like the sough of the lowest notes of an Aeolian harp—we were so far away and the night so calm and clear.

I think, also, the perilous place from which we viewed all this beauty put something in our hearts that had not been there before.

We held each other's hands, because, as it appeared to me, the place where we stood was palpably unsafe. And so, indeed, in the event it proved.

'Joyce,' I began, and then forgot what I had set out to say, and fell silent again in the kindred silence of the hills and the moon's red beauty. Then I confessed to her that I had forgotten what I had begun to say. Whereat we both laughed—and I heard her heart beat!

At that moment something happened.

I know not whether she had ventured a trifle too near the precipice. Usually Joyce was as sure-footed as a goat; but certain it is that a part of the insecure rocky foundation of the path crumbled beneath us, and if it had not been that I caught her in my arms, she had fallen over the verge, a couple of hundred feet or so, on to a stone slide that tailed off steeply towards the ravine.

'Oh, Max!' she cried, for the first time using the shorter name; and, before either of us knew, her arm was about my neck, having come there in the effort to sustain herself, and—my lips were upon hers!

We did not kiss—that is, not in the ordinary sense; but these are the facts, unexpected, overwhelming, altogether revolutionary.

The pleasure of it? Well, I do not know. It was like fire in my veins.

We could not fall apart instantly. Even the shock could not effectuate that. The path was too narrow and perilous. So I kept my arm where it was, and her hand was still on my neck but we did not look at each other any more. The weight of a great embarrassment lay heavy on both of us.

We had not proceeded more than a score of the short steps that men and women take together before they grow accustomed when, at the corner of the path, just where it widens towards the Shiel of the Dungeon, a dark figure sprang past us, with a whirr and rattle of loose stones. Something long, sinewy, and snakelike distinguished the man's movements even in his haste and dim light. I could feel Joyce shrinking a little towards me. I remember the sensation distinctly, because it was the first time I had experienced it. The girl had always seemed infinitely stronger than I. Yet on this occasion, most undeniably she shrank towards me for protection. And for almost the first time in my life I had a sense of pride in myself as a man.

As I say, Joyce shrank against me. It was almost, on that narrow path, as if I had held her close against me from knee to shoulder—a detail in the roll of conquest to a bold lover, but to me utterly subversive of all the feelings and resolves of a lifetime.

'Harry Polwart!' she exclaimed under her breath, with a kind of gasp.

'And who is Harry Polwart?' I asked, a new thing in my voice, and a new and wholesome anger in my heart. And then I first knew that I was as other men. A girl was afraid and I was not. An instinct of possession and protection surged upward in my heart.

And I kissed Joyce Faa for the first time—the other did not count!

Who Harry Polwart was it was my destiny to find out ere I was an hour older.

Joyce said no more to me then. Indeed, for a long time after these occurrences we did not speak, and I think that we went homeward to the swallow's nest of the Shieling a little dazed and light-headed. To make matters worse, Meggat was short with us, growling out to Joyce that if she took any interest in such matters, she might care to know that Hector had almost arranged my ransom with my father, and on such favourable terms that they would all be able to return to France.

'No that auld Meggat Faa will ever stir oot o' the land o' the Scots—na, na, though they should end by hangin' her at a rope's end in the Grassmarket o' Edinburgh! But young folk that are sae fell fond o' gallivantin' athort the country will dootless be glad to gang whaur they will get their fill o't!'

The malice of Meggat Faa's intention was obvious enough, and I fell to wondering whether, indeed, Joyce would be glad to return to France—the country of her birth and her education, the country of her mother. It was none of my business, of course, but I felt that I would like to know. The problem interested me more than many herds and beeves full-fed, and all the landed properties in the world. Once more the feeling came strongly upon me that I, Marwell Heron, the son of Patrick and his wife May, was a changeling. Somehow and somewhere their true offspring must, like Rhymer Thomas, be kept in servitude to the Queen of the Little People. He would appear one day and I vanish in a puff of sulphur reek and an unpleasant odour.

Joyce did not answer Meggat, either yea or nay. She ate her supper without interest, and presently took an opportunity, when there was a slight disturbance without, to slip off to her own curtained cell (for, indeed, it was little more—accommodation in the Shiel of the Dungeon being somewhat severely restricted).

It was in my mind to follow her example and forthwith proceed to mine. But something stifling in the air of the cavern-dwelling, a choking in the blue, thin, charcoal smoke that bellied beneath the low roof and eddied uncertainly from chimney and door ere it dispersed itself up the face of the rock, suddenly filled me with loathing unspeakable. I simply could not abide where I was. Restlessly I changed the position of my creepie-stool till I was beside the cruisie lamp which Meggat had lighted. I pulled my one book out —a little Testament of my mother's. I tried to read; but the tiny characters, though, indeed, marvels of type-cutting, ran together into little whirlpools as if I had looked at them through knotted glass.

At another time I should have taken this as a sign that I was overcome with sleep, and had better get me immediately to bed. But I knew better now. There were strange things to be seen and recalled out there in the moonlight of the empty hills. I would go again to the comer, where—where Joyce had so nearly lost her life, and where I also had lost something, and gained—what was it that I had gained? I wanted to have some one answer that question.

I got my wish—it may be my desert.

On the far silent hills the moon rested, her sifted light filling the glens with a dreamy vapour. There was a solemnity about everything, the largeness of simplicity; yet with something eminently human withal about it, like the heart of a good man as it is known to his God.

I walked slowly, now with a kind of triumphant feeling that my lips had indeed tasted of the fruit of the tree of knowledge, anon with sharp teeth of self-blame mordant about my heart—reproach that I had so long forgotten my mother and those who were doubtless anxious on my behalf down by the shores of Solway.

Why should I not take my life in my hands and escape? I believed—quite wrongly, as I now know—that I could easily escape Hector Faa's watchers.

The mountains I looked upon were wide and lowering, bossed with granite, and caverned with heather and peat-hags. Lochs, deep and solemn, cut across the glens and wider straths. What hill-gypsy could swim with me, who had breasted Solway surges ever since I was a little lad of six—my only manful accomplishment? My word passed to the daughter of an outlaw—well, surely every man has a right to make an effort for his life. Besides, had Joyce Faa not said that I was welcome to escape, if I would? Ah! that was just it— if I would! But did I wish to?

Then I took shame to myself when I thought to what infinitesimal proportions Joyce's kiss (I suppose I must call it that) had in a moment reduced my remorseful thoughts about my mother. I wonder if mothers expect this—if they ever think of this when they themselves are in love? But I suppose that in this, as in so much else, things square themselves if let alone, and that the ingratitude of the young to those who brought them into the world is paid for in kind when they themselves are parents in their turn.

So at the corner of the path I stood triumphant, subdued, remorseful, smiling, somehow altered from myself, and foolishly happy, because at last I had tasted life's sweet common good, when, swift as a bird's shadow, something dark leaped upon me from the cliff. I saw a flash like driven steel a moment cold in the moonlight. Then one fiery rending pang, and immediately I knew myself to be falling—falling—falling!

Yet I did not think of death. It was all much like a dream. I clutched upward and caught something—hair, I think it was. For a moment I saw before me the distorted, angry face of a man—my murderer—hang over me! Then the features seemed somehow to mingle with the red moon, and I knew I had met my death on the spot where an hour before I had first tasted life.

'Joyce!' I cried. And again, 'Joyce!'

And knew no more.

The kiss was paid for.

CHAPTER THIRTEEN
JOYCE FAA BRINGS ME HOME

But I did not die. Of course not, or I should not now be writing these memoirs of my life. My murderer was only my murderer in intent, if even so much. But it was long before I came to myself out of the confused tracts of whirling vapour and a certain stinging torment of Whiteness that oppressed my brain. I can still recall scenes I saw during these nights and days when I hovered on the confines of the Things that are Without.

I should like to tell of them, but meantime I should certainly scatter my readers. Still, I do remember a white city set on a hill, with towers and spires of churches here and there, a long white road thrown in loops and wimples, up which men toiled with eager, drawn faces towards the gates, few and narrow, of the city. And as they toiled aloft they wiped the sweat from their brows.

But ever and anon, here and there by the way great black paws at the end of hairy arms were stretched out from deep cavern and bosky hollow, and lo! all suddenly the road at that place was empty, and the moiling pilgrim was not!

I thought a deal upon this till I remembered that a certain man named Bunyan had seen much the same thing on hot summer nights in Bedford Gaol, when the fever held him. Then knew I that I had not really forgotten my mother and her teachings. (Afterwards I was told that during these days I called often on my mother, and murmured many childish prayers—a thing which, had I not been told it, would have seemed impossible to me.) For it was not my mother's hand that I held in mine when at last I awoke. It was—and the reader needs no telling—the hand of Joyce Faa.

And from this point, of course, as books are written, the story, with an eddy or two, ought, according to all the canons, to flow equably to the sea which is Peace and Love and Mutual Concord.

But so it was not to be. For though I had, as it

were, proved the right of my manhood to share the common good of the race, I was not a man like my father, to rive my way onward like a plough through stubborn soil. I, Maxwell Heron, born of the race of Scots who led the charge at the Battle of the Standard, and died in the van about King James at Flodden, was in many things weaker than a woman. And in all (save perhaps a certain composure in the face of danger, which I could not help being in my blood) I was ever the least heroic of mankind. If at any time I got credit for bravery, it was because I was taken by surprise, and had not time to do more or worse than simply stand my ground.

Well, as I say, when I awoke, Joyce Faa held my hand. And the face that I looked upon was full of a rich, wrathful tenderness. I know not how better to express it. Her countenance was not strikingly pale. It was rather of the hue of old ivory, but with the tinge of health through it. Yet the rich flooding red was gone from her cheeks and the lips had less of their accustomed vermilion. Perhaps it was that which suggested to a disordered and moidered brain my first spoken words.

'My dear,' I said, 'you are pale. You should put a poppy in your hair.'

Nor would I be appeased till she had put a bunch of red bell-heather in the raven masses coiled so densely about her head. She set it in Spanish fashion, just above the ear, and smiled a little wanly down upon me.

Then I asked another question.

'How did I come here? Tell me.'

'You were found wounded almost to death,' she said. 'You were carried hither from the foot of the precipice over which you had been thrown.'

'Who threw me?'

'Harry Polwart,' she answered, shortly, looking at the floor.

'But why—what harm have I done him? I never saw this Harry Polwart between the eyes, that I know of.'

Then Joyce looked away from me a long while,

and a slow carnation mantled her cheeks.

'He—saw—you—kiss—me!'

So that was how a perfectly natural action—or, rather, an involuntary and instinctive motion of protection—had been interpreted by the person most deeply concerned. I saw that I had yet much to learn.

But not being wholly void of sense and gratitude, I drew her hand nearer to me and laid my cheek upon it.

'Pardon me, dear Joyce,' I said. 'I had forgotten how expensive the article was up in these wilds. But I have paid the price.'

'Hush!' she said. 'You are very weak—you must not talk.'

I had just one word more to say, and I said it ere deep sleep—the grey, troublous, uneasy sleep of wounds and weariness—fell upon me.

'Dear, it was worth it!'

And I thought that she might have kissed me again, perhaps, for that. I seemed to have dreamed of such things happening before I awoke. But she did not—at least, not that I know of.

It was not till three or four days after this that I heard what had actually happened at the corner of the path. And then it was old Meggat who told me. Joyce herself was entirely reticent upon the subject.

'Bedded were we safe and siccar in the Shiel,' began Meggat Faa 'Na, I wasna sleepin'. Auld banes allow but little sleep when ye come to the age o' four-score years an' ten. But I thocht that Joyce was lang asleep.'

I asked Meggat a question here.

'Na, an' troth, that gied me nae concern. For I kenned that Hector's folk wad watch ye weel. There's no' a man o' them a' wad daur to gar Hector lose your ransom-siller, were it no that deil's birkie that smote ye, Hairry Polwart Faith, he is none feared even for Hector himsel'; only Silver Sand himsel' can fear Hairry, an' it tak's him a' his time.

'But after a gye while I hears Joyce moving in her bit chaumer.

'It's the disease,' thinks I, 'and a sair peety. For

77

Romany is bound to mate wi' Romany while the world lasts. But the fever o' young folk's blood wha can check? Then Joyce hersel' puts her head oot frae the curtains, as it were, answerin' my thocht.

'Is he no comed in yet?' she says.

'What should I ken?' says I. For it wasna in my mind to encourage her. Then Joyce she says never a word o' guid or ill, but pits on a wilicoat abune her nicht gear and slips oot canny as pussy. I think I maun hae dozed a wee, for the next that I kenned was the door faain' back on its hinges wi' a clash that near hand brocht it doon, and there stood the young lass wi' you claspit it her airms and the heart's bluid o' ye on her white goon. Sirce, sirce! It's an unco thing what love will gar a young lass do for a lad —him, maybe, no carin' ony mair for her than for the leaf that the wind o' the back end o' the year blaws against his face.'

She looked at me sternly as she spoke, and I sustained her gaze, knowing full well that I intended no harm to Joyce Faa.

Meggat resumed her tale.

'I hae fetched him' she says to me, wi' a kind o' sab, and wi' that lays ye doon on her ain bed. 'He is dead, and by the God that made us, Meggat, I am gangin' oot never to come back till I hae killed the black hound that murdered him—Harry Polwart!'

'And she was juist gettin doon her faitherns gun (that she can shoot wi' near as true as himself) to pursue after Hairry Polwart, when I cried on her to bide a wee. It is the maist strange thing that, though she brocht ye frae the foot o' the Slide on her ain back or in her ain airms— ye can speer at her whilk yin it was—she never jaloosed but that ye were by wi' it for this life, an indeed, ye lookit fell like it. For besides the drive ye had gotten frae Harrys gully-knife ye had cuttit yourself faa'in' doon thae dreadsome rocks, and, ta'en by and large, ye werena bonny to look upon.

'But for a' that, when I lifted the lid frae the e'e in your head, it wasna set and it wasna glazed. 'Deein', ye may be, laddie,' says I, 'but deid ye are no!'

Sae, wi' that, Joyce an' me gat ye to bed. And here ye are, as croose as a cock on a new-turned midden, my young Laird o' Rathan.'

'You may count on me to do that which is right,' I answered her, stupidly enough, for I was far too sick to rise to the height of her argument. But, indeed, what was right to do I knew not—nor did I know then (nor for long thereafter) the beginning or the middle or the end of the heart of Joyce Faa, the daughter of Hector the Outlaw.

As for me, as I grew better in body I seemed to grow more lonely in spirit. Hector came home the day after the assault and immediately departed again, vowing vengeance upon Harry Polwart for so nearly defrauding him at one blow of his ransom and his revenge.

After that only the stated sentinels and spies were at their posts, and the Dungeon itself was as quiet as the inside of a kirk on a week-day.

Joyce was more shy of me now, and our old cheerful comradeship was utterly broken. A first kiss may be like the laying of the foundation-stone of an edifice, but it may also be the pulling out of the key-stone, which dooms the whole bridge to destruction.

I had lost something; of so much I was sure. But I had not made up my mind whether I had gained anything, or (despise me who will) whether, indeed, I desired the thing that I had gained.

The English of which is, that I was a young fool and needed a lesson. And for such a kind Providence generally provides a competent preceptor.

CHAPTER FOURTEEN
THE MUSTER OF RASCARREL

Shortly before midnight the great muster was set at the cross-roads of Rascarrel. The younger and bolder sort of the Levellers were to be united for the first time under a leader of skill and daring—so at least the rumour ran. The walls of Jericho were at once and literally to fall down flat. The lairds, sons of Amalek and of the Philistines, were to be smitten hip and thigh.

The chief of these oppressors of the brethren were the Earl of Kirkham and an English officer of late come in his wife's right to the possession of a Galloway estate, by name Colonel Gunter, of Dunbeith. Now these gentlemen, eager for progress and especially diligent to lay field to field, forgot in their haste that measures which had succeeded well enough with the more obedient and servile peasantry of the southern English shires, were foredoomed to failure with a population so fierce and turbulent as that of Galloway, the natural wildness of whose nature had received a stern and solemn twist in the direction of fanaticism from the ill-judged severity of the second Charles and his brother James.

In these struggles the local lairds had, with but few exceptions, separated themselves from the common folk, and, instead of taking the hills with Peden and Alexander; Jordon, had chosen to remain and drink to the death of rebels and the confusion of all Whigs, in company with rough-riding Lag and Captain Windram, that admirable, hard-drinking six-bottle man who at Kirkcudbright commanded in the interests of King Charles's right to appoint bishops over the flock of God.

And now, fifty years afterwards, the Galloway lairds were paying the penalty for the sins of their predecessors. And part of the price—the first instalment, as it were— was to be paid on the night of the Muster of Rascarrel.

It was a curious sight, and one long memorable in the annals of cot-house and farm-ingle.

The cross-roads of Rascarrel were no more than the meeting-place of two green tracks that wimpled and lingered among the heather—by day a little greener and smoother on either side, and in the midst worn more rough and red by the plunging hooves of cattle and the pattering trotters of droving sheep; but by night scarce to be distinguished from the leagues of circumambient heather.

But there were several erect boulders in one of the angles made by the meeting ways, which gave the place its alternative name of the Standing Stanes o' Rascarrel.

The gathering was not without a certain rude pomp of its own. High on the highest standing stone was seated a figure dressed in a strange garb, looking in the flickering light of torches and the brief glimpses of the moon as the fleecy clouds scudded across her face, like a monstrous witch playing before the Master of Witches himself.

A huge poke-bonnet covered features, which, moreover, were blackened, while the whole figure was wrapped in a ludicrous parody of feminine attire, designed in sackcloth or the bags in which meal was carried to market. And this Witch of Endor, high placed above the throng, elbowed and smirked, as with infinite lilt of gracenotes borrowed from the Celtic pipes, she played 'The tailor fell through the bed, needles an' a',' 'The Broom o' the Cowdenknowes,' 'The wind that shakes the Barley,' and other fast-running, jigging tunes.

When the two maids Mistress Grisel Heron and the false Dick o' the Isle came within sight of the gathering, I think that at least the former was more than a little daunted. But the bearing of her companion quickly reassured her. For as soon as they heard the sounds of mirth Captain Dick quickened his step. (It is best for the present to adhere to the masculine pronoun.) He firmed his lips one upon the other, and with a quick drawing in of breath laid his hand upon the bunch of blue ribbons which he carried at his sword-hilt. When they came in sight of the levy, Grisel saw that not only the figure on the rock with the fiddle, but all others of the Levellers, wore the same costume as herself—that is, a huge bonnet concealing the face, and a peasant woman's cloak without sleeves belted the waist, leaving the arms free for any emergency.

Only Captain Dick of the Isle was differently arrayed, and wore his close-fitting suit of blue, his sword and his pistols with distinction and ease. Though the many bearded and mustached faces seen under the poke-bonnets revealed a preponderance of the masculine element, at the same time it was clear that there were many women in the throng. These were generally not armed, but kept together in small companies of two or three, and carried huge ox-poles, or, in some cases, ropes of twisted hide, by which these last were to be fastened together.

Half a dozen youths carried aloft torches of rosin roots dipped in tar, which they swung vigorously about their heads to quicken into flame as often as they smouldered. The entire concourse could not have numbered less than two hundred—all, except the women, being well provided with weapons of some sort or other.

They received their leader with a shout of welcome. Harry Polwart and his party had sung his praises well, and, indeed, the whole bearing of the young man was capable and daring. He alone had chosen to appear without mask or blackening of the face. These common folk felt that he was risking much for their sakes. Moreover he was wise in counsel. He it was who had bidden them bring to the muster the great ox-poles fifteen to twenty feet long, the purpose of which was so mysterious, and which had been the subject of so many jests and muttered imprecations as they were hurried cumbrously over hill and dale to the cross-roads of Rascarrel.

'Are you all here?' cried Dick of the Isle, taking command at once. The captains of companies briefly responded in semi-military fashion, and Dick told them off, according to a plan of his own, assigning picked men to the various portions of the great enclosure which had been erected by Colonel Gunter about the former holdings and pasturages of the expatriated cottiers of Dunbeith.

A sore bewildered man was Sammle Tamson when Captain Dick set him in charge of those who were to watch the mansion house of Colonel Gunter, situated on a rising ground, from which, had it been daylight, they would have had an admirable view of the destruction of the doomed fences.

'The voice is the voice of Jacob,' murmured Sammle, shaking his head; 'but the skin is the skin o'—deil tak' me, gin I ken wha's skin it is!'

But nevertheless Sammle moved off obediently enough with his company of scouts, charged with the duty of warning the Levellers of the approach of the forces of law and order.

Then Captain Dick initiated the remaining divisions of his forces into the secret and mystery of the ox-poles. Two or three of these were to be lashed firmly together. A company of twenty or thirty able-bodied rebels was told off, ten to each pole. Then at a given word the whole of these were to put forth their strength as one man, and the hated fences would be levelled with the ground. This they pledged themselves to do as often as the landlords continued to rebuild them.

At last they stood at the place where the campaign was to begin. The Earl's dry-stone dyke stretched away east and west, looming up under the clouded moon vast as the Great Wall of China—though, indeed, it was in no place much more than six feet high.

In silence the Levellers took their places, swank young herds and horny-fisted working women of the fields, all attired in the same absurd and outlandish costume. They manifested the utmost confidence in their youthful leader, and obeyed his orders without scruple. Probably this would not have been the case had the men concerned in the affair been the elders of the cause. But as most were young, and the element of adventure entered largely into their motives, and they were ready without question to follow so gallant a captain wherever he wished to lead them.

'Order out the bars!' cried Dick of the Isle.

The huge poles were placed in position behind the dykes.

'Man the bars!'

Thirty of the Levellers set themselves in position to push simultaneously.

'When I say three—let go, all! One, two. Three!'

'And over she goes!' chorussed the Levellers hoarsely at the word.

The huge, sky-mounting ridge of newly built dykes, not yet settled down on its foundations, swayed a moment uncertainly. A few stones toppled over upon the feet of the attacking force, and then with a slow, majestic bend, almost like that of a breaking wave, a furlong of it fell over in one piece, with a far-resounding crash, and lo! the green hill-side again stretched from horizon to horizon unbroken under the moon.

After this there was no concealment, or, indeed, any attempt at it. And this was the policy of Captain Dick of the Isle. By his very carelessness of observation he meant to strike terror into the Enclosers.

'Here they come!'

A messenger from Sammle Tamson's outpost near the mansion house of Dunbeith informed the Levellers that they were not to be allowed to continue their career of destruction without opposition.

But here again the young chieftain of the rebels proved himself worthy of their confidence. He placed a party in ambush, and at the head of a score of well-armed young fellows, willing to dare anything, he advanced to meet the Laird of Dunbeith's men.

Now Colonel Gunter had served in the foreign wars, and was a very headstrong old man, particularly ill to advise, and slow to acknowledge that circumstances were too strong for him.

'Who are you that come trespassing on my lands and destroying my property?' he cried. 'For this I will have you all hanged, drawn, and quartered!'

'Your lands you have bought or inherited,' answered Captain Dick, unabashed, 'but not the souls of the men who have dwelt on them for generations, nor yet the right to destroy their bodies and cast out their carcasses upon the waste!'

At this open defiance the Colonel was nearly beside himself with frenzy.

'If I could see you more clearly, young man!' he cried, 'I would not await the verdict of the judge to execute justice upon you!'

Promptly Dick of the Isle stepped out before his men. His features were hidden by his broad bonnet of blue, but the gallant defiance of his bearing could not be mistaken. This was the born chieftain—none other.

'I am here at your service,' he said; 'wait till the moon reaches yonder clear space in the heavens, and then execute your commission. You will find us ready. You will discover that men fighting for their homes are at least as trustworthy as any pack of pensioners and hirelings you can muster!'

Colonel Gunter strode forward, an imposing figure in a cloak of military blue, holding himself erect and stiff in spite of his age and honourable wounds.

'Halt, there! I warn you, sir,' cried young Dick, 'keep to your own side of the road and wait for the moon!'

It was upon the verge of a green drove-road, through the heather, that the old officer found himself halted, and now he stood fuming and glancing aloft in an agony of angry impatience.

The moon ploughed her way through the fleecy streamers as if running before the wind.

The tall, gloomy figures of the officer and of the slim young Captain of Levellers fronted each other, waiting for that clear shining.

At last it came. The moon sailed out, and the soldier lifted his arm with a pistol in his hand.

'Before you fire,' said Dick of the Isle, 'let me tell you, sir, that you and your men are entirely surrounded and at our mercy. You are less than a dozen, all told; we are more than two hundred. Our men are better armed, as you see. But we are no murderers. Go back to your home. We will return to ours. But remember that so often as you shut us out from our ancient privileges, so often will we put the bonds aside as a man's hand shreds the morning gossamer.'

'Your claims are as ridiculous as your language, sirrah!' cried the angry soldier. 'You are rank rebels against his Majesty King George. You shall all go to the gallows, and to hell thereafter! And now I am going to shoot you where you stand as a warning to others! God save the King!'

Colonel Gunter paused a moment, to give the young man time to reply or surrender. He did neither, only lifting his left hand to motion his followers to remain quiet. Then the officer again pointed his pistol at Captain Dick. But before he could pull the trigger his young adversary had fired a pistol, resting his wrist upon his hip in a way it had taken him many months to acquire, practising all through the afternoons of one summer upon the wild shores of Isle Rathan.

The distance was, indeed, no more than ten paces, and the accuracy of the aim no more difficult in the daytime than it would be to hit the square face of an empty Hollands bottle. But with the uncertain glinting of the moon, which alters all distances, and the soldier's threatening arm uplifted, it says something for Captain Dick's nerve that his ball, shot without direct aim, clipped the pistol neatly out of Colonel Gunter's grasp, numbing his arm to the elbow, but doing the old man no other harm.

Then, with great grace Captain Dick bowed, and asked the Colonel if he were satisfied. The old soldier returned the salutation curtly enough, and answered that, while he could hold no parley with manifest rebels, still he recognized that he was to some extent in their hands. He would see to it that they had a fair trial, and such small chance of his Majesty's clemency as they could expect.

'And as for you—who doubtless call yourself a captain among your crew, let me tell you, sir, that your speech and manner, though I confess I know not your face, betrays the gentleman. There may be some excuse for the ill-doing of the ignorant clowns I see disguised around you; but for you, a man of education and breeding, let me tell you, it sits ill upon you, sir—yes, damnably ill, sir!'

With this the old gentleman moved off, taking no notice of Dick's lifted bonnet. At the distance of a hundred yards he turned, and, shaking his finger at the youth, he cried, 'If I were your father, sir, I would break every bone in your body!'

'There is much to be said in favour of that view of the case,' responded Captain Dick, smiling and bowing courteously.

CHAPTER FIFTEEN
THE ANGERS OF EPPIE

In the midst of all these strange events it did not seem to occur to any one that there might be yet another point of view upon Isle Rathan—that of Mistress Eppie Tamson. This strenuous lady was not the woman to be left at home by her husband and step-daughter without a clear understanding of whys and wherefores.

It was possible, of course, for the culprits to enlarge upon the number of interests which needed to be seen to 'ower by at the new hoose,' and especially in the case of the younger delinquent the close friendship of their master's daughter Grisel could be made to cover a multitude of absences.

But by the constant sum of explanations, each in itself adequate and satisfactory, a general impression of distrust was created in Eppie Tamson's mind—distrust so complete that when next arrangements were made for a simultaneous excursion to the mainland by Sammle and his daughter, Eppie resolved to be of the party.

She did not mention her purpose, and, indeed, took considerable pains to conceal her arrangements. Any one acquainted with her abilities as the head of a household will not be hard to convince that these were thoroughly practical, and, indeed, showed evidences of the highest kind of strategy.

It was a slumberous autumn day, and Sammle, after declaring his intention to 'gang ower by and see to the stackin' o' the corn on the Whinny Knowes' dawdled about till it was past the middle of the afternoon; while as for Mistress Marion, who, in this matter, had Davie Veitch also to consult, she had so often put off her visit to her friend Grisel that she drove her step-mother almost to despair.

'If ye are gangin', gang! and if ye are bidin', bide.' she cried, 'but for Guides sake keep frae rinnin' to the door ten times in the meenite to see gin there's a white cloot waved at Balcairry Point! I never was in a hoose wi' siccan daftness gaun on, and I'm no gaun to coontenance it at my age! Sae I'm tellin' ye! When I hae the cakes bakit I'm gaun to lie doon, and then ye can baith gang to Jericho gin ye like for me!'

This was so extraordinary a proceeding for Mistress Eppie, in the middle of the afternoon, that Marion asked her if anything were the matter with her.

'Maitter!' she cried, sharply. 'What should be the maitter, except that I am fair seek to my stammack o' leevin' within the same fower waa's wi' twa clean daft folk!'

Discussion was vain in the house of Rathan with its mistress in such a frame of mind; but there was a general feeling of relief when, having accomplished the baking of the cake, and also the proper firing of it, Eppie finally betook herself to her bedroom.

That Eppie had small intention of remaining there will afterwards be abundantly manifest.

And so it came to pass that the next conclave of the Levellers held with all due solemnity in the Caldron of Ben Tudor, found itself unceremoniously invaded by a stout but determined woman, armed with the kitchen 'beetle,' or round-headed wooden club used for bruising or mashing potatoes, a formidable weapon in the hand of one accustomed to wield it every day of her life against the round 'dowp' of an iron pot.

'Come oot o' this Sammle Tamson! Hear ye me? Did ye leave the decent hoose o' Rathan that ye micht waste your time that is your maister's, your character that is your ain (what there is o't), and your guid health that ye owe to your duty to your wife?'

No man calling her in question she proceeded.

'And as for that young birkie wha (they say) has led ye astray, dinna let me come across him wi' this beetle in my hands, or I will learn him something that will serve him better than breakin' doon dykes and defyin' them that are set in authority over us! Bonny to look on, is he? Fegs, I wad sune mar his beauty gin I get hand o' him!'

For Eppie was emphatically on the side of the

powers that be.

But her threat remained words only. For Dick o' the Isle, a lion in courage when he had only an old war-dog like Colonel Gunter to face, seemed to have as little desire as his seniors to underlie the formidable 'beetle' of that very righteous woman, Eppie Tamson, formerly of Mossdale, now of the Old Tower of Rathan, when her angers were loosened upon her.

It so chanced, however, that one of the more influential of the Levellers, by name Jacob Trimmer—an argumentative, mouthy man, the lawyer of a lawless movement—interposed himself, and, greatly daring, drew upon himself the ire of Eppie.

'Woman!' he said, 'remember where you stand! Beware how you interfere with the representatives of the folk of Galloway in free Parliament assembled?'

'Free Parliament!' cried Eppie, raising the 'beetle' threateningly. 'Ye peetifu', wee, snarbled craitur, I'll learn you to talk to me aboot yer 'Free Parliaments.' Wha elecktit ye, I wad like to ken? An assembly of rebels that, gin ye gat your deserts, wad swing at the hands of Saunders Lennox, the common hangman o' Kirkcudbright! 'Free Parliament!' says you. Guid's truth, Jacob Trimmer, I wonder ye hae nae mair shame in ye! D'ye think I dinna ken that there was never onything free aboot ye, forbye the stick ye tak' to your puir wife! My certes, sirrah! it wad hae been tellin' ye gin ye had had for your guidwife juist this same Eppie Tamson that's standin' before you! The verra first time ye had lifted hand or fit to her, she wad garred your bits o' brains play clash again the wa' like a jabloch o' cauld parritch! And a great an' lasting benefit to the world that wad hae been!'

The argumentative man offered a remark in this place. It was not well-timed, nor yet well received.

'And wad ye daur to counter Eppie Tamson wi' your ill-talk, ye wee thrawn-faced atomy? Certes, I'll learn you! I'll level ye, bonny Levellers, gin ye anger me! By the faith o' an honest woman, gin I win at ye wi' this pitato beetle I'll learn ye something aboot levellin'! Levelling indeed! By honest John Knox, I'se do some levellin' mysel' the noo, an' wi' this verra beetle!'

And with no more preliminary than this Eppie rushed upon the upholders of a Free Land and a Free People, and, with the sternest and soundest of arguments, persuaded, not only Jacob Trimmer, but many others, that, whatever virtue there might be in these sounding entities, there abides a power in the cudgel of a woman free and able-bodied which even reformers and philanthropists have occasionally to reckon with.

So not for the first or last time in the history of the world, representative institution yielded to superior force. Providence exercised its ancient preference for the heavier battalions by declaring on the side of Eppie and the potato beetle, while in the general tumult the council of the Levellers broke up in some confusion.

'An' noo, Sammle Tamson,' said his wife, when she had him by the arm, 'come you doon the brae wi' me, and I'll explicate to you the inwardness and the ootwardness o' your iniquity, and point oot till ye, forbye, what will happen gin ever I hear tell o' ye again in siccan company as I found ye in this day!'

Sammle was understood to murmur some objection which concerned conscience and the rights of the individual.

'See here, Sammle Tamson,' answered this extremely convincing lady, 'I'm no carin' a docken for a' your fine words and prick-me-denty whimsies! But I, Eppie Tamson, will talk to you in words that ye will understand—ay, an' the wayfarin' man, though as big a fule as yourself, will mak' nae mistak' aboot them! See ye here! No' a breakfast will ye get in the hoose o' Rathan, unless ye promise me on your Bible oath to hae naething mair to do wi' things that are unlawfu'! And never a chack o' supper will pass your teeth but ye accoont to me, as ye will ae day to your Maker, for ilka hour o' the twenty-fower an' ilka minute o' ilka hour. Ay, and mind you, I'll no be pitten aff wi' ony story, faceable or unfaceable; nor wull ye be able to get through in the crood, as ye micht houp to do on That Day. I ken ye, Sammle Tamson! I'll no hae sae mony on my mind as Him; an' I'll be the better able to gie ye my undivided attention, as the lawyer bodies say, 'all and hale.' Sae try nane o' your lees an' equippitations wi' me, Sammle Tamson!'

Sammle visibly quailed at the prospect before him. The years stretched themselves ahead, one long eternity of domestic inquisition, and Sammle felt that he was not sufficient for these things. Nevertheless, all unmoved, Eppie went on her way.

'Ay, and what's mair—leavin' you oot o' the accoont for the present—there's that lass Marion! Do ye think I am blind and deaf and stupid, as the adder that stoppeth her ears? That lassie is no rinnin' here and watchin' yonder withoot some auld-farrant ploy in the head o' her. And what I say to you, I say to her. I hae gane through Davie Veitch with a hazel rung, as if I had searched his inward pairts wi' a lichtit candle and it's wonderfu' what an amount o' information ye can get oot o' the craitur juist by diligence in your vocation and a willin' airm. Noo, I willna hairm the lassie. Gin she was my ain, as she is yours, and no mine—I wad lang ere noo hae kaimed her wi' a bane kame! But ye didna, and I wadna. Sae Marion Tamson is the lassie that she is this day. The Lord that kens a' things, keep the puir bairn frae bein' misled, for I'm sair feared she is walkin' in a devious way!

'As I say, Eppie Tamson will never lift a hand on her —no, though she tak's to robbin' the mail-coach on the King's highway! And by what Davie Veitch lets on to me, she is no that far frae that even noo!

'But gin she is to bide in the hoose o' Rathan, suppin' o' my good brose an' stappin' the horn into my sonsy kail-pot, she maun e'en behave hersel' seemly, as becometh a douce and solate maid. That she is a bonny yin, a' fowk sees that has e'en in their heid; and a' the mair because o' that does it behoove her to be byordinar' douce. For the better-faured a lass is in this warld, the mair ill will folk find to say aboot her, and the less excuse will they mak', gin her foot slips in the way! Sae mind ye, Sammle, tell the lass that when next ye forgather wi' her! For it will come better aff you nor me—you bein', as it were, airt and pairt, if no heid and front, in the same transgression!

CHAPTER SIXTEEN
MAY MISCHIEF CONTRIVES

And indeed, it was just at this time that Marion of the Isle, though deeply attached both to her father and step-mother, recognized the impossibility of remaining longer in the ancient tower of Rathan under present conditions. It followed that she went direct to Orraland, where Grisel Heron rejoiced with a great rejoicing.

There was nothing unusual in such an intimacy among our simple Galloway folk. As everyone knows, my father and mother had been deeply interested in Marion from the time of the Great Raiding. Indeed, my father has elsewhere written fully the story of her childish adventurings. In consequence of this, and also because of his wife's liking for the maid, my father, Patrick Heron, had Marion brought up along with my sister. They attended the same schools, sewed at the same samplers, followed the same copy lines, and became greater and closer comrades every year.

They were the better friends that their characters were quite opposite. Grisel, as sweet a maid and loyal a sister as ever drew the breath of life, was ever of lighter and more sportive mind than Marion. Not that the maid of the Isle could not be mirthful and tricksome too upon due provocation. But it was upon occasion, and was apt to alternate with periods of depression and extreme blame of self. Grisel Heron, on the other hand, was ever a springtime maid, wanton of jest and prank as a lamb on the green April pastures. Marion grew up a true September beauty, fertile of resource, rich in thought, prodigal of self in the cause of those she loved, but inclined by nature to certain oft recurring storminesses of mood—as in her birth-month serene autumnal days are apt to alternate with the sudden turbulence of winds equinoctial.

It was natural enough, therefore, that Marion and Grisel should be much together. And the arrangement was favoured by my mother, with whom

Marion of the Isle was a prime favourite—so great, indeed, that to her much was permitted or overlooked which would have brought the swiftest condemnation upon others.

'I am glad to see you, Marion lass,' said my father, for his share in the welcome; 'this gives me two daughters instead of one!'

All this time Patrick Heron and his wife did not say much about my absence, and that to those who knew them was the truest gauge of what they thought. The negotiations for my ransom were conducted through Silver Sand, and that wise counsellor had advised no overt movement against the outlaw of the Dungeon in the mean time. He was convinced that my liberation could be effected better without bloodshed. The county was quieter than it had been twenty years ago, when the country rose against the hill gypsies. Hector, driven to extremities, was a more desperate outlaw than any of those who had sojourned about the Dark House of Craignaimy, and if his scouts brought him word of the advance of any armed party against him, it was ten to one that he would cut my throat out of hand, and forthwith remove himself out of the country.

Besides, Silver Sand expressed to my mother his confidence that I would certainly be well looked after by Joyce and Meggat, the two women who dwelt with Hector Faa in the Shieling of the Dungeon.

And my mother, though at first the notion of ministrant womankind in my afflictions appeared to comfort her, grew restive as the weeks rolled on, and finally declared her intention of going to the Shiel of the Dungeon, alone and unaccompanied, if none would help to bring her son home to her.

And she developed this idea more than ever after Marion came to the Orraland. For in her my mother found a sympathetic listener and a ready helper in any madcap ploy.

But, as was their custom, the three women said nothing to my father—who, to tell the truth, had a little settled down upon the lees of his comfort about this time, and desired nothing so much as that all things should be done decently and in order. For one thing, he had made up his mind, by the advice of Silver Sand, that the offer of a reasonable ransom was the best way to get his son home again. If he had been advised that the matter could better be settled by an armed invasion of the outlaw territory, no man would have enlisted, equipped, and led a band more swiftly, more boldly, or more successfully, as has indeed been proven over and over again.

But Patrick Heron had gotten past the wildness of his adventurous youth by this time, and was glad to take the straightest and most easily trodden path to his goal, without very much care whether or no it led him through scenery particularly picturesque. But so it is with most who have spent a gamesome and various youth. When the body begins to clothe itself with its natural over-coverture of fat, what wonder if the mind also begin to incline a little to a kindred adipose.

So the women of the house of Orraland took counsel with each other, admitting no breeched thing to their secrets, and specially swearing, all three of them, not to breathe a word of their intent to my father or Silver Sand. At the right moment, if it should be judged necessary, Jasper Jamie was to be admitted to so much of the high mystery as it was good for him to know, my sister Grisel and Marion of the Island jointly and severally offering to be his vouchers.

'We can do what we like with Jasper Jamie!' cried Grisel, with a little touch of scorn. At this time they were all for Hector Faa, Harry Polwart, Captain Cleveland, and, in general, such as were accounted desperate adventurers, so that even poor Jasper's broken head and bloody clouts gained him no great consideration from these freaksome lasses.

But a little sojourn at the Shieling of the Dungeon, particularly in the stable-caverns thereof, is the best cure for such foolish, romantical notions. For though I deny not that some of the women there are indubitable angels, yet if the men folk be such, at all events they are by no means of that sort which lost

96

not its first estate.

'I see not what there is 'twixt here and the Dungeon to hinder us,' said my mother; 'why, when I was May Maxwell, and a younger woman, I have ridden all the way, and thought little enough of it.'

'Ay, mother mine,' said Grisel, who was sitting at her knee in the pleasant little parlour that overlooks Rathan and its bay; 'but then you were in love!'

'And, pray, what am I now, Mistress Malapert?' quoth my mother; 'do you think a woman would do more for her sweetheart than she would twenty years after for her son? If so, you have much to learn!'

'Let us argue it out, pros and cons, as men do,' my mother went on, after a pause. 'Marion, you have the mind to advise; let us hear your thought upon the matter. First, then, there is the difficulty of getting away—'

'That we may leave to Jasper Jamie,' Grisel interrupted; 'if he fail, so much the worse for him!'

'Then there is the journey,' said my mother; 'that, I think, we will manage very well. One night at the Ferrytown of Cree, one at Bongill or the Borgan—a long day up to the Dungeon—and back again!'

Marion of the Isle laughed out suddenly. 'Oh, that is the point at last?,'she said; 'and back again. But then the question is, would you get back again at all? 'Tis a queetion that has two sides to it.'

'Let all hear them, Marion,' said my mother. She had great belief in the practical wisdom of the girl's advice. Perhaps, indeed, more than she would have had if she had known all the surprising story of Dick o' the Isle and his bonnet of blue.

'Why, then,' said Marion, 'there is this in it—if one prisoner at ransom bring in so much money to Hector Faa, how much more will four bring in? 'Tis a sum in Rule of Three, and perhaps Mr. Patrick Heron of Rathan might not like the answer to it!'

'But I say no,' said my mother, who had set her heart upon the venture. 'Hector knows as well as we do when he is at his tether's end, and he would never risk raising the country, as he would do if a couple of fair maids and one well-considered dame were held to ransom among the hills of the Dungeon. Besides, methinks. Silver Sand might have a word to say if his brother kept not his courtesy to us.'

'Why should Silver Sand do more for us than for poor Max?' said Grisel, who never could bear that I should be slighted, even in seeming.

'Silver Sand knows far more than all the rest of us,' said my mother, loyal as ever to her friends; 'and we have proved him with the proof of five and twenty years, remember. He will do, and is doing, what is best for Maxwell, whom he judges to be in no great danger as to his person. If the worst happened, he would also do the best for us!'

'But, why?' said Grisel; 'if Max is in no great danger, and in the way of being happy with a vastly pretty girl (for so Silver Sand reports of her), why go all that way and run risks for that which will doubtless come right of itself?'

My mother looked at Grisel with a certain amused contempt.

"Tis little that bairns ken aboot law-burrows!' as your father says,' quoth my mother. 'Do you think that I can bide to have my one son so long in the house of a fremit lass I have never seen? Grisel, I canna rest in my bed till I hae looked into the e'en o' this Joyce Faa, and kenned whether or no she be true woman!'

And it seemed to my mother that Marion of the Isle nodded an assent.

CHAPTER SEVENTEEN
IN WHICH I MAKE A POOR APPEARANCE

While all these various events were happening upon the Solway shore I remained with Joyce and Meggat Faa upon the rocky side of the Dungeon of Buchan.

The real negotiations for my release were not carried on among the hills, but at some of the low-country haunts frequented by Hector Faa and known to his brother Silver Sand.

So I knew nothing of them—nor, indeed, did Joyce and I greatly wish to know. God wot I am no hero (as will too often appear), and in nothing am I less heroic than in making provision for the future. My own mother has often warned me of this.

'If your meat be well readied. Maxwell, your bed made, and the day fine, a book to read or a lass to talk to—there ye are! Your heaven is accomplished—ay, though your father should break his heart and her that bore you lament like Rachel and refuse to be comforted.'

This reproach may be true enough as far as concerns myself, and I do not deny that constitutionally I am content too easily. But my mother hath the faculty also, and I am well convinced (and informed) that, as a matter of fact, my mother did not lament like Rachel nor did my father utterly break his heart. In fact, he would not allow anyone to take a hopeless tone about me at all.

'There never was an ill but there micht be a waur,' he said, in one of his frequent proverbs, and as for my mother, the reader knows in what manner she refused to be comforted. But this is ever the lot of those who are born out of their due time or who cannot run in beaten tracks all their days. Their sanity is doubted, their sincerity sneered at, their motives questioned. They are called selfish, foolish, vain, and, though it be with them but the sixth hour of the day, they have oftentimes to bear the brunt of the midnight excesses of others. At least, so it has been with one such, whom I know well, to which statement of fact I, Maxwell Heron, adherit my name and style.

And this is why, in the Shiel of the Dungeon, I abode with my friend Joyce Faa, not wholly happy, yet by no means ill-content. It was already autumn, and that and no other is the crown of the Scottish year. The front of October, so be it brings with it a week or so of still, gracious weather, is very height of living. Oh! these early crisp mornings up there at the Dungeon, when the hoarfrost lay for the better part of an hour grey on the heather, and then was lifted suddenly away with such an elation of golden sunbeams set aslant from over the edge of the world, and such brisk whirring of muirbirds (which I went out to shoot for our larder, Joyce following after, like a young roe upon the mountains), such inexpressible freshness of the clean high air, such nearness of the sky—which, nevertheless, when you lay on your back and looked upward at it became instantly infinitely removed. Will ever such good days come again? I wot not. We have grown old.

For one cannot run the wheels back upon the tracks of life, nor again be two-and-twenty, and out on the hills with a maid whose hand meets yours by instinct at each steepy turn of the brae.

Was I in love with Joyce Faa? A hard question, and one not lightly to be answered. Perhaps ay and no at the one time. I was most like a young colt in a field of red and white clover. I had had such abundance of clover all my life that I began to question whether after all I did not prefer plain meadow hay.

Jasper Jamie, who had the masculine faculty of being able to be in love, principally with one and subsidiarily with half a dozen others, as opportunity afforded, all at the one time, would have had no doubts. He would have forgotten (for the time being) that there was another girl in the world besides Joyce Faa, and, to use his own inelegant phrase, would have 'gone it deaf and blind.' Now I know not why this should be accounted a better way than mine. For Jasper Jamie, being at Orraland, would have been equally ready to do the same with my sister Grisel, with Marion of the Isle, or, indeed, with any of the pretty maids about—who could be induced to listen to him, that is. But of these there were not many, for Jasper's little frailty had become known, and the girls wickedly confided to each other his stock phrases of passionate devotion. So that on more than one occasion our minx of a Grisel prompted him when he paused for a word or disremembered a quotation, 'By heaven and earth and all the powers that be—'

(Here Jasper halted, being afflicted with a butter-finger memory).

'I—I—ah! Mumm...'

'I swear that never have I loved but thee! That is what you said to Marion.' Thus, in somewhat disconcerting fashion, Grisel would continue Jasper's quotation for him.

Now to me the futility of such proceedings cannot be expressed. More than that, and what is perhaps of more importance, the thing itself did not greatly amuse me.

So it came about in September I was no more to Joyce Faa than I had been the night before the affair of Harry Polwart—a confession of extraordinary weakness, as most men count weakness.

It was at this time that Silver Sand appeared in the Shieling of the Dungeon with his proposition. It had been long delayed, it seemed; but when it came, then for the first time I seemed to see Silver Sand in his true colours, and all his lifetime of loyalty and service to my parents, and incidentally to myself, was swept away in a moment.

I have said that in many things I was delicate as a girl. Yet all the more, there was in me a subsoil of obstinacy, and when I thought myself wronged, no one could resist with more zeal or determination. Indeed, I often enough bested Jasper Jamie at this game. For he, being large and good-natured, would give in rather than fight the matter out. The which I do not deny that I took advantage of to weary him into doing as I wanted, a thing which, though primarily for my advantage, yet generally turned out to be for his also. For his judgment was by no means equal to mine.

It was a keen autumn morning, about six of the clock, the sun just rising over the top of Millfore to the east. I went out to observe, as my custom is, the dawn. It was a true autumnal sunrise, rich and smoky, with the pinks and reds of summer all deepened to russet and misty gold, infinitely more lovely withal, like an awkward school-girl miss who, to her own surprise, grows beautiful at twenty. With a keen sense of enjoyment I stood watching the moorbirds busy about their avocations, the snipe circling and quavering far overhead, the knot and dotterel going twittering down to the shallow pools to wet their legs, the herons standing like statues in the lochs to spear eels and young pike, and—what was as much part of the scheme of nature and life up in these solitudes, the blue smoke-drifts from the Shieling, which rose along the rock-scarp of the Dungeon and disengaged themselves impalpably from the verge, like mist drawn upward by the sun's heat, ere they melted into a yet bluer blue too fine for human sight to follow them further.

'Silver Sand!' I cried, and ran to him as soon as I saw him come up out of the east as it were backed by this ruddy sunrise.

He reached a hand to me, palm downward as usual.

'What brings you here so early? You must have travelled all night.'

He smiled his patient smile—not an old man's smile, though he must have been nigh on to seventy. Silver Sand did not look any particular age. One might have guessed him anywhere between forty-five and sixty, for no look or action suggested old age.

'Ah!' he answered, 'I was born on the hills. I shall die, as I hope, on the hills. The clean-strae death of the house-dweller is not for Silver Sand. Yestreen I rested in a cave on the side of Lamachan, and thought upon many things. And I had good reason to bethink me, for today I am to risk the friendship of my oldest friends, and the good-will of a lad whom I love.'

He paused awhile in thought, and looked so sad and so gentle withal that my heart went out to him.

'If it be anything that concerns me,' I said, 'make yourself easy. Be not afraid. I know your good heart. I will do even as you bid me.'

He shook his head gently.

'That you say because you do not yet know the thing it has been laid upon me to propose. It is my brother's last word. Ransom in money he will not accept from any of your house—'

'But—but,' I exclaimed, greatly surprised, 'I thought —my father wrote that the matter was in the way of being arranged! And it was Hector Faa who gave me the letter himself. I am sure that at that time, at least, he had no very implacable thoughts with regard to me!'

'No more has he at this present,' said Silver Sand. 'He has changed his mind about accepting money, that is all.'

'And tell me, then—what he will accept?' I said, laying my hand on his arm. 'Tell me quickly Silver Sand.'

'Some folk would not consider it any hardship— I should not myself, at your age. It is that you marry sweet Mistress Joyce yonder!'

And with his hand he pointed in the direction of the Shieling, and lo! at the door stood the girl, shading her eyes with her hand and looking out towards us. She was a tall maid of her inches, lithe as a panther, and so soon as she caught a glimpse of us she came bounding along the narrow rocky paths and threw her arms about Silver Sand.

'Uncle! Uncle!' she cried, 'this is the gladdest sight I have seen for many a day! What has brought you here, and where have you slept all night? Are you hungry for breakfast? I am glad—so glad to see you!'

'These are too many questions all in a breath,' he answered, gravely smiling, while I stood a little aback from them, dumb and frozen; 'the wind of seventy years or thereby doth not avail to answer all these. But if you will make a choice of one among so many, I will answer that. Choose it carefully, as you

103

would choose a sweetheart.'

But instead she replied with a new pair of questions, not on her former list.

'How long are you going to stay, and is my father with you?'

'I am alone, and how long I must stay depends on the convenience of this young gentleman.'

As he spoke Silver Sand looked warningly at me.

Joyce Faa looked at me in a kind of bewilderment, with which a certain apprehension seemed to be mingled.

'Is he—has Mr. Heron been ransomed?' she asked. I glanced at her in surprise. The words were not spoken with her usual slow, sweet intonation. They fell somehow shortly upon the ear.

'It was upon such an errand that I came hither,' said Silver Sand; 'that is, on behalf of your father, I have made a proposition to this gentleman to which he has not yet replied.'

Joyce appeared to gather from her uncle's tone that he desired to be alone with me, and with a bright little nod and smile betook herself to her duties indoors. Silver Sand and I were again left on the hillside.

Yet the whirling chaos of my mind was not appeased, but rather increased by the sight of Joyce Faa, and the look that she cast at me out of her eyes. It is strange to think that it was at that very moment that I made up my mind for the first time of what colour they were, though I had often enough disputed the matter with her before. But at that instant of time, when I knew that she was afraid within her that our comradeship of the months was at an end, and I (be content, God has punished me!) was beginning to cherish hard and unworthy thoughts even of her—I discovered that her eyes were the exact colour of the dark under-bark of the silver birch—that which is revealed when the top skin curls up and reveals a rich brownish purple underneath, soft as moss velvet.

Why this so chanced I do not know, but the fact was so, and not otherwise.

'Well,' said Silver Sand, 'you have heard what I had to say Maxwell, and I presume from what my brother tells me that the offer can hardly be unacceptable to you. Joyce is a fit mate for any man of any degree. She was well educated in France, in a fashion to which few of the maidens of Scotland, even our own fair pair at Orraland, can lay claim. That she is fair to look upon, I do not need to inform you. That she is good, you have not been so long in her company without finding out. That she is ill-fitted for the rough life here, goes without saying.'

'I own all that,' said I, speaking at last; 'and yet I cannot answer you.'

Were it not that I have also to record my remorse and my punishment I could not bear to write down here cubbish impertinences.

'Come—come,' he said; 'surely this is not a hanging matter. It should not take a young lad of spirit long to make up his mind upon an offer so much in harmony with his conduct during the last three months.'

'I cannot. Silver Sand,' I said, with what I thought creditable firmness. 'I will be married to no maiden against my will!'

'Is that all you have to say Maxwell?'

I cried; 'surely no—a thousand times no. I have more to say—much more. I have also several questions to ask.'

'Which I will answer to the best of my knowledge,' said Silver Sand, unmoved.

'First of all, then—does my father know of this—and my mother?' I was certain that my father knew nothing of the matter—less sure of my mother. For she had ever many whimsies.

'No,' said Silver Sand, shortly; 'they do not know— yet!'

'Then I tell you I will have nothing to do with the affair!' said I.

Silver Sand laughed—the easy, tolerant, entirely sapient laugh of the man of the world who has seen many things and knows their outcome.

'Of one thing I can inform you, Master Heron;

your father and mother were not troubled with any such fine scruples at your age,' Silver Sand said, and there was something of contempt in his voice as he spoke. But to that I was accustomed, and cared little for it. I had only one life that I knew of, and I must do the best with that, as it seemed to me, without considering too much of what this one and that other would think of me.

'That is possible,' answered I; 'but then I am not my father and my mother—and so have perforce to arrange my own conduct as best I may.'

Silver Sand smiled.

'It is an error of the very youthful,' he said, 'that they can improve off-hand upon the ways of their forbears. You will allow that I am well known to and approven by your father and mother. I am trusted by them, and am not likely to venture anything to cause that trust to be withdrawn. Will you believe me when I say that if they knew all that I know of the matter, I am certain they would unhesitatingly add their entreaties to mine, and, if need be, their commands.'

'Even so,' I replied; 'one would be as vain as the other, unless I had made up my own mind. Moreover, how do you know that I have not another affair on my hands, and another sweetheart left behind me to whom I am betrothed? I may not have spent these twenty-two years in vain, any more than many another young man.'

He seemed for the moment a little nonplussed, and his countenance fell.

'Surely not,' he said at length; 'after all, you are the son of Patrick and May Heron. And—I have heard of the affair of Harry Polwart, and who it was that saved your life. I can tell you this—if you have played the hound, neither she nor I will be able to save it a second time.'

'Well, we will pass from that for the present,' I said. 'I may have no sweetheart, and yet decline to insult a woman by offering her an empty, loveless heart!'

'I am informed that you have acted as if your heart were very full indeed!'

'As to that, you are at liberty to inquire of Mistress Joyce, whether by word or deed I have done aught to give sayin' to that assertion.' I own he looked at me steadily for the best part of a meenit.

'I suppose that, for a likely young man, and a lad of your inches, ye are aware that ye are making a remarkably poor appearance.'

'I am aware,' I answered, 'that many might think so. But I did not count you among the number, Silver Sand. It is, as I have seen the world, better to be a little cautious beforehand than have the livelong rue afterwards.'

'Have you anything more to ask me?' said Silver Sand. ' I see that it grows nigh breakfast-time, and, indeed, I have cause to be ready for that same, besides, it is an exercise more useful for the mouth than this barren questioning.'

'That I have,' said I; 'and, first, what does the young lady herself know of this demand?'

'Nothing whatever!' said Silver Sand, emphatically, and, for the first time, with some anger at my persistence.

'Then,' said I, 'I am willing to abide by her verdict when the proposition is made to her!'

Silver Sand flashed a look at me, as though he had not expected so much finesse from my father's son.

'Which of us is to put the proposition before her, let me ask?' he queried, shrewdly, in his turn.

'You,' said I, to the full as dryly as he.

Now this seemed to me at the time the best solution. For I had every confidence in the delicacy of mind which I had noted on all occasions in this daughter of an outlaw. No spirit could be more graciously full of proud reserve than Joyce Faa's. She would shrink even as I from a compulsory marriage, and I should be delivered from the false position in which I was placed.

'I am content to leave it so!' I said. 'But, finally, tell me what is the alternative of my refusal?'

Then, for the first time in my life, I saw the gypsy blood leap up quick and savage in Silver Sand's eyes. It was something beyond anger—a pity for the ignorance of my race.

'My brother does not offer you any alternative—save that.'

He pointed to where, over the shoulder of the Rig of Enoch, we could just see the lean, leaden oval of the unplumbed Murder Hole cutting the autumnal russet of its fringing reeds.

'That is your alternative,' he repeated, with a certain grim solemnity.

CHAPTER EIGHTEEN
I DECIDE THAT I AM NO HERO

It was not till breakfast was well over that anything more was said upon the subject which Silver Sand had sprung upon me so suddenly. During the meal Joyce regarded her uncle with sparkling eyes and it was plain that he was a high favourite with her as indeed he was everywhere. Meggat Faa, though obviously no little in awe of the head of the name and clan, chattered incessantly, sometimes in some dialect unknown to me (for these gypsy folk have a language or jargon of their own) and sometimes in the ordinary Scots' of the country-side.

It struck me as curious that upon his first entrance into the Shiel of the Dungeon, both Meggat and Joyce took Silver Sand by the hand and kissed a thick silver ring which he wore upon his little finger. I knew not the meaning of this rite then, nor did I ask, for I had other things to think of. But I doubt not it was some relic of the ancient fealty to the anointed King of the Gypsies—the true Rey Assoluto, of the most ancient monarchy in the world.

Yet all passed without any notice taken, being as quickly over and done with as our shaking of hands, a thing too common to be either noted or dwelt upon.

Joyce, in the intervals of her serving, sat at the table's end, her pretty chin sunk upon her hand, and her eyes shining with good-will upon her uncle, yet not wholly disregarding me, where I sat opposite, glooming with the black dog on my back, grinding my teeth to think what a fool I was and yet for the life of me not able to help it.

However, so long as the breakfast lasted and the three of us abode in the Shieling, we got no further forward, though all the time I was cudgelling my brains as to what I should say or do. Joyce Faa was my friend of many weeks, my comrade, the companion whom in my walks I certainly preferred to all others. But equally certainly life is a longish journey and (till recently) I had felt no overwhelming desire to possess this girl and none other, such as the poets had led me to believe was the necessary sign and corollary of love.

Yet I had set my word to the bond betwixt myself and Silver Sand, and stand to it I must.

Grice Baillie and the other retainers of the Shieling came in, ate and drank silently and awkwardly, more like sullen, faithful dogs than men of intelligent human kind. Then they slouched out again, making the same acknowledgment of rank to Silver Sand, as in the case of the women. He said a word or two to them in the jargon which I did not understand, and presently there was Joyce busily washing up the dishes and listening to the tales of Silver Sand about the great, brave days before the world grew old and dull.

To me it seemed neither one nor yet the other. Indeed, I could have wished it more of both. For here was I, a young man romantically captive, in charge of a fair jailer—in fact, provided with all the accessories and opportunities of a hero, and yet—I heartily wished myself well out of it, and a decent citizen of Dumfries with a shop-counter in front of me and the curves of a capon-lined stomach interfering between my eyes and toes.

Yet I was, in a manner of speaking, a hero. Every man must be, of the tale he tells of himself. Yet what sort of appearance did I make in the two great requisites of a hero. A hero must vanquish his enemies and make love to his sweetheart. Whereas I had merely gotten me a clout on the head, and been brought to my prison-house like a bale of goods without striking a blow.

Still worse, here was a maiden fair as the goddesses of old time, in a manner of speaking, at my disposition— yet I did not know whether I wanted her or not, and, like a poltroon, hung tardy-foot on the apex of my fate. Truth to tell, my mother had spoiled me. I had been so continually with women, and they had made so much of me, that, like an apprentice in a sweet-stuff shop, I had grown not to care about any of them.

God forgive me for being such a conceited ape! But at any rate, in the dry of the leaf, I was made to smart for it.

I could see Silver Sand edging the conversation round to get us both out of the house. 'Would Meggat come out on the hills for a breath? It was years since she had trodden the white beaches of Loch Enoch. It would remind her of the days when he travelled the country with his donkey, and by selling sharpening' for the strakes' of the mowers, earned his name of Silver Sand.'

'Na, na,' cried old Meggat, holding up her hands in horror of the suggestion; 'never on this side of Daith's river will the e'en o' Meggat Faa, that was born o' the Kers o' Blackshiels on the Border Side, seek to rest on the bluidy shores o' Enoch, or on the Pit o' Sheep frae whilk was ta'en oot nae fewer than seventeen bodies o' strong men. Na, na; it's bad eneuch as it is, to ken that it lies awa' back there ahint the cliffs o' Buchan's Dungeon. But how you, John, that's a Faa born and the King o' a' the folk o' Egypt, can bide to look on that valley o' destruction is mair nor I can tell! But gang ye, gang ye blithely. Maybe ye will learn the second generation to mind what the first has forgotten, and, indeed, what nane but puir auld Meggat, that is as good as dead, ever gies a thocht to!'

So, thus despatched, the three of us went out again into the wide, wholesome morning, full of living breath and the crying of birds. It is pleasant to be on Enoch-side when the sun shines—not so marvellous, indeed, as to see its surges through the driving snow-swirls as the short fierce afternoons of winter close in. Still, even so, and in the summer weather, there is ever a sense up there that somehow heaven is near, and the evil things of the earth remote. 'Not with change of sky changes the mind of man,' saith the ancient. But where Enoch is held up to the firmament as upon a dandling palm of granite rock by Nature, the Great Mother, the souls of men seem insensibly to grow larger and simpler, if not conspicuously wiser.

This is what we looked upon.

Beyond to the west, the massive buttresses of the Merrick descended to the water's edge in myriad scarp and counterscarp, bastion and piled earthwork, laid out by engineer greater than that French Mons. Vauban now so highly acclaimed.

Green snatches of turf, narrow selvage of granite-sand shining silver white, granite piers stretching out every way half across, with water enough alongside each to float a king's ship—fret and babble and lisp of live water all through this bright stirring autumn day—while above, continuous as the wavelets, the swoop and cry and blithesome clangor of muirfowl. Such was Loch Enoch as we saw it. And the sight has remained in my mind, from which so many things more important have utterly faded.

For the better part of an hour Silver Sand said nothing about the question he was to put to Joyce. The girl leaned happily and unsuspectingly upon his arm, or sprang on ahead, alert as a young goat to point out something new and strange on the hill-side, or to bring back a handful of purple blackberries, late ripe at these altitudes, to give her uncle pleasure.

'But you have not been very lonely of late, Joyce,' said Silver Sand at last, 'with this prisoner of yours to look after?'

'No; I have not been lonely,' she answered, simply, looking directly at him, and speaking without embarrassment.

'You two have been good friends?' asked Silver Sand, as directly, but with a certain obvious meaning beyond what the words conveyed.

The gypsy girl flushed a little—a ripe dark flush in which, as it were, one saw the rich colour of the under-running blood. It was, to my mind, one of her rarest beauties.

She glanced once at me, perhaps to condition her reply according to whether I was near enough to hear her words. Then she replied to me, and not to Silver Sand.

'We have been good friends, you and I—is it not so?'

She turned upon me as she spoke with a quick

spriteliness of questioning unmistakably foreign. I had been lingering sullenly a step or two behind, making, as Silver Sand had truly remarked, no good appearance for one of my age and parentage. And I did not reply to her question,

'Joyce,' said Silver Sand, without an alteration of voice, and as if he were commenting upon the scenery, 'your father has ordered you to marry this young man. Are you willing to obey?'

She uttered a little quick cry, and in a moment straightened herself as a wild fawn might do, stricken while peacefully grazing by the hunter's bullet. If I might say so, the words of Silver Sand seemed to splash her very life's blood.

Then, if I had been anyways hard-hearted, I might have distinguished a complete study of emotions. But, foolishly indurating my heart, I saw nothing except that this proud, shy creature of the hills and glens had certainly known nothing of the matter. She was more innocent of it far than I.

For some time she tried hard to regain composure and ask a question, but her tongue refused its office. She could only look helplessly from Silver Sand to me, and from me back again to Silver Sand. I cursed her uncle for the brutal abruptness of his question. But now I see well why he did it thus. God-forsaken, worthless fool that I was, he did it to shame me by the very dumbness of the sweet, wild, young creature's pain.

A cat-o'-nine-tails across my back would have fitted me better than such consideration.

But at this time I had no bowels—and by that sign I knew myself for a man. Yet, to do me justice, I never meant in aught to wrong or hurt her, or to do anything that had not in it both right and honour.

'I do not understand,' her lips said at last, the words, as it were, straining past many barriers to win out.

'Your father demands, as the price of this young man's freedom, that he should marry you,' said Silver Sand, with his pitiless precision; 'what have you to say to such a proposal?'

Joyce Faa lifted one long, very long glance at me where I stood petulantly kicking up the white sand on the margin of the baylet among the rocks of Enoch. It was such a look as had never crossed me before. It seemed to explore me to the depths of my soul. The eyes of the maid, for well did I know her to be the purest and the truest maid God had made, rested on me a long moment, as if to make certain of my mind with regard to her—or, it might be, to give me space for repentance. But I, pitiable hound, did not respond to her eyes—not, it is some small comfort to reflect, from any lack of love, but because my wretched pride would not allow me to take even the thing that I most desired upon compulsion. So at least I told myself.

Well, I wot, if my appearance had been poor before, it was absolutely dastardly now. I let Joyce Faa's appeal fall to the ground. And, as I say, the only consolation is that I have suffered, liver and skin, soul and marrow, for that moment's cowardice. As, indeed, I richly deserved.

Then at last she spoke, drawing herself up haughtily and like a princess, as, indeed, she was. Pride, woman's best coadjutor, had come to her aid, and any love there might have been in her heart for Maxwell Heron was, for the time being at least, sent to its own place.

'I will never marry this man while heather grows and woods are green,' she said; 'no, not though I were to be all my days a handmaid in the house of the stranger!'

And I thought that as she spoke these cruel words Silver Sand nodded his head approvingly.

But he went on to do his commission according to the terms thereof.

'I do not think you understand,' he continued, gently; 'this young man, Maxwell Heron, younger of Rathan, is presently held a prisoner under ransom. Now, this present offer is not an alternative between the payment of a sum of money and a proposition of marriage. This young man must choose whether he will marry you—or die!'

'And he has chosen Death — rather than me!'

There was divine fire in her eyes as she spoke, and she drew herself up till she seemed tall as a queen of tragedy.

'He has chosen Death rather than me!' she repeated.

Whereupon I made haste to explain that I had not yet given any answer. I tried to tell her that I had left the answer to her, and promised to abide by her word; but she would listen to nothing. And I am bound to say I admired her for it. She was wholly and perfectly in the right.

She waved her hand with the back towards me, as if to keep even my words at a distance.

'You did answer—or, rather,' she said, 'if you did not answer, that is all the answer I need—now and to all eternity!'

And, being, in some measure, made crosswise, as a woman is made, I admired her more then than during all the months I had passed in her company.

Then she turned her about.

'I will leave you two to continue your discussion,' she said. And with that walked proudly away up Loch Enoch-side, leaving the two of us standing like statues gazing after her. And I scarcely need to say that no queen going to execution, with the consciousness of the proud obligement of race and conscious wrong upon her, ever walked more nobly erect than this daughter of Hector Faa, the gypsy outlaw, to her poor swallow's nest of clay and wattles among the cliffs of the Dungeon.

CHAPTER NINETEEN
THE STABLE-CAVERNS

Silver Sand and I stood looking at each other. I think he smiled a little, but the eye that met mine was like the edge of sharp steel. He nodded slightly and coolly, as to a compulsory acquaintance.

'Well,' he said, 'as neither of you will wed the other, this pleasant sojourn of mine at the Shiel is finished. I have no more to say. I must return to my brother. Meantime, it is my duty to commit you to the care of Mistress Joyce Faa's successor, and I hope you will like the change.'

He paced slowly to the men's quarters—certain caverns, rudely square, half-natural cavities, half hewn by gradual enlargement out from the rock. Here dwelt Grice Baillie, Orr McCaterick, the drunken dominie, and others of their kind, the chief of them being this tongueless, sleepless, loyal Grice, to whose custody I was now to be committed.

On my way thither I made a final appeal, but I had better have kept silence.

'Silver Sand,' I said, 'you have called yourself my father's friend. You saved my mother when her years were no more than mine! Can you let their son perish before your very eyes, or, at least, as soon as your back is turned?'

A little expression of disappointment overspread Silver Sand's countenance when I began to speak. He walked somewhat faster, as if to escape my words, so that I judged that shame moved within him.

'I think you do not understand my position,' he said, with a sort of firm suavity; 'I came hither simply as an ambassador. I have no power or influence with my brother, who has barely been even friendly with me for years. I undertook this embassy because it seemed to me that your father's friend might have more influence with you, and—and—with the young lady, than another and a rougher go-between. But since you both refuse—why, my task is the sooner ended. I can only endeavour to use my good offices with my brother and try to obtain some milder solution of the difficulty than a plunge in the Murder Hole down there, which, I tell you frankly, was the threat on his tongue when I left him.'

'But, Silver Sand,' I urged, 'if it be come to this, my parole is returned to me. You will help me to escape? I could have done it a thousand times before, but for my passed word to Joyce. I am under no promise now. Let Grice Baillie and his kind keep me, if they can.'

'Young man,' said Silver Sand, solemnly, 'when once I am gone from this Shiel of the Dungeon I will move heaven and earth to save you! Meantime, I am here as a trusted ambassador, and I would not stir hand or foot to help you till I am out of Hector Faa's country—not though a score of Maxwell Herons were to plumb the Murder Hole tomorrow morning!'

This little better tang of temper seemed to relieve Silver Sand considerably, and it was in an altered voice and with a more kindly demeanour that he resumed.

'Nor do I think that you asked this thing seriously,' he went on, 'and in any case it would have been in vain. See here!'

He put a couple of fingers to his mouth in the moorland way. The note of the whaup rang out, three times repeated, as true and perfect in tone as my father had told me concerning it twenty years before. I had often asked Silver Sand to perform it for me; but he appeared to attach something sacred or superstitious to the gypsies signal, and though he would readily mimic all other birds he could never be induced to imitate the whaup— perhaps because in Scotland the whaup with his long crooked neb is regarded as in some ways 'sib to the deil.'

When Silver Sand made his signal there was an instant boiling up of the seabirds that come inland to nest along the little creeks and islands of the loch. The moorbirds also sprang aloft with clamorous cries, angry at being disturbed, and lo! I saw a watcher stand upragged and tattered as a scarecrow, indeed, but well-armed with gun and pistol, and (I doubt not, though I could not see it) with a jockteleg snugly

117

ensconsed at his hip.

'But,' I urged, not willing to lose my life upon a quibble or for the lack of asking, 'if you have this power to whistle him up from the wide heather, why cannot you also send them away for an hour or two, so that my father's son might escape? Surely he would obey you in this, if they obeyed you in the other!'

Silver Sand smiled grimly.

'Well, we shall see!' he said, between his teeth. And we marched together to the outlying caverns, one of which was now to be my residence in place of the snug Shieling, sheltered from every wind and perfumed like a holy place by the rich sweet presence of Joyce Faa, whose very commonest household duties carried distinction with them, as of a princess condescending to hew wood and to draw water.

Grice Baillie lounged by the door of the rude abode which I was to share with him.

'Grice,' said Silver Sand, 'will you take a score of honest lads and go down to the Lodge of Trostan this nicht to bring hame a fat wether or twa for the larder? We have need of such.'

'A' wull not,' said Grice, without raising his head from the scrap of harness he was repairing.

'And, pray, why? Am I not the chief of your clan?'

'Ay, maybe, ye are a great man, John Faa, an' ye may hae great poo'er gi'en ye, but Hector Faa wad certainly kill me gin I war to gang a fit frae the Shiel o' the Dungeon withoot his orders!'

'But I come here by Hector Faa's instructions. You must obey me!' said Silver Sand.

'Let us see hand-o'-write on't then! A' canna reed, maybe, but Orr McCaterick can, him that was yince a dominie to the Yerl o' Eglintoun, and wad be hangit even yet if his lordship could catch him, a' ower the bit maitter o' his lordship's madam that he keepit aboot the castle.'

'Then you will not obey me, Grice?'

'No, that a' wull not!' And will any of the others, think you?' Na, no a man o' them; they hae mair

118

respeck for their necks. And maybes a scummer o' gaun to hell afore their time, and o' gettin' a scowder frae the deil's fire-irons afore it comes to them in the coorse o' natur'!'

Silver Sand turned to me with a wave of the hand and a hoist of the shoulder that were never, I am sure, learned within fifty mile of the cross of Dumfries. He did not need to speak. I understood that he had done what he could, and that I must look for safety elsewhere than in his protection, so long as I remained in the cavern-prisons of Hector Faa among the rocks of the Dungeon o' Buchan.

Nevertheless, the knowledge strengthened, and in a manner saved me. Since even the ancient ally of our house had deserted me, I stiffened my lip and resolved to take without murmuring whatever might be before me.

So I bade Silver Sand good-bye with an assured countenance, being resolved that, if he had thought badly of me in the matter of Joyce (where I had acted according to my conscience), at least he should have nothing unworthy to report as to my bearing under the threat of death.

Yet the one came far easier to me than the other. And this is the strange thing, that I have often been admired for a courage which cost me nothing—a certain frosty indifference as to what might happen—whereas I was despised for doing that which cost me more to do than all the other acts of my life. I loved Joyce Faa, or, at least, I felt towards her as I had never done to any woman. But I would not marry her on compulsion, nor be driven to the bride-bed at the point of the bayonet. Yet, by doing as I did, I had earned the contempt of a sane, knowledgeable man like Silver Sand, and, as I venture to compute, of nine-tenths of the men and women who read this over-true chronicle.

Yet a woman—any woman might have done as I did and never been blamed. Nay, more, she would have been applauded for a proper pride. She but used the weapons and privilege of her sex.

Has a man, then, no privileges of sex? Can I,

119

Maxwell Heron, be blamed that in some points I am nearer to the nature of the woman than the man? Ah, well! if it be so, I cannot help it. And here I shrug my shoulders as like to Silver Sand as I can.

Yet I do my complaining now, long years after; I did not do it then, which is perhaps the best thing that can be said for me. Nevertheless, I put it on record that what was chiefly the matter with me in my youth amounted to just this, that in opposition to the almost universally approved custom, I declined to let my desires take the reins out of the hands of my reason—an unpopular attitude in a young man, yet one not necessarily criminal.

(Except, that is, in delaying the story while at intervals I pause to expound it.)

That night I realized acutely the difference in my position as I shared Grice Baillie's uneasy couch in the second cave to the left, a hundred yards or so east from the Shieling.

'Hand up your fut!' said Grice, who came from the Mull of Cantyrre, to which the southwest wind has blown over from Ireland more than a whiff of the prevailing accent.

Because there was nothing else to be done I held up my foot, and the great brute shackled my ankle with a rude circle of metal with overlapping ends, which, being worked inward with a key, could be made to compress the leg, and, if necessary, to crush the very bone.

I explained to him that this was not necessary, because I had had abundant opportunities of escape if escape had been in my thought. But my explanation availed nothing.

'Aweel, that may be,' said Grice, sullenly, going on with his task, 'but, you see, it wasna me that had the keepin o' ye then. It's me that will be keepin ye noo!'

I made the plea of pity. How could I sleep with an encumbrance like that on my leg?

'Juist the way that a' wull sleep mysel!' said Grice, stolidly, proceeding to affix the corresponding shackle to his own ankle, the two being connected by a stout chain.

'Juist you watch me!' he said. And without a moment's hesitation he threw himself on his back on a heap of heather and was asleep and snoring in five minutes.

And though I appreciated fully the humour of Grice's suggestion, I found considerable difficulty in complying with it. The cavern had, recently as well as anciently, been used as a stable, and numerous tokens of such occupancy remained. A stinging odour of animal ammonia seemed slowly to pervade my system, until, as it seemed to me, my very immortal soul stank within me. Not till I had slept a night in a Spanish 'paradour,' where muleteers congregate, did I encounter the like, and even that was the mere refined essence of a suggestion compared to the claimant iniquities of the stable-chamber of Grice Baillie and his brother-outlaws.

That endless night I had ample time to bethink myself, and I thought many thoughts. Never had Joyce herself seemed so dainty or so adorable, the sense of her presence so full of desire and the graciousness of life, as during the hours when I was chained to that foul, hulking hound in the stable of the Shiel of the Dungeon. I had time enough to repent, and a score of times during that night I made up my mind to send for Joyce, if they would let her come to me. I would tell her how truly I loved her, and how I asked nothing better than to spend my life with her—in fact, that I could not live without her.

But ever as I thought, it would come over me anon that in another sense it was true that I could not live without her. She was my alternative to the Murder Hole of Loch Neldricken. I must marry her—or die! And at that point I stopped. No, I would show them. I would not do that which I most desired, at the word of command from any bog-trotting desperado that ever drove stolen cattle and poached other men's mutton.

So the night ended where it had began.

I rose unrefreshed from the dirty bundles of heather, wherein dwelt a restless army of insects of every sort that preys upon the skin of man. I was in agony; but Grice and his comrades manifested no impatience, or at the most composedly did their scratchings in their sleep, as it were, merely shifting pasture.

Yet this was with me an argument more compelling to make me come to terms than all appeals to decalogues and codes of honour. For, as is the case with women, my little fears and privations are far more compelling than my great ones.

I am not personally afraid of mice, but I can quite understand and appreciate the feelings of those who are. Yet these same women can look forward to a life of child-bearing with happy and even expectant hearts. We are strange creatures, both men and women of us, and there are few things for which we can afford to laugh at each other.

I had a sore and uncouth life of it all the time that I was in Grice Baillie's keeping—that is, for nearly a fortnight, or, as it seemed, a hatful of eternities. Joyce I did not see at all. I do not think she ever came within the range of my vision during the weary days I abode in the stable of the Shieling of the Dungeon.

Our meals were brought out to us, generally by Orr McCaterick, whose conversation—for at one time he had been a learned man (almost a clerk, indeed)—was the one redeeming feature of my life. He and I talked of many things, especially, it is curious to remember, of the characters of the kings and queens of England and Scotland— Orr, the disgraced dominie, being all for severity and sternness, especially towards the women of them.

'Eh, but she was a besom, if a' tales be true!' would be his summing up of many a long tale told out of the Latin of Buchanan or from Froissart's 'Chronicles' the former being Orr's specialty and the latter mine.

Once old Meggat came forth to spy out the land, as I think, but nominally to bring me a better dinner than usual, in which, with a curious irritated feeling of ill-usage, I recognized Joyce's hand.

'Ye hae dootless benefited by your change o' residence, Laird o' Rathan!' said Meggat, grimly rejoicing in the change in my appearance. 'Them that willna stammock wheaten bread, will come to want sowens!'

With this proverb she left us, and without a remark the dominie Orr turned again to the character of Mary Queen of Scots.

'Eh, but she was a besom, and yince—what is warst o' a'—I saw her picture, when I was in Enbra' wi' my Lord Eglintoun, and, d'ye ken, man, she wasna sae bonny as she has been crackit up to be. Eh, that was a sair disappointment to me, for I was a gye het-livered younker at that time and keen on the weemen-folk.'

Grice Baillie had been sitting meantime whittling a hasp for a gate-post, and, as we thought, scarcely listening to our talk. But at this point he raised his eyes— red, heavy, sullen eyes, jowled beneath with a dogged surliness. He looked at the dominie with a kind of masterful and saturnine humour that had nevertheless something lowering and threatening in it.

'Ah, Orr McCaterick, you are the man that's a judge o' besomd! But gin ye say anither word again' Mary, that bonny quean, I'll gie ye a jag that will gar ye wuss that the Yerl o' Eglintoun had gotten ye, the time ye ran frae the castle yett in your sark tails!'

It came as quick as tick-tack, the two men sitting opposite to each other on a heap of straw. I saw Orr McCaterick smite Grice fair between the eyes, and even as knuckles thudded on frontal bone the whittle in Grice's hands was sheathed in the dominie's ribs.

It was among such men that I had now perforce to practise what of manhood had come to me by ordinary generation, or as I had acquired on my daily pilgrimage.

CHAPTER TWENTY
JOYCE LOVES ME

More dismally even than usual loomed up the interior of the stable bedchamber which I shared with Grice, my gaoler, the wounded dominie, and an innumerable company of other animals. The wet, reeking straw, the sodden bundles of heather, the walls running with brown moss-water, the dripping, sooty thatch, seemed deader and dismaller and more hopeless than ever before.

To lie and listen to Orr McCaterick's groaning was all my distraction, and as a steady amusement it could not be termed of a cheerful boy.

'And am I come to this, me that was brocht up a colleger at St. Anders, that aunciend seat o' lear—me that has set copy-heads to mony a great man, me that bonny women and grand women hae favoured—whilk hap was my undoing. I wonder if Yon Yin minds the day amang the booers o' Castle Eglintoun—and the Ode to Chloe that I wraite to her (she didna read honest John Donne— na, na, or she wad hae faud it there!) And noo I hae comed to this o't—that a dumb dog that canna bark in any articulate speech may stap his knife in me, that kens twa dead languages, and never be checkit for't! But I mind the words o' the poet that wrote: 'Chloe, the aureate tresses of thy hair— ' I forget how it gaed after that. But she approved—and Heaven forgie me, she was fell bonny—as bonny as I was young. But his lordship cam' at us unawares—and— what's that I hear? No Hector Faa's fit? Lord, if it be, help puir Orr! For he's as guid as deid, and kens it. 'Dinna fecht at your posts,' says Hector, or there will be some fechtin' when I come back, to speak aboot!' Noo he will come back an' find me here. Waes me for puir auld Orr, that yince was the belovit o' weemen an' wraite poetry!'

The door of the miserable hovel, which had been ajar so that one could see the continuous slanting of the rain, was rudely driven wide, and Hector Faa stood before us. There was a deep frown on his face.

'First I will attend to your case, friend Orr,' he said; 'Grice Baillie will no stab a man for some time to come. You were brawling, I hear—and after what I said to ye?'

'Nay, by my faith and honour,' said the dominie, in the extremity of terror; 'Grice struck me before I was aware!'

'There is a bruise between Grice's eyes that tells another tale—what have you to say to that?'

'I did it in my death agony after I was stricken with a knife! In God's faith, it fell out so. This young gentleman will bear me witness!'

But, having no wish to mix myself up in any such ravelled business, I held my tongue. I was also most undesirous of prejudicing my own case, when (according to the gypsy's word) it should come up for judgment a few minutes later.

'Well, Master Orr, learned son of Caterick, I shall have a word with you presently. There is a swift and easy way with those who love blood-letting. I may need a little done on my own account presently. You are a learned man, I hear, Master Orr—well, if it turns out so, you shall be my leech.'

Then Hector Faa addressed me with that mixture of fine-gentleman courtesy and bullying bravado which he is said to have learned from his first commander, the famous Captain Yawkins.

'So, sir,' he said, 'I am given to understand that you consider the outlaw's daughter, of the best blood of an older land than this rotting dunghill of Lowland Scots, not to be good enough or fair enough for the son of the laird of Rathan!'

'Then, if that be so, sir, you have been given to understand that which is not true,' I answered him. 'Mistress Joyce Faa is infinitely too good for me to aspire to. She is too beautiful and noble. I honour her above all women, and when in honour I can humbly ask her to marry me, it will be the happiest day in my life if she accept my hand.'

In those days I was the greatest don at set speeches. I think I gat the lilt of them out of an old book of my father's (with some poetics in it, too, very curious and rare—at least, I hope they are the latter) called the 'Gentleman's Pocket Mirror of Wit and Eloquence.' I studied it oft, and learned screeds of it off by heart, all to please my mother, who, in the days of my hobbledehoy-hood, used to dress me as a page, with ribbons in bunches at my belt and knee—making, as my father said, 'A fool of a decent enough lad.'

But the speeches out of 'Wit and Eloquence' (let my father scoff at them as he will) were quite to the taste of this Captain of Outlaws. Perhaps, in old days. Captain Yawkins also had a copy of the 'Pocket Mirror,' and instructed his youthful lieutenant.

'You speak well,' he said; 'but I have my idea, and it is that the society of these clowns, and even of this wondrous learned man (who, however, scratches himself to the full as often as the others), may have had something to do with these handsome sentiments.'

'Again you misunderstand my position,' I said; 'when in honour I can ask Mistress Joyce's favour, ask her I will. But then, Captain Hector, I cannot bring myself to do that, to which another compels me without choice of my own. Besides, the lady herself hath refused to have aught to do with me. When Silver Sand put me matter to her, she denied me point blank, as, indeed, I own that I well deserved.'

'These are fine birds indeed, but I will plook them of their gay feathers,' the gypsy said, quoting another proverb. 'I made you an offer, and that by the mouth of your own chosen intermediary. You refused. Two alternatives were placed before you. Still your answer was the same. With what my daughter may have said, or her reasons for saying it—I have nothing to do. With my offer and your response I am prepared to deal.'

He turned about to the wounded dominie, who lay with dropped jaw, interested as to my case, yet doubtless in painful doubt as to his own fate.

'Learned doctor,' said Hector Faa, with suave and dangerous deference, 'I need not ask whether so wise and practical a man has a knife about him with an edge upon which a man may rely on in case of need? I have forbidden you to carry such except when on duty, for you are an unruly set, and apt for ill deeds among yourselves!'

The dominie at first denied, but, being pressed, he rolled sulkily over, and, groping among the damp and reeking straw of his bed, he disinterred a piece of whity-brown paper. This he unrolled, and there lay Grice's whittle, with its curved edge and the spring catch, a ghastly object, for Orr's own blood was yet uncleansed from its blade.

'Ah,' said Hector Faa, 'this will not do. I know well where you meant to drive that the first time you caught Master Grice asleep. But I have another purpose for it now. I have not too many rascals up here in these wilds, and few of them are of the right tiger blood like Grice. I cannot afford to lose him. Therefore, to make up the quarrel between you, you shall share a little piece of work. This young gentleman hath had his choice betwixt bride-bed and the bottom of the Murder Hole. He has had the bad taste to prefer the latter. So now you must see him handsomely on his way.

'Now, as you are a little hipped at present, Orr, my lad, I should advise that you use your knife as you meant to do upon Grice, when your prisoner is asleep. And be good enough to make a clean job of it. Then Grice, in his turn, will disembarrass you of—the Thing which Remains! The Murder Hole will tell no tales as to that!'

Hector Faa stood as easily against the door-post and spoke as smoothly as if he had said ' 'Twill be a fine day tomorrow,' the while he was uttering these atrocious sentiments. But the dominie, in spite of his wound, started up.

'I cannot—I cannot—God's truth, I cannot slit a man's throat in cold blood!' he cried, 'and we have been none such bad friends either, he and I. I cannot do it, and so I tell you. Hector!'

The outlaw leaned a little over, and with a kind of sigh, murmured, confidentially, 'Ah, well, then, I suppose I shall have to do it myself—after your decease, Orr!'

'You would not murder me, Captain?'

The words came like a cry of terror. Lame as he was, the poor dominie was half on his feet by this time, his teeth clicking together in sheer terror. 'You would not murder a man who has worked for you, and done your bidding faithfully for years?'

'That is just the point,' said Hector, with the same deadly chill in his voice. 'Done my bidding faithfully, you say. Well, you swore to do it when you joined the band, did you not—under penalty of death? Now, if you refuse to do it, you cannot complain if you are called on to suffer that penalty. It is no more murder than the plain choice offered to this gentleman, which he has accepted and will doubtless stand by like a gentleman!'

While he had been speaking. Hector had picked up Grice Baillie's knife, wiped it on an old rag which had been thrust into a dripping crevice of the cavern. Then, having assured himself as to its point and edge, he nodded significantly.

'Grice keeps good tools, and also sharp ones—though his wits, God knows, he keeps dull enough. This will finish the business out of hand; and Grice, who will be in waiting outside, can report to me at the Shiel after his part is done. The women are not to know, of course!'

He spoke these final directions in a tone somewhat louder than before, whether by intention or not I do not know. At all events, scarcely were they out of his mouth when the side door of the shelter, which had been partially closed during the colloquy, was burst open, and Joyce Faa entered, her black hair dishevelled and falling in great raven coils about her face and over her neck. She seemed quite unconscious of anything but the horror of the words she had overheard.

'Oh, my father,' she cried, dropping on her knees and holding him by the skirts of his long sea-captain's coat of blue, 'father, you do not mean this! You have always been good and kind to me. That you have slain men, I know; but it has always been in fair

128

fight. Surely you will not shed this young lad's blood as he lies bound and helpless in your power! That were too cruel, cowardly, murderous—'

Hector Faa pushed her away, but even on her knees she moved a little nearer, and would not let him go.

'Father, you must hear me—you must listen,' she sobbed. I had not believed that tears could come at all into the proud, splendid eyes of Joyce Faa. Meantime, I lay there wonderfully composed, with manacles upon my feet and my wrists tied with rope so tight that the fingers swelled, just as that great nowt Grice had left me. But, believe it who will, this part of my trial was easy, or, at least nothing to many things that had gone before—or that followed after.

Indeed, a little proud pulse beat somewhere within me near my heart, but more towards the bottom of the throat. I have felt it a time or two in my life, and always when I have thought that I was behaving well.

Hector Faa took his daughter by the shoulders, and lifted her up with a kind of sternness, at once scornful and bitter.

'Joyce,' he said, 'I thought you had more pride than thus to humble yourself to seek the life of the man who has despised you.'

'I do not,' I cried, 'and I never did. Before God, I love and honour—'

But my words could no more turn this man from his intent than the cheeping of a mouse in the corn-mow is able to prevent its overthrow when the threshers stand waiting on the earthen floor.

'Listen, Joyce,' he said; 'from this man's father I and mine suffered the greatest wrongs man can lay upon man—expatriation, pursuit, death. By his mother was put upon me the greatest of slights. Now their son, their only son, is in my hands. I am an outlaw, and every man's hand is against me. Yet I not only spare him, but I offer him my daughter in marriage to heal the ancient breach. I ask him to make choice between that and death. And he chose death! Is this the man for whom you plead, Joyce

Faa? Let me tell you that the true child of the gypsy would rejoice in the death of her house's enemy, the righteous condemnation of the man who scorned and slighted her!'

At the words that I had chosen death rather than her I saw Joyce wince, as she leaned with one hand on the lid of the corn-chest which stood in the angle of the cave.

But she rallied bravely, like one resolved at all costs to carry through the thing that was in her heart.

'Indeed I do plead,' she said. 'I would go down on my knees to beg him to marry me rather than that he should die upon a mere point of honour. I would not have him die, even if he does not love me. There are times for a woman to cherish pride, but not now.'

She turned to me where I lay helpless on the heap of filth which had been my bed.

'Maxwell,' she said, clasping her hands, 'you will not still hold out? You will promise to marry me and not die? God help me, I never thought thus to speak to any man. But I do not care. Why should I care—what is pride to a gypsy maid? But do not be afraid that I will hinder you on your way through the world. I will go away afterwards, and you will never be troubled more with Joyce Faa.'

Then, even as she spoke, there came for the first time the rushing of a mighty love into my heart. My soul swelled within me, and the tears stood large in my eyes.

'I love you, Joyce,' I cried, looking at her through a blur of salt water; 'God knows, I am not worthy to love you—not worthy to wed you—not worthy to touch the hem of your garment. But if you will take me, you shall have all the love of a man's heart therewith!'

And in a moment, with a sweet, sharp cry of thankfulness, Joyce Faa was upon her knees before me, trying with her trembling hand to unfasten my bonds, and the hot tears splashing down upon my face, broad and solitary as the first droppings of a thunder-shower.

'Bless you—bless you!' she whispered; 'say

130

these things over again to my father, and he will believe you. Be not afraid to speak. I will not hereafter trouble you!'

And this saying of hers I could not fathom at the time, but set it down to perturbation of spirit.

And when for a moment I hesitated, for such things once spoken are difficult to repeat—' Say it! Say it! Let my father hear it!' she murmured in my ear.

So I took heart of grace, and addressed Hector Faa directly as he stood looking silently and grimly down.

'If this maid, whom with all my heart I love and honour, will consent to marry me, I offer her all the love of a man's heart, and all I have in this world of goods and gear.'

'Thank you—thank you—that is well said. My father is turning—I know his ways. He wishes to be convinced to save you. But he is set on this.'

And the girl who had seemed so proud, dropped her head upon my hands, and because she could not untie the fastenings quickly, she bit at the cords with her teeth.

Seeing which, with a quick-fading, bitter smile. Hector Faa lifted the knife of Grice Baillie, which had been destined to cut my throat, and slit my bonds with it instead. The leg-irons he slipped off with the assistance of the dominie, who smiled, well pleased to be rid of a job he had no pleasure in—and then the next moment his mouth was twisted awry with the pain of his own wound.

CHAPTER TWENTY ONE
I LOVE JOYCE

Out of the muckly litter I rose somewhat uncertainly to my feet, with a glad heart, yet feeling (as to the corporeal part of me) the meanest, dirtiest, most downtrodden piece of stable refuse that ever insulted the wholesome eye of day.

Hector Faa said no more at that time, but, with a return of his old sardonic smile, he turned on his heel and left the stable. Joyce and I followed him more slowly, the eyes of the wounded dominie enviously upon us.

As we crossed the space which separated the stable-caverns from the well-kept Shieling of the Dungeon I said to Joyce, pressing her arm, 'Dearest, you have saved my life! I thank you, and love you with all my heart.'

Judge of my astonishment when she quietly disengaged her arm and answered, 'There is no need of that now; my father is out of hearing!'

'But I do truly love you, Joyce!' I said, speaking the thing that was in my heart.

She opened her eyes upon me, as if with a single, hopeful, searching glance, but immediately smiled again with a fixed bitterness which recalled her father.

'You do not need to keep up appearances with me!' she said. 'It is not necessary, and I do not expect it from you.'

'But I love you, Joyce!'

She looked at me with that single-eyed glance, so sweet, lingering, yet for no reason known to me, all so soon melting away into that same bitterness of soul. Then, nodding slightly, as if taking the statement for what it was worth (and finding the value a slight one), she moved quietly away towards the house.

A thorough cleansing of my person in an alcove arranged by Meggat, the donning of a good suit of clothes never made or meant for Hector Faa (which, however, fitted me very well), and Maxwell Heron was a new man again. Also, but for Joyce's inexplicable behaviour, I should have been a happy one.

Hector came to see me an hour after as I sat in my old seat and new array, looking out of the window of the Shieling, Meggat and Joyce meanwhile moving silently about at their household tasks.

'So,' he said, leaning against the door-post, without sitting down, 'you are again arrayed according to your quality—or, if I remember the circumstances aright a little above it. Well, son-in-law, we have a work to do, and it behoves that it is well done. For me, I should have been content, like our forefathers, with the gypsy wedding, without priest or minister. But our far-travelled Joyce here, has other ideas. So I have sent to arrange with the Minister of Minnigaff, who sits, as it were, under my hand, and will not deny me the favour I have asked— that he marry you according to the fashion of the Scottish kirk on the third day from now. I have granted this delay to please my daughter; but remember, young man, if you play with Hector Faa, you play with death.'

Joyce turned a swift look upon me, half over her shoulder. I thought she smiled.

'You need fear nothing from me,' I said. 'I shall only be the happier man every instant that the event is hastened.'

'I had not thought it of Grice and Orr,' said Hector. 'Let no man after this judge of the talents of another.'

What the fear of death and the proffer of love could not do, one short week of Grice and Orr hath most pleasantly effectuated.

And again over her shoulder as she passed I caught the glance of Joyce Faa, pleasantly approving. So, with little talk, but great comfort of body, ended the day. Could I only have understood the meaning of Joyce Faa's actions and demeanour I should have been altogether happy. But this I could not do. So long as her father was near—either in the house or moving about the doors—no sweetheart could have been more loving, no wife more devoted.

133

She would lay her hand on my shoulder and appear to read from the same book. She permitted me freely to take her hand, a thing she had never done since the kiss at the rocky corner—that for which I paid so dearly.

But no sooner was her father a hundred yards down the path than, with the quietest determination in the world, she would disengage herself, and draw off, either to her own chamber, or, if she remained at all, it was to intrench herself behind Meggat and sit silent and distrait over her sewing.

Never had I dreamed of being so treated, and when I bethought me that in the latter parts of the business I had behaved not that ill (and I think so even to this day) to be slighted and scorned—and to have my devotion, as it were, thrown in my teeth— why, it was hard, indeed, for a young man to bear.

But there was more, and worse, yet before me.

I strove all the afternoon to get a word with her alone. But I doubt not that she had forewarned Meggat—so that, do what I would, at kitchen-ingle or bakeboard, peat-stack or rock-larder, where one was, the other was, and my desire was continually balked. Did I see her lifting a wooden pail, three parts empty, from the corner behind the door where the well-water was placed to keep cool, I started to my feet. Formerly we would have gone off pleasantly together, a pail in either hand, and a 'gird' or hoop to hang it outside, in order to keep the brimming water free from spilling as we brought them back. But now, when in a few hours we were to be all in all to each other, I was coldly permitted to go alone, and to bring back the pails gloomy and sick at heart.

I could not imagine that this was the maiden who had offered to throw herself at my feet, beseeching me to marry her, rather than that I should die by her father's edict.

But at the eleventh hour, as it were, she did speak to me, though her communication was one that mystified me more than ever.

'Do not take off your clothes tonight,' she said, softly, in my ear, 'and be ready for a journey!'

134

She was looking over my shoulder at the time as she spoke, as I sat by the fire. Meggat had gone out, and Hector Faa stood in the door-way looking down the glen, his broad shoulders filling the aperture from side to side.

I caught the girl's hand.

'If I have seemed not to love you hitherto,' I began, 'it has only been that I dared not.'

'Remember what I say,' she interrupted, paying no heed to my words, 'do not take off your clothes, and be ready when I call you!'

Then, with a quick disengaging of her waist and an avoidance of my detaining hand, she was gone. Yet I will take my Bible oath that as she went, this bewildering girl actually turned and, in full sight of her father, blew me an audacious kiss from her finger-tips, a gesture she must have learned among the nuns or other light people in France, for I never saw the like in this country-side. Yet, withal, it was monstrously pretty to see.

Nevertheless, the dull hours lagged even more tardy-foot. For who could be cheerful with Hector Faa wandering here and there like a detached thunder-cloud, and Joyce behaving like the very Sphinx of Egypt in petticoats and a red silk snood.

But after the stench of the stable-caverns, God knows the Shieling was a pleasant place enough, and I have no fault to find therewith. But I am a man who loves greatly to understand things, and whichever way I turned I found myself badly bogged in mysteries.

I could not comprehend why Hector Faa was so set on my marrying Joyce. That he had some purpose to serve was certain. I did not understand why Joyce, who had begged my life with such fervour, now blew hot and cold, and gave me no more than, as it were, the parings of her favour.

But on the other hand, for the first time in my life, I clearly understood myself. There was no doubt about the matter any more. I loved as other men love—nay, better, for my love was once and for all. And the woman I loved was not Marion of the Isle, nor any other but Joyce Faa, the daughter of the Outlaw of the Dungeon.

That was so much to be certain of, at any rate, and a gain to me in my spirit. But there was greater gain on the way, and if bitter waters are good for souls, verily mine ought to have profited greatly.

Hector retired with the setting of the young moon to his own particular swallow's nest. For ever since the last raid of the Ayrshiremen he had kept one private and particular cover known only to himself and perhaps one trusted lieutenant, who could find him at all hours to make reports and to take orders.

Then, the night being very dark and no light anywhere without, I came back in-doors, and sat idly watching the red glow of the peat fire on the hearth as it fell in gradually upon itself and noiselessly took smaller bulk.

I could see or hear nothing of Joyce or Meggat. I did not greatly desire to see the latter, but in my father's memoirs, and in various books of the romance order, I had read that there were pleasant elements connected with the nightly leave-taking of persons betrothed in marriage. Also, for all Joyce's recent strange behaviour, I had sundry memories, and, in especial, she had not taken my kiss so greatly amiss that moonlit night by the cliff's edge. I had a greater right now, yet Joyce was nowhere to be seen.

So after waiting for the better part of an hour, till, indeed, the red of the peat ashes—the 'grieshoch,' as we say in Galloway—sank to the dull red of cooling iron, and finally grew scarcely distinguishable from the darkness about, I groped my way to my couch.

Here I threw myself down without undressing and waited. It is difficult to wait in the dark with strained attention and expectant ear, and I fancy I must have dozed a little.

For it seemed only a moment before I felt a hand on my arm, and a voice in my ear said, 'Hush.'

Within me my heart leaped, for I knew it was Joyce Faa.

'Else,' she said. 'You and I must escape for our

lives! I have all things ready! Do not waste a moment!'

I did not answer, but, feeling her breath sweet on my cheek, I drew her to me. For a moment she resisted, and even somewhat indignantly tried to push me away. Then all at once I heard her whisper, 'Only this once! I deserve it!'

And I kissed Joyce Faa for the second time. But, though her lips were sweet, the fire was quite gone out of them. They were salt with tears, and she kissed me more like a mother who kisses her son whom she sends forth to the battle from which he will never return.

God help thee, Joyce! That dark midnight I felt the love leap between us, and yet even then I knew little more of the great spirit of Joyce Faa than when for the first time I saw her eyes bend darkly over me, at once splendid and pitiful, the fit index of her heart.

CHAPTER TWENTY TWO
THE NIGHT JOURNEY

I shall try, and I know in vain, to describe that wonderful stint of night-travel upon which we now entered. We set out immediately, leaving the narrow shelf of the Dungeon Shieling, not by the way I had arrived, along the line of lochs, each deep-set in its own rock-basin, but by a track which led away to the east, a way narrow and difficult. Joyce it was who took my hand, and at the first I could just see her before me, a dark figure blotting out the stars.

Twice we heard the solitary whistle of the curlew, and twice it was answered with a significant variation—not by Joyce, as it appeared to me, but by some other person, who, though unseen, was of our company.

It occurred to me once or twice that after all I was being taken, as it were for facility of transport, upon my own legs to the Murder Hole. But instantly I put that thought from me. Joyce was there, and therefore nothing but good was intended towards me.

Once, however, there came the sound of a verbal challenge, human and natural, which the unseen person in our care answered cavalierly—indeed, even with something of anger and surprise in his reply—both challenge and reply being still in the unknown gypsy jargon.

Our route was swiftly downward, and then, turning to the right, I got a glimpse of steely grey waters sleeping far below, as if the very stones my feet stirred would drop with a splash into them. For the moment I could think of nothing but our precipitous road, and of the necessity I was under of keeping close to Joyce. For this was the first time I had made so long a journey since my wounding.

Many times I tried to press her hand and to draw her nearer me; but she went ever the faster, murmuring only, 'Hush! Let be! We are not yet out of danger!'

And I tried to extract some comfort from the 'we,' but the yield was small when all was done, and of poor quality. I was always conscious of that other, our leader and guide, who now went on in front; and in spite of all Joyce's kindness there was a stand-off feeling in her touch which grated upon me. For I minded how differently a certain May Maxwell had acted when she fled in the dark down from these same mountains with one of my race.

But this at least was Joyce Faa's way, and it is her story I am telling.

Sometimes, on the less steep places, muirbirds would fly upward with a startling 'Brek-kek-kek,' and sometimes an old ram, rushed out of sound slumber, would break away with the rush of a war-horse into the deeper dark, a trail of stones and dirt rattling down after him. We heard the thunder of the torrent throwing itself over the steep, the white spouting of the 'jaws' (so the hill-folk call them), as if the mountains were venting their waste waters to feed the thirsty plains. Once an eagle or some other heavily flying bird passed across us, almost brushing our faces with his pinions. A raven cried 'Olonh-glonh' with a wearying iterance away to the left, perhaps encouraging us to break our necks for his behoof. And I noted all these things instinctively, like one in a dream.

What I really wanted was to find out whether Joyce Faa loved me, and whither she was taking me. Besides these questions there was one other.

Who was the unseen guide who had answered the sentries with his whistle, guided us down the wild mountain slides, and was now leading us across the trackless, plunging morasses by a path safe enough and practicable, if not particularly dry.

Presently we passed a stunted thorn-bush, from which I learned two things—first, that we had reached the upper limit of trees, which meant also of cultivation; and, secondly, that the night was growing slightly less dark than it had been.

I could now see the dark shape of Joyce going before, and, still more dimly, the shadow of our leader leaning forward, pole in hand, and striking this way and that among the morasses to test the way. There seemed something familiar about the figure, too, and I wondered where I had seen it before.

So, hour after hour, the three of us held upon our way. A cloud settled down over the east into which we were journeying. After the temporary illumination it grew darker again. The silhouettes of my companions dropped back into darkness and we all plunged blindly on, now through the deep hags of infinite morasses, anon crossing by means of the leaping-pole some sluggish 'lane' or deep, black streak of oily water, in which I could dimly see the lilies set like white jewels when I could discern nothing else in heaven or on earth, not even my own feet.

A step or two farther and I was breaking my shins among an infinite wilderness of granite blocks and smooth-weathered stones, slipping upon the 'corklit' moss, and from time to time almost breaking my ankles in the 'traps' betwixt stones which abounded all over the dreary moorland. There was no slackening, no ceasing all that night. We kept at it as men run a long race—silently, determinedly—for a great prize, as, indeed, one among us was doing.

It had been no more than the first breaking of the blackness—not dawn, but the false dawn that looks out of the windows of the east for a moment to see what kind of morning it is and then forthwith goes back to bed again.

Presently we came to a little farm-steading, or rather something as much smaller than that as my lady's spaniel is less than my lord's hound. The group of square-set buildings seemed to be castaway, deserted, left forlorn and derelict amid that world of heather. And yet it was evident that folk lived there, and folk, moreover, not ill-provided with the necessities of life. Within some stables close at hand we could hear the sound of horses shifting their iron-shod hoofs in the butt-end of the dwelling-house, and beyond that again cattle munching in their stalls. It all sounded to me good and friendly, and of the lowlands, though, indeed, we had descended upon the place out of the very heart of the wilds, and, as I afterwards found, the heather grew right up to the door on all sides.

The name of the place was Craigencailzie, and there was a well-marked track from it across the waste to the great Irish drove road which runs by the New Town of Galloway to Dumfries.

Now I come to a part of my tale which must be written, and yet which even now makes a pain and an emptiness about my heart as I write it.

The walls of Craigencailzie byre were whitewashed, and I could see Joyce well enough as she stood looking stilly at me. I was weak with our journeying, and had perforce to lean against the rough-cast rough stone and lime, little better than a dry stone dyke. Our companion, whoever he might be, had gone off to rouse the inmates, or at least to have some private conference of his own with them. So Joyce and I were left alone. For a while we did not speak—I being exhausted, she watching me silently.

'Whither do we go from here?' I said at last

'You take horse, and ride as soon as may be, south into your own country.'

'And you, dearest Joyce?'

She moved impatiently at the caressing word like a spirited horse at the touch of a whip.

'There is now no need of that!' she said, bitterly. 'All is past and done with. I go back to mine own place and mine own folk. For me there is nothing else left.'

'But you must come with me, home to Rathan, to Orraland, dear Joyce. You have saved my life. None other shall ever be my wife. My father and mother will rejoice to welcome you to their home. I know their hearts.'

She laughed a little scornfully.

'They will welcome the news you take them much more,' she said, and stood a step farther off.

'The news I take them, sweetheart? What can that be, save that I love you, and that we are to be married as soon as may be!'

'You may be married, truly—doubtless you will soon provide yourself with a bride—if, indeed, is there not one waiting for you now upon the Solway shore?'

'Truly, Joyce, you speak only to try me! Never have I loved a woman before. None shall be my bride except your sweet self!'

She shook her head, but with less anger, as I think, than before.

'Perhaps you do mean it now,' she said, with something like a sigh, 'in your way, but you will soon forget! But love me you do not—not as I understand love. Perhaps you will learn some day. Pray for that time, even if it come to you in as bitter pain as it has come to Joyce Faa!'

'Then you love me?'

'Love you?' She laughed a little. 'Well, have I not brought you hither? Have I not delivered you— at a price if I have saved your life— at a price! Love you? Well, you can think it over as you ride home to your mother—and— any other who may be waiting for you!'

'I know that you have saved my life, sweetheart—you, and you alone. But you spoke of a price, dear Joyce—what is that price? Nothing that can come between us two, surely?'

'A price—ay,' she said, 'not a great price; a price little and worthless, but long, very long, in the paying. The price of saving you is—myself!'

I held out my arms to clasp her to my heart, for I thought that in these words she confessed her love for me.

'I thank you, Joyce,' I said. 'I will make it the sweetest price that ever was paid, and the longest in paying—every day of our lives a new happiness.'

The light was coming clearer now, and I saw her lay her hand hastily upon her heart, and sway a little, as if suddenly taken with, a dwalm of sickness. But she recovered herself and stood upright again, proudly as ever.

She set the palm of her other hand against her breast. 'It is too late. Maxwell lad,' she said, smiling kindly. 'Had you found out sooner—well, it might have been. But you let it slip, and now—there was no other way to save you from the death which had been determined against you. He that helped me would

142

take no other price. So I must pay—and pay I will!'

She leaned her elbows upon the barn-end, and dropped her face into her palms.

And as I stood watching her thus, and wondering at her emotion, which even then I but vaguely understood, Harry Polwart, Hector Faa's sometime lieutenant, came round the corner of the steading leading a horse saddled and bridled.

As soon, as he saw us he checked himself, but immediately changing his mind, he came on towards us, a scowl on his handsome gypsy face.

'Here is your horse,' he said, in a tone of challenge.

'When you reach Orraland, let it be tethered outside the gate on the third night after your arrival, and it will be fetched. Further than that, do not concern yourself.'

Then he turned to Joyce, who had not moved.

'Have you told him?' he said, but not roughly, as he had spoken to me, rather gently and with a certain grave deference.

The girl let fall her hands, and looked from the one to the other of us with a dazed expression.

'Tell him,' he said, more firmly.

Then, as if she had been a child again repeating a lesson she knew by heart, she said: 'I promised to marry Harry Polwart, if he would help me to save your life. I could have done nothing without him. You would surely have died. My father had no pity.'

She paused, and the young gypsy took her by the hand.

'Come!' he said, with a not unkindly constraint. Then he looked up at me with a certain light of defiance in his eye.

'You need not be afraid to trust her to me. Harry Polwart can hate, as you know, but then he is equally good at loving. And she will be happier among her own people!'

Then again he bent a little towards the girl, and said, 'Come, Joyce!'

A quick, fierce sob shook her frame, almost like a man's weeping.

143

'I have saved him,' she said, throwing up her head, and looking at us both boldly and fully. 'No one can take that from me. And now—yes, I will pay the price!'

She dropped her head again, and for the third time the gypsy took her hand. 'You must come away!' he said, more firmly.

She seemed to nod an acquiescence, and without looking up, or speaking another word, Joyce Faa went slowly round the corner of the wall out of my eighty her hand in another man's hand.

Then I mounted my horse and with a reeling brain and only the empty ache of my heart dinning in my ears, I rode along that mountain southward towards Rathan. But I did not once look behind me.

CHAPTER TWENTY THREE
MAY MISCHIEF MAKES SOME

This which follows is the more cheerful tale of the three who rode northward from the house of Orraland, on the Solway shore, to effectuate, after their own fashion, my liberation. A more gallant trio pressed not saddle-leather that day on any bridle-path or highway military throughout broad Scotland. To wit, there was Mistress Heron of Rathan and Orraland, my fair and gracious mother; Grisel, our dear Miss Minx, light of heart, light of heel, and—more than occasionally—flight of head; also, thirdly, a most dashing cavalier, one Dick o' the Isle, riding out into the eye of day as unabashed as if there had never been a lawless muster betwixt Saterness and the Quarry Hole o' Cassencairy.

My mother was gay—'abune hersel',' as Eppie, our old dependent, would have said. Her youthful keenness for a freakish ploy came upon her like a seizure, and lo! she was again May Mischief, as of old.

The spirit of mirthful daring had come upon Marion also. Her more serious work was for the time being done. Every obnoxious dyke was flat on all the southern estates, and in many cases the landlords patrolled their policies with armed train-bands of their own raising to keep even their park walls intact. Dick o' the Isle—the bold, brave, handsome Captain Dick—had grown suddenly famous. His name was in every mouth, his praises sung at every inglenook. So that this was not Dick o' the Isle, but another Dick—even one Captain Richard Heron, of his Majesty's Fencibles.

The blue bonnet and sash, the rig-and-fur stockings, the Puritan array of the young leader of ploughboys and cottiers' sons was a disguise manifestly unsafe. Yet it was altogether something too much akin to my mother's heart to forego, that in her quest after a lost son, in danger from a beauteous but detrimental gypsy maiden, Grisel and she should be escorted by a dashing cavalier as handsome as he was mysterious.

Many were the discussions at Orraland as to the garb which Captain Richard should wear, till at last it struck Grisel that the King's uniform—which had been got for me in the year of the troubles concerning my Lord Kenmure's rebellion, in order that I might go out and fight for King George and the Protestant succession (not to speak of the safety and well-being of the loyal House of Heron)—might possibly, with a little shortening and a good deal of making over, be made to fit the figure of the soidisant Dick of the Isle—Captain Dick, rebel and Leveller, now setting forth on a new adventure as a gallant squire of dames.

As sure as I tell it, these three madcap wights, one of them (and, verily, the maddest of all) the mother that bore me, sat up secretly at night, or during the day hastily pushed seams under couches and behind curtains at the sound of my father's footsteps, till there was never a more spruce or well-set-up officer on his Majesty's roster than young Captain Heron of Rathan and Orraland. For in appropriating my uniform these three harpies had also made free with my birthright, so that on my arrival I bade fair to find myself without either name or fame, character or cleading.

'And so, for a day or two, good-bye, dear Patrick!' cried my mother, as my father helped her to mount. 'No, indeed, and you shall not ride any part of the way with us.

We do not need you, and you know you must go over to the Isle and oversee Sammle Tamson. I have a message, too, for Eppie, which you can take. Tell her not to be anxious about Marion for a day or two. I will look after her. She is to meet us at the change-house of Causeway End.'

For to her husband Mistress May had reported that she went to visit an ancient crony, the Lady Grace Gordon, at her new mansion house of Greenlaw. It was so long since they had seen each other. The Lady Grace had written frequently—she was so anxious to see Grisel. And so on and so forth, as is the custom of that larger portion of humanity who (with intent or without it) habitually tell only a part of the truth.

For to the new house of Greenlaw—a plain-faced, whitewashed domicile with an ancient staircase, the two were indeed bound, but also, in intention, somewhat farther.

And now, who gayer than Mistress May Mischief (late dame of Orraland and Isle Rathan), when, with Captain Dick at her right hand and her daughter Grisel on the left, she rode away northward. For though there never were two people more made for each other than Patrick Heron and his wife May, I judge that my father's well-contented staidness was sometimes a trial to the more lightsome and freakish spirit which shared his fortunes.

For however well two folk may love each other, to the more sportive nature of the two a masquerade once in twenty years or so is congenial, and to be considered good ground for a certain elevation of spirits.

But this day my mother was completely 'fey.' She insisted on Captain Dick telling the adventure of Colonel Gunter's pistol (of which she had vaguely heard), of the breaking of the dykes, and all the other incidents of the agrarian strife. So much did she enter into the spirit of the matter, that Grisel judged it an opportune occasion to reveal her own part in the Muster at Rascarrel, and was graciously pardoned upon Captain Dick entering into a covenant not to repeat these performances without the approval of the mother of that stout private of Levellers, Mistress Grisel Heron.

And then who so handsome as Captain Dick? The King's scarlet and gold setting him as (God wot!) it had never set its original wearer! Out of the way-side cottages tumbled hordes of bairns to stare open-mouthed. Maidens fair (and of full age to appreciate such things) stood apron at lip, smitten to the heart at the mere sight—so my mother declared.

'Faith, and I do not wonder!' she cried, after they had passed in this fashion through the little village of Gelston, which stands at the end of the Loch of Carlinwark; 'an' it were not that I ken what I ken aboot ye, my handsome Dickie, Patrick Heron might have cause to rue the day he trusted his married wife to the like o' ye! And as for Grisel here, I fear ye hae spoiled her for a' the braw callants that will come chappin' at our yett, for a score of years.'

And indeed he was very handsome, that same Captain Dick. Being slight and well set up, he looked taller on horseback than on foot, and he rode with the grace of a born light-horseman. True, the mustache which he caressed was wellnigh invisible, but the upward swirl of his dark eyelash matched in effective fierceness the swaggering frown of many a cuirassier.

It was at another crossroads before the entering in of the village of Causeyend that fate came suddenly upon them. Here two paths meet, at a place called the Furbar, one from Kirdcudbright, and the other that upon which our three were travelling towards Greenlaw and the Lady Grace.

Tall trees, beeches, and ash-trees mostly, grow there, and the place of meeting is deeply shaded. They were all talking and laughing gayly, wholly wrapped in themselves, as whatever foolish and unobservant men say women often are.

But suddenly there was a clatter of hoofs before them the neigh of a horse and they found themselves face to face with the Earl of Kirkham and his daughter.

CHAPTER TWENTY FOUR
LOVE AND SYLVIA

The first stun of surprise was quickly followed by a feeling of relief. For although the Earl of Kirkham was bad enough, Colonel Gunter would have been ten times worse. Because to the military eye, the standing and service of Captain Richard Heron would have suggested conundrums which it would have been very difficult for his companions to solve without more or less of preparation.

'Good-morrow to you, fair mistress,' cried the Earl, a man of forms and observances, but with much antiquated coquetry about him; 'good-morrow to you all. Well do I remember you Mistress Patrick Heron, and the ball at the Dumfries Assembly Rooms, where you made me so happy by dancing the coranto with me.'

'Your courtesy is better than your memory, my lord,' said my mother, 'for it was my daughter you danced with.'

'But it was you I talked to, my lady of Rathan,' returned the peer, taking off his hat ceremoniously; 'the fairer mother of a fair daughter, eh? No, I have not forgot either you or this fair maid. But this young gentleman in his Majesty's uniform—I do not think I have met him before.'

'Tis my son Richard, or, as we call him more often, Dick,' said my mother, blushing. 'He has been long from us, being with his uncle, who is in the French service.'

'Ah! bad, bad; infernally bad!' cried the Earl; 'Love and Sylvia makes a young fellow either a Jacobite or a jack-a-dandy, eh—ha, ha! That is what I always say. Good, is it not? I said it myself, eight years ago, of a cousin of mine who went to France, and it hath been my joke ever since.'

'Father,' said his daughter, 'I am sure this young gentleman is neither one nor the other.'

'How do you know, Sylvia, ha, ha?' cried the peer, laughing with a noise like a rickety spinning-wheel. 'Tell me how you know that?'

The Lady Sylvia Kirkham was a maiden, as one might say, a little over-ripe. A wrinkle or two had to be kept track of, and the smoother side of her face exposed upon important occasions. There was a touch of colour, too, upon her cheek, a tinge that did not deserve the name of rouge, but which, as it were, recalled to the beholder the evening glow of the sun upon warm-tinted rocks. But still, in her own idea, Sylvia Kirkham was young and fascinating. Good-tempered she was, too, kindly natured, generous, impulsive; her only fault a liability to the fallacy that every man she met was certain to fall in love with her.

So when her father put this question she bridled a little, turned her mare's head aside, and answered: 'The young gentleman is no jack-a-dandy, one can see by his countenance; and as to his being a Jacobite—why, he wears the King's coat, and, besides, he is the son of Mr. Heron of Rathan. And you know, father, I have often heard you say that there was not a more loyal man than he in the county.'

'Nor is there, Sylvia—nor is there! But I have great pleasure in making the acquaintance of—what is your rank, sir?—Captain Richard Heron.'

'I shall call him Dick,' said the Lady Sylvia, simperingly; 'may I, Captain Dick?' Richard always reminds me of the bad King with the hunchback who killed the little boys.'

And she looked so beseechingly that the gallant officer he had perforce to agree as joyfully as he could, lest his repute for courtesy should fall beneath contempt.

'You must turn aside to Castle Kirkham, and give me the pleasure of your company at dinner,' said the Earl, in his turn; 'we dine always at two o'clock of the day. 'Tis somewhat late, I know; but then, Sylvia prides herself on bringing to these wilds some of the manners of St. James.'

'I thank your lordship,' said my mother, now eager to be gone, 'but we have a long travel before us, and must proceed with some considerable speed. We are covenanted to sleep tonight in the house of the

Lady Grace Gordon, at Greenlaw.'

The Earl's daughter gave a little, eager cry.

'How wonderfully diverting!' she cried; 'indeed, it falls out like a Providence! Now I can go with you. For my father was to send me thither yesterday to that very place, but owing to the depredations of this Dick o' the Isle (all Dicks are sad rogues, I fear!), he had to bide at home, and young Theophilus Gunter as well, so I could find nobody to take me to Greenlaw. Things have come to a pretty pass when the Lady Sylvia Kirkham has actually to pray for an escort and be refused.'

'Now, childie,' said her father, who held his daughter's views as to her bewitching youth—or, at least, found it convenient to pretend to adopt them— 'you know well enough, little one, that it was not Theo's fault. He had to abide by his father, who had been shot at and half murdered by that villain Dick o' the Isle, the Captain of Levellers, as he calls himself. As soon as he gets him hanged, Theo Gunter will be at your feet all day and every day!'

'Well, father, at any rate we are safe now!' cried his daughter. 'Here we have a brave young man for our escort—a King's officer; and if the wicked Dick so much as set his head round the corner—why. Captain Heron would shoot him dead.'

'Indeed I would,' cried the gallant youth, rising to the occasion. 'I swear to shoot Dick o' the Isle the first time I meet him face to face!'

'Ay, and he would be as good as his word, I can vouch for that!' cried my mother, proudly gazing at the handsome lad, who sat blushing as red as his scarlet uniform.

"Tis more than most mothers of my acquaintance are able to say!' cried the Earl, gayly. 'But if you will be so kind, madam, as to permit this silly child of mine to accompany you on your journey, you will confer a very considerable favour upon me, and one which I will be slow to forget.'

'But,' said my mother, to gain time, 'the young lady's outfit, her dresses?'

'Oh, as to that, do not annoy yourself,' cried the

Lady Sylvia, quickly; 'my father sent all these on ahead yesterday with Antony, his man, my maid Trixy riding on a pillion behind him.'

'God help that horse, then!' cried my mother, unawares, 'for Antony is twenty good stones weight, to begin with!'

But my lord never minded, being set upon the Lady Sylvia's new idea.

'I am much indebted to you, madam,' said the Earl, taking off his hat, and making ready to depart. 'During these troubles, this is no place for a young girl of rank and beauty, and you do well, madam, to carry off your daughter till a better spirit is abroad in the land.'

He was a very wearisome old gentleman, yet (though they thought it not now) the time came when the Orraland trio would gladly have welcomed him back to the company.

And now the three who had started so gayly, and been so bright and gallant with each other, especially when riding through the great stretches of moorland silence, had become four. But a brace of pairs in this case proved no good company. For the Lady Sylvia, without a word to the others, appropriated Captain Dick—who, for his very manhood's sake, could not permit her to ride on ahead unattended, while my mother, her madcap humour suddenly dampened and her purpose blunted, rode somewhat gloomily along with Grisel, whom bottled indignation was fast converting into a perfect little spitfire.

'The wizened old maid,' she said to her mother, with the prettiest spitefulness, 'to force herself in where she was not wanted, and to carry off Marion just when the sport was at its finest! Ugh! I could strangle her! The Lady Sylvia Kirkham, indeed! I wish it would come a shower of rain, and we could see that pink-and-white complexion somewhat spattered! I have no patience with such people!'

'We will get rid of her at Greenlaw,' said my mother; 'that is one comfort!'

'Oh, do not be so sure of that!' Grisel cried; 'she

will be up to her ears in love with Dick by that time.'

'Dick—Dick! What Dick?' said my mother, whose mind had been busy contriving ways and means to extricate herself from the difficulties into which her 'fey' humour had brought her, and who had momentarily forgotten Dick o' the Isle. Morning nearly always brought counsel to my mother, but never interfered with the mad humours of the night.

'Why, Captain Heron, of course! Your so handsome son—otherwise our Marion there!' said her daughter, pointing with her stick to where the scarlet and gold of the brave cavalier and the blue riding-habit of the Lady Sylvia gleamed through the dancing lightness of the birchen sprays, which they shed like green waves on either side of them.

As they looked, the Lady Sylvia half turned in her saddle, and tapped her companion lightly on the arm with her riding-whip.

'See that!' cried Grisel, fierce and quick as the greeting a cat gives a strange dog; 'she is at it again! If that does not sicken Marion—well, she is stronger in the stomach than I take her for! And then, she will have to contrive sweet speeches in reply! Ha, ha! I would that I could hear them at it!'

'But,' sighed her mother, dolefully, 'I would rather that we were well out of this business. It is a mad ploy, at the best. And what will Patrick say?'

'That, madam, you should have thought on sooner!' snapped Grisel, who at the moment was not in the sweetest of tempers.

After this passage of arms the couple proceeded a long way towards the house of Greenlaw, without further interruption to the silence which fell upon them.

But with the couple in advance, the Lady Sylvia and our gallant Captain Dick o' the Isle, matters went very differently.

At first Marion (to call her for once by her own name, that we may catch the point of view) had been a little nervous. But as the glamour grew in the eyes of the Lady Sylvia, and it seemed impossible to penetrate her disguise, the words and acts of a young home-returning Scot came the more easily to her, that she and Grisel had spent two entire winters in the gay city of Paris. So Captain Dick straightened his shoulders, and answered with an assurance which practice soon made perfect.

Sylvia had arrived at the age when she preferred very young men. And this in itself marks a stage. It happens most frequently to married women who sigh for a little innocent admiration of a more demonstrative sort than is supplied by well-accustomed domesticity. But sometimes it arrives to a maid who has passed her prime, and then the type produced is of a very curious sort.

Sylvia's methods of love-making were those of the bold buccaneer. It consisted in extorting compliments and declarations at the point of the bayonet, and then, with the same weapon, pinning her unfortunate victim to his own words.

'And so, Captain Dick,' she said, with a tender glance up at him, 'you have come back from France. Ah! I am sorry for that, for how can we poor innocent young maids, who have been all the time tied to our mother's apron-strings, hope to vie, in your travelled heart, with the beauties of the Court?'

'I am sure that the Lady Sylvia Kirkham has nothing to fear on that score,' said Captain Dick, gallantly, praying to the gods for aid.

'Ah, you are a deceiver!' cried Sylvia. 'La! how can men be so false! Not one in twenty of you ever mean what you say. And especially you, Captain Dick, who have practised all sorts of taking sayings on the madames of the Court of King Louis—who, if all tales be true, are little better.'

'Indeed, I have never done anything of the kind,' said Dick, hastily, and with perfect truth.

'And am I really the first, then, in whose innocent ear you have whispered these sweet nothings? I cannot believe it, to look at you! No, that I cannot!"

She sighed as she spoke.

'The very first,' said Captain Dick, mentally consigning the daughter of an earl to a place where soft nothings are not supposed to be current coin.

'If only I could believe you! But, la! men are such unconscionable gallants nowadays!' said Sylvia, in a very lackadaisical manner, languishing at Dick from under her bold, black brows, knowing that the deep shade of the trees kept the crows' feet from showing.

The devil at this point tempted Dick to answer: 'I suppose men were very different when you were young?' But a good angel intervened, and he said, instead: 'Men are certainly very much alike where the Lady Sylvia is concerned.'

At this point the Lady Sylvia stretched across to her cavalier a gloved hand which was certainly very small and sufficiently dainty. Dick could not do less than bend over in the saddle and kiss it, having at the same time an acute consciousness in the small of his back that the two behind were laughing consumedly.

'You must come back with me to Castle Kirkham,' said Sylvia. 'All day we will roam the woods, and by the purling brook we will gather us flowers. In the evenings I will tease my father to have you advanced in rank. He has great influence in the army.'

'I will certainly come to Kirkham Castle,' said Dick, thinking, however, that when he did the lady might not like it so well as she anticipated. And, as if speaking his thought, the lady clapped her hands, and cried: 'That will be splendid! We will not be afraid of Dick of the Isle any more when you are there—and Colonel Tredennis also, who is coming with a regiment of King's soldiers to make an end of the rebellion!'

'When does he arrive?' asked Captain Richard Heron, looking at his companion with more interest than he had yet shown.

'Oh, it is a great secret, and my father would be angry if he knew I had told: but as you also are a King's officer, it does not matter. Colonel Tredennis is lying at Ruthwell, near to Dumfries, with his men, and is to march on the evening of the eighth day from now, at the dark of the moon, going round by New

155

Abbey to surprise a muster of the wicked Levellers. There will be a great battle, all the rebels will be taken prisoners, and very certainly Dick of the Isle will either be shot or hanged!'

'You will be glad of that?' asked her companion, looking away from the Lady Sylvia in what appeared to her to be a curious manner for a man of his evident breeding and gallantry.

'Surely,' she cried, 'you and I can have no sympathy with these godless villains? We have nothing in common with them? They are dirty, unwashed, ill-bred, and quite lacking in reverence for their superiors! But you are a gentleman—gallant, handsome' (here it was that she tapped him on the arm) 'and since you are the son of Mr. Patrick Heron of Rathan, who has lately bought the estates of Orraland, I am sure that—that—if you behave openly with my father, and—la! how I blush to mention such a thing!—but if you speak to him of—of—of what you have been saying to me, I have no doubt that he will bestow my hand upon you, though you are but a commoner! Perhaps he will get you made a lord, who knows? He has a mighty great influence with the government.'

Here Captain Dick, with a limp back and a perspiring frame, tried to combine mental agony with the enthusiasm proper to an accepted lover.

'Good Lord,' he thought, 'here am I, not only the leader of the rebels, but engaged to marry the daughter of their chief enemy!'

And then a certain thought rose with a great bound of relief in the mind of Dick of the Isle—alias Captain Richard Heron, alias Mistress Marion of Isle Rathan—a thought connected with the mutability of all human affairs, and especially with the exceeding mutability of borrowed riding-breeches and coats of scarlet and gold worn by officers of his Majesty's Fencibles.

And for the first time in her life Marion thanked the powers that have permanently arranged the conditions of sex under the decent concealing draperies, yclept petticoats —and for the added covertures called gowns and padua-soys.

Her old lindsey-woolsey gown became to her as an ark of safety.

'She surely will not insist on marrying me then,' she said.

CHAPTER TWENTY FIVE
JASPER JAMIE PLAYS 'CROSS-TIG'

But any such deliverance as this was long deferred and far to seek. The true god out of the machine appeared an hour or two before they expected to come in sight of the comfortable white bulk of the new house of Greenlaw, ensconced amid its green plantations, still little larger than fir-cones stuck in the ground. Jasper Jamie was the deliverer, not of intent, but of compulsion; and the motive power which sent him to dare his fate with the Lady Sylvia was the wrath, malice, and all-uncharitable-ness which had been accumulating in the breast of that pretty fury—my sister Grisel.

Now for this a brother would not have cared a doit, or replied only with an advice to our Grisel to do such jobs herself, if she wished them well done. But with Jasper it was different. The mere flutter of a petticoat put him in a tremor. I have seen a servant-wench at an inn-ordinary order him about (after she had taken his measure) like her own kitchen scullion.

I have suffered much in my time for my childish insensibility to womenkind and their influences, but—the Lord preserve me from the disaster of Jamie Jasper's temperament!

It will be seen, then, how little chance he had in such a company as that upon which he now made up, his beast in a lather with his frantic haste, just where the by-way to Threave debouches out of the woodlands of Cross Michael.

It was Grisel who was chiefly in Jasper's thought as he rode. Not exclusively, of course. For, owing to the defect of organization of which I have spoken, he was in love also with Marion of the Isle. But a certain austerity in that damsel having checked his blood in the initial stages, his passion for Grisel had had, as it were, a considerable start, and now bade fair (not being interfered with) to become a 'passion'—as that word was understood by Jasper Jamie.

For love to Jasper was of the nature of the

children's game which is called 'cross-tig.' This consists in the pursuer following one quarry only till another darts between pursuer and pursued, when the hunter instantly turns his attention to quarry number two, till such time as the trail is crossed once more by quarry number three. It is an enterprising game and exhilarating, with a resemblance to Jasper's love affairs which is certainly striking.

But on the whole, at the time when he caught sight of the cavalcade of four on the green track ahead of him, it may be taken for granted that his uneasy heart was chiefly held in spell by the charms of Grisel Heron.

'Jasper Jamie, you have to rid us of that cat!' the last-named outspoken lady declared, as soon as she had dropped behind to give Jasper his cue. 'If you do not—well, I shall never speak to you again. You can go back to your father, and learn to clean paint-brushes with turpentine!'

'Grisel,' said the young man, looking eternal devotion with all his eyes, 'you speak cruelly, but you mean to be kind. Tell me what you want me to do, and I will do it. I am not clever—'

'God knows I' said Grisel, agreeing fervently.

'But you know that I love you, and would give my life to serve you!'

'Love me!' Since when?' cried Grisel, scornfully. 'Since you bought the dominie's Toinette that pretty lace collarette out of Robin Grieve's, and stole a Latin poem to send with it—out of Nichors collection, misspelling six of the words, so that her father, Henry Gowdenlock, declared that if you had been still at school, he would have had you horsed round the yard for such carelessness till you howled amain?'

'Tis false, dear Grisel—false!' cried Jasper, cut to the quick; 'this story was all a lie of Max's, made up out of spite, and to damage me in—in—'

'Ah, yes—in Marion's eyes!' retorted Grisel, like a flash. 'I remember. It was that same week you told Marion that she was 'like Ariadne on a sea-girt isle,' and she asked you what other sort of isle you were familiar with. It was a quick conceit of Marion's! Just to think that then she was all bright and well—and now, alas! poor Marion!'

'What is the matter with her?' said Jasper, anxiously.

'Ah! there you are! You see—you still love her!' said Grisel, who, to tell the plain truth, cared not a solitary doit one way or the other.

'I do not,' said Jasper; 'but I would not have her ill or misused. I—I respect her.'

Grisel laughed heartily.

'I will certainly tell Marion. She will sleep the better for that knowledge. But indeed, of a surety, she is—how shall I say it?—sore vexed with a devil!'

'Vexed with a devil?' queried Jasper, still more mystified.

Grisel pointed with her index-finger, where, on the edge of the woodlands, my mother had joined the gay young cavalier and his lady, presumably somewhat to their chagrin at being thus interrupted.

'There,' Grisel said, 'your work lies yonder. And it is also a wager in intellects. Jasper, if you can separate that cavalier from the lady at his side, I will give you— I will give you (with a quick burst) the kiss you have been pestering me about this week of Sundays! There!'

The reward was certainly a great and exceptional one, and worthy of the highest enterprise, but the very offer made Jasper suspicious.

'You wish them separated,' he said. 'Who is this young officer? He wears a gay coat. Perhaps he has also been given a kiss for pleasing you?'

'He has, and many of them!'

'Grisel Heron, you are right shameless! All is over with my heart. You have broken it I And that, too, when you knew that I loved you! I demand that you tell me who is the young man whom you have kissed so often— after what you promised to me last Friday fortnight among the nutwood hazels!'

'What if he be my new brother—Captain Richard Heron, of the Fencibles—newly come home from France?'

'A likely story!' cried Jasper, his nose in the air;

'this is the first I ever heard of your having a brother Dick, and Max and I have had the self-same lodging ever since we were birched together by Dominie Gowdenlock!'

'Well,' quoth Grisel, tauntingly, 'you are a sporting man—what say you to laying a crown on the matter?'

'I would rather cry double or quits on our last wager,' said the artful Jasper.

'Aha, lad! double or quits! I admire your impudence!' said Grisel. 'Indeed, it will be time enough to speak of that when you have won the first trick. But meantime, if that youth there in the scarlet does not answer to the name of Captain Richard Heron, you shall buy me a pair of Flemish gloves the first time you ride into Dumfries.'

'Done!' said Jasper, who, indeed, asked no better than to spend his father's money on any pretty girl—a generosity not uncommon amongst sons.

'And what do you give me?' cried Jasper, immediately, for upon second thoughts the wager seemed somewhat one-sided.

'That,' said Grisel, 'we need not condescend upon, for it will not happen. When we ride away from Greenlaw without the Lady Sylvia—'

'The Lady Sylvia Kirkham?' queried Jasper, laughing.

'Why, do you know her?'

'I have narrowly escaped dancing with her once or twice, as a man flees for his life, at the Dumfries assemblies; and once, in Edinburgh, she had my sedan while I walked beside it down from the High Street, bareheaded, in a northerly rain.'

'Brave boy!' cried Grisel; 'you will do well yet, Jasper. I think, after all, I was well advised not to make it double or quits.'

Jasper gazed at her with widely interrogative eyes. With the best intentions in the world, he could not always follow her swift speeches, and moods that varied and quavered like a sunbeam in water.

'I mean,' said Grisel, 'that you are the very man for the task! Go, with my blessing; go, Jasper Jamie, and when all is done, and well done—why, come with a bill of attachment, and see if you can collect your debt. If I am not dyvour and man-sworn by that time, well— you shall be paid!'

Still somewhat mystified, but with the usual belief in his powers of love-making (which all these lumps of bone and flesh have), Jasper set spurs to his beast, and set out to overtake the three in front.

My mother was riding with the Lady Sylvia, and listening to the praises of her son Richard with mingled feelings, wondering, as usual, how she should get out of the scrape, and what Patrick, her husband, would say to it all. Their cavalier, Captain Dick, had been detained by a stone in the shoe of his mare, and had only just remounted when he was overtaken by Jasper Jamie.

'Captain Richard Heron,' cried the latter, as the officer was for spurring forward out of his reach, 'I desire a word with you, sir.'

Very unwillingly, Captain Dick wheeled about. He had upon him all the trouble his nerves would stand, in the double fact that he was at once attainted for treason and engaged to demand from the Earl of Kirkham the hand of his daughter.

At the sight of him, Jasper Jamie reined in his steed as if he had been stricken with lightning. Surprise, wonder, mystification coursed through his mind, and emotion chased swift emotion across his ingenuous countenance.

He saw before him a face that (for the better part of a month) he had once thought the loveliest in the world, a figure he had dreamed of (yet never seen in such fashion before), a pair of laughing, defiant eyes, an upper lip touched with dusky down like to the markings of a young swan's bill. So, completely bewildered, he blundered as usual into audacious speech.

'Good Lord!' he cried; 'Marion! What are you doing here with Max Heron's breeches on?'

They were now approaching the woods of Greenlaw, and Jasper was still laboring at the oar. He had, by the rudest of methods, ousted Captain Dick from his cavalier-ship of the lady, and Sylvia, by no means insusceptible to the advantages of competition, anticipated the good effect upon her handsome Captain of the openly expressed admiration of a rival wooer. And of a certainty there was no false modesty about Jasper Jamie.

But his methods were indeed more than a thought crude. Jasper always tickled his trout with a pickaxe all the days of him.

'He is handsome,' said the Lady Sylvia, indicating Captain Richard over her shoulder with a toss of her head. And she had brought the battery of her bold eyes to bear upon Jasper with quite as much good-will as on Captain Dick, and with an equal care in the shading of crows' feet.

'Handsome? Why, well enough!' cried Jasper; 'but-' Here he shook his head with a grave warning.

'What do you mean?' cried Sylvia, eagerly taking him by the arm.

'He comes from France!' said Jasper, with meaning.

'That is rather a recommendation, I find,' said Sylvia, drawing a breath of relief; 'he has such charming tales to tell of the Court.'

'Ah!' said Jasper Jamie.

'He knows all the great ladies of fashion.'

'And none of the gentlemen!' said Jasper.

'You mean to say—?'

'I do not mean to say anything,' purred the suggester of evil, 'but his tales were all of nuns and ladies and fair maids, were they not?'

'All that had any particularity in them, I must avow,' admitted the Lady Sylvia. 'But what of that?'

'There is a sailor proverb: "Many ports, many wives"!' said Jasper, meaningly.

The Lady Sylvia started, and, reigning her horse, faced Jasper Jamie.

'You do not mean to infer that Captain Richard is married already?'

'I did not say so,' quoth the thrice wicked Jasper, 'only that he is more at home in the boudoirs of the ladies in France than in the quarters of his mess. A soldier, indeed! I warrant he does not know how a bombard is horsed on its way to a siege, nor yet can he distinguish between scarp and counterscarp in a fortification. Ask him!'

'But then I should not know whether or no he spoke the truth. And I would as lief believe in him as you, at any rate. Master Jasper! For why? He is so handsome!' And the lady sighed.

'Well,' said Jasper, 'ask him on which side of a window a man puts the looking-glass when he shaves. Bid him unbutton and button his surtout; he will button it again not on the right as a man doth but on the left like a woman. Did you ever see him put on his hat without a mirror? He is a very coxcomb, that hath done nothing all his days but dangle after and deceive foolish women.'

'Then he shall not deceive me!' cried Sylvia, veering suddenly. 'I am sorry that ever I listened to his lying tongue, and I do not think he is so very handsome, after all! When one looks upon a true man—a real man of substance and—and avoirdupois—ah, that is a different thing.'

Stout Jasper puffed his cheeks, and sat a little more erect in the saddle.

'I did not mean to wrong my friend, not yet to speak to his discredit,' he said, 'but, knowing his predilections and customs, I could not bear to see him aspiring to the favour of one so beautiful and accomplished as the Lady Sylvia Kirkham.'

The lady blushed through the slightly over-permanent colour of her cheek at the fervor of Jasper's words.

'You must come and see us at Kirkham,' she said. 'You are going to be a lawyer at the Parliament House, I hear. Ah! I will speak to my father; he has much influence with my Lord Advocate. He will do anything for your advancement in—ah, the government interest.'

'I am infinitely obliged,' said Jasper, gravely.

'You will stay meanwhile at Greenlaw,' said the Lady Sylvia. 'I had intended to go farther, but now I shall remain here. You must positively stay with me.'

'I am sorry that I do not know the Lady Grace Gordon,' said Jasper, promptly; 'and, besides, Mr. Heron of Rathan put his wife and daughter in my care till the completion of this journey.'

'In that case you must come to Kirkham as soon as possible after your return,' she answered, with her hand on his arm. 'Then we will wander in happy converse by the babbling brooks and commnne together beneath the moon's pale ray.'

'I shall live for that happy moment,' said Jasper Jamie, aloud. But to himself he said: 'I wish Grisel had taken my double or quits. But we shall see.'

So, just because that young lard-barrel Jasper dealt thus with my character, the Lady Sylvia abode at the new house of Greenlaw, and only these four rode northward upon their quest—to wit Mistress Heron of Isle Rathan, Grisel her daughter, Jasper Jamie, and, in scarlet and gold. Captain Dick of the handsome face and the sorely damaged reputation.

When they were going the Lady Sylvia drew Jasper aside.

'I can never be sufficiently grateful to you,' she said; 'you have saved me from a villain! When my Lady Grace offered him her own serving-man to wait upon him and sleep in his anteroom (the house being so full), he replied 'that he was only accustomed to women about him.' A roue! A manifest villain, who makes it his business to go about inveigling foolish and innocent young hearts!'

But all the same, as they rode away the Lady Sylvia sighed, and confided to her hostess, 'It is a pity, for, after all, he is so handsome!'

'That is just it,' said the Lady Grace Gordon, who had a celebrity for plain-speaking which she felt bound to keep up; 'old women like you and me, Sylvia, cannot afford handsome young husbands with the reputations of rakes. For my part, I do not believe a word the fat youth said; but, all the same, if you must catch 'em young, you would be safer with him than with any handsome Captain Dick new landed from France.'

'But his father is a painter,' sighed the Lady

165

Sylvia.

'Well, I do not think that you, at least, can afford to cast stones at that profession!' quoth the apostle of plain speech.

Upon which the Lady Sylvia blushed through her rouge and was silent

CHAPTER TWENTY SIX
THE FIRE OF GOD

Dismal and bitter as were the thoughts that coursed like a mill race through my heart as I rode southwards over the Flowe of Craigenkailzie, those with which Joyce Faa accompanied her companion were darker and more bitter still.

Bitter remorse for opportunity lost, love slighted, anger against destiny – contempt of self, these were no pleasant journeying companions, and they were mine.

But Joyce Faa looked forward to a life to be spent with a murderous desperado – one of her own race truly but a thousand leagues from her in education, feeling, manners.

Nevertheless with the, instinct of the gypsy woman she followed him without complaint, taking as her part of her duty the great 'kent' or 'leaping pole' with which they must cross the slow running 'lanes' of water on their way to the distant home which Harry Polwart had provided for his wife.

The morn had broken wild and uncertain, a drift of slaty blue clouds edged with white shouldering up from the south west, low across the landscape. There was not much wind, but the clouds drew down upon the mountains and far in the west there was the occasional growl of thunder like a ruffle of drums.

Joyce heeded not, a physical callousness, the reaction after vehement emotion, taking for the time being complete possession of her. She followed as in a dream. The tall, hawk-faced young gypsy stepped out across the heather, keeping to the southward of the great valley of Glen Trool. He had his course accurately marked, and after passing Loch Dee, he bore away up the side of Curley-wee, the peewits scattering and whinnying before him as he went. He followed a little stream which came down the mountain, dispersing its waters into spray a dozen times, again collecting them, apparently undiminished in volume, sending them to sleep in half a score of shallow lakelets and one deep unruffled tarn, and finally in one great white spout of foam, dropping itself into the valley far below.

Without a word spoken on either side, Joyce and her companion took this goat's track up the mountain-side. They were just on the border lands of Lamachan and Curlywee. Above them the blue thunder-clouds streamed eastward at a uniform height along the side of the huge precipitous ridge of Bennanbrack. Up, up they went, Joyce scarce wondering whither they were going, but blindly obeying, and in a certain sick and weary-hearted way glad to obey, if only to do anything, and to keep on doing it.

Harry Polwart did not slacken his speed till the stagnant airs of the valley began to give place to an occasional puff of icy wind blown downward from above. He was marching right upward into the thunder-cloud. Joyce felt more than once the sting of hail in her face. Suddenly a whitish-grey tongue of cloud came rushing towards them, at sight of which the gypsy uttered a warning cry, and Joyce caught at a projecting corner of rock which gave under her hand.

In a moment the gypsy had sprung to her side, and pulled her down behind a huge boulder, which, after sliding thus far, had remained perilously poised on the mountain-side. He put his arm about Joyce and forced her into the most interior crevice of the rock, standing in front of her. The threatening arm reached out as if to snatch them from their refuge. As it came nearer, Joyce saw a funnel-shaped cloud, its point spinning like a top along the mountain-side. It rushed upon them. The next moment, with a tremendous explosion of sound and a blinding pale-blue light, the world seemed to end, and the heart of Joyce Faa gave a bound of thankfulness. God had surely heard her prayer. The end was come! The thunderbolt had smitten them both!

But the next instant, against the rushing steam-vapors of the cloud, Joyce saw the figure of Harry the Gypsy stand out with a certain wild nobility. His hands were outstretched, and as it were striking palm-forward against some imminent horror. The great boulder behind which they stood had disappeared in a wild debris of fragments, chips, and granite dust. The ground was torn up in all directions—here in great gashes as if a gigantic ploughshare had passed that way; there, in a myriad of shallow tunnels, apparently as purposeless and wandering as mole runs. There was a smell of powder everywhere that made Joyce gasp and catch her breath, and beneath her, on the next slope, the heather was on fire.

Meanwhile Harry Polwart was standing with his hands now pressed to his eyes, now driven out, in angry protests against God and destiny.

'I am blind, Joyce!' he cried, in agony. 'God's truth, I cannot see! Tell me that it is dark, Joyce—surely it is very dark!'

Yet nevertheless, as if to stand between her and danger, he kept his place in front of her, so that she had perforce to remain yet awhile in the cleft of the rock where he had placed her.

For, to do him justice, the man was true in love, and wholly without fear.

Joyce put out her hand, being stricken with sudden pity, and drew the blinded man back into the covert, where they crouched close together. She saw him by the constant white and lilac flick-flack of the lightning flashes. His face seemed to be seared an ugly white, white as bleached bone, and his sightless eyes rolled ghastly and large this way and that.

For Harry Polwart, who a few hours before had led us through the meshes of the moss hags in the darkness of midnight, now stood blind, groping, and trtmbling like a frightened steed. For the finger of God had touched him suddenly.

He could not even see the ripples of fire that played level all about them, running from scarlet and lavender upon the leonine haunches of Curlywee to blinding and burning opal as the flame ran along the ragged cloud edges beneath the ridge of Bennanbrack.

A constant rattle of falling stones accompanied

169

the storm as the thunderbolts shot every way along the mountain-side. Every moment's safety seemed to Joyce a miracle; and Harry Polwart, like a child in fear of the dark, caught at her hand and nursed it to his side, saying, over and over, 'You will not leave me now, Joyce! You will keep your promise?'

'I will keep my promise,' she answered; and he heard her even amid the loudest roaring of the storm, yet was not satisfied.

'Promise me, Joyce! I am blind! I cannot see you, or follow you! But you will keep your word to Harry the Gypsy, who dared death and kept his word to you?'

'I have said it,' answered Joyce Faa.

The thunder-storm was a long one, and did not move with the wind. It seemed rather to hang heavily between the hills about the head of the great glens, venting itself after a while, not in short, sharp, frequent explosions, but rather in long brooding silences, which were followed by tremendous outbursts of sound and flame.

And through the aching silences Harry Polwart, the gypsy, spoke his heart into the ear of Joyce Faa.

'I have loved you, Joyce—ever since your father brought you, a little white maid, from the foreign ship. It was I who made you rush-baskets, woven from the spretty bogs. I swam in to bring you water-lilies. I scoured the hills to find you birds eggs. I was with you night and day. Then you went to France, and when you came back it was (as I knew it would be) a different Joyce. But you had grown tall and beautiful—a true gypsy maid; and, though I had not your learning, nor your foreign ways, I loved you a thousandfold more than before. And when this young man, Maxwell Heron, came—so like a woman, with his love-locks, and his talk of books and men and cities, all that you knew and I did not—I swore an oath that if I was not for you, he at least should not have you while steel would kill or water drown.'

'But if you hated him, why did you not let my father slay him?' said Joyce, speaking for the first time.

Harry Polwart passed a hand across his brow as if to clear his brain.

For that he had a reason, too, if only he could remember it.

'And what would that have advantaged me?' he said. 'You would have been no nearer me. But I made this bargain with you, for I knew that you loved him: 'Your life for his!' I said. I would save him, you should give yourself to me. A fair bargain, clearly understood between us, was it not? And now, though I never again see the light of the sun or of your eyes, you will keep your part, Joyce, even as I, Harry Polwart, have kept mine?'

'I have told you that I would keep my promise,' said Joyce Faa, still letting him htld her hand.

'Then you will take me to the Manse of Minnigaff, and there the minister will marry us. For not otherwise will I be wed to you, Joyce Faa, but even as was your own choice when your father would have given you to the young laird's son!'

The storm passed away as it had come with scattering peals, a dying flicker of lightning far away to the east, and gusts of cold wet wind that rumbled about the rock clefts and soughed eerily through the deep glens on the flanks of Caimsmuir.

All about them there was the glimmering haze, which is the rain driven into spray as it danced off the boulders and was exhaled from the soaked and sodden heather.

In this fashion, hand in hand, Joyce Faa and the blind gypsy took their way towards the Manse of Minnigaff, where that very day another bridegroom was to have stood up beside her.

CHAPTER TWENTY SEVEN
DEVIL'S WORK

It was part of the strange ordering of events that at the exact moment when I was breasting the last brae which leads to Orraland upon the grey horse which my gypsy guide had borrowed for me at Craigencailzie, Joyce and Harry Polwart were descending the slopes of Carnsmuir towards the Manse of Minnigaff and my mother's relief expedition had passed the Fleet and was riding slowly towards the noblest cliffs that line the shores of Solway.

Jasper and my mother led the way, for she had recovered all her hopefulness and gracious humours so soon as the party was rid of the Lady Sylvia. Indeed, the whole party were in other spirits, and though Jasper had been unable as yet to bring the faithless Grisel to count and reckoning, he looked confidently forward to evening, as being the time when such debts are most amicably and satisfactorily settled.

The King's officer and Grisel came behind, their eyes upon each other, almost like the eyes of lovers. And a pair of lovers well-mated they appeared to the on-lookers, so that the good-wives of the Gatehouse nodded approvingly as they rode through, and said, 'It is evidently a settled thing atween thae two!'

Grisel and her companion were upon that pretty wooded elbow of path which meanders round by Rutherford's ancient kirk, when there befell one of those chances which make a story worth the telling. For if we had the making of our own lives as men skilled in the trade make a tale to be read, they would never be interesting enough to relate. It is men's disasters rather than their successes which interest the world.

Now Grisel Heron and this handsome Captain Dick were taking their horses slowly under a green roof of leaves. The cushie-doves coo-rooed in the silence. There was the sweetness in the air which only comes after thunder, when the heavens are cleaned down of their cobwebs, and a breath from somewhere beyond the blue blows over all the face of the world.

As they came round a corner suddenly they were stopped by the words of a woman's beseeching. A cottage had been unroofed and the doors and windows carried away. A pile of furniture, still dripping with the rain of the morning, lay piled up by the way-side.

A little back from the path stood the torn and dismembered fragments of a byre, the stalls still fairly complete. But the mangers were empty, and a hayrack above had a hole driven through it by a man's foot, from which a wisp of straw hung down forlornly. A stable also there was a little in the rear, but all equally ruined and desolate.

An old man stood with his hands clasping and unclasping each other in front of him, and his forehead leaning against the cold stones of the gable. Beside him, with one hand laid pleadingly upon his shoulder, was a woman of a like age. The old man was sobbing like a child, deaf and blind to the world.

'Oh, the bonny bit! Oh, the heartsome—that was my faither's an' my faither's faither's! There was the verra winnock-sole where my mither set my parritch to cool afore I should eat them in the summer nichts! There is the rockin'-chair wherein she nursed us a', and where I set you, my Nanny, the nicht I brocht ye hame.'

'Guidman! guidman!'—his wife's voice was gentle and comfortable in his ear— 'dinna quarrel wi' the Lord! Dinna fecht again His wull, Tammas! For we hae had mony mercies, you and me, a canny bairn-time, a hame bien an' comfortable for forty year—a heartsome hearth-stane—'

'Na, na, Nanny,' said the old man, lifting his head and trying to smile, 'dinna fear—I'se no quarrel wi' the Almichty! But ye see I am nane that sure that He has had ony hand in this. It's mair like to deil's wark—this rivin' up o' hearthstanes, and tearin' doon o' roof-trees that the laird's sheep and black nowt beasts may get their bite and sup, where the bairns played and the joes coorted thegither at e'en. Mony a score o' ingle-nooks are as desolate as this o' yours

173

an' mine, Nanny, just that young Allister Mure may bigg anither too'er to Cassencairy and hae siller to spend amang the great folk i' London toon!'

'Devils' work, indeed!' cried Marion of the Isle, who, with a wave of her hand had imposed silence upon her companion as they sat their horses and listened to this colloquy, 'for who but devils would so pluck up by the roots a goodly tree that hath flourished here for generations. By whose order is this done?'

The old couple turned, and regarded with surprise the handsome youth who spoke. But suspicion instantly clouded faces which had momentarily brightened at the sound of Sympathetic words.

'I am not what I seem,' cried Marion, forgetting everything in her anger. 'I wear the coat of a soldier, it is true, but my heart fights for the rights and liberties of the poor folk of Galloway!'

'Ye are indeed unco braw to take part with men ruined and dispossessed,' said the old man, 'though I dare say ye mean weel. But there is little ye can do for the like o' us. The cadger's poke and the cauld wat bed ahint the dyke are to be our portion till we die! But I judge that it will no be lang! The lord grant it sae!'

'Perhaps I can do more for you than that,' said Captain Dick. 'But what have we here?'

A company of horsemen swept up to the ruined cottage at a rattling trot.

'What! not out of this yet, you infamous old rebel?' cried a slim dark youth in the regimentals of junior officer.

'Be quiet, Theo!' said another officer, a man of forty or thereby, with a mustache touched with premature grey, and keen grey eyes looking out under the stiff dragoon's crest which decorated his helmet. 'You are inclined to be over-hasty, sir. Besides, you are not in command here, pray remember that!'

'This is indeed pretty work for officers and gentlemen!' cried Marion, riding forward, Her indignation getting the better of her discretion. 'Tis,

174

indeed, something safer than fighting the King's enemies in the Low Countries!'

The soldiers turned round with great surprise, for the overhanging trees on the opposite side of the road, and their haste, had prevented them seeing Grisel and her companion till now.

'And whom have we here?' cried the younger— he whom his brother-officer had called Theo; 'Fair Mistress Grisel Heron, and—Heaven help us! a Dumfries Fencible rigged out all as trig as a stage-lancer, with his hair curled as point-device, and none-so-pretty as a stick barley-sugar wrapped in a silver paper! And he dares to stand in the way of his Majesty's forces doing their duty! Your name and rank, sir?'

'I have as much right to demand yours!' retorted Marion. 'I ride upon my occasions, and am not liable to interrogatories upon the highway!'

'Nor are men doing their duty liable to such comments as you indulged in a moment ago, young sir,' said the elder man, gravely. He had never taken his eyes off Marion's face.

'This is my brother Richard, lately home from France, Ensign Gunter said Grisel, sharply. 'I pray you pardon him, for he is yet ignorant of many things here in his native country, and, besides, is apt to speak over-hastily.'

'Your pardon, Mistress Grisel,' said the young man, 'but if that be so, why does your brother Richard wear your brother Max's clothes while he is still in the hands of the outlaws—as I hear?'

'Why, as to that, 'tis a plot of my mother's,' said Grisel, readily. 'She has an idea of effecting Max's liberation by that means.'

'But how? In what fashion?'

'That,' said Grisel, mysteriously, 'is a secret which I have promised not to tell.'

And it was certainly a promise easy enough to keep, for the young lady had not the remotest idea of how Captain Richard Heron's wearing of ex-Captain Maxwell Heron's clothes was to deliver the latter from captivity.

Nevertheless, such was the repute of my mother in the Stewardry for freakish doings that Grisel could observe young Gunter leaning over to whisper the jest to his superior officer, who slightly smiled and nodded.

'Enough,' cried the latter, saluting Grisel, 'let us proceed. We have other work to do.'

He turned to the old couple, who had been standing silent listening to the colloquy.

'It is my orders that you have till sundown to clear all your possessions off the lands of Mr. Anthony Mure of Cassencary.'

The old man raided his bonnet politely, with a certain air of austere dignity and respect for law.

'You but follow your commission, sir,' he said. 'In that I do not blame you. But all my property—and it is not much—I have already removed furth of the bounds of Anthony Mure's properties.'

'But it lies on the King's highway!' cried the young man Theo, furiously. 'You are an old rebel, and I doubt not were heart and part in the muster at Rascarrel! I tell you, if you and all your possessions are not clear of the bounds of the parish by six o'clock this evening, I will take a file of men and burn every rag and stick I find on this spot I Now, I have warned you!'

'You will do no such thing so long as you are under my orders!' said the elder man, turning upon him sternly.

The youth curled his lip.

'Thank Heaven!' he retorted, 'I am not in your company, and if you are too stiff in the stock, Austin, to lend me a corporal's file—faith! I can get a half-dozen game-watchers—fellows who will ask no questions, but have this rubbish heap blazing in twenty shakes of a cow's tail—ay, and some of these pullets roasting merrily above it for their own suppers, too!'

During these amenities, the face of Marion of the Isle had passed through a score of changes—shame for the masquerade dress in which she had perforce to appear in serious affairs and in the eye of day, anger and scorn of the destroyers of ancient peace and humble well-doing, consciousness of her own impotence, and (above all) concern for what she might bring upon her companions by her rashness.

Nevertheless, she could not deny herself a last word.

'I can only hope that your further work is of a more reputable sort than this,' she said, pointing to the broken chair which lay on the top of the pile.

'That is no more our work than yours, young sir,' returned the officer. 'We are neither sheriff's officers nor yet bailiffs. So we can well spare your comments. If you have any right to the coat you wear, you are aware that the first duty of a soldier is to obey his instructions without query or question, and also that I have power to order you under arrest for your words. I choose rather, however, to waive my rank and official errand here, and to say that if you or any man have aught to urge against me or my actions, my name is Austin Tredennis, Captain in Ligonier's Horse, and that I shall not stand upon my rights as to choice of weapons! I wish you a very good-day, sir, and to you, madame, my humble service!'

He bowed to Grisel, waved his hand, and presently, with unanimous clatter of accoutrement, the squadron was gone.

'That man is a man!' murmured Marion of the Isle, thoughtfully, as she looked after them.

There are few fairer spots by nature on the face of this land of the Scots than the site of the Manse of Minnigaff. It is, indeed, a mere outpost of a vast rearward territory of parish, but it sits with some coquetry on a pleasant knoll looking down on the waters of the Cree through a wilderness of birch and alder copses. It is (or rather was, when these things happened) a little low dwelling of three chambers and a garret, all covered down tightly with a nightcap of thatch pulled close about its ears. The minister, Mr. Hugh Penpont, was considered a prop of orthodoxy in these wavering times, and, moreover, was a man keenly alive to his interests in both worlds, for no man in all the whole Presbytery knew better how to harmonize the moral law and the commandments of the heritors.

Mr. Penpont was writing his sermon, and had advanced to 'seventeenthly' in the elucidation of the city of Jericho, considered as a type of the Popish and Prelatical Kirk which, till the never-to-be-sufficiently lauded Revolution had lorded it over the heritage of the saints, when a yet more revolutionary thing happened to him. Greg Payter-son, the minister's 'man,' beadle, and general reporter of all the ill and well doing of the parish, rushed in with the intelligence that 'thae gypsy folk had comed to get mairried, juist themsel's two—an' nae Hector Faa wi' them ava.'

'Gin I war you, minister' advised Greg, with his usual freedom, 'I wadna gie them either prayer or benison, the ill-contrived, thievin' blasties.'

'Greg,' said the minister, pausing with his pen between his fingers, 'it's little that you ken o' the responsibilities o' a public man.'

'And pray ye, minister,' said the offended Greg, 'wha is a public man if it be na the kirk officer o' the parish o' Minnigaff, I wad like to ken?'

'Ay, ay, I dare say,' said the minister, pacifically, for being dependent on Greg for the most part of his gossip, he did not choose to quarrel with him at such a crisis; 'but yet ken that gin we offend thae savage folk o' the hills, there's aye Hector Faa himsel' to reckon wi', and, mair nor that. Silver Sand, forbye. And though he has won wonderfu' far ben wi' the great o' the land, he is aye a gypsy, when a' is said an' dune! But tell me, Greg, what like are they?'

'To tell ye Guid's truth, minister, the lass is no that unfaceable-like ava—I micht hae ta'en a notion o' her my-self—a comely quean, an' hand's her head high. But the gypsy loon—Lord keep us!—he's a gashly sicht. I kenna whether the vengeance o' the Almichty has fa'en on him or whether he was born to this heritage. But I never saw onything like him. Yet the lass leads him by the hand as cannily and couthily as if he were a' her care.'

'And where hae ye left them a' this time?' asked the minister, toying with his quill and dotting the i's of 'seventeenthly' lightly and with a loving touch.

'They are juist on the road there oot bye!' said the minister's man; 'd'ye think I wad let two wandering do-nae-gaids aff the heather hae the run o' my kitchen, or gang into your benroom where ye keep your buiks and silver, forbye the sonsy greybeard o' undutied brandy that ye hae laid awa' for your winter boasts—'

'There, Greg, I hae telled ye oft and oft that ye will be the daith o' me! Ye want me to get a jag in the ribs frae Hector Faa's jockteleg. Maybe ye wad get a kinder maister! To keep them standin' there! Them that Hector Faa sent to tryst me to mairry! Fetch them ben this minute I order ye, and offer them cake an' wine! Hear me, Greg!'

Greg Payterson went out obediently, muttering only under his breath, 'Cake an' wine, indeed, to wild hill gypsies! Set them up! I'm thinking scones and tippenny sma' ale will hae to serve them!'

Thus the first of the three parties which (all unknown to him) were converging upon Mr. Hugh Penpont's manse had arrived, and stood on the road-way waiting Greg Payterson's pleasure.

There had been little talk between Joyce and

her lover as they descended the long green valley of the Penkill, leaving the great open hill pastures, and passing through benty bottoms, where the burn, dammed by some fallen-in 'rickle o' stanes,' had turned a score of acres into a swamp. Finally, emerging from the rough country of the hills, they passed the little park enclosures of Pulgap and Cumloden, climbed the manse brae and stood before Greg Payterson.

The reception they met with we know.

Meantime, our four adventurers of the Rathan expedition were riding along the plain King's highway by the Ferry Town of Cree. They had reached Clashdookie, and my mother was explaining to Jasper Jamie the inwardness of the word, and implying that his varied imperfections were to be set down to ignorance and neglect of opportunities on the part of his tutors and governors, when all of a sudden she clapped her hands, and cried, 'I declare I never thought o' it till this minute! We juist canna pass the door o' my auld frien' Hughie Penpont withoot a handshake!'

'Is it that Hugh Penpont who never married for the sake of you, mother mine?' said Grisel, who knew many things and guessed others.

'Havers—juist your faither's silly havers!' cried the mistress of Rathan, well pleased. 'When ye are aulder and wiser, and hae a guidman o' your ain, ye will ken that the men-folk aye like to think ither men wad hae gi'en their e'en and front teeth for what they themsel's gat for the asking. And your faither is juist like the lave.'

'But it is true, is it not, mother?' persisted Grisel. 'Hugh Penpont was a sweetheart of yours when you were young?'

'When I was young, lassie!' cried my mother, feeling the smooth full under-curve, which she always denied was a double chin, 'you cheepin' chicks think nae woman young unless she is as jimp aboot the waist that ye could span her wi' your gowpens. But men that set themsel's up to ken, like something a thocht mair substantial. When they eat sugar plooms

180

they like them ripe, no green an' hard—sae ye will maybe mind that a woman may hae bairns o' her ain (and impudent, upsettin' gorbs they are!) an' yet be far and far eneuch frae the sere leaf an' the yellow!'

'Come away then, mother!' cried careless Grisel, falling herself into the country talk, 'and let us see your auld admirer hirplin' on his stick, or aiblins meeting us in the manse loaning wi' a dog and a string to lead him!'

My mother did not deign to answer this remark, but nevertheless, the whole cavalcade turned towards the Manse of Minnigaff in answer to her thought.

Destiny was closing her nets, and those who were to be taken in the toils knew it not.

But the final tug was given to the strings when a sly, deceitful-eyed game-watcher named Gleyed Lowrie ran across an open space of meadow, holding up his hand to the officers of the squadron of horse. Captain Austin Tredennis halted his company impatiently, but the informer passed him by, and holding by the stirrup of young Theophilus Gunter, he poured a lengthy tale into his private ear.

Meanwhile, in the little study and oratory of the Manse of Minnigaff (where in the corner before a little wooden shelf, made large enough to hold a Bible, there were a couple of hollows worn smooth and round by the knees of godly ministers long gone to their account) Hugh Penpont, ancient bachelor and minister of the kirk, replaced his pen with care in his great silver ink-horn, and fortified himself with a glass of Hollands before venturing out to be (according to his possible) the instrument of Destiny.

In the 'ben'-room sat Joyce Faa, strange-eyed, grey-lipped, inert in the grip of her fate. Harry Polwart, for whom there was no physician of any pretension nearer than Dumfries, stood erect, his hands pressed to his seared forehead. Moreover, Surgeon-barber Christopher Kitman, had the gypsy thought of consulting him, would probably have prescribed a poultice of the brains of bats braised small, together with the wings of beetles and the galls of three newly killed stoats, to be applied to the eyeballs thrice a day. But neither Joyce nor Harry Polwart even thought of a doctor. They had trusted all their lives to simples and the rude efficient surgery learned from Meggat and the crones of the tribe. In such a case as this, however, there was no idea of seeking a remedy. Harry, at least, would have connected something like impiety with the notion. The god of the lightning and thunder—Shiv, the striking god—he had put forth his hand, and there was an end. Shiv's hand had closed. All was ended.

And Joyce, though in part convent bred, had in extreme youth been reared among these simple nature worshippers, and whatever beliefs and thoughts she may have kept in her heart, she was far from mentioning to any of her kith and kin.

Greg Payterson (by birth Paterson, but so pronounced) was also an instrument of some occult Providence—whether of Shiv or Another. The minister had sent him to bring an additional witness, and, wishing to do the job thoroughly (and also to please as many as possible of his cronies in the hamlet of Cree Bridge), he had returned with Peter MacGill the miller, Allan Blair the smith, Easton Darvell the weaver of broadcloth, together with their several wives, all hastily attired in aprons and clean 'keps,' added to their work-a-day dresses—altogether much too large a company for the little ben-room of the Manse of Minnigaff.

Greg, however, mindful of his master's repute for hospitality, had carefully guarded his position in the issuing of invitations.

'Ye see, lads,' he had said, 'this is to be nae penny weddin' spree, mind ye that! It's eneuch, and mair than eneuch, that Maister Penpont should demean himsel' to mairry them ava' an' gie siccan heart-breakin' pagans a Christian benison, withoot haein' himsel' robbit by a wheen drouthy tykes frae the Clachan, that hae nae mair mense than to sup up guid French aquavity like sae muckle well water! Sae mind, lathies, ye come for the pleasure o' the sicht, an' no to get onything oot o' it for your bellies. Gin ye are no content—faith, ye can gang up to the Dungeon o' Buchan and settle your claims wi' Hector Faa himsel'!'

So in such circumstances and with such witnesses, Joyce Faa stood up to be married to Harry Polwart in the little green walk before the Manse door, shaded with beach-trees, now thinning a little and yellowing, while the path itself was thick carpeted beneath with their fallen leaves. Their feet made no noise upon these as they took their places, guided by Greg Payterson, who, having dry-nursed his minister through thirty years of helpless bachelordom, was naturally fully expert in the mysteries attending wedlock.

'A wee to this side, Maister Gypsyman—a kennin' farther wast, mistress. There, ye'll do the noo. When the minister comes in his black silk goon, wi' tassels, ye are to step twa steps to the front and gie a bow and a kurtshie, according to yer eddication and abeelities. This sort o' thing is maistly thocht the maist decent in the pairish o' Minnigaff, a kind o' soopin o' the grund like a wifie dusting the meal aff farles o' cake wi' a feather brush. But some toon-bred folks favours a kind o' dook on your hunkers, like a half-fu' tub jinkin on a mill dam—'

'Joyce,' whispered Harry, 'if that fellow has mnch more to say, let me get a hand on the haft of my knife and another on his neck!'

But the girl's hand, laid gently on his arm, calmed and quieted him. And, in truth, the rasping self-sufficience of Greg Payterson's official voice was doubtless very irritating to nerves tried as the gypsy's had been that day.

Then the minister sailed with dignity out of his front door. He was attired in his Sabbath blacks. A clean neckcloth had taken the place of the ink-stained article, on which in fits of absent-mindedness he sometimes wiped his goose-quills. He had put on the decent Genevan gown, which covered him down to his feet, and a little red pocket Bible that had been ready to his hand ever since college days, had a finger duly stuck between the leaves at a favourite passage in Ephesians, which he administered as a kind of extreme unction to those about to wed.

For Hugh Penpont, alive to the necessity of dwelling at harmony with all the world, was not the man to neglect the outward and ordinary means, even where only a couple of gypsies were concerned. Altogether, had he known that his ancient sweetheart and (comparatively speaking) heart-breaker was within a mile of his house with purport of visitation in her heart, he could not have ordered himself more elegantly. Which thing shows the advantage of having no respect of persons in the matter of toilet, for such are often privileged to entertain angels unaware and in befitting raiment.

'Let the parties to this contemplated engagement in holy matrimony stand up,' said the minister, with dignity.

Greg Payterson signified that the command was part of the ritual by jerking his elbow, and finally taking the bridegroom by the arm and moving him forward a pace to the front.

'Keep your dirty paw off me!' hissed the gypsy out of the corner of his mouth, with an accent so fierce that Greg fell back as if he had been struck fair in the face.

'They are no chancy, I telled ye sae, Greg—thae wild gypsies!' he muttered to hiriiself. 'Lord, he has pitten me mair in a trimmle than when I drappit the Psalm-buik on the Yerl's head as I was gaun up the pulpit steps! Oh, the murderin', misleart runnagate! Nae man can be decent wi' a face on him like yon! He looks like a man dead and damned a guid twalmonth an' mair!'

'Can any man allege and support any just cause or impediment why these two persons should not be wedded according to the law and judicatories of the Kirk of Scotland as by the Revolution Settlement established?'

The minister's question came forth solemn and official.

'I can!' cried Jasper Jamie, riding up with the face of an accusing angel. 'The man before you is a murderer! And I call upon you all to help me to arrest him! I will hold you six men responsible if you do not! Minister, this is Harry Polwart, the gypsy smuggler, who, with mine own eyes, I saw lead off the two excisemen—Supervisor Craig and Bobin Trevor—with intent to cast them into the quicksands of Barnhourie!'

At the first sound of Jasper Jamie's voice the blind man snatched his hand out of Joyce's, turned his head every way as if to locate his enemy, and drew a knife.

Then, as Jasper continued speaking, Polwart launched himself straight, as he thought, at his accuser.

But Jasper, still on horseback, easily evaded the charge, and the gypsy rushed straight upon Greg Payterson, that worthy but inglorious stoop of the Kirk, who, thinking the assault delivered solely on his account, gave vent to a yell and tripped backward over a row of the minister's cabbages.

'Help! help! He is on me,' he cried; 'he is killing me! Murder! Death! Destruction! The wild gypsy has broken lowse! Grip him! Hand him! To prison wi' the randy! In the King's name, baud him! I order you by my authority as beadle o' this pairish!'

So, nimbly scrambling to his feet, and uttering all the time these valorous calls to arms, the minister's man disappeared down the little manse loaning, and, finding the kirk door open, he rushed through it into the vestry and there locked himself within.

Then, throwing open the window, which consisted of a single pane, and through which a cat would be hard pushed to intrude itself, he continued to shout directions at the top of his voice to whomsoever it might concern.

'He's blind, I tell ye! He canna do ye ony hurt, lads! Tak' firm haud o' him, and aff to prison wi' the murderous rogue! Grip him richt aboot the legs and throw him! Syne tie him up firm wi' a rape!'

But even these directions of Greg Payterson's, in themselves something futile and impersonal, had their uses. For the sound of them, borne upon the

185

light wind, carried from the Kirk knowe across the shallow Penkill Water and down to where at the change-house of Minnigaff a certain squadron of that famous regiment of King George's dragoons, afterwards called Ligonier's Horse, was easing girths and cooling throats in the narrow village street.

The clachan of Minnigaff is certainly one of the most ancient in Galloway, and at that time it resembled nothing so much as a boulder-strewn hillside, with the spaces between the blocks of stone rudely roofed over and thatched with brown heather and yellow oat straw. A few of these huts had their gables to the road (which passed up the left bank of the Water of Cree), but the greater number were set at an angle, as if showered from a pepper-caster.

But whether duly oriented or dispersed at random, every domicile possessed another and often far larger erection before its door. This was the family midden—those edifices which in these latter days wise men have begun to study for what they tell of the life of the folk of bygone ages, but which, when considered contemporaneously and by means of the ordinary senses, are not pleasant objects for prolonged contemplation. These Minnigaff middens, I say, were in nearly every case larger than the parent house, or compound of dwelling and cattle-shed, whose inhabitants, human and bestial, had supplied the materials for its erection. Most of these middens, also, were set like mountainous islands in a sea of liquid green filth, where ducks dabbled and squattered all day long, and in which patient calves stood winking the flies from their inflamed eyes or apparently enjoying the coolness and the light aromatic breezes as much as though they had been chewing the cud knee-deep in some rippling river or lily-bordered lake.

In front of the largest of these, that belonging to the change-house. Captain Austin Tredennis held his nose, and swore with heavy cavalry point and vigor at the poverty of the accommodation upon which he had been counting, and, alternately, at the infamous kind of work which local authorities set a gentleman to do.

The good-wives made manifold affidavits that most of the men-folk had gone off to the manse, and the troopers, with a bad grace, were carrying water for their beasts and grooming them in person—-duties which they are wont to delegate upon occasion to the able-bodied male inhabitants of each village where they found themselves quartered, while they proceeded to make themselves pleasant to the women-folk, as the duty of cavalrymen is all the world over.

All this was going on when, wafted upon the winds from above, came repeated calls of 'Death!' and 'Murder!' from the heights of the kirk lands.

It did not take the men long to saddle and ride out in the direction from whence came the outcries, the spy who had clung to young Gunter's stirrup leading them.

And so it chanced that there in the manse garden of Minnigaff, where the ink was not yet dry upon the minister's peaceful quill, and the last sentence of 'seven-teenthly' lay unfinished upon the desk, the hand of Destiny shut down.

As Austin Tredennis rode at a rapid trot up the hill, his men scatteringly following, he came upon a striking sight. In an angle of the little walled manse garden a tall, dark man, his eyes staring wildly, a long and shining knife in his hand, crouched low on his hams. His lips were compressed, and with his sightless head turning slowly about in a listening attitude, he strove to catch every movement of his assailants.

These, with one exception, were not too painfully eager for the attack. The half-dozen villagers had armed themselves with any weapon that came to hand—a garden mattock, a hammer, a scythe—as chance directed, while Jasper Jamie alone held a sword in his hand. The gypsy was bleeding at the shoulder from having thrown himself in his first furious anger upon the point of Jasper's weapon. It would have been easy enough to kill him, but Jasper cried out to take him alive—a recommendation which was converted into a command with the authority of law by the minister.

'Ay!' cried Mr. Penpont, who had picked up the skirts of his gown in order that if necessary he might the sooner place himself in safety; 'take the fellow alive! Let him be tried! I am a justice of the peace, and order you!'

Joyce Faa stood a little apart, her hands clinched, her eyes flashing. Harry Polwart had, at the first sound of alarm, bidden her keep at this distance. But with the instinct of her breeding and the wild life she had led at the Dungeon of Buchan, she never even thought of deserting him. Her sympathies were all with the blind outlaw, now in imminent danger of being caught in the hunters' toils. In a rapid undertone, and in their own language, she kept him informed of every movement of his assailants, and had there been no interference from without, there is no saying how the fight might have ended. For the two hill gypsies kept edging all the time nearer to the deep, tangled ravine of the Cree Water, and it was in the heart of Joyce that if she could get Harry once into the dense thickets of the Wood of Cree they could there defy all pursuit. For the first of Bonunany laws is this: 'Thou shalt help thy fellow-gypsy well if he be thy friend, but if he be thine enemy—better! Afterwards ye may settle your affairs.'

Beside the minister stood his ancient sweetheart, May Mischief, who had ridden on ahead, with Jasper Jamie, perhaps that Grisel might not too critically observe the meeting, but Marion and her daughter had not come up yet.

As soon, however, as the squadron of cavalry jingled into the little enclosure, the blind gypsy recognized that all was over so far as his chances of flight were concerned. He threw down the long knife at his feet, folded his arms placidly across his breast, and with a slight upward jerk of his chin summoned Joyce to his side.

There they stood, the only calm and impassive figures within sight, the two outlaw folk within the ring of their enemies. And such was the power of kinship that Joyce never once thought of not taking upon herself an equal responsibility for any crime with which her companion might stand chargeable under the laws of the King.

'What have we here?' cried Captain Tredennis. 'A murderer? Say you so? Hold him there, sergeant! Bring a pair of handcuffs. His companion also!'

But to himself he said: 'By gad! a handsome wench. What eyes these gypsies have—black as a starless night!'

The two gypsies yielded themselves without any trace of emotion, and the cunning spy, Gleyed Lowrie, hummed 'Lillibullero' as he gleefully clicked the Bow Street 'hold-fasts' upon their wrists. Lowrie was a well-known informer and officer of the law from Kirkcudbright—the best-hated man in a score of parishes.

At this moment there rode up Grisel Heron, and with her, gay in his scarlet and gold. Captain Richard Heron, called of his Majesty's Border Fencibles.

In a moment the spy had his little, keen, pig's eyes fixed upon him.

Captain Austin Tredennis rode forward to where against the dry stone dyke of Mr. Penpont's garden the two gypsies stood manacled, fronting their accusers, much as in a day of battle and execution they might have fronted a firing party.

'Your names!' he demanded, brusquely, but not unkindly.

The male gypsy did not answer, maintaining his attitude of contemptuous indifference. But the girl spoke out directly as one speaks to an equal. My name is Joyce Faa,' she said.

'Daughter of the outlaw. Hector Faa, attainted for murder?'

'If my father be a murderer,' answered Joyce Faa, defiantly, 'so are most men of your profession!'

The soldier seemed to be surprised at hearing such words so clearly spoken by a gypsy girl of the hills. But he turned away, saying only: 'it is my duty to carry you to Kirkcudbright, where questions will be put to you by those of more authority than I. Meantime, do you deny knowing anything of these two missing men Mr. Sapervisor Craig and Trevor the exciseman?'

'I have not heard so maeh as their names before,' said the girl.

'I trust that may turn out to be so,' said the soldier, gravely. 'Murder in the first degree and maidens of your appearance consort but ill together!'

At the first sound of the name of Joyce Faa my mother started forward. She had heard the word 'murder' used several times, with an indistinct idea that somehow it must concern me. So now she sprang forward, shaking off in a moment the minister's restraining hand. She ran to the girl and seized her by the wrist.

'Where is my son, Joyce Faa?' she cried. 'I bid you tell me if you have killed him! Where is he? If you have murdered him, I will kill you with my hands!'

At the sound of the new voice Harry Polwart turned his sightless eyes full on my mother, and his mind seemed to endeavour to pierce the black blank in which he was wrapped.

But Joyce did not reply at all. Whether she even understood my mother is doubtful. At any rate, she spoke no word. So my mother shook her in her unreasoning anger. For these fits sometimes took her when none could restrain her—that is, save my father only.

'Tell me—tell me I or I will surely kill you!' she cried.

Then rode Captain Austin Tredennis slowly up to her.

'Do not forget yourself, madam,' he said, courteously; 'remember that the woman is a prisoner and bound.'

But my mother was not to be turned from her purpose.

'She has killed my son! I know it! She held him prisoner for months—there in their horrid dens and caves! And now I only ask if she has slain him, and she will not answer—no, nor even tell me where they have put his body?'

Then once again the soldier turned to Joyce

190

Faa.

'Do you know anything of this lady's son?' he said.

'Who is this woman?' answered Joyce, no muscle of her face moving—only her lips, that lay like twin geranium flowers upon the ivory pallor of her cheek, paling a little.

'She is Mistress Patrick Heron of Rathan and Orraland,' yet another voice put in—that of Captain Richard Heron of the Fencibles, who had just ridden up.

'She is my mother,' added Grisel. 'And pray, what have you done with my brother Max?'

'She has killed him!' cried my mother.

'More likely married him!' quoth Grisel.

Then there came a slow, rosy flush, deep and gradual, over the face of Joyce Faa. The red quite faded from her lips, but all the more stood confessed along her cheek and neck. With it there came a smile, the first that had crossed her face since she bent over to wake me in the Shiel of the Dungeon the night of my capture. She had done so much, and this was her reward from the people of my race and name.

'If I reckon aright,' she said, speaking quietly and without heat, 'about this time he will be riding over the hill to Orraland Gate upon a borrowed sheltie.'

'Mount the prisoners and let them ride forward, Sergeant Pratt; detail twenty men and the same number of the least tired horses to convey them to Kirkcudbright without delay. I will accompany them myself.'

'Aha, Austin! still with an eye to beauty! Fie, fie! and at your age!' cried young Leo Gunter, who thought that he had kept silence long enough.

But the spy, Gleyed Lowrie, had something yet to say.

'Stop a moment. Captain. I give you another prisoner!' he cried. 'I deliver into your hands Dick o' the Isle, the leader of the Levellers' rebellion! I saw him at the muster by the cross-roads of Rascarrel. Ask him. He will not deny it!'

191

He pointed directly at Captain Hichard Heron of his Majesty's Border Feneible Regiment, who sat his horse calmly, twirling an all but imaginary mustache.

'He will not deny it!' he cried, triumphantly. 'I saw him stand out in the moonlight and shoot his pistol at your father—Colonel Gunter!'

'Oh, he is not, I tell you—he is not— !' cried my mother, and stopped.

For the difficulty of explaining who Captain Richard Heron was not, seemed nothing to the impossibility of explaining who Dick o' the Isle was. But the young man of many aliases made a slight movement of his hand to his friends to indicate that it would be advisable for the present to let things take their course.

'I do not deny anything,' he said. 'I am Dick of the Isle, and I did shoot a pistol at Colonel Gunter at the muster of Rascarrel, though not with intent to do him bodily harm.'

'And if that be true, by the Lord, you shall explain what you are doing here in that King's coat!' cried Captain Tredennis, angrily, for this was a point of honour with him.

'I have as good a right to this coat of the King— ay, though it came warm off the Royal Hanoverian back an hour ago,' said the false Dick of the Isle, 'as to any other coat in the universe!'

'And that,' he added to himself, under his breath, 'is just no right at all!'

CHAPTER TWENTY NINE
THE PROVOST'S SPIRITS

Few men had been worse used by fortune than Captain Austin Tredennis. Born to an ample fortune—so far, that it, as expectations go (and in his ease they did not go far), Austin had the further misfortune of nominally inheriting an involved title and an estate not worth a penny.

At a time when money did most things and influence the rest in the British army, he found himself still a captain of dragoons at thirty-nine, with nothing to show for his twenty years' active service but a sword of honour given him by the Prince Eugene, that excellent ally of England, and a bullet wound in the right thigh, which gave him a slight halt in walking, and kept him informed when he might expect the wind to change into the east.

A man not overwhelmingly in love with life, one who owed little to the great, yet who felt himself the superior of many set in authority over him, Austin Tredennis was a man who never made a complaint that life had treated him badly. He was in all things scrupulous to obey, rigorous to exact obedience, liked for his grace and certain courtesy by his inferiors, and, besides being trusted by his men as all good officers are, his unquestioned personal courage carrying him safely through many a strait place. As a swordsman he had few equals in Britain at a time when every man was a fencer. He had no equal at all as a shot with a pistol. These facts, becoming widely known made for peace.

His father, Chieseley Tredennis, had made a fortune in the West India trade as it was then—sugar, tobacco, and imported negroes. He had designed his son to follow in his footsteps. But one voyage to Jamaica, and a single month's experience of the methods of an enlightened British plantation under half-breed overseers, had satisfied young Austin. Come what might, he could not be a sugar-planter. He would be a soldier, if he had to serve in the ranks. There was an interview between father and son which comprised some picturesque language on either side, and then Austin Tredennis, of all his father's great fortune, took only the price of an ensigncy of horse—the purchase-money of which he afterwards repaid out of his meagre pay to the uttermost farthing.

His father, being an exact man, gave him a receipt upon stamped paper for the amount. As for his other relatives, his uncle, Lord Tredennis, had a daughter by an early uncovenanted attachment, which fear of his father, also a hard man, had prevented him from making regular till the death of the mother rendered it impossible.

In order to compose all family divisions and quarrels, this girl, when but a child, had been designed by Lord Tredennis for his nephew. But the West India planter discovered an objection—the nobleman had thrown all his energies into a successful attempt to legitimatize the girl, and to convey to her his recently granted earldom. It was in pursuit of an attempt to prove an early marriage by consent under the more elastic laws of Scotland, and to induce the government of the day to grant him his desired succession to heirs general, that Lord Tredennis embarked for Greenock at London Bridge in a vessel which was never more heard of.

Nevertheless, the machinery he had set going worked for him, and all that he had desired was granted after his death.

In the mean time there remained nothing but a disputed succession to the son of the West India planter. His father, now an old man, had so pickled an originally pregnant temper in spices and hot condiments that he remained alive solely to plague and vex his son. He was a benevolent man, too, in his way, which made it worse. There are fine marble palaces out near to the physic garden in Chelsea which bear his name, where widows of sailormen lodged in almhouses, and blessed all day (and especially at meal-times) the name of Chieseley Tredennis. He built a school, also, out at East Gidding for the children of persecuted enthusiasts, and his name is mentioned with honour in all the calendars of the company of Christian people called Wesleyans.

But he so arranged matters that he should not have one stiver to leave to that poor captain of horse, his only son Austin, who on his part neither blessed his name nor made any pretence of doing so. On the other hand, with a fine equanimity, he drilled his men, did as he was bid, or saw that others did as he bade them; fought battles, rode on chargers, plundered a little or a great deal, as he had opportunity—according to the wont of the horsemen of the period. Yet he was not a man of cruelty, and no wife, maid, or widow in any captured town laid her scaith to him. He did his business, which was the business of the government, as well in Galloway as he might have done it in the Low Countries, without partisanship and without heat, but with a dispassionate attention to instruction and a liberal reading of human kindness into the letter of the law— so far, that is, as he could square the result with his duty.

All this till the day when from the House of Destiny, the Manse of Minnigaff, he rode eastward by the shore-road to the prison of Kirkcudbright.

At this point the old Austin Tredennis and the new part company.

The common prison or Thieves Hole of the burgh of Kirkcudbright was as a later visiting philanthropist said, 'a disgrace to any civilized land.' But then, till the last few years so was every jail in Scotland. Now it seems as if the fashion of the time had run to the other extreme, insomuch that nowadays the able-bodied rogue universally prefers prison to the workhouse erected for the reception of honest poverty.

But Captain Austin Tredennis, having done his duty in riding to Kirkcudbright upon escort duty with his trio of prisoners, discovered upon opening the door of the Thieves' Hole that all the space available for those under his charge was a dripping, noisome den, already inhabited by a dozen rogues of both sexes, the sweepings of the bounds of municipal rascaldom, a stray debtor without friends to enlarge his privileges, and, dispersed over all, an innumerable company of the accumulated vermin of the ages.

'Sir,' said Austin Tredennis, to the chief magistrate at whose door he had knocked with his sword-hilt on his arrival, 'in England we would not lodge our scent-dogs thus—no, not the hogs in our styes.'

The provost laughed a little, low, gurgling laugh. He was a jocose man, and fat of his habit, a well-to-do owner of coastwise shipping and herring boats out upon fair and doubtful ventures. And in his time he had seen many English captains of horse, who had grumbled at many things within the bounds of his burgh.

But the mistake that Provost Roy McCaskie made was that he had never seen an English captain of horse in the least like Austin Tredennis.

They were standing together at the door of the Thieves' Hole. For the soldier had drawn back in disgust from the miserable interior and the reeking abominations that struck him in the face with more than the pain of a blow.

The provost's gurgle settled matters. It irritated Austin even more than the accumulated odors of the Thieves' Hole of Kirkcudbright.

'Observe,' he said, laying one gloved finger in the palm of the other hand, 'I am in this shire of Galloway with certain powers of command, and I can suit my actions to my conceptions of military necessity. I can call upon you, as the responsible head of this burgh council, to assist me! Now I will not dispose of these untried prisoners—one of them a woman, and another evidently of gentle birth and breeding—like beasts that are driven to market! If you do not find me some safe and decent place where I can lodge these prisoners in ward—by the Lord, sir provost, I will quarter them, every one, in your own house, and set a picket outside the door!'

The chief magistrate fell back in absolute astonishment.

'Do you ken to whom ye speak, captain?' he

cried. 'I am Boy McCaskie, a second cousin o' the ex-provost o' Paisley, and whenever the Yerl o' Kirkham comes to the toon he never yince passes my door! So ye had better caa' canny, wi' your English assurance! I can tell ye, my man, I hae gotten brisker laddies than you cashiered for less.'

'I do not give a candle-end,' said the soldier, 'for a score of provosts, with all their councils at their tails (and not a clean-washed man among them)—no, nor yet for earls of Kirkham either, by the gross or bale! I have my instructions and my discretion. Do as I bid you, Mr. McCaskie, or I will quarter these my prisoners upon you— ay, and see that they are kept in the best of bed and board at your private charges till such time as you provide fitting accommodation for them elsewhere!'

Thus brought up upon the short rein, the provost suddenly remembered an alternative which might otherwise have escaped him. He held up his hand, and the whole expression of his face changed.

'Dear me, Captain Tredennis,' he exclaimed, 'dinna stot all like a baa' aff a gableend. I declare I shall forget my ain name next. I am no fit to be Robin the toon's drummer, let alane provost! It is true that the gaol o' Kirkcudbright is nocht less than a fair disgrace. But, ye see, the common guid o' the toon has been in a sair state for a while, what wi' the Levellers dingin' doon the park waa's and but little comin' in! But after this year the thing will be diiferent. For Treasurer Bailie Todd and me hae ta'en the parks on a lang lease atween us, and gin I'm spared till Martinmas I can assure you, major, that the Thieves' Hole shall be pitten in a state o' thorough repair!'

'But, my excellent provost,' said Austin, grimly, 'Martinmas is a long way off, and in the mean time you may be as tired of providing house-room for my prisoners and their guard, as I shall be of seeing to it that everything is done to my satisfaction.'

'Oh, colonel,' said the now alarmed magistrate, 'I didna mean that—I was far frae meanin' that. But— to tell ye the truth—there is a place where they might be warded safely eneuch. But—I hardly like to mention it to a braw King's man—the fact is that Bailie Todd and me, and a wheen ither decent men wi' an interest in the common guid o' the community at lairge, hae a kind o' private store o' barrels, juist bits o' casks and puncheons an' sic like—some o' them fu' an some o' them empty—that we are no juist anxious to hae ony exciseman's gaugin' stick mixin' and mellin' wi—'

'In fact, provost,' said Captain Tredennis, smiling, 'you have in this town a Thieves' Hole and a Smugglers' Hole, both under the direct patronage of the magistracy! Well, well! I am no exciseman, but a plain soldier. I have no commission to tap your casks, though I would advise you to lock them carefully in a part of your cellars where my lads cannot get at them, or you may chance upon an empty keg or two, and I find the sergeant's guard hopping at the triangles. But lead the way, provost, and let us see these, your private cellars.'

' 'Deed, to tell ye the truth, General,' said the anxious magistrate, 'it's neither mair nor less than juist in the auld castle—what folks caa's Maclellan's Wark. It was biggit some fifty or a hunder years syne by the grand auld Maclellans, that were Lords o' Kirkcudbrie for mony's the year. But afore ever they gat it plenished, so the story gangs, the siller gaed dune, or the bottom fell oot o' the meal ark—or something—and whush—the Maclellans were a' gane! Nocht left but an auld sang, and thae waa's up there that hae never been ony doom's guid to leevin' sowl!

'But here we are, captain, an' gin ye will tell your troopers to baud a kennin' farther aff, and gie their best attention to the prisoners, I'll be terrible obleegit till ye. There's maybes a bit anker or twa o' brandy that micht be seen if the door was opened untimeous-like. I hae had the muckle yett sealed wi' the toon seal, whilk I cairry convenient-like in my pooch here for the purpose, wi' a guid wad o' the excellent sealing-wax that we use for our charters. For it is oor plan in the municipawlity that a' thing be dune decently and in order, and, 'deed, that has aye been my ain aim an' motty—.'

'Very right, provost,' said Austin Tredennis.

The chief of the burgh magistracy looked cautiously over his shoulder to see that no curious spectator approached too near. Then he drew forth a book from his breastpocket, and, opening it, read hastily and in a loud and solemn tone somewhat as follows: 'Let all spirits of evil depart from this dwelling, and suffer only such things as are of good report to dwell here! I exorcise the deevil! Michty, I forget the rest— There will be horse and hiring fares in the following places in Scotland at the undermentioned dates: Airberdeen the 20th o' Aprile, Alyth the 6th o' June, Biggar the 29th o' September!' At this he looked about and shut the book with the same caution as before. 'I think that will do, captain! We can gang in noo!'

'And what, in the name of fortune, may be the meaning of this idiocy?' cried the captain of horse, who had an idea that he was being played with.

'Haud your paitience a wee langer, captain, and ye will see. Ye understan' they are a verra superstitious folk here in Kirkcoobrie, an' what's pitten into folk by the Powers abune is there to be made use o' by somebody. Noo, the bodies will threep doon your throat that this auld biggin' is haimtit wi' speerits. And so it is—conjunctly and severally— though no by the kind o' speerits they mean. Nae ill speerits ever comes across the sea in my boaties! And sae a wise magistracy, wi' the common guid of the toon at heart, do their best to preserve sic auncient and weel-befittin' feelin's atween the dead and the leevin'. Forbye, there's no yin o' the craiturs wad pit a fit inside the place at nicht for a' the gowd o' the Indies. We hae seen to that oorsel's!'

'But what was all that nonsense you read out of a book? And was it not from the Bible? I thought you Scots folk were monstrously particular about blasphemy and such things?'

'The Bible! Hear till the man! Na, na! It was' just the Belfast Almanack, and when I forget what auld Andrew Cameron (that was the great hand at exorcesin') used to say, I e'en gang on wi' the list o' fairs, and times when the tide is fu' at the pier o' Leith, an' siclike things as that. There's neither Bible nor Psalm-book about the maitter. I wad hae ye ken that Roy McCaskie, thrice provost o' Kirkcoobrie, has mair respeck for revealed releegion than that!'

By this time they were in the great hall of Maclellan's Wark, and truly there were many reasons visible to the least suspicious eye why an enlightened magistracy should not wish to have the officers of his Majesty's excise admitted to the secrets of their haunted towers.

'Bide ye here a wee, captain,' said the provost, 'an' I'll gang fetch Bailie Todd and Dean of Guild Georgie Sproat, that is as decent a lad as ever lifted a toddy ladle to see gin the sugar was meltit. I'm getting' a wee short i' the puff myself, and I canna face the removal o' a' thae barrels single-handed.'

During the provost's absence Austin Tredennis poked about in various recesses here and there in the ancient walls, and among other things discovered that a dozen of rooms had recently been roughly boarded off, and that five or six of them could easily be rendered available for cells and guard-rooms. But what amused him most was to find in a recess of the first floors a singularly cosey apartment, fitted not only with a table, chairs, a fireplace and kettle, but with the very toddy ladles and rummer of which the provost had spoken, and, indeed, all the necessaries for producing an immediate and considerable elevation of spirits among the members of this deserving and enlight-ened magistracy.

But several robes of extraordinary appearance next drew his attention. These had apparently been manufactured out of white sheeting, deeply stained with red. Next came a double length of plough chain of unusual thickness, and a sheet of thin iron all crinkled and bossed like a sheet of paper that has been wet and dried again, which last completely puzzled him.

He was still standing with the stiff white sheets in his hand when the provost returned, with two men following close behind him. One man was old and very sober-looking, with a formal upper-lip, which was, however, slightly contracted by the twinkle of sly humour in the corners of his eyes. Him the soldier set down at once as Treasurer Bailie Todd. Nor was he far wrong, for the introduction was immediately accomplished; while his comrade, a tall, good-looking, buirdly young man, with rosy cheeks and an infectious laugh, was stated to be 'Maister Dean o' Guild Sproat, and the best falla' in twal' coonties!' added Provost Roy McCaskie, slapping his back with joyous particularity.

'I see ye hae gotten haud o' oor ghaist's claes, captain,' said the chief magistrate. 'Ye see, we are a set o' quaite folk hereaway, and a wee thing gangs a lang gate. And, faith, gin it werena for the terrible ghaists in Maclellan's Auld Wark, there wad be nocht to pass the time o' day aboot in the burgh, but the day an' date when Aggie Muir's cat is gaun to kittle and wha's Tam was the daddie o't! But as we that are in the magistracy ken weel, Satan finds wark for idle fowk's tongues as weel as for their fingers. Sae we like to gie the guidwives something to keckle aboot —no ower aften, ye ken, but maybes twice i' the month, that familiarity may no juist breed contempt, as the sayin' is.'

'Geordie, there, in a white sheet an' a splotch or twa o' guid cairt red dreepin' frae his breast is eneuch to scaur the verra saunts abune frae their harpin'! Fegs, he gars the hair on my auld pow rise up like bristles, and when we three are at it full blast, wi' Geordie standin' bleatin' like a dementit sheep on the riggin o' this auld pile, and the bailie—decent man— dancin' on the sheet iron like a hen on a het girdle, and me doin' my best at trailing the pleuch chains alang the board fioors and up and doon the stairs—I declare it's fair Pandemonium an' Gehenna spoken thegither in auld Maclellan's Wark. But it's at its finest in a thunder-storm. The verra minister, when he cam' to pee it, gaed hame that wat wi' fear that they had to pit a' his claes oot on the line neist mornin' early! Man! it's juist doom's graund, that's a fack! And then we hae a bit drappie ben here, and, syne to settle the drinks weel doon, we gang oot every hour or twa an' tak' anither turn at the speeritual eddication o' the burgh!'

'You do well, provost and magistrates!' said Captain Tredennis.

CHAPTER THIRTY
A MASTERFUL MAN

Within an hour the boarded chambers of Maclellan's Wark had been freed of their hoard of kegs, ankers, puncheons, and casks, while within the same period the three leading members of the enlightened magistracy of Kirkcudbright were in a state of profuse perspiration. In some cases the rooms, especially those on the ground floor, had been originally planned but left unfinished, and in others they had been, as it were, carved out of the general space of the interior.

The prisoners, upon being taken into Maclellan's Wark, were placed each in the chamber set apart for them. The room appointed for Marion was placed midway between that of Joyce Faa and the gypsy Harry Polwart, possibly with an idea of preventing these two complices from communicating. The guards were established in a large open space beside the main doorway, and Captain Austin Tredennis, who did not desire to put himself under any obligations of hospitality to the provost or other citizen, took up his quarters in the chamber which they had apportioned and provisioned for their private revels.

Throughout the town, many were the dismal prophecies of what would happen when once 'the ghaists o' the auld Maclellans,' discovering earthly intruders upon their domain, should arise and wreak their vengeance. While the fact that during the whole of this tenancy the spectres did, indeed, cease to gibber blood-boltered on the battlements was put down to Joyce and Harry being gypsies, and, therefore, 'sib to the deil, wha is aye kind to his ain.'

Of the three captives, Harry Polwart, a thorough fatalist like all his people, threw himself on the pallet-bed which had been hastily provided by the provost, and lay there sleepless through the night watches, his hands pressed upon his aching eyeballs. He had no hopes, no fears, and it was not in his nature to be afraid of that which only might be. Whatever came, it would find him ready.

Joyce was chiefly conscious of a reprieve. The marriage to which she had sold herself for the sake of another's life had not taken place. But, nevertheless, she held herself pledged to Harry Polwart, and was as determined as ever to carry out her promise if, and when, opportunity should occur. Whether or no the man was a murderer did not greatly trouble her. If this thing were true, it had been done by her father's orders; and, knowing Hector Faa as she did, she would not greatly blame any of his followers for obeying him. But, meantime, the four massive walls of Maclellan's Wark, the solitude, and the time of respite, were not unwelcome. Joyce did not think much, for, as she has borne witness since, she had determined to shut the thought of a certain Maxwell Heron out of her heart.

Marion alone set herself down to understand and define her position in all its bearings—her chances and dangers, her present situation and future action. My mother and Grisel had remained with her as long as they were allowed, and it was only the absolute order of Captain Tredennis which prevented both of these loving and impulsive women from remaining all night in the prison. When my mother found herself extruded she sought out Jasper Jamie, and, bidding him get horses, insisted on setting out immediately for Orraland.

'It is barely eight mile over the hill, and the time an hour from sundown! Think shame o' ye, Jasper Jamie, that ye wad let puir Marion die for the want of guid advice!'

To know my mother in such a mood was to obey her— that is, save in the case of my father, who had his own methods.

For, though May Mischief retained her old proclivity for getting into scrapes, and sometimes to his very face voted her husband slow and matter-of-fact, yet she had more than her ancient respect for his opinion, and often came running to him, not only with her own, but with other people's difficulties.

If Patrick Heron could not help—why, there was

no help in man! So at least thought May Mischief after twenty-five years.

The autumn night held a chill in it, and in the grim old keep of Maclellan's Wark the mortar dripped damp upon the walls. The unplaned boards wept at the seams. A pillow hard as a door-mat, a pallet-bed on which a maidservant might have slept, an old torn blanket—these constituted her equipment of the night. And since, through the unglazed but barred window, the wind blew in fresh and wet from the sea, Marion shivered. Yet, to do her justice, discomfort, and not fear, caused the tremor.

That she had incurred the extreme penalty of the law by the crime of rebellion, she knew well. That Colonel Gunter would pursue the Chief of the Levellers to the uttermost she was sure of also, for such was his approven character. Whenever she thought determinedly upon the matter it seemed a terrible thing enough that she should die so young, but yet somehow the idea did not remain long with her. Her mind wandered off to other things, and more than once she found herself smiling. The scene at the manse had certainly been amusing. She wondered if she would ever again see Greg Payterson. Oh yes! of course—at the trial. Then she fell to wondering if she would be tried at the same time as the gypsies. What a beautiful girl! No wonder Maxwell loved her. But that she should love Maxwell Heron—a girl like that— Marion thought it unlikely. The blind gypsy, now, to whom she had been on the point of being married! He was a dark, lowering fellow enough; blind, too, and with a terrible look as of one recently smitten. But, after all, Marion could not imagine any one being long in love with—at least, not after knowing.

She meditated a while here, and found herself returning to the point from which she had set out.

Did this beautiful Joyce Faa love the blind gypsy or— Max Heron? She wished she could ask her. With Marion of the Isle to resolve was to act immediately—that is, if action were at all within the realms of possibility.

She remembered that she had seen the soldiers

put Joyce into the chamber to the left of her own.

Could she hear if she called, or, hearing, would she answer?

She tapped lightly on the woodwork with the knuckle of her finger. There was silence for a moment, and then a low voice answered:

'Harry, is it your eyes? Do they pain you?'

'It is not Harry It is I—Dick of the Isles,' said Marion.

'I do not know you—I have nothing to say to you. What do you want with Joyce Faa?'

'With Joyce Faa nothing. Only to know if she loves Maxwell Heron?'

There was a deep silence over the prison, and the rough laugh of a trooper in the outer hall jarred upon both of them.

'By what right do you ask that question, Dick of the Isle, if that be your name? What is it to you?'

'It is nothing to me, and yet I ask it,' came the answer back.

'It is a woman's question?' said Joyce Faa, 'and yet you are not a woman. Did any one by the shore of Solway—one whom he loved—bid you ask that question of me?'

'No one,' said Marion, instantly relieved in her turn from a fear that she had discovered her sex. 'Max Heron never loved any one in his life—save himself.'

'That again is a woman's bitterness,' said Joyce, 'and yet you are not a woman! Why do you hate Maxwell Heron? Did he ever do you an injury?'

'Max Heron! Nay, verily!' I fear her tone was a little contemptuous. 'He would no more do any one an injury than a mavis that sings in the meadow copses.'

There was a long and quiet pause in the chamber of Joyce Faa. Then came the words: 'You are a woman! You cannot deceive me, who am a woman also! And if you do not love Maxwell Heron, sure I am that your heart swayed towards him once.'

Then it was the time of silence in Marion's chamber. She was debating with herself whether to confide in this wild girl of the hills—who stood accused of murder, and might go to the gallows. Then Marion smiled a little bitterly. For that was also where she had some likelihood of finding herself, and what right had she to be proud with Joyce Faa? She was alone, in prison, and the girl might help her. At least there would be two of them.

'Put your head down and listen very closely,' she said at last. 'There is a crack in the partition here. I will tell you, if you will also tell me the thing which I asked you.'

She could hear Joyce Faa moving to obey her.

'It is true—the thing you say—I am a girl,' said Marion, 'and once, before I knew what men there were in the world, I was in danger of—of loving one who could not have loved me—who cannot love as men love! But I stayed myself in time!'

Beyond the partition there was a sound like a quick sob in the listener's throat, and the words came back:

'And I did not stay myself—till it was too late!' murmured Joyce.

'God help all women—let men take care of themselves!' returned Marion, devoutly.

So, in this fashion, two women drew themselves to one another within the grim, damp heart of Maclellan's Wark.

And while they communed thus there came the sound of a padlock being unlocked, then the click of the dropping hinge, and the door of Marion's prison-room opened. It was Captain Austin Tredennis who entered. He was still in his campaigning dress, which, though the full uniform of his corps, was of rougher and stronger material than is common among young captains of horse. For it had not been Austin Tredennis's hap to be able to afford many suits of uniform.

'Good-evening to you,' he said, his stern face relaxing a little. 'It appeared to me that, as I understand that you are of some birth and breeding, I might be able to afford you such facilities for communicating with your friends as my duty allows, or in some other way of enabling you to meet the grave charges which are preferred against you. If there is any way in which I can do this, pray command me. You will find that I am a man who means what he says—it may be a little more, certainly no less.'

He set down the lantern he carried, having first of all opened the case and stuck the candle on the top in a place appointed for it. Then he pulled an empty keg out from an angle of the wall, and sat down upon it in the strong, easy attitude of a man accustomed to all chances by land and sea.

'Do you sit also and let us talk,' he said. 'I have had a great deal of experience, and know well that young men will often venture their necks in very poor causes for the sake of the adventure. But there may be ways out. There generally are when one is one-and-twenty. I hear you are a pretty shot. Young Gunter tells me you disarmed his father in the moonlight at ten paces. If you fence as well as you shoot, young man, you should be dangerous on the grass at daybreak.'

'I can play a little with the sabre' said Marion, modestly, 'but I hardly know how to hold a foil. Moreover, my wrist is not strong enough for fence.'

'Let me see,' said the soldier, and, ere his prisoner realized what he was doing, he had her hand in his, and was giving serious regard to the pretty, slenderish fingers and the palm, which Marion of the Isle would have given a thousand pounds at that moment to have rendered strong and coarse.

But after all he said nothing. He only looked a while at the blue-veined wrist and the taper fingers. Then he let them drop abruptly, and with a yawn and stretch he drew a little, oblong metal box out of his pocket,and rolling a twisted paper of tobacco, fine almost as dust, he looked at his prisoner and said, as he licked the edges together, 'A foreign habit, sir, and a good one. I learned it from a Spaniard in the prison at Namur, in the Low Countries. You should acquire it. Nothing passes the time so well when one is not one's own master.'

'Then you also have been in prison?' said

Marion, smiling, and glad to change the subject on any terms.

'More times than I care to think of,' said Austin Tredennis. 'I have not followed the wars for twenty years without many ups and downs, and, indeed, this is the only peaceful business I was ever in.'

He smiled as he spoke, as it seemed to the girl, a little indulgently.

'I do not call it a peaceful business!' cried Marion, hastily, 'when men born and bred on their little cottage plots and tenements are turned adrift to die on the hillside! It is no time to cry 'Peace! peace!' when there is no peace! Some one must fight for them—why not I? Some one must lead them—why not I?'

'I think there is an obvious answer to that last question,' said Austin Tredennis, 'but I will not give it now.'

He inhaled the smoke of the little roll of Spanish tobacco and breaiiied it softly through his nostrils, till it came into Marion's mind (who had never seen the like before) that it was like the breathing of cattle on a frosty morning.

And looking at Captain Austin, she seemed to herself the most pitiable and laughable imitation of true manhood. Accustomed chiefly to men inferior in station, like the cottiers whom she led, or somewhat younger in years like Jasper Jamie and myself, Marion felt that this man somehow shamed her. Each act and trait of this masterful soldier deepened the impression. The deep scar cut into his chin, instead of being a disfigurement, seemed the guinea-stamp of manhood. The very way he had with his tobacco smoke seemed delightfully masculine and insolent. The worn sword-hilt and notched scabbard he threw upon the little table, the patched uniform and threadbare accoutrement, the rubbed riding-boots a trifle down at the heel, the loose and jingling spurs—all seemed part of a larger personality than she had ever known.

How pitiful, paltry, miserable a masquerade it all had been—this dainty scarlet and gold of a regiment that had never faced a foe! And even to that she had no right. She was Marion, the daughter of Sammle Tamson of Isle Rathan, the commonest and poorest daw tricked out in peacock's feathers, which yet could deceive no one.

She wished that this middle-aged, plain-featured war-captain would take himself off! What right had he to intrude himself upon his prisoners? She was prepared to die—on the scaffold, if need were. But to have this large, cool, masterful man sitting breathing smoke gently through his nostrils, and taking her measure as a tradesman takes the size of a foot before he begins to cut his leather—it was more than our poor Marion could bear.

She shivered a little involuntarily, at which, without a word, he undid the clasp of his great, blue military cloak and threw it with careless kindness in her direction. It had a criss-cross curb chain that jingled, and huge brass buttons with the arms of King Gteorge upon them.

'Take that,' he said; 'I do not feel the cold. I have come from America but lately, where ofttimes we slept comfortably enough among the snow.'

It was the last straw—that and the jingling of the curb chain. Marion rose to her feet. She had been sitting upon the edge of her pallet, and trying to conceal as much of her knees as possible with the ragged coverlet.

'I do not want your cloak!' she cried, flinging it viciously on the ground and stamping upon it. 'You insult me by coming here at all. I hate you! I know why you came, and I despise you for it! It was a spy's act! Do you hear—a spy's act, and unworthy of a gentleman!'

The girl stood a full minute gloriously defiant. Then something clicked somewhere in her throat, like the spring of a watch when it breaks in the winding. And the gallant Dick of the Isle, Captain of all the Levellers of Galloway, rebel, criminal, and probable martyr in the cause of liberty —burst into tears!

In a moment Austin Tredennis had sprung up. Quick as thought he was beside her, his arm was about her.

'My child, my child!' he was murmuring, 'what is this? Tell me, what is this?'

CHAPTER THIRTY ONE
THE SON OF A KING

Captain Austin Tredennis, of Ligonier's Horse, was steady as steel in the face of danger. Any man of his regiment would have told you as much. But he could also be fierce and indomitable upon provocation. Once he had fought a duel to the death with a huge German of the Palatinate Regiment, and left that maitre d'armes for dead on the field. But here in the little, bare, damp cell of Maclellan's Wark he was certainly strangely affected, and that without manifest cause. He felt all the agitations and tremulous forebodings of a stripling girl first touched by love.

Leaving Marion a moment to herself, he stepped swiftly to the door, and let the gleam of the lantern with which he went his rounds fall on the heaped casks and barrel-staves which still cumbered the hall. He saw nothing, but, nevertheless, in the feeble light, it seemed to him as if a shadow darted behind a hogshead between him and the great door. He went to the spot, but found nothing save a heap of matting and straw. Yet Austin Tredennis was not wholly satisfied, as he went back thoughtfully to the cell where he had left the bold Chief of the Levellers sobbing, with her face between her hands.

Had he dared, he would have posted a sentinel within the great hall as well as without. But it came to him with a sudden shock that he might find himself constrained to certain acts contrary to his commission and the articles of war, in which case it would certainly be better to be without the restraint of a witness.

'And now' he said, sitting down beside Marion, 'tell me all about it, little one.'

Pride made a last rally.

'I will not,' said the girl, pushing out her hands, 'I will not! I would die first!'

'Very likely,' said Austin Tredennis, quietly, 'nevertheless, you are going to tell me—and at once, for there is no time to be lost.'

And so resolute was his manner, so assured his

demeanor, that Marion of the Isle, mastered for the first time in her life, found herself telling this King's officer all that she had carefully hidden from her own father— her discontent with her position, her anger at the treatment of the poor cottier folk—indeed, everything she had done and what she yet hoped to do.

Austin Tredennis sat upon the low truckle bed and listened gravely. He did not, however, repeat the first involuntary caress with which he had taken the girl in his arms when she burst into angry tears. But he had wrapped her closely in his great, blue military cloak with the brass clasp, the same he had thrown so carelessly across to his prisoner half an hour before. For this hard-featured captain of horse, whom the neglect of superiors and the fierce accident of campaigning had left little different in appearance and manner from a common soldier, was yet at heart a gentleman among fine gentlemen.

But when he had heard the last word of Marion's tale and the sobs had somewhat stilled themselves, he still sat thoughtful and grave, his mind poised between the long discipline of duty and this sudden eruptive lava-burst in his bosom which constrained him to break with the regulated traditions of a lifetime.

At last, in sheer perplexity, he rose and paced the room.

'I must help her,' he muttered to himself, as if she had not been present, adding, a moment after, 'whatever it may cost me.'

But the quick, ardent spirit of Marion of the Isle rebelled against this tone in a stranger.

'No, no!' she cried, recovering herself; 'you shall not assist me to your own cost. I will not have help on such terms. God knows, I am not afraid of anything— only bitterly ashamed to be seen in this dress of masquerade. I am ready as any one to die, but oh! I do hate to be laughed at!'

Wherein she spoke the feeling of many, not only of her own, but of her assumed sex.

'I am thinking it out,' said the officer, without

213

looking at her or attending to what she said. Look you, I do not care a jot for your petty local politics of cotmen and grazing rights, commonties and plantations. But I own that I am concerned for the first time in my life not to obey orders. Yet this also will I do for you, if I lose the King's coat off my back for the deed!'

And there was something in the grave eyes which made Marion turn away her head-something direct and masterful, yet soft also, and with power to pull at her heartstrings like the ropes which foresters affix to a tree to direct its fall.

'I ask of you but one thing,' he said, with averted eyes. 'Permit my friends, Mistress Heron of Isle Rathan and her daughter Grisel, to send me the garments proper to my sex, and I shall ask for nothing else.'

'Yes, yes!' he said, still striding up and down, and pulling at his great mustache, 'it shall be done. I will ride over there myself.'

The girl started involuntarily.

'Oh no!' she cried. 'Do not go away! I would rather that you sent a letter!'

It was a subtle, though unintentional, compliment, and the grave man blushed a little under his martial tan. It was the first time for twenty years when his presence or absence had made a difference to any human creature. Yet Marion had intended nothing more than the simplest statement of fact. This captain had penetrated her secret and seemed inclined to keep it. Others who might be left —blatant young officers or inquisitive townsmen in authority— might do the same, without his reticence or his desire to serve her. In brief, she did not wish Captain Tredennis to ride away on a message which one of his troopers would perform just as well.

But the course of events was suddenly altered by an occurrence in the court-yard. As these two remained together within the narrow limits of the cell, or, rather, as Marion sat and Austin Tredennis strode savagely about, clanking his spurs as he went, there came from without a noise of the clattering feet of horses, shouts, neighings, and all the pell-mell attendant on the arrival of a considerable cavalcade. This was followed by a vehement pounding upon the outer door of Maclellan's Wark.

'That must be the General Fitzgeorge!' said Tredennis, speaking in a low and genuinely alarmed voice. 'I had notice of his coming, but did not expect him to arrive so soon. For Heaven's sake, let him not see you, or have any suspicion of who you are! I could do nothing then! Lie down on your bed, and muffle yourself up closely in this cloak!'

'The general,' Marion was beginning. 'Why should I care for a score of generals?'

'Do as I bid you—do you hear?' commanded Tredennis, in a voice so hard and changed that Marion hardly recognized it. Nevertheless, after a moment's hesitation, she meekly obeyed. And, thinking the matter over afterwards, she decided that she rather liked the little sensation of fear which struck through her heart when she heard him speak thus to her.. She knew now how he spoke to his soldiers in time of danger.

Then with a great clanging of superfluous doors and clanking of scabbard, Captain Austin finally appeared at the door of Maclellan's Wark, somewhat ostentatiously rubbing his eyes, and with a button or two of his tunic unfastened.

It was indeed the distinguished general commanding all his Majesty's forces in Scotland, as Tredennis had supposed, and as, indeed, was easy to be seen, even by the dim light of the lanterns which were being hurriedly brought from the troop-stables.

General George Fitzgeorge was known to have royal blood in his veins. Indeed, it might even be perceived, richly florescent, on his countenance. He was also, as became his ancestry, a professed admirer of 'the sex,' and his manner of receiving any reasonably well-looking woman suggested that he was considering her in the light of a possible conquest. He had (it was whispered) been horsewhipped once or twice; but for men in the service this was an expensive luxury, while others were deterred by

General Fitzgeorge's early fame as a duellist. Nevertheless, there was that on Austin Tredennis's face when he opened the door of Maclellan's Wark which might have caused even so ancient and chartered a Hanoverian as General Fitzgeorge to pause, if he had not been too excited by wine to notice it.

'Ah, Tredennis! Sly dog—sly dog! he cried. 'What do you mean by keeping us waiting? Young Gunter tells me that you have a deucedly pretty girl here as prisoner in this old, tumbledown stone box. Keeping her all to yourself—eh, my friend? Well, you know that cock won't fight with George Fitzgeorge, so pick up your lantern and let us have a look at her!'

Behind the general appeared my Lord Kirkham—correct, immobile, and with infinite respect for the ancient blood royal, even as, somewhat degraded in quality, it coursed through the veins of General Fitzgeorge. Also, wonder of wonders! The Lady Sylvia was of the party. The fascinations of Jasper Jamie had proved as tow in the fire when she heard that the handsome young officer, pretended son of Patrick Heron of Isle Rathan, was indeed a dangerous and rebellious Captain of Levellers. The Lady Sylvia scented a mystery, and thought it positively charming.

'General,' said my Lord Kirkham, persuasively, 'is it not time that we should make our way to my town house? You know that I sent on a servant to make preparations for our visit there? Supper will be on the table by this time!'

But he appealed in vain to the pleasures of the table. The general had other fish to fry.

'Nothing of the sort!' cried this arrogant, cross-barred descendant of kings. 'We will see on the instant how and with whom Tredennis has been passing his time. Open the doors, you dog, and let us see this pretty gypsy lass of yours.'

Full of his recent discovery with regard to Marion, Austin Tredennis had, for the moment, quite forgotten Joyce Faa's existence. And when the general began to speak to him each word conveyed to him the impression that the secret which he had thought his own was no secret at all, and that this party of great folk had come to Maclellan's Wark thus untimeously for the special purpose of shaming Marion in her gallant's attire of scarlet and blue. But no sooner did he perceive that she was still undiscovered than his spirits rose, and, manlike, he hastened to sacrifice poor Joyce (for whom he cared no jot) upon the altar of curiosity, that the girl for whom he did care might be safe.

'You are welcome, general,' he said, gravely saluting his superior officer, and standing aside for the party to pass within; 'the arrangements here are necessarily but temporary, and of the rudest kind. But I took it upon myself to refuse to quarter my prisoners in the wretched thatched hut they call the common prison, or Thieves' Hole, of this burgh.'

'Quite right, sir, quite right!' cried the general. 'These little provost folk need keeping in order, and by the blood of my royal father, sir, I think you. Captain Tredennis, are the man to do it! A minute ago you looked as if you were about to bar the path of your commanding officer. But, as my lord observes, do not let us waste time. Exhibit your beauty, captain. Let us see if she is what she is cracked up to be. Theo Gunter there declares her a none such, but at his age anything that wears petticoats is held worthy to be a King's mistress!'

Austin Tredennis moved slowly forward, swinging his lantern, and muttering bitterly between his clinched teeth, 'If I were in your place General George Fitzgeorge, I would not speak so freely of King's mistresses!'

'Do you wish to see the gypsy who is accused of the murder of the exciseman,' he said aloud, 'or only the girl who was captured along with him?'

'Oh, the girl by all means!' cried the general. 'It will be time enough to see the fellow when he is in the hands of the common hangman. But the girl—the girl, of course, and immediately! What else would have kept us so late from the claret but to catch a glimpse of this most renowned paragon?'

With a second salute, in which there was no small degree of scorn, Austin Tredennis threw open the door of Joyce Faa's cell.

CHAPTER THIRTY TWO

A DERELICTION OF DUTY

After the conversation conducted through the wooden partition with Marion of the Isle, Joyce Faa had thrown herself listlessly down on the rough wooden settle or bench, which in its primal capacity had served for a second row of the small ankers of smuggled municipal brandy. Her hands were clasped behind her head, and though her eyes remained open, the darkness which surrounded her was absolute. It was thus that they found her.

She had heard the noisy entrance of the cavalcade into the little square in front of Maclellan's Wark, but her heart neither bounded with hope nor was pinched by fear. The bells struck the hour of midnight, and the sound entered in alike from the ancient steeple and from the comfortable eight-day clocks of sleeping burgher folk, but Joyce Faa never hearkened. She was aware of the clanking spurs and clashing swords that approached her door, but she gave no heed. Motionless she waited fate. Not till the door was flung wide open by the hand of Austin Tredennis, and a flood of light illuminated her cell and showed the girl a crowd of curious heads looking in upon her, did the outlaw's daughter spring up.

There was something of the wild animal in the vigorous and instantaneous grace of the action, as well as in the disdain with which she eyed the general and his company when, cloaked and belted, they stood gazing over their lanterns at her as though she had been shut up for their inspection in a cage.

'Well, my girl,' said the descendant of royalty at last, his red face and loose underjowl shaking like turkey wattles, 'what is this—what is this? Accused of murder in the first degree, I Never heard of such a thing! A girl of your appearance, too, by gad! might have found something better to do. By my royal father, yes! So she might. Speak, girl! Why don't you speak, and tell me what you have to say for yourself?'

The highly descended Fitzgeorge had certainly caught the Hanoverian manner of speech, and was possessed of about the average quantity of Georgian brains.

'I must first know to whom I have the honour of speaking, and why I, a woman and a prisoner, cannot be left alone at night,' said Joyce, in the full soft tones that consorted so ill with what her visitors expected to hear from a wild gypsy of the hills.

'Girl, restrain your insolence! Do you not know that this is General Fitzgeorge, commanding his Majesty's forces in Scotland, and that I am the Earl of Kirkham?' broke in that dignitary. 'Captain Tredennis, pray be good enough to conduct my daughter, the Lady Sylvia Kirkham, to my town house, which you will find open and prepared. This is no place for her!'

He was, indeed, in mortal terror of what the general might say next, for upon that semi-royal tongue a spade was wont to be called a spade. But to her father's scruples the Lady Sylvia vigorously demurred.

'I will do nothing of the kind, papa!' she said, with determination. 'I have got eyes and ears as well as you, and mean to use them for the same purpose! Make your reckoning with that, papa!'

Joyce Faa stood against a background of the rough stone of Maclellan's Wark, a narrow barred window above her head. Her dark eyes were large and haughty as those of any princess. Her bosom heaved perceptibly beneath the crossed shawl which covered it, and her pretty head was poised upon her full white neck like a lily upon its stem. The general commanding his Majesty's forces in Scotland devoured her with little, twinkling eyes.

'Go on,' he said. 'I have the power to order your release. Speak freely. Do not be afraid.'

'I am brought here for having taken part in the death of two men whom I never saw and whose names I never heard, upon the mere word of a common informer! That is all I know of the matter!'

There was nothing of fear in Joyce's voice; only the calm, clear enunciation of a woman wronged who asks for justice.

'These are perilous times, my pretty one,' said the gallant general, 'and you must not be too hard on our worthy officer. Captain Tredennis. His methods may be a trifle rough, but he means well. Moreover, they tell me that you are the only daughter of Hector Faa, an outlaw who has maintained himself among the wild hills for a number of years and committed great depredations. What have you to say to that?'

'I am the daughter of Hector Faa, indeed,' said Joyce, more defiantly than before, 'but I have yet to learn that there is anything criminal in that!'

'Oh, it has been held—it has been acted upon more than once—the sins of the fathers, you know,' said the general, 'but on this occasion we are not inclined to be too severe. Captain Tredennis, see that this—this young lady has every comfort before you leave her. Then report to me at my lodgings, and, that you may not feel oppressed with constant watchfulness, Ensign Gunter will assist you in your responsibility for this prison and its inmates.'

At this order the countenance of Austin Tredennis suddenly fell. He was, of course, too good a soldier to dispute an order directly, but he did what he had never done before in all his years of service—he ventured a remonstrance.

'But, general,' he said, almost stammering in his eagerness, 'these are my prisoners, taken under my special commission in the matter of the Levellers, and I cannot share any responsibility for them with Ensign Gunter or any other till I have handed them over to the civil arm!'

'Nonsense, nonsense!' cried the general, airily, but not displeased. 'I understand your unwillingness, Tredennis. It does credit to your manhood. Never yet was a good soldier who was not fond of a pretty girl. But I am new to this troublesome Galloway. I need your advice myself, and you must be free to give it. Deuce take it, man, you have more head-piece than a score of these cantering young asses of my staff!'

Captain Tredennis saluted, and said nothing more aloud.

'It has taken your Highness a long time to come

to that conclusion,' he muttered below his breath, as he fell back into the gloom of the great hall of Maclellan's Wark. He felt that for the present there was no more to be done. 'But, for all that,' he added, fiercely, still to himself, 'may I roast in hottest pit fire if I leave these two girls to the cubbish impertinences of Theo Gunter and the senile insolences of General George Fitzgeorge! I would not stand by and permit it—no, not if it were his royal father himself come back from Gehenna!'

As he stood looking out under his brows at the general and his friends, he reiterated his determination.

'Hanged if I do—no, not though I be broke for it,' muttered Captain Tredennis, and it was with a great sense of relief that he escorted the distinguished party to the door of Maclellan's Wark, from which a slippery plank or two afforded uncertain access to a dirt-encumbered roadway, the despair of successive generations of provosts.

'Finish quickly and report to me,' said the general. 'You will find me at my lord's town house. I will send over young Gunter to take your prisoners off your hand for the night'

Once more Captain Tredcnnis saluted and was left standing in the door-way with the dark of the hall behind him and the sky glittering with stars above him.

He hastened back at once to the little cell in which Marion had been locked all the while listening to the colloquy in the next chamber. He found her still wrapped in his own great cloak, and restlessly pacing the narrow bounds within which she was confined, evidently deep in thought.

'You must get away at once,' he said. 'My authority here will be over in half an hour—for tonight, at least. Be ready to follow me the instant I can have a beast saddled for you.'

Marion stayed him, laying her hand on his shoulder with a curious new equality that, even at that moment, affected him strangely.

'One thing only I ask you to do for me, and I will

obey,' she said, stopping in her walk and facing him. 'Let me, for the few minutes that remain, speak with one of the other prisoners—with Joyce Faa.'

'And why?' returned Austin Tredennis, chafing visibly.

Marion for the first time permitted herself to smile one of her strange, winning smiles up at him.

'I am trusting you a good deal,' she said, 'trust me also thus far. I have a reason.'

And she had, but it was far from being a reason which would have commended itself to Captain Austin Tredennis.

Marion followed up her advantage the moment she saw that she had obtained it.

'Ah, then, you will?' she whispered, laying her hand on the cuff of his military coat. 'I shall not forget your kindness.'

'Well,' he said, 'I suppose it must be so. But, remember, every moment is precious, and you must be ready by the time I return with the horse.'

'You shall not have to wait,' said Marion of the Isle, again smiling her subtle smile. So, with her hand still on the cuff of his coat, he handed her courteously out, and in the darkness of the passage she waited till he had opened the door of the chamber wherein was Joyce Faa.

'I can leave you no more than this single rushlight,' he said, laying down a little iron lantern, as Joyce rose in some confusion to receive her new visitor, 'but that will be sufficient for what you have to say. Do not let the light shine beneath the door nor yet through the bars. And, above all, be ready when I come for you.'

He touched his helmet in salute, exactly as he had done to his superior officer, clicked the key in the lock, and they could hear the jingle of his spurs growing fainter and fainter across the hall. Then came the dull, sombre sound which announced the closing of the outer door, and for the first time the two women about whom this history turns were alone together. Yet of their conversation this chronicler has nothing to report. The details have not been confided

223

to him.

Half an hour later Austin Tredennis returned, moving more swiftly and noiselessly than any one would have given him credit for. He opened the cell door. All was dark and silent within, but the voice of Marion of the Isle reassured him.

'The lantern has gone out,' she said.

'No matter,' he whispered. 'Follow me!'

There was the low sound of a kiss—a sob, and then 'Good-bye, Joyce! Be of good heart!' The words were spoken clearly and calmly.

And as he stood in the doorway a tall, slender figure wrapped in his own military cloak, went noiselessly past Captain Tredennis. He did not wait to reillumine the lantern but, noting simply by the pale light that the outlaw's daughter had resumed her former position upon the truckle bed, he locked the cell door, and followed the slim figure in the cavalry cloak out into the open air.

Austin Tredennis and his charge waited till the sentry had disappeared round the corner of the ancient unfinished castle. Then he took the girl by the hand, hurried her across the wide, vague space, still littered with blocks of building stone, and plunged into a little alley, from the further end of which they emerged to find a horse tied to a tree in the shadow of a little wood of fir-trees.

All this while no word was spoken. The officer assisted his companion into the saddle and put the reins into her hands. Only after he did so he drew one of them a little aside and kissed the slender fingers.

And this was the sole reward which Austin Tredennis claimed from the girl for whose sake he had endangered his commission and disgraced the King's coat.

CHAPTER THIRTY THREE
THE LEVELLERS TO THE RESCUE

And this curious dereliction of duty, or, more exactly, aberration of judgment on the part of Captain Austin Tredennis, of Ligonier's Horse, explains why on the morning of the following day Jasper Jamie and I, riding at the head of fifty or sixty young fellows of the countryside, all well armed and sworn Levellers, met and halted a certain tall young soldier whose coat of red showed at intervals through the great blue military cloak he wore.

It was on the brae-face above Loch Fergus that we met him, and I had in my heart a kind of fearful pride, for to my thinking I was engaged in the most reckless and daring act of my life. How it came upon me I cannot tell. For both in idea and execution the thing was mine, and (though the supposition is, at the first blush, a much more likely one) Jasper Jamie had nothing to do with the matter.

I will, however, tell you how it happened, and the impartial reader of this history shall be left to judge, bearing me witness that I have not spared in other parts to animadvert upon the womanliness and pusillanimity of my character. I may, therefore, be trusted not to give myself more praise than is my due for my single act of manhood.

It came to me as soon as my mother and Grisel rode into the court-yard of Orraland with the news that Joyce Faa was fast held in the prison of Kirkcudbright.

I would raise the Levellers, and the imprisonment of Captain Dick and Harry Polwart were the arguments I would use with that organization. So I made my way to Sammle Tamson, over at Isle Rathan, and the reasons I made use of, without betraying his daughter's incognito, were such that the long man promised to put me in communication that very afternoon with the chiefs of the Levellers.

So it came to pass that the son of Patrick and May Heron attended a meeting of rebels, convoked in the shady dell behind the famous nutwood on my father's own property of Orraland. The younger men, to the number of nearly six score, were enthusiastic and eager for action. What to them was a company of horse scattered here and there about the closes and lanes of Kirkcudbright?

So that night we met as before at the crossroads of Rascarrel, the spot of the first great muster. And if I did not go forth with my father's blessing, I am sure that he blessed God that I had so much spunk in me as to take my life in my hand and ride out to strike a blow for a couple of young lasses, neither of whom were any kin to me.

For my father, though now all for order and the King's laws, had had his time of wildness like every other good fellow, and had not forgotten how much better smuggled brandy and stolen waters taste when compared with the ordained and dutified article.

So, though he might easily have stopped me, he said no word, but came downstairs again in his shirt and breeches after he had gone to bed. He took a new and favourite pair of pistols from their case and gave them to me.

'I will show you how to load them. Maxwell,' he said. 'They shoot to a quarter of an inch at twenty paces, but, allow, they are something kittle at the loading.'

And with great gravity he showed me the proper quantities of powder, and how to insert the ball and hold it in place.

'This is only in case ye should need anything of the kind,' he said. 'Mind, Maxwell, keep out of all quarrels and bickerings. Live peaceably with all men, and, above all, mind that the pistol with the cross on the stock does with a pinch less of powder than her sister, and throws a trifle high and to the left. God bless ye, lad.'

And with that he went upstairs, my dear and excellent father, and, as my mother afterwards told me, would neither let her go to the window nor in any way betray herself, but went himself, and stood by the little barred lattice of his dressing-room and watched me saddle my horse and ride away with Jasper Jamie without a sign of emotion on his face. Then he came to bed, and said to my mother as he composed himself to sleep, 'Mary, I think Maxwell's trip to the Dungeon of Buchan was the best day's learning he ever gat, and that a month up at Hector Faa's Shiel is worth five year of Edinburgh College.'

So, I may say, I rode away from Orraland, if not exactly with my father's blessing on my lawless act, at least with something very like it.

And as the morning broke fresh and blithe, with a touch of an earthy chill in the faint, unequal breeze, we passed from the stern and rocky country which stretches away from Orraland towards Ben Tudor, and entered a land which speaks to me even more completely of Galloway, and is, to my mind, like none other in the world. Green holms, far-stretching and smooth of turf, break here and there into broomy knolls round which the plough has moved for unnumbered generations. In the midst of these islets, on a little, flowery eminence, there usually stands a white thorn-tree, gnarled and solitary—in the spring blond and foamy with May-blossom as with a larger growth of meadow-sweet, in the autumn and early winter russet with haw-berries and the haunt of chattering hordes of fleld-fares and redwings.

To the right and the left the holms fall away into dells and dingles, all equally smooth and green. In these the thorn-trees stand thicker, and are alternated with delicately tendrilled birk and ancientest crabbed sloe, spreading its twisted arms abroad, and, as it were, feeling its way along the ground like a beggar blind and lame, crawling to his stance of alms.

Well, it was even in such a place as this, and, as I say, on the brae-face, above Loch Fergus, that we gat sight of a young soldier riding on a good beast, and as it were directly forth to meet us.

As we breasted the brae he turned his horse's head, and would have ridden off to avoid our company. But, as a Leveller for the time being, I had the sense to know that the game we were playing did not admit of our leaving any spies behind us. So, snatching my father's best pistol, and bidding Jasper Jamie and the two of the better mounted of the Levellers to follow us, I rode away after the fugitive. His beast was a fat, round-barrelled rouncy from the English border, and but ill-adapted for our Galloway gullies and mossy quags.

'Stand!' I cried, as we gained on him. 'Stand, or we will shoot you!'

It was curious how, when the thing came of its own accord (as it were), I took the lead even of Jasper Jamie, who was a fighter by nature. But so, for the time being at least, it was. Well, the soldier in blue and scarlet continued to flee, and I should most certainly have fired upon him, and done what I know not of mischief, if it had not been that his heavy mare, unaccustomed to the soft ground, laired in a green moss bog and stood still, with both forelegs strained stiffly, in spite of all that the rider could do with whip and spur to get her out.

As yet we could see nothing of the appearance of the soldier. For, as I mentioned, he was all enwrapped in a great mantle of blue, which, in the chill blowing of the wind, sometimes flapped back at the comer and revealed a tight-fitting suit of military scarlet beneath.

Seeing that I could not safely approach him over the soft ground, I leaped from my beast and, running at him, with one hand I held the pistol at his head, and with the other snatched back the great capote or hood by which his features were hidden.

It was the face of Joyce Faa that was revealed—now pale as drifted snow, now dyed with quick-fading crimson.

'Great God, Joyce!' I cried, letting the pistol drop from my hand in sheer astonishment, 'why are you here?'

At that moment Jasper Jamie came up, and what with the wind and the convulsive movements of the mare trying to extricate herself, the cloak blew back, so that the slender figure on horseback was revealed from stock to stirrup, and Joyce's long, black hair fell over her shoulders.

'Heavens!' cried Jasper Jamie, 'what can have gotten into the wenches? Maxwell, here is another of them trigged out in your old Fencible breeches!'

But Joyce said not a word of good or bad. She scarcely seemed to hear. Her simple nature, accustomed to disguises, and touched with the wildness of the hills, found no shame (or at least showed none) in a situation which would have driven Marion or Grisel distracted.

Instead, let me take her hand, and lightly dismounted on one of the stray tussocks of bent grass which studded the treacherous morass. In a moment more the cloak was round her again, and securely fastened with an inner strap about the waist. She even assisted us to relieve the mare from its dangerous position, and I sent back two of the young Levellers to the squadron to inform them that it was one of Hector Faa's company escaped in disguise from the prison, and on his way to safe hiding.

Then I turned again to Joyce.

'You must go to my father and mother, at Orraland,' I said; 'they will right gladly welcome you. In the future you may choose for yourself, but in the mean time you need, before everything else, a place of immediate safety and repose.'

But Joyce only shook her head firmly and sadly.

'I cannot go to the house of your mother,' she said. 'Do not forget that it was but the other day that she saw me stand up to be married to another man.'

'But I have told her that you sacrificed yourself to save me, Joyce,' I said. 'But, thank God, you are not yet married to Harry Polwart!'

'It was I who stopped that!' muttered Jasper Jamie, under his breath.

Joyce again shook her head, but this time with the faintest of smiles upon her lips.

'That which has happened changes nothing,' she said. 'I have passed my word to Harry Polwart. For so much I promised to give so much. He has performed his part. Shall Hector Faa's daughter fail to keep her bargain because a man is blind and helpless? No, not while life lasts to her. But, all the same, I thank you, Maxwell Heron. You mean the best and kindest. It was in order that I might find means to break his prison that I took the chance deliverance which fortune put in my way.'

'Joyce,' said I, 'listen to me. Here we are, a hundred of us, riding to Kirkcudbright to break down the walls of the Castle. If we fail, what can you hope to do? Attired as you are, you would only be a hindrance and a danger to us. Your disguise is known, and will doubtless be advertised on every kirk door throughout broad Scotland. If you will not go to Orraland to my mother—which I still think to be the best plan—you must accompany Davie Veitch to Marion's mother, at Isle Rathan. She will hold you safe, provide you with suitable clothing, and thank you for news of Marion.'

From motives which I could not fathom at the time, Joyce did not look at me as she replied:

'Who is this Davie Veitch? Let me see him.'

So I called Davie forward, and at the sight of his broad, honest, porridge-and-milk visage, Joyce was immediately reassured.

'I will go with him to the Isle,' she said. 'I have, indeed, a message to deliver to one dwelling there.'

I guessed that her message was for Sammle Tamson, but, with an impulse of selfishness that I afterwards regretted, I did not tell her that Sammle was in the cavalcade of Levellers which waited, impatiently enough, their figures silhouetted against the dawn, upon the summit of the brae. But, to tell the truth, I was afraid that if Joyce were able to deliver her message she might insist upon returning with us to the rescue of Harry Polwart—an enterprise to which, even as it was, I looked forward with no very sanguine anticipations.

So, in a few minutes more, the figures of Joyce and her chosen companion were lost behind the red berries of the solitary hawthorns, and I was riding with my company of Levellers towards the prison of Kirkcudbright.

CHAPTER THIRTY FOUR
AUSTIN TREDENNIS, MUTINEER

I think the men were all inclined to be a little sulky about the delay and the loss of Davie Veitch, who, though in years little more than a callant, was yet exceedingly lively and mirthful of his mood, and inclined to be a good soldier by nature, keeping all about him in humour on the march with his whistling and snatches of song. But I told them of the necessity for putting so famous a person as Hector Faa's daughter into a place of safety (for after she was gone I saw no great harm in revealing her identity), and enlarged upon the news that Joyce had brought from Kirkcudbright—to wit, that Dick of the Isle and Harry Polwart were lying, not in the common prison or Thieves' Hole, but in the much more easily broken stronghold of Maclellan's Wark.

In a way and for the nonce the Levellers had accepted me as their leader, chiefly, I think, because it was I who had summoned them, but, for all that, they did not permit me to be present at any of their private colloquies. So, when they desired to speak apart among themselves, Robin Galtway, a fine old cottier from the wilder uplands of Rerrick, would touch his brow with something of a seafaring reverence that proved him one who in his time had set his Majesty's revenue laws at defiance upon many a smuggling brig.

'Maister Maxwell, an' you, young sir, wha's name I canna mind, ye will pardon us,' he would say, 'but there is a word or two that we Leveller lads wad speak as it were, atween oorsel's!'

And so it happened now. The Levellers drew together in a little hollow place near a burn that flows by the ruins of an ancient castle. Jasper Jamie and I were left alone on the drove road, which we could see making a green, waving track from farm-town to farm-town upward towards Whinnyliggate and the broomy knowes of Hartburn.

'Can they mean to betray us?' asked Jasper Jamie of me, in a low voice. For Jasper, though bold

231

in action, never had any great head-piece to boast of, and was, moreover, generally cautious and rash in the wrong places.

'Betray us! No, you gomeril! cried I. 'They only want to talk over their plans with some freedom. For what is, after all, a holiday frolic to you and me, being our fathers' sons, may very easily turn out a hanging matter to every man of them. We want Marion, and if we do not get her by force—why, we will make her leave off gallivanting, put on her proper petticoats, and do our best to shame or intimidate the sheriff into setting her at liberty. For this Harry Polwart of theirs (to be candid) we do not care a doit. He may hang for it, as far as either of us care. We are not Levellers any more than we are Papists, and these fellows do well not to trust their secrets to us.'

While we were thus talking old Robin came back to us, and said, with another touch of his forelock, 'Sirs, it will not do for any of us lads to be seen in Kirkcudbright or in the neighbourhood before dark. We are agreed, therefore, to make for a certain howe that we ken o', nigh to the Buckland Burn and lie there safely till nicht, when, if ye bring us back news of good intent, we will make oor attempt.'

'Very well, Robin,' said I. 'My friend and I have the matter just as much at heart as any of you. We will go over to the Buckland Burn and lie hid with you.'

Robin seemed a little put out at this and hesitated, shuffling his feet.

'The lads were thinkin',' he said at last, 'that maybe, gin your honours were willin', ye might slip doon to the toon and kind o' see how things were faain' oot. There's nocht again either o' you, and ye micht mak' up to some o' the sojer officers and hear what their dispositions were to be for the nicht. That wad help us maist mightily.'

In itself it was indeed none so ill thocht on, and though at the first blush it seemed rather a mean errand for a laird's son thus to become little better than a spy, yet since it was for Marion's sake (and indirectly for my mother's and Grisel's), I nodded a

232

quick acquiescence. Jasper and I were, indeed, too deeply in to draw back now.

'Where shall I find you on your return?' I asked Robin Galtway.

A quick flush passed over the old man's face. He drew nearer to us as we sat on our horses by the way-side.

'I was bidden not to tell ye,' he said, 'but to send yin o' the lads to meet ye oot yonder on the highway. Yet I wad lippen my life on the faith o' your faither's son, sir. Ye wad never sell them that hae trusted ye, into the hands o' their enemies. Ye will find us when ye like amang the birks aneath the auld Castle o' Bombie.'

Jasper Jamie and I, therefore, went our ways down to the ancient burgal town of Kirkcudbright, where it was our hap at the door of the Red Lion to meet with young Theo Gunter, lounging against the lintel-post of the inn, and eying attentively all the women who picked their way daintily past over the rounded cobble-stones of the causeway, strewn from side to side with the ends of carrots and the refuse of ancient cabbages.

'Hola, young Rathan!' he cried, for we knew each other of old at the college of Edinburgh, 'whither away? To see this same fine young woman from the wilds? Well, I do not wonder. Ah! by the way, is she not the same who nursed you in your imprisonment? By my faith, a romance all ready-made! A fine chance this to show your gratitude, Master Maxwell—only, alas! you come a day after the fair.'

'How so, sir?' I asked him, indignantly. For Theo Gunter was a fellow whom I had despised ever since the time I could truss my own breeches. He never could speak honestly concerning any woman—no, not about his own sister—but always with a jest and a fleer and a sidelong look that I hated worse than the devil.

'How so?' he laughed. 'Because you must wait till your betters are served, my fine lad—escaped prisoner, grateful for your deliverance and all the rest of it, though you be! You are a laird's son, it is true,

233

like myself. 'Tis well enough in its way! But hark to this: There is a king's son before you! What think you of that?'

'A king's son!' quoth I, amazed, and thinking of Joyce on her way to the safety of Isle Rathan with honest Davie Veitch for a companion. 'What mean you by talking of a king's son in connection with Joyce Faa?'

'I mean the thing I say!' cried young Gunter, clapping his hands upon his thighs at my discomfiture. 'He is with her now—General George Fitzgeorge, no less, commanding his Majesty's forces in Scotland. If he is not a king's son, his mother is more than usually belied.'

I turned me about and looked at Jasper, and Jasper looked at me. His mouth formed the word 'Marion' so clearly that I could almost hear him speak it. But when Gunter glanced at him he pretended to whistle, which was Jasper's idea of- unconscious, tactful innocence.

Throwing the reins of our beasts to the hostler of the Red Lion, and hastily promising to return and dine with Ensign Gunter at three o'clock (a promise which was never kept), Jasper and I set out in the direction of Maclellan's Wark. I had no idea how I was to obtain permission to enter, for it was now nine of the clock. Joyce's escape must have been found out long before that time, and the hue and cry raised, though idle Theo Gunter had not yet got word of the matter. But that did not in the least surprise me. For all the days of him he cared for naught save to be thought a devil of a fellow, and to stand in a door-way ogling the women as they passed by upon their occasions.

But as luck would have it, at the door of Maclellan's Wark, in colloquy with Saunders Lennox, the burgh officer of Kirkcudbright, we saw a tall man in well-worn regimentals, whom Jasper Jamie informed me was Captain Austin Tredennis, of Ligonier's Horse.

'Introduce me,' I bade him, in a whisper, and Jasper, who (when he understood) always implicitly obeyed me, instantly did so.

The captain bowed calmly, yet with an air of distinct hauteur that I thought strange at first.

'Mr. Maxwell Heron, I am honoured to make your acquaintance,' he said. 'I had, I think, the advantage of meeting two ladies of your family when— when we took these prisoners at the Manse of Minnigaff.'

'It is on business which intimately concerns one of these that we are here today,' I said, and then hesitated how I should continue, for, indeed, the matter was a difficult one to open out diplomatically.

'Ah!' said Captain Tredennis, wryly, measuring me with his eye, as if wondering how much better I would look ten paces away over the trigger of a pistol.

I hastened to add (for I could see from the dryness of our reception that his mood was no ways favourable to our cause) how that I had nothing to say in favour of the gypsy Harry Polwart, who, indeed, on one occasion had attempted to take my life; but that, on the other hand, I was much interested—

'In his companion, the daughter of the outlaw Hector Faa,' interrupted the officer, harshly. 'I think I heard as much. But I warn you that I can do nothing on her behalf. The commander-in-chief of the forces in Scotland has taken the case into his own hands.'

There was a curious light in Tredennis's eye as he spoke, which I understood afterwards to result from an angry contempt for his superior, mingling with a rejoicing certainty of the safety of the girl in whom his own heart was thus early interested.

'No,' I answered, not doubting that as custodian of the prisoners he already knew of Joyce's escape, 'it is not of Hector Faa's daughter that I would speak, but of another maiden, very closely linked by aflfection and kindness with our house!'

Then, in a moment, the fighting spirit leaped clear into the eyes of Captain Austin Tredennis. His face flushed and paled again. He had been leaning carelessly against the wall by the great door of the castle, but in an instant he drew himself up to his full height and laid his hand menacingly upon his sword-hilt.

'Of whom do you speak?' he said.

'Of Mistress Marion—called Marion of the Isle,' I made answer, 'who has been to my mother as a daughter and to my sister Grisel as a twin sister.'

'Also, mayhap—' he sneered a little here, twisting his mustaches the while— 'also as something equally near and dear to Master Maxwell Heron, younger, of Rathan, and (so they tell me), general lover!'

But I was too anxious to help Marion out of her difficulty without bloodshed, to be in any quarrelsome vein, so I only laughed at his provocation as at a goodly jest.

'No,' said I, smiling, and speaking the simple truth, 'Marion of the Isle is well, and very well, but neither of us ever weared two thoughts upon the other, till first one and afterwards the other of us got fast in a prison. Then, for my mother's sake, Marion rode out in her company to deliver me from the Dungeon of Buchan, even as now, for my mother's sake, I in my turn plead her interest with you,'

Again Captain Tredennis smiled, but in quite another fashion than before.

'In that case I have what cannot prove other than good news to you and your family,' he said. 'I have just been informed by the caretaker that the temporary cell occupied by the young lady to whom you refer has been found empty. As nothing has been heard of her, I have little doubt that she is by this time in a place of safety.'

'Good heavens!' cried Jasper Jamie, in high excitement. 'Then they have both of them escaped?'

'Both?' queried the captain, a little hoarsely. 'What do you mean?'

'Why,' said Jasper Jamie, before I could warn or stop him, 'this morning we met Joyce Faa on a dun mare riding as hard westward as she could go!'

'You met Joyce Faa?' There was a sudden wonder and anxiety in the eyes of Austin Tredennis.

He turned to the door of Maclellan's Wark and clanged hastily upon it with the hilt of his sword.

'Open there!' he cried.

A voice issued from the wide keyhole, at about the level of his knee, with a curious whistling sound.

'It's the general's orders that nane are allowed to enter here save and except himsel' and them that hae his pass!'

'I will stand between you and the general. I take the consequences upon myself,' said the captain of horse. 'Open the door this instant, Saunders Lennox! You know the prisoners were first of all mine—brought hither by me!'

'Weel, they canna hang me for 't,' grumbled the voice, as a faint fumbling of rusty iron made itself heard within, 'for I am the hangman's sel', and—faith I wad juist refuse to operate! That's yae comfort!'

It was Saunders Lennox's one joke but all three of us were too anxious to honour it.

We passed him hastily, without a word, and, following Austin Tredennis, strode across the wide, empty hall to the doors of the little cells which had been formerly occupied by the magisterial kegs and ankers. The door of one stood open.

'That's whaur the young birkie escapit frae yestreen,' said Saunders Lennox, explanatorily. 'But hoo he did it, or whaur he has gane, I declare it wad puzzle the Auld Yin himsel' to tell!'

There was the nest of the flown bird indeed, plain to be seen—the rude bench, the straw mattress, and the sack coverlet. But the question was, which of the birds had flown? Jasper and I knew the answer already, and Captain Austin Tredennis was very suddenly and surprisingly to obtain satisfaction, or rather, in this case, dissatisfaction.

As we crossed the wide, dusky spaces of the hall the sound of voices in angry debate rose high and clear. The words which reached us first were those of a woman.

'Come a step nearer, and, by Heaven, I will stab you to the heart!' the voice said.

More hoarsely, a man's answered it: 'What! What! Blood me! An intolerable vixen!'

Tredennis tried the door, shaking it fiercely. It

was locked inside. But, with a quick stoop, Austin Tredennis made sure that the key-hole was clear.

'Here, Saunders, quick!' he cried. 'Give me your master-key a moment!'

'It were as muckle as my life's worth, if I did!' faltered the burgh officer.

'Your life is in greater danger this moment if you do not!' said Tredennis, savagely. 'Give me the key, or I will throttle you and take it, you vagabond!'

With some unwilling alacrity Saunders selected a strong key from a bunch, and, shaking it clear of the others, handed it to the soldier. In another moment it was in the lock and the wards turned. The door flew back before his strong arm.

A girl was standing in the farthest corner of the little cell with a dirk in her hand. Nearer us, his arm raised before his face, either in self defence or in a half humorous deprecation, stood the gallant if left handed scion of a kingly race General George Fitzgeorge.

In another moment after one brief glance at the girl's features, Captain Tredennis took his superior office by the collar of his gold-laced coat and with a single swirl of his arm, swung him clean out of the cell where he accurately measured out the breadth of his back in the dust of the hall.

I will acknowledge that at this act of daring insubordination my heart stood aghast. I expected no less than that the captain of horse would be instantly had out and shot against the wall. But, strange to relate, the high officer gathered himself up out of the dust with something approaching to a smile upon his face.

'You are overhasty Captain Tredennis — what? what?' he said. 'Did you not see your superior officer engaged in interrogating a prisoner—one, indeed, who is under strong suspicion of aiding and abetting the escape of her companion, a notorious rebel, during the night? You are hasty, sir—infamously hasty! You should keep better eyes in your head, Captain Tredennis! I have a great mind to put you under arrest, sir! Yes, and I would do so too—were it not that I do not wish to magnify a simple incident to undue proportions, or to cause a scandal concerning one of the officers under my command!'

'Not under your command, genera,' answered the other with a grim and smileless face. 'I would have you remember that I am Captain Austin Tredennis, of Ligonier's Horse, detailed for special service in the province from my regiment, presently quartered at Carlisle. I can, therefore, only take orders from my lieutenant-colonel, and can only be put under arrest by him!'

'Your captaincy has the enlistment regulations and the articles of war by heart, I see. I congratulate you. It is more than ever I could master,' said the general, mildly. By this time he had picked himself up, and was dusting himself with no very ill grace—even with a certain appreciation of the occasion. 'If you have the goodness, in conjunction with your two young friends, to say nothing about this little affair—why, I on my part will be delighted to inform those whose interest it is to know, how admirable an officer his Majesty has the good fortune to possess in the person of Captain Tredennis, of Ligonier's Horse.'

'As to that last,' said the captain, shortly, 'you can, of course, please yourself. In any case you can count on us not to speak of the matter. These young gentlemen are friends of the lady's family, and it is not their wish.'

'Heavens! I never once thought of that!' cried the general. 'The lady is far too charming to need such a thing as a family tree; indeed, I have none to speak of myself—on the female side, that is.'

The descendant of kings smiled around him with universal benevolence, and then, turning to Marion, who stood with her hands dropped to her side, he made her a profound bow before speaking again.

'I regret, my dear young lady, that you should so far have misinterpreted my most respectful offer of service and good offices as to suppose that I—that I could for a moment cherish any but the profoundest sentiments of respect and esteem for one so blest by

239

nature with beauty, of person, and so highly endowed with, I am sure, the purest and noblest of moral qualities. Permit me to express my sincere regrets, and again, and in the presence of these gentlemen, to offer you the utmost service that is within my power.'

'By doing so, general, you will escape the mistake your Excellency made last time,' said Captain Austin, a little ironically. 'Such offers to friendless girls are best made before witnesses. But, sir, as it happens, you are in a position to give effect to your wishes, which I have no doubt are sincere.'

'And in what manner, sir, can I have that pleasure?' said the general, who had by this time finished dusting himself and settling his discomposed stock in its place.

'Simply by ordering, on your discretion, the temporary release of this young lady. I have the pleasure of informing you that not only I myself, who am no more than a poor soldier, but these gentlemen, representatives of two of the best families of the county, will hold themselves responsible for her appearance at any time.'

'I do not in the least doubt it,' said the general, smiling. 'If the young lady had been willing to trust herself to me, why so should I.'

Captain Tredennis bit his lip savagely, but with a supreme effort controlled his temper.

'Your Excellency will grant her release then—conditionally, of course, upon joint and personal undertaking to produce her when called upon?'

'If the young lady will deign to accept an unconditional freedom at my hands, I should be better pleased!' said the gallant general, who liked titles which were only his by a considerable stretch of courtesy.

But instead of making him the least sign of gratitude, our haughty Marion turned her back full upon her benefactor and stared out through the narrow-barred window of her prison.

The general waved a hand towards her indulgently.

'I cannot look for anything else,' he said; 'I well

know that ladies' prejudices when once formed are ineradicable. I can only hope, madam, that some of your three sponsors will be more fortunate than—ahem! the son of a king!'

And with these words the old buck saluted grandly, even regally, and forthwith marched himself out of the Castle, swinging his gold-headed cane, as it were to the beat of drums, jauntily, as if he had been walking down the Mall arm-in-arm with his own royal father.

CHAPTER THIRTY FIVE
MARION DISCHARGES HER DEBT

In the little cell in Maclellan's Wark there remained the three of us—and Marion of the Isle. But here was the difficulty. For though men, taken by and large, do business easily enough together, yet the merest flutter of a petticoat deucedly complicates matters. And, in spite of my disclaimer, I could see that the large cavalry captain was in no mind to permit us to ride off in company with his prisoner—at least, till she had explained the mystery of Joyce Faa and her escape.

Nor had Jasper and I easy parts to play. For, first of all, we had given our promise to the honest fellows presently lying under arms, and ready for the fray on Marion's account, under the birk and broom bushes of Bombie glen.

Then there was our undertaking to the general, made jointly with Austin Tredennis, to keep the young woman out of mischief (which, in the long run, proved the most troublesome of all). And lastly, there was Marion herself, at best a very uncertain quantity, and one well fitted to bring the best-laid plans of three wise men to naught. Neither father nor mother had ever had the least influence over her. It remained to be seen whether a committee of three would be able to manage any better

So it came to pass that I was witness of the interview between Austin and Marion, much (as I could judge) against the will of the former. Jasper Jamie, who would not in any case have tasted the delicacy of the occasion, was despatched to look after the horses and have them in readiness against our departure. And I flattered myself by thinking that my presence gave some courage to Marion —or, as it may be named, contrariness. For as I have often said (in the course of this narrative), I am by nature so like a woman in many of my feelings, that women do not commonly consider me in the way upon occasions when they would be glad of the presence and support of another woman.

So, be it to my credit or no, it is a fact that I believe Marion was pleased that the first interview with Austin Tredennis after the deceit she had played upon him, took place with me for a witness.

And the reader who cares for these things will, I trust, find the explanation of much of my unsatisfactory behaviour in this fact, and make some allowance for my uncertain and fitful courtship of my sweetheart, my wavering march towards the goal to which most men speed straight as an arrow shot, my frequent fainting by the way, and my very occasional accesses of courageousness. All these, as well as the curious sympathy I have for their ways (apart, that is, from love-making), prove to myself that I was born with some part of a woman's nature and character awkwardly enough contained within or superimposed upon the outward framework of a man.

But there I am—at it again, as usual, explaining myself when I ought in fairness to the reader to be hard at the essential matter of my tale.

Well, as I say, Marion was pleased to see me. Captain Tredennis, if equally delighted, certainly dissembled his pleasure with some considerable success.

After the general's departure Marion had not sat down, though she had managed, without attracting attention, to conceal Joyce's dirk somewhere about her person, and now she turned to face us with a smile on her face. But Tredennis was more than usually grave. His expression might almost be spoken of as glum.

'Well,' he said at last, finding that Marion did not speak, 'considering what passed between us last night, madam, I little expected to find you here.'

'Well,' said Marion, proudly, 'and pray what passed between us, sir?'

Captain Tredennis half turned about to me with a frown which meant, as plain as printers' ink, 'Be good enough, sir, to go to the devil!'

I felt the difficulty of the position, and though I had a very woman's curiosity to know the beginning and the end of the matter, I was preparing to remove

243

myself on the pretext of seeing where Jasper Jamie had gone to, when Marion, with a quick, imperious movement of her hand, fixed me to the spot.

'Maxwell Heron is my friend!' she said, with wonderful dignity. 'He will permit me, though of another sphere in life, to call him that. We have been comrades and playfellows since childhood. There can be no secrets, sir, between us, whose acquaintance is but that of a day, which is not fit for him to hear!'

Austin Tredennis cast another annihilating glance at me as Marion was speaking, but I only bowed, and said that I was wholly at her service. Thereupon, Captain Tredennis laid his hand suggestively on the hilt of his sword, as if he would much like to argue the matter out with me on the green in front of the Castle with other weapons than the tongue.

'It is true I have no such long-standing claims,' he said, dryly. 'I only risked my whole career—nay, my life —for you last night in order to free you from prison and possible death, and doubtless the reward I have deserved I now receive—deceit, double-dealing, shame. You must forgive me, mistress, if I speak roughly. I have no skill of words to please maidens of such slight purpose. But I speak out that which is in my heartland I tell you frankly, madam, my heart is sore and disappointed within me. And you are the cause.'

'Indeed!' said Marion. 'And is that all you have to say?'

'It is, madam,' he answered, gravely, 'and, having said it, for my part I desire no explanation. As you heard just now, your safety has been arranged for in another way. Save that upon this occasion I have the advantage of being associated with this young gentleman (your ancient playmate, I think you said), I expect no more gratitude now than formerly. But at least I may express a hope that in any engagements you may enter into with Mr. Maxwell Heron he will find that you are more inclined to keep your plighted word—as you did not, madam, when a certain poor fool put his life and reputation in peril for you last night.'

'You have entirely finished?' queried Marion, calmly. And, by her tone, I could have sworn, having oft played with her at piquet, that the young woman held the better cards. I looked to see this rash captain of horse piqued and repiqued, rubiconed and capoted, till he should throw down his hand in sheer despair. And, indeed, so it fell out.

To her inquiry Austin Tredennis only bowed an affirmative, setting his lips grimly enough, however, beneath his great mustache.

'Well, then, Captain Austin Tredennis,' said Marion of the Isle, 'in the first place let me recall to your mind that I made with you nothing of the nature of a compact.'

'You asked me to trust you,' he interrupted. 'I did trust you! And...' Instead of finishing the sentence he stretched his hand out towards Joyce Faa's empty cell.

'You mistake,' said Marion, swiftly countering. 'I promised only to be ready when you came. I was ready— only ready to remain, not to go. From the first you had taken me for a light thing—a child to be petted and dandled, whose tears were to be dried with dainties and sweetstuffs. You had overborne me with your boastful manhood and found pleasure in it. And I—well, I was resolved to show you that a poor weak woman, one from whom you could at will wring pettish tears of weakness-tears at which you laughed.'

'I deny that!' said Austin Tredennis.

'Yes, tears of shameful folly, at which doubtless you were right to laugh—I do not blame you at all,' repeated Marion, conserving the immemorial advantage of her sex and utilizing a denial as an admission. 'But all the same, I was resolved to do a deed which would be to the full as manful as any swaggering braggadocio of the camp or point-device of etiquette which you gentlemen learn who follow the wars.'

('She loves him, of that I am sure!' I thought to myself at this point.) And I looked at the captain of

245

horse to see how he was taking it. But there was no change in his face that I could detect, save that, if anything, the lips under the heavy mustache were a little more grimly compressed. Marion went trampling on.

'So, instead of stealing off like a child taken in a fault, and in fear of the rod, I bade a woman take my place who was in some danger—some real danger, I mean. She had a reason for escape. I had none, or, at least, none that weighed at all with me, after I had arranged a certain matter with her. You found me in a dress in which I had appeared a score of times. Yet, of set purpose, sir, you made me feel the shame of it. Well, Captain Tredennis, I exchanged my chance of liberty for this (she gave a proud little swing to the skirt of my poor Joyce's old gown, which nevertheless set off her tall figure to a marvel) And I think the exchange was well worth making, in that, though I am still your prisoner, I can now talk to you on equal terms.'

'You call this talking on equal terms, do you?' he said, with more subtlety of ironic vein than I had given him credit for.

'I do,' said Marion, not to be diverted from her purpose even for a moment. 'You found out my secret last night and you had no pity on me. You flung your coat at me as you would have flung a crust to a starving dog! You looked at me with a look, of contempt! Heavens!' cried Marion, suddenly breaking off,' I would rather hang by the neck till I was dead than see another such look on your face—on any man's face.'

'You prefer that which was on that of his Excellency the general just now, perhaps?' said Austin Tredennis, softly.

'His Excellency!' Marion's scorn grew to something like fury. 'I beg you to remember that I was speaking of men! I know very well how to protect myself against brute beasts! It was you, sir, not your superior officer, who took advantage of my position—played upon my helplessness as a prisoner, my weakness as a woman.'

246

'You bade me go, with your man's scorn for my sex's frailty. I remained, to prove to you that your compassion was as misplaced as your scorn!'

'I thank you,' said Austin Tredennis, simply, after waiting a moment as if to make sure that she had finished. 'I will now leave you with your comrade and playmate till I complete the necessary arrangements for your liberation. I promise you that these will not detain you long. This is only a temporary prison, and the general's signature to an order of release will be sufficient for all purposes.'

He saluted, and turned to go. As he went out into the outer hall Marion made a single step as if to follow him.

'You have nothing to answer?' she said, checking herself quickly, and speaking in a slightly more subdued tone.

'I have nothing to say,' answered the soldier, and again gravely saluted, immediately going to the outer door and locking it behind him. Without taking any notice of me, Marion sat down on the low truckle-bed and stared thoughtfully out after Tredennis into the semi-darkness of the main hall of Maclellan's Wark. She seemed once or twice on the eve of speech, but refrained and remained silent.

'I think, Marion,' I said, after a long pause, 'that you were quite unnecessarily severe with him. After all, and according to your own telling, Captain Tredennis risked a good deal to be of assistance to you.'

'I did not wish him to be of any assistance to me—nor do I now! I would die first!' she flashed out upon me, stamping her foot as if I were to blame. 'Surely you understand! He sat there and looked me over as if I had been a beast in the drovers' stalls at Dumfries Cattle Tryst. He penetrated my secret, and he played with me, I sitting before him all ashamed in that—that thrice abominable travesty of fools' motley! He knew it all the while, and he was laughing at my shame! I could see he was, and I would far rather have had the old general's insolence a thousand times! Well I knew how to deal with that. But this

247

man held me at an advantage, and had no mercy. He humiliated me, and I will never forgive him—never!'

The door was flung open, and Austin Tredennis stood within the portals. We could see him against the light— a tall, dark figure, girthed solidly about the chest like an oak, but, in spite of his great size, erect as a pine.

'You are at liberty, madam, to go where you will,' he said.

'I have no doubt your playmate will be able to make better arrangements for your safety and happiness than it has been the fortune of Austin Tredennis to do!'

CHAPTER THIRTY SIX
BY THE BUCKLAND BURN

'That word seems to stick in his gizzard,' I whispered to Marion, when we had passed out of the prison, and were making our way towards the Red Lion, where Jasper was ready with the horses to convey us to Orraland.

'What word?' said Marion, sharply. She seemed to be thinking of something else—perhaps of some taunt she had forgotten to ply the unfortunate soldier with.

'That you called me your 'playmate,'' I made answer.

'God help me, I have played too long!' was the girl's unexpected reply, in a kind of breaking voice.

Yet all the while I comprehended as well as another woman her swift change of mood; all the inconsistency and apparent ingratitude of her behaviour to one whose actions on her behalf had been so much at variance with his official position. So now, when she had exhausted the outpouring of her wounded pride, it was natural that into the vacancy thus created there should flow the gratitude of a strong and sweet nature.

But it was too late. Captain Tredennis was gone. We saw no more of him that day, nor, indeed, for many days. As we rode away towards Orraland, leaving the little grey steeple and multitudinous gables of the old Dutch-like town huddled beneath us, Marion seemed more than usually sad.

It was the fine mellow dusk of an October day, a grip of early frost already refreshing in the air, the woods reddening of their own proper intent as well as incarnadined by the sunset, when I detached myself from our cavalcade of three—Marion, Jasper, and myself—and, with a swift look over my shoulder to see that I was not followed, rode without drawing bridle up the little crooked sheep-track by the side of the Buckland Burn.

It puzzled myself how I should content old Robin Galtway and the company of Levellers, who had accepted me as in some sense a leader for the nonce—what I should say to them with regard to Marion, and in what way I should rid myself of the necessity of joining in a useless assault upon Maclellan's Wark in order to release Harry Polwart. For I had been more than human if I had desired any better fortune to befall the blind gypsy than that he should be comfortably cared for in his Majesty's prison till such times as he should answer for the deaths of the bold excisemen Craig and Trevor.

It was a curious thought to me, as I made my way towards the solitude hidden by those yellowing leaves, with the Buckland Burn running white and brown alternate as deep pool succeeded rocky fall, that, had I been a soldier of King George's instead of, for the moment, art and part with rebels, yonder bosky silence of woodland would have exploded at my approach into rattling volleys of musketry, and this clean upland air, sweet with thyme and heather, have been poisoned with the reek of gunpowder.

But I was quite safe, and I knew it. Though, of course, as was my wont, I told myself tales, exciting myself like a child with imagined dangers, while the whaups cried overhead on their way down to the sands of the Isle which the tide was just leaving bare, or a belated humble-bee went blundering by, last of his race, homeward bound, with his back-burden of ravished sweets.

'Ah, lad!' the voice came from above, where, all alone, Robin Galtway had been keeping watch, 'and what news do ye bring? Guid, or I am nae judge o' the lichtsome lilt o' your whistle.'

I had, all unknown to myself, been whistling a tune as I came—not, I am sure, to keep my courage up, for there was nothing akin to fear in my heart, though very considerable perplexity as to what I should say and do. Ae to these last, however, I had now to make up my mind.

'Good! in so far, at least,' I said, as brightly as I could, 'your captain has escaped—has disappeared—no one for the present knows whither.'

The old man turned him about, and, with a

wave of his arm, cried to the unseen company in the hollow out of my sight, 'Lads, half our task is done! Dick o' the Isle has escapit, and a' the King's horses and a' the King's men canna lay hand on him, far or near.'

Some of the younger and rasher would have set up a cheer, but this was forbidden by a second and more imperative movement of the old man's hand.

'And what of that wild cat o' the hills, Hairry Polwart?' he said.

'I fear I have little tidings of him that will afford any comfort to his friends,' said I. 'The case abides thus, as I have been able to understand it—Harry Polwart is attainted for no business that concerns the Levellers, but for murder in the first degree, rank and staring. Indeed, the beginnings of the fact I saw myself, and Jasper Jamie, my friend, saw more than I. Therefore, I see not that either you or any well-wisher of the cause will advance matters a whit by running into danger of life and limb for Harry Polwart's sake. If he has killed excisemen Craig and Trevor—why, let him stand his trial, like a man! Now Dick o' the Isle is out of prison the business of the Levellers at Kirkcudbright is ended. For the rest, let every herring hang by his ain heid, say I!'

While speaking thus I raised my voice so that those in the hollow could hear me and as soon as I had finished there arose a strife and contention among them, some (and they the elder and more grave) arguing that the Levellers should accept my advice and retire for that time to their homes, but others of the younger sort eager to assault the Castle of Kirkcudbright, and take their chance of an encounter with the military.

Seeing that it would take the Levellers some time to decide this point, and knowing also that they liked to discuss their plans in private, I withdrew softly a pistol-shot from the dell where they were assembled, and so it chanced that I was able to descry upon the face of the moorland towards the north the passage of a considerable body of cavalry, riding loosely and easily, as if they had been upon a

251

march of considerable duration.

With all due care and circumspection I descended instantly from the little hillock and, running on all fours like a rabbit, made the best of my way to the dell, where, as I had anticipated, the dispute was waxing ever more fast and furious.

'There is a good half regiment of dragoons passing down there,' I said, 'on their way to Kirdcudbright. I fear me your Harry Polwart, willy-nilly, must bide where he is for the present. Let every man give thanks for his own safety and that of your captain. There never was an ill but there might have been a waur, as the proverb says. And if I had not seen these redcoats on the road down there some score of you would have gotten a short summons and a long sleep this night, I'm thinking!'

And, the kettle-drums birling up at that moment, my words wanted not their effect, so that each man began to make his own hasty preparations for flight. Whereupon, without further parley, I summoned Sammle Tamson to my side, and, bidding them all a fair good-e'en, we took our way anglewise across the hillside to intercept Marion and Jasper upon the road to Orraland.

And there have been few days of my life on earth that I saw close with less regret than that one.

CHAPTER THIRTY SEVEN
MORN ON RATHAN

My father has always said (and I agree with him) that there is no prospect in the world more beautiful, with a beauty that savours of the city whose gates are twelve pearls, than that from the tower of the old House of Rathan when the sun is rising. Encircled by the sea on all sides, the foreshores of Orraland distant enough to clothe themselves in soft haze, the points of the Ross on the one hand and Satterness on the other, so far away that they are indistinguishable from the golden and amethystine cloud-bars through which the sun rises, bare Rathan at such times grows immaterial as the clouds themselves, while the sea to the eastward, tipped with multitudinous silver right into the sun's eye, becomes a broad highway to a lost Avalon or to the purple islands of an unknown sea, like that which Cortez saw.

It was very well to note down the preceding sentence in my note-book at the time, and argues a praiseworthy diligence, but the fact is I had not come to Rathan to observe the sunrise. Neither health nor landskip had aught to do with the matter. Joyce Faa was there, and I had come to see whether the love which had proved so potent in the Dungeon of Buchan would revive, to my advantage, on the shores of Solway.

How Joyce came to Rathan I had better tell at once, and in a few words. Davie Veitch, as I anticipated, had proved entirely faithful to his promise, and with infinite good humour and a sufficiency of caution, had conveyed the young officer in the cloak of military blue safely past Orraland House—where, on the terrace walk, they could see my father walking to and fro, and ever pausing at the point nearest to the Kirkcudbright road to gaze along it for any messenger or other sign of our return.

But, because of the shy pride of her heart, Joyce would on no account permit herself to be made known to him. So the two struck away to the right, so as to come out on the shore through the hazel woods near-by the rocky point of Balcary. Here, in that same little glade from which my sister Grisel had been wont to make her signals to Marion of the Isle, Davie Veitch, with steel and tinder-box, lighted a fire of leaves and dampish twigs, or, as he termed it, a 'smudge.'

It was a clean-aired autumn day, the sun bright but not powerful, and the House of Rathan looked exceedingly bien and comfortable, built on a rocky knoll, its grey tower set against the green breast of the island pastures, and Eppie's blue pew of reek wafting full daintily upward till the bluer sky of mid-noon swallowed it.

'It looked a bonny place, and a heartsome,' said Joyce afterwards; better than the great new house of Orraland, with its acre-wide gardens, its flowery pleasaunces, and green plantations.

Meantime, Davies 'smudge' mounted high into the heavens, and had doubtless been observed and wondered at by lonesome sailor-men on tall ships far out at sea, as well as on land by many watchful gentlemen of his Majesty's Preventive Service, long before there was any response from Isle Rathan. But, no ways discouraged, Davie gathered dry wrack in yet greater plenty. He went up among the hazels and brought armful after armful of twigs, with the leaves already beginning to turn and the husked nuts still attached to them in clusters. Of these last Davie proffered store to his companion.

'If ye canna crack them, sir,' said the youth, cheerfully, 'I'se be glad to crack them for ye. I hae graund teeth.'

And opening such a crescent-shaped mouth as is only to be found along the shores of Merrick, Davie showed so fine a store of ivory that even Joyce, with her heart very heavy in her bosom, could not help smiling with him—his gladness at finding himself at home again was so genuine and contagious.

'I thank you,' she said, kindly, and letting her eyes dwell upon his honest face with pleasure. 'I shall be very glad of the nuts, but I can open them for myself.'

'Bless my clog-soles and heel-cackers!' cried Davie, 'but whaur do ye come frae? I declare ye speak juist like oor Marion, and faith, if ye haena gotten on her claes that she rade awa' frae Orraland in! Deil tak' me—if ye hae murdered oor Marion, but I wull slit your thrapple wi' my ain gully-knife, that I hae used thae twa winters for shaw-in' turnips! Ay, that I wull—see ye here! Tell Davie Veitch whaur is oor Marion, an' hoo ye cam' by thae claes, afore ye gang a step farther!'

And so excited was the honest fellow that he actually drew the aforesaid ancient gully-knife from his pocket and opened it, meanwhile standing and stamping his foot on the sand of the little hidden bay from which he had made his signal.

Joyce Faa sat still upon a tussock of the barren brown sea-side common in that place.

'No,' she answered, gently, 'I have not killed your Marion. But I am a woman, like her, and she made me change clothes with her that I might escape.'

'That was juist like her—juist like her!' cried the youth, whirling the gully-knife round his head with a joyous whoof of delight. 'It maun be true, too, for Marion was aye doin' things like that. She yince gied me a peerie (top) to stop me greetin', and then a cuff on the lug because I askit her to gie me the strings tool But where is she?'

'She is in the prison at Kirkcudbright,' said Joyce, smiling at the boy's earnestness in praise of his mistress. 'But Mr. Maxwell Heron, and all those men who are with him, have gone on to rescue her, so, perhaps, she will not stay very long there.'

'Oh! Maxwell Heron is nae great things at the fechtin, I'm thinkin',' said Davie, a little contemptuously; 'but there's plenty wi' him that can fecht. Yon Jasper Jamie yince gied bluidy noses to a hale crew o' smugglers frae the Isle o' Man that challenged him doon at the Scaur! Oh! an' he is juist a fair terror for the lasses.'

'I think there is some one coming across in a boat from the island,' interrupted Joyce, to check the torrent of somewhat over-curious reminiscence, the mere memory of which was making Davie choke and gurgle in his throat with suppressed merriment. So that it is impossible in this place to give Davie's recollections of Jasper Jamie's amatory performances, by which in all probability the history is no loser.

At Joyce's words Davie turned instantly and shut up his knife in a great hurry. He took off his great, broad Kilmarnock bonnet, and began using it as a scoop to throw sand upon the smouldering fire.

'Dowse the smudge, for your life, man!' he cried, forgetting the sex of his companion. 'I can tell ye that the mistress is far frae canny when she is roused! And be ready to answer when she speers at ye. Mind ye that! The last time she askit ony questions at me, and I was inclined to disremember, I declare I was ruled doon the back in blue lines frae my collar to my shins, for a' the world like yin o' Dominie Camochan's copy-buiks! And for sax lang weeks I had to look for the saftest bit o' a board afore I could sit me decently doon on a lang settle. Oh, she's nane canny, the mistress, and sae I'm tellin' ye!'

When the boat neared the land Eppie Tamson atood up in it and with several sweeps of an oar on either side, using the lower blade in the fashion of a paddle, she kept the boat steady about a dozen yards from the land.

'A heartsome mornin' to ye, sir,' cried Eppie, whose sixty odd years had not a whit abated either her natural force of tongue or strength of arm. 'What brings ye to Rathan Isle this day so early? The guidman is frae hame, and it's no' my custom to hae young men that I dinna ken aboot the house. But, dootless, ye hae a reason. Let me hear it.'

Davie Veitch had judiciously retired during the first hostilities (or amenities as the case might be), so that Joyce, still in her military cloak, stood alone on the shore, the little waves lisping and hissing at her feet, and Eppie, in front of her—kindly, rosy-faced, and irascible—steadying the boat against the broad and shining plain of the sea.

'I have, indeed, a reason for being here,' said

Joyce, 'as I dare say your eyes tell you. I am no soldier, but a woman—a woman hunted for her life, and yet without having done any crime. I have been delivered from prison by one noble and strong as an angel of light—your daughter Marion.'

'What!' cried Eppie, 'did Marion send ye here? Where is she? She is nane o' my dochter, nor is she ony mair like an angel o' light than Davie Veitch there (Guid forgie me for sayin' sae I). But it is the Lord's truth that I, Eppie Tamson, wad gang through fire and water for that lass! She never was like ither lasses frae her cradle, and canna be controuled. Yet, oh! I am that fond o' her! I never ken how fond, till she is awa'!'

'She is in the prison called Maclellan's Wark, in Kirkcudbright town,' said Joyce. 'She is charged with being at the head of the Leveller folk, and with having led them on the night when they broke down the laird's dykes at the muster of Bascarrel.'

'Guidsake me! Losh-gosh! Lovenenty!' cried Eppie, putting all the superlatives of her astonishment together. 'Do ye tell me sae? Oor wee Marion, that creeped into my bed when she was a bit wean at Mossdale, and was lost takkin' her faither's dinner ower the hill, to turn oot a rebel and a Leveller! It maun hae been the years she spent amang yon ootlaw renagates the Faa's, up on the hills, that gars her do siclike things noo! Waes me—waes me, for oor wee Marion!'

As she was speaking these words the mistress of Rathan was sculling in her boat with powerful strokes, and presently the bows grated on the white shell-sand of the bay. Joyce Faa steadied the little craft a moment, with her strong hand laid on the planks of the bow.

'Before I come on board,' she said, 'I must know that I am welcome. I am Joyce Faa, the daughter of Hector Faa, one of the outlaws of whom you were speaking. Perhaps you would not wish to trust one of that name on your quiet Isle of Rathan?'

Eppie looked a moment into the dark and steady, yet passionate, eyes of Joyce Faa, and then, with a leap that would have done credit to nineteen, was on the bench by her side. She put her arms about the girl with a strong and hearty good-will, and, though caressing womenkind was not common with her, she kissed the gypsy's daughter heartily on the cheek.

'Lord bless me!' said Davie Veitch, from his lair among the broom, 'I wuss I had thocht on doin' that, instead o' threatenin' the lass wi' my gully! Oh, Davie, Davie! what a gomeril ye are! She's a lass weel worth gettin' a kiss frae, yon yin, I can tell ye, though she does wear the breeks!'

Down on the sand Eppie was speaking softly into the girl's ear the first words of hope and comfort she had heard for many a day.

'Come awa' ben to auld Eppie,' she was saying; 'she kens a' aboot it. Gypsy or gypsy's dochter maitter no' ae whit when there is sorrow in a lass's heart and that look in the e'e that Eppie kens sae weel! Hoots, hoots, bairnie! Never greet! There's no a man i' the wide world worth it —unless he is there himself to see ye. Then greet gin ye like! Greet your fill, and I'se warrant ye will get your ain way. But in the mean time come your ways hame wi' auld Eppie, and— whaur's that guid-for-naething, ramshackle, oot-jointed thief o' the world, Davie Veitch, that I saw wi' ye? Deil hain me, gin I do na scarify his hurdies for the lazy, ill-conditioned—! Oh! here ye are! What do ye mean by skulkin' there when ye see your mistress and a veesitor tryin' to drive a boat into the water? There— tak' ye that! And thae' (putting a pair of oars into his hands), 'and see that ye bring us straight as a die to the Shell Cove o' Rathan, or by my certes the same identical hazel-oil I anointed ye wi' last time is ahint the kitchen door unto this day!'

So it was in this fashion that Joyce Faa came home to my ancestral Tower and Isle of Ratban.

CHAPTER THIRTY EIGHT
THE AUMRY OF THE ISLE

But it was quite otherwise when, as I began to tell in the beginning of the last chapter, Marion and I landed together. We took my father's boat from Orraland pier, and, with Sammle Tamson to row us, we crossed very early in the morning, reaching Rathan Tower while the October rime still lay white even on the prickly hollies and spiked seabents of the pasture edges.

But knock as we might on the spiked outer door of Rathan, and call as we would up to the narrow windows set deep in the vast thickness of the walls, there came to us no answering greeting. No thin shaft of kindly smoke took the air from Eppie's kitchen chimney in the sheltered gable-end. Never a clog-shod heel clattered responsively down the stone turnpikes of the staircase. Our hearts began to tremble within us, with we hardly dared to think what of peril and terror.

It was Sammle Tamson who spoke first, as we looked stupidly at each other.

'The Aumry,' he said, suddenly; 'something will hae disturbit them. They'll maybe be in the Cave o' the Aumry.'

And I must admit that when I remembered Grice Baillie's stable-cavern in the Dungeon of Buchan a stound of fear shot through me. I involuntarily shuddered as I thought of Joyce, and Marion's eye, quick to note all things, observed the movement. She laid her hand kindly on my arm.

'The Cave of Isle Rathan is no ill-place of harbourage,' she said. 'Come with me, and you shall see.'

Of course I knew by heart all the famous history which my father had written when he was a young man, concerning Rathan Great Cave and all that happened there. During the quiet years that followed the raiding it had even become a kind of show-place for idle Sunday pilgrimages, till one August day certain Orraland callants (who ought to have been decently in the kirk listening to honest Master Hallyburton) undertook to swim within the water entrance of the cave when the tide was running seaward like a mill-race. Three of them were never heard of or seen again, and the body of another—a bonny lad called Donald Cavan—was cast up on the Orraland beach almost in front of his mother's door. So after that my father forbade all ingress to the Isle or its caverns, save by permission and under escort of Sammle Tamson or his wife Eppie.

I expected, therefore, when Marion spoke of the Cave of the Aumry, that it was to this famous place of whistling winds and unquiet tides we were about to adventure in the boat. So I was manifestly astonished when Sammle took his way, cannily, and apparently as confidently as if we were going to fodder the cattle, through the little rearward yard of the tower. Then, entering the cow-shed, he set his hands to the side of the byre farthest from the light. It was, like all the rest, walled with split 'stobs' with the rounded side outward, and the rough bark was polished as smooth as the head of a walking-stick by the rubbing of the cows' hairy sides as they went in and out of their stalls.

With a firm and knowledgable hand Sammle lifted half a dozen of these 'stobs' bodily out of their places six inches or so, when, to my surprise, they swung back upon a pair of well-greased hinges and revealed a low door of impainted wood. Upon this he knocked in a peculiar fashion and it was not long before it was opened from the inside, and I saw, peering out into the darkness of the byre, the comfortable face of Eppie Tamson.

'Save us!' she cried. 'What's this? Marion, how gat ye hame, lassie? Come your ways in! I hae juist been settling a bonny lass in the Aumry—that you, Maister Maxle, will be proud to see, or ye are no' your faither's son.'

Bidding us, therefore, have a care of our crowns and walk circumspectly, the old lady turned into a long, dark passage cut in the rock, which presently turning at right angles, I found myself ascending steps so high and so many that, taking the height of the tower-yard where we went in, I knew that if we went on we must soon come out upon the top of the Isle.

Now I knew well that all our island of Rathan and the opposite coasts of Portowarren and Douglasha' are riddled with caves and holes. So I was in no wise astonished at this new proof of the subterranean resources of my native isle. I only followed on, eager to see where Joyce had been bestowed, and, with a strange constriction of the heart, to find out how she might receive me.

All at once Eppie came to another door. It stood half open, and lo! a light beyond showed me a wide and pleasant house-place—a fire in one corner, some chairs and stools, not ill-made, and in a screened recess all roofed and boarded with wood a couple of beds, each large as a family coach—and not so very unlike that conveyance, either, in being screened from draughty with heavy curtains and ascended to by a flight of steps.

Eppie turned her about and smiled a welcome upon us all.

We were in the Aumry, it appeared, a place which had been made by the ingenuity of my father and the labor of Eppie's husband, soon after Patrick Heron brought his bride to Isle Rathan.

'There were mony dangers in thae days by sea and land, ye ken,' said Eppie, with meaning, 'and Patrick Heron was no the man to lose his wee white hen the second time.'

But I had neither time nor inclination to listen to Eppie's historical explanations as to the construction of the cave, but hastened to where by the window Joyce Faa stood, clad now in one of Marion's frocks, and looking, though pale, sweeter and lovelier than even in her own Shiel of the Dungeon.

Marion was before me, and had already taken the girl in her arms, and whispered something in her ear which brought the colour flooding to her cheek.

Then I went up and held out my hand.

But Joyce went pale again as she reached out her own past Marion, yet for a long moment her eyes, great and dark, looked unflinchingly into mine as I stood holding her fingers.

'I am glad to see you again, Maxwell,' she said.

But, without a shade of coquetry or self-consciousness, she permitted me to retain her hand a full minute before withdrawing it. There could not have been a sweeter, simpler, or more unaffected greeting. Yet, for all that, there was something in her eyes which struck me to the heart. I felt that there could be no hope for me. I knew that I loved this girl with all my heart. I believed that she loved me. But somehow it seemed too late. This was not my lightsome Joyce, who had run the mountains of the Dungeon with me like a young roe, whose eyes had turned pleasurably to me as we came slowly homeward in the twilight, or paused, finger on lip, in a pretty endeavour to disentangle from her store of nun's French the name of some small mountain flower.

This was a woman (so it seemed to me as I looked at her) who had passed through the fire—who, having tasted of the Waters of Marah, had found the tree of healing cut down, and the waters yet more bitter there.

Her lips might smile but hopelessness remained as it had been intrenched in her eyes. It was a thing not good to see on the face of a young lass—still worse to know that all might have been otherwise but for my own folly.

That, at least, was my thought, as I greeted Joyce Faa in the comfortable Aumry which my father had constructed ere he would trust his bonny May on 'Rogues' Island,' as in those days Rathan Isle was often called.

But in addition to what he had done, during these last years our wilful, wayward Marion had spent much time contriving comforts and securities for this true Cave of Adullam. At first it had been little more than a child's play with her, but since she had grown older and become more deeply concerned in the business of the Levellers, she had suborned her father to help her, and between them they had completed a couple of rooms boarded, and with a raised floor of hewn logs, to keep out the damp. The outer of these could only be used in fine weather. It contained a long opening, roughly hewn to imitate nature, oblong to the measurement of something like from four yards vertically to half as much perpendicularly. Behind this the rock-dwelling opened spaciously with benches of wood and seats hewn out of the native rock. But, of course, the winds and frosts of a Scottish October made this ante-chamber only occasionally habitable. The inner room, however, was completely different, being lighted by two windows, small, but of good glass, and containing a fireplace whereon a fire of charcoal had been recently lighted.

This was to be the abode of these two maidens during certain days of peril, while one of them, at least, was sought for far and near.

After a few minutes within the Aumry I signalled to Sammle, and we two made our ways back again through the underground passage which my father had constructed after the closing of the former entrance by the great fall of rock now called 'Captain Yawkin's Quarterdeck.' So skilfully had this been done that even when examining the work with a lantern I had some difficulty in distinguishing that which was natural from what had been wrought by the hand of man. Sammle stood at the outside of the barn, and told me with quite unwonted enthusiasm how he had been sent to bring good quarrymen and stone-cutters from Workington, in Cumberland. He pointed out the exact blowing patch of reek on the distant English coast where some of these men still dwelt.

'Though, considerin' what characters thae Englishers are, wi' their warslin' an' dowg-fechtin' and cock-fechtin' and set drinkin's, it's mair nor likely that there's no yin left abane the sod to tell the tale o' the queer den that they helpit to mak' mair than twenty year syne upon Isle Rathan.'

I ventured to say to Sammle that it was a wonderful thing that my father had never spoken of it to me. He laughed a little, and turning on his long storks' legs as on a pedestal of which only the top joints would work (and these but partially), he answered me.

'Faith, Maister Maxle, ye maun ken your faither but little if ye think he canna keep a secret to himself when need be. At the first it was a compact between us that this hidie-hole that we ca' the Aumry was to be keepit between himsel' an' me. But when Eppie and me cam' here to bide, of course it behooved that she should find it oot, sae it was the simplest plan to tell her. For ye are acquaint wi' oor Eppie. What she is no telled she will find oot, and, generally speakin', a deal mair than ye were na prepared for!

'Sae I gat your faither, Maister Patrick Heron's, consent to tell Eppie, and yae day when we were ganging into the Aumry to pit things to richts (for it's a place that by the nature o' the case tak's a heap o' keepin'), Eppie sent Marion as usual doon to the sands to play. But the wee witch followed her, keeping close to her tail, and jookin' aneath a buss o' broom or heather as often as Eppie turned to look. And by my faith she slippit by her mither somewhere, and was in the Aumry as sune as her. The besom! She should hae been lickit for that. But somehow or ither I never could bear to lay hands on the bit thing in anger. No, nor Eppie, either—though whiles Eppie hasna spared her wi' that guid-gaun tongue o' hers. But I never kenned ony differ that it made to Marion. She has aye been the lass that ye see the day, neither mair nor less.'

'The girl who, to save a friend's life, could risk her own,' I said, thinking to please him.

Sammle smiled a queer, far-away smile, as if he could see farther into his daughter's character than I.

'It may be sae,' he said, 'it may be sae. But I kenned Marion a gye while, and though she wad be willin' eneuch to save anither lass's life, she wad aye hae some fish o' her ain to fry, too—or Sammle Tamson is muckle mistaken!'

Then at that I smiled, too. For I knew that the fish Sammle spoke of clinked cavalry spurs and blew tobacco smoke through its gills!

CHAPTER THIRTY NINE
EPPIE TAMSON, COUNSELLOR AND AUTOCRAT

The days that followed were days of great activity and danger upon the mainland, and especially in the vicinage of the ancient burgh of Kirkcudbright. For though the presence of the new regiment sent south from Glasgow to compel immediate attention to the mandates of the commander-in-chief prevented any direct attack of the Levellers on Maclellan's Wark, yet the substitution of another commissioner of higher rank and more pronounced opinions for Captain Tredennis, was manifested immediately in the increased severity which was shown to the Levellers and all their works.

Workmen brought from a distance began, under escort of mounted soldiery (who rode unwearyingly to and fro while the others built), to restore on a much more extensive plan and in a more solid style the dykes which had been destroyed after the muster of Bascarrel. The new commander, Colonel Collinson, was brother-in-law to Colonel Gunter; and mainly through his influence with General Fitzgeorge a series of domiciliary visitations was begun, by means of which the lairds hoped to get into their hands the chiefs of the Leveller movement, so that the common sort, deprived of their leaders, might gradually settle down with some content to the new state of affairs.

Indeed, that was happening in the Lowlands which happened a quarter of a century later in the Highlands. The common folk of Galloway recognized, indeed, that the land belonged in some sort to the lairds, but they had not yet got rid of the ancient idea that it was held by the chief of the sept or clan in trust for his people. Especially was this so with regard to the moors and wide hills incapable of cultivation, which had always been considered common grazing for the poor folk's sheep, and where every little valley and green gusset of meadow-land between two waters sheltered its croft or holding where in times long gone by a family had squatted, and by centuries of labor had won a few scanty parks from the surrounding wilderness of bog and leather.

But all was now to be changed. The lairds were no more of the people. They had taken the side of what all Galloway considered an alien and persecuting communion during the reigns of Charles and James. Thus in most cases they had been divorced in sympathy from the clan or sept with which they were ancestorily connected.

Add to this that many of the original landlords had either been dispossessed as disloyal to some party or other during the long troubles, or had been driven to sell their lands to strangers from a distance. Hardly ever had additional property passed into the hands of a Galloway man of aboriginal stock save in the case of my own father—Mr. Patrick Heron of Rathan.

The newcomers, such as my Lord Kirkham and Colonel Gunter, of course, considered these settlers on these lands and hillside crofters as so many incumbrances. They set their lawyers to work, and, discovering that the poor folk possessed no claims to their little holdings save that of having entirely created them, built up every stone and sod of office and dwelling-house, and cultivated in peace their two or three scanty parks and meadows of rough grass for centuries, they proceeded to clear their lands of them and all their works.

A few of the more kindly disposed—having human hearts within them—gave sites whereon the dispossessed were permitted to erect other cottages, huddled more closely together. And this was the origin of many of our Galloway villages of today. But the greater landlords did not desire any such settlements near their borders, regarding them solely as refuges for the disaffected, as nurseries of poaching, smuggling, and general unprofitableness.

So the edict 'To be Banished Furth of Scotland' began to figure at every court of justice to which resistance to inclosure was reported. And poor families, expelled from their little cottages, had to wander into England or endeavour to find some ship's captain, who, in return for the right to dispose of their services in the colonies for a period of years, was willing, as a speculation, to transport them to Massachusetts or Connecticut or the growing settlement of New Amsterdam, farther to the south.

But naturally there were many—young fellows of high heart and courage—accustomed to the use of rude weapons and hardened by field labor, who could not be brought thus tamely to submit. And when Colonel Gunter and my Lord Kirkham, by arrangement with the government, proceeded to carry out their policy of 'Thorough,' naturally enough they had to face such roving bands, officered frequently by some old Covenanter, who in his time had trudged into Edinburgh to defend the Convention of the '89 against the troopers of Clavers and the more dangerous parchment bonds of the Bluidy Mackenzie.

But there was little chance, unless a true leader chanced to appear to draw the Levellers into some kind of cohesion, that they could make any head against regular soldiers. And in the mean time there were many searchings of heart and waggings of head throughout the wilds of Galloway when the 'hated red-coats' were again seen crossing the moors to visit a solitary cot-house, or beating the heather-bushes and searching the moss-hags for some celebrated fugitive.

As old Robin Galtway meditated, looking down from his hiding on the side of the Bennan Hill and watching the scarlet jackets of the dragoons filing up the side of the Loch of Ken 'Verily do I remember what guid Maister Alexander Peden, that remarkable seer of things to come, prophesied, as I myself heard him by the thorn-buss o' Priarrainion, 'A bluidy sword for thee, O Scotland, that shall pierce to the hearts of many! Many miles shall ye travel, and see nothing but desolation and ruinous wastes. Many a conventicle has God weared on thee, puir Scotland, but now Qod will make a covenant with tiiee that will make the world tremble.'

Thus over and over to himself mourned Robin Galtway in his heather-bush, recalling the things that had been.

But over on Isle Rathan there was little bruit of these things. For my father's high repute in the country, and the good odour in which he had stood with the government ever since the former troubles, made Colonels Gunter and Collinson somewhat loath to meddle with him. And as for Lord Kirkham, he had once, when a young man, refused my father's challenge, accepting in lieu thereof certain strokes of Mr. Patrick Heron's malacca cane. So, not unnaturally, he had some delicacy in meddling with one who still carried a similar weapon about him.

But one day there arrived in the house of Orraland a perquisition in name of the commander-in-chief of his Majesty's forces in Scotland, setting forth 'that whereas a certain noted rebel, called sometimes 'Dick of the Isle' and sometimes 'Marion' of the same, being a person of doubtful sex and various disguises, was suspected to be lurking, in companionship with one Joyce Faa, the daughter of a noted outlaw. Hector Faa by name—a party of H.M. Dragoons would visit Mr. Patrick Heron's property upon a day afterwards to be fixed.' The day was purposely left doubtful, and in the same communication (General Fitzgeorge called upon a subject of such known loyalty as Mr. Heron, of Rathan, to assist the authorities, by every means in his power, to capture the said offenders and restore them to the prison of Kirkcudbright, from which they had feloniously escaped.

My father was on the Terrace Walk when this citation was delivered to him by an orderly. He perused the document with his usual care, refolded it, and stood regarding the soldier for a moment or two thoughtfully, flicking the paper across the palm of one hand with the fingers of the other.

'Mr. Patrick Heron's compliments to the commander-in-chief,' he answered, 'and be good enough to tell him that both he and every honest servant of the King is welcome at Orraland any day and every day.'

Then my father called for a tass of brandy for the messenger, slipped a silver groat in his hand, returned his salute punctiliously, and with a somewhat disturbed heart watched him ride away.

So excellent was the report which the orderly carried back to the commander-in-chief that no party of perquisition ever came near Orraland or Rathan, and we on the isle lived in as much security as if we had been on foreign soil with no trouble within a thousand miles of us.

But it was thought prudent that my father should know nothing (officially) of these ongoings, being a magistrate and liable to be put on his oath at any moment. So when any of us spoke at table of the Aumry, or concerning Marion of the Isle and Joyce Faa, he would feign a mighty ignorance, and say, 'Who may these young persons be?' Or it might be, 'Maxwell, I wish you would not show your learning by speaking in tongues. Pray remember that I am a plain man—and a magistrate!'

My mother, on the other hand, was so happy at getting me safe back that she went frequently over to the island, and was good enough to say that Mistress Joyce Faa was a modest maiden, and, considering all things, wondrously well educated—though (here spoke my dear mother in her properest person) not quite so remarkably beautiful as she had been led to expect! As for my sister Grisel, the girl was in the heights of delight at having not only Marion, but such another companion as Joyce within reach. And it was only my father's absolute command that kept her from taking up her abode permanently at the Aumry, the arrangements of which she admired with girlish enthusiasm.

'I think,' she said, one day to Marion, 'that you should be the happiest girl in all the world. You have everything that earth can give. Why, the Garden of Eden could hardly have been better. You wear doublet and hose when you will.'

'The costume of Eden might be considered even more remarkable,' put in Marion, smiling, but my sister was in too great a hurry to notice the interpolation.

'You live in a cave, hidden from every one, with

parties of soldiers looking for you everywhere! The handsomest one of all is in love with you! Oh yes, he is! I know he is! Maxwell says so. Oh! I do wish I could be anything else than what I am—a commonplace, comfortable, break-fast-dinner-and-supper girl, with the same old snuff-coloured frock to wear every week-day, and a nasty green silk paduasoy skirt for Sundays!'

And our Grisel, being greatly disturbed in her mind by the manifold disadvantages of her position, burst into tears.

As for me, being as it were in the plot, my presence was almost essential upon the island every day. I slept (when I did sleep) at Orraland, but by earliest daybreak I would be up and loading a basket with provisions which my good mother had gathered together over-night. Then, leaving the house by a back door, I went down to the little pier my father had built, rowed across to the island, beached my boat, and lo! there I would be knocking up Eppie when the early cock had hardly done crowing upon the office riggings of Isle Rathan.

'Eh, laddie, ye mind me o' your faither,' the old lady would cry with delight, for I was a favourite with her. 'I never thocht before ye had as muckle o' the auld man's spunk in ye. Bide a wee till I get on my stockings, can ye no, ye graceless whelp? Wad ye shame an auld woman weel on in her fourth score o' years, besides giein' her her daith o' cauld, a' to let ye in a minute sooner wi' your bundles and cook-me-denties? Fie, for shame, lad! Yet it's a blythe day to my heart to see ye sae gleg aboot a lass. I was aye feared that ye wad turn oot a sumph, wi' your buiklear an' gatherin' o' crabs' legs and sea-pyes' eggs, and never ony word in the country-side o' ye takin' up wi' ony lass, gentle or semple!'

Eppie's meditations coincided in quantity with the stage of undress at which I had surprised her. Presently I would hear her come shuffling to the door, her 'hoshens,' or wide, loose house-slippers, making a faint rustling on the stone floor.

'Come in wi' ye, then,' she would say, opening

the door wide in pretended indignation; 'raising decent law-abidin' folk oot o' their naked beds to ready breakfasts to you, and a couple o' hizzies that daurna show their faces like honest lasses at kirk and market! What hae ye gotten in that basket? D'ye think Eppie Tamson haesna as guid bacon-ham—ay, and mutton-ham, too—as ye can fetch frae the braw hoose o' Orraland? What! that's venison, is it? Weel, and that's nae news to Eppie Tamson! Do ye think I hae comed to my time o' life, and had a man that leeved sae lang on the flowe o' Mossdale, withoot kennin' honest venison when I see it? But tea—save us! kimmers, that's an unchancy foreign drink! I canna bide it, and they tell me it's doom's dear, too! Weel, a' brews are guid for something; some to cure the sair heid and some to mak' a heid sair. For me, gie me my honest dish o' brose. Parritch-an'-milk is guid eneuch for puir auld Eppie. But young idle folk maun pamper the flesh wi'their foreign stews an' ragoos, their sugar-ploom custards an' Ejrtalian kickshaws! Lovenenty me! It's gettin' to be a bonny world!'

Nevertheless, there was nothing that Eppie liked better than to set out for our delectation a noble moorland breakfast, with the addition of flounder fresh in the pan which her husband brought up from the tidal flats to the landward of Rathan, where my father had caught the like so many years before. There was the platter of mutton-ham cut so fine that a breath of wind would blow it away in flakes, a braw hearty ashet of ham and eggs, together with three or four kinds of scones and oatcakes. All that I could have wished in addition was that when the two girls came from their chamber, through which the sweet airs of the sea had been blowing all night and morning, they should have brought with them such appetites as I had, after my early rising and long pull at the sculls through the dour and lumpy waters of the bay.

But I could not conceal from myself that neither Marion nor Joyce, though they could walk all day in perfect safety on the seaward side of the island, had quite their former brightness of eye and gladsome spring of carriage. That Marion was anxious and fretting it was easy to see. She said no word either of the Levellers or of that sturdy captain of horse and hard-bitten soldier, Austin Tredennis. Nor for a while could I make out which of the two subjects was most on her mind.

As for Joyce, I had not been often upon the island before I saw that she had covenanted with Marion not to leave her alone with me. Yet, mingled with the disappointment, there was a kind of pride also. For I knew that she would not have shunned an interview unless she had been in a manner afraid of my influence over her.

But it was in Eppie that I found my gallantest and most thorough-going ally.

'I am an auld woman, me that yince was young, and (the lads said) not uncomely, but yet have I never seen ony guid come o' haudin' to an oath hastily sworn. Had Sammle come to me and said, 'Eppie, my woman, I hae made a mistak'; it's no' you I want to mairry!' I wad e'en hae said to him, 'Sammle, Guid's blessin' that ye found it oot noo and no later!' And gin this lass o' yours has trysted to mairry that red-wud Hielant reiver they caa' Hairry Polwart, it's nocht but an ill-promise and a hasty word— like the vow o' that eediot Jephthah in Scripture, wha for the sake o' his oath cut aff the life o' that puir young thing his dochter, and should hae been hangit high as Haman or that rascal Hairry Polwart will be the next week as ever was! Sae bide ye here, till ye see what will happen. We will send ower Davie Veitch to the hangin', and he will bring us word. Then we will see what this Mistress Joyce o' yours will say to that. Yet I opine, whatever she may say, she will be a glad woman and a prood woman to hear the last of Hairry Polwart and her vow thegither!'

For, though I had kept the matter from the maids, my father had been in at Kirkcudbright, and brought us word that the blind gypsy had been condemned to be hanged on a new gallows, in front of Maclellan's Wark the following Monday. The trial for the murder of the gangers had been a brief one.

Polwart had refused to plead before that or any tribunal, and when asked if he had anything to say, remarked only 'I saw not the men killed. I know nothing of the matter.' Nor would he at all reveal who were his co-partners in the deed.

So Davie Veitch was despatched to report on the proceedings. For my father could not abide such scenes, and, besides my private disinclinations to be present, I judged that it might look vindictive if I went thither, and perhaps prejudice my cause with Joyce Faa.

Eppie was an extraordinary comfort to me during all this time, and many a long afternoon did I pass beside the bake-board, listening to the dunt-dunt of her roller-pin as it spread out the doughy and hearkening to her brave talk, all compact of Scots sense and strength and vivid expression. I have forgotten much of it now, and even when I remember and set it down the essence of the matter seems to have evaporated. For it was less her words than the whole scene, the clapper of the waves coming up briskly beneath the tower, the crackle of the wood and peat under the iron girdle, the warm, comfortable smell of the readying scones and cakes, and (I may as well own it), above all, the sense that at any moment Marion and Joyce might come out of the Aumry, arm in arm, and set themselves down anent to me on the lang settle that made the impression memorable. And I think that more than anything these long days of converse with Eppie (for I saw not much of the girls) made me cast off many shreds of dandification which I had learned by being kept hedged too close within the pale of my kind mother's anxieties.

For Eppie, homely in person as she was, of speech unpolished, and sometimes stormy in debate, had nothing ungracious or acerb about her. A kinder or a kindlier woman met I never one. And she would tell me tales, one after another, as long indeed as I liked to listen, of old days when she dwelt about the Moat of Parton, and of her courtships by many others beside Sammle. 'This was afore his time,' was the formula with which she introduced these. Or, still oftener, she would tell me of my own kinsfolk, of the boyhood and girlhood of Patrick Heron and May Maxwell, of my grandfather, John Heron, whom I had never seen, but whose memory she greatly revered, and of all that gay, fast-running, eventful time which made these present trials of Levellers and dragooning seem to her but light and evanescent.

In especial there was one subject on which she was inimitable. I think I hear her yet.

'Let nae man mairry oot o' his degree,' she would lay down the law. 'That may not be the first and great commandment, but it is like unto it, hear ye that Maxwell. And what for then, say ye, is Eppie Tamson, that is auld eneuch to ken better, doin' her leevin' best to help you (that's a laird's son and will heir a' Rathan and Orraland) to mairry an outlaw's dochter, a gypsy o' the Egjrptians, a lass tainted wi' the ill-doing o' ithers that are her kin? But bide ye, lad; I will redd up the maitter. This shall not always be so. If Silver Sand means what he says (and I never kenned him do ither, heather-gypsy as he is), be you assured that the lassie is o' as guid kin as yoursel'! And if no, what then? There the lassie is. Ye see her. She is bonny to look upon, and desirable—at least in the e'en o' Maxwell Heron. Then she is so weel edicate, Marion tells me. No the like o' her in the countryside. She can bake and eke brew, and at a fine seam— faith, I can tell ye even Eppie Tamson couldna do better in her best days! And that is nae starved boast! Weel, suppose Silver Sand be wrang, and the lass's kin are but sheep-stealers and cattle-thieves after a'—what o' that? Tis scarcelins two hunder year since the Herons o' Rathan were nae whit better! And, mair nor that, what guid can a wheen auld ancestors do ony man, lyin' up in the kirk-yard yonder? Allow that ye willna mairry Joyce, for the sake of your grand forbears, will the coats o' airms on their tombs console ye when ye think on the wimples o' the silken hair that curls aboot her brow, or gar ye forget the lang look oot o' the glancin' e'e or the hand laid confidingly in yours as ye gang up the brae o' life thegither?'

'But, Eppie,' I said, 'I am not thinking at all of these things. In such a matter I do not give the value of a plack for all my ancestors put together. The shoe pinches quite the other foot. Joyce will not marry me. She thinks herself bound in honour to this—this blind gypsy. She will scarce permit me the poor grace of a word with her. What shall I do?'

Eppie laughed a little, but there was a kind of contemptuous echo in her tone, as if she held that a man ought not to need instruction in any such simple matter.

'Gypsy here an' promise there,' she said. 'Saunders Lennox's tow rape will break mony a promise on Monday mornin' by nine o' Kirkcudbright clock. Bide till then, laddie; say no word. And even if he get a reprieve, put your trust in auld Eppie. She has kenned the world for mair years than the age o' the pair o' you foolish young folk pitten thegither. When a lass deals wi' a lad as Mistress Joyce Faa has dealt wi' you, Maxwell—it is no a random tryst wi' a blind gypsy that will twine them!'

'Ah, but Eppie!' I said, a little sadly, 'you do not know Joyce. She is not like other maids.'

'I have never yet kenned a lad that thocht his lass like ither lasses,' said Eppie, smiling, and refusing to be discomforted. 'He wad be a puir stick if he did. But be at ease. This Joyce of yours has made a crony o' oor Marion, and—'

'Has Marion told you anything?' I cried, starting up eagerly, for this would have been information at first hand. Eppie put me down with a contemptuous gesture.

'Ye little ken Marion if ye think sae,' she said. 'Na, na; it's nae carried tale, but Eppie Tamson has e'en in her head. And brawly she kens what it means when twa lasses keep oot o' the road when a lad comes aboot the hoose, yet watch him frae the tower window when his back is turned—ay, even till he has drawn up his boat in Balcary Bay—then, syne come their ways doon the stairs wi' their airms linkit, whispering the yin to the ither, as if a' the secrets o' the universe were on their bit silly minds.'

And Eppie laughed again—a kind, self-gratulatory, pleasant laugh, good to listen to.

'Na, na!' she said, in conclusion; 'siclike things had a meanin' when Eppie Tamson was young. I say not what that meanin' is. But gin ye hae ony difficulty o' interpretation, ye are a greater gomeril than I tak' ye for!

'Davert, I hae letting my cakes burn, talkin' clavers wi' you! Oot o' this wi' ye!'

Verily a comfortable counsellor was Eppie, High Autocrat of the Isle, and there is small wonder that I sojourned often in her kitchen during these bright, brisk October days when I waited upon fate.

This is the report of Davie Veitch, commissioner extraordinary from the house of Rathan, who was charged to attend the execution of one Harry Polwart, convicted of murder in the first degree and to return the same night with a full accotmt of the last words and testimony of the aforesaid.

It was late when Davie arrived, and the girls, Marion and Joyce, who knew nothing of the matter, had long gone to their hidden apartments in the Aumry, to which I had never been invited since that first morning when Sammle and I came home with Marion.

As had been arranged, I met Davie at the landing-place, being under a solemn covenant with Eppie to allow him to speak no word till she and I could catechise him together, and so, as it were, start fair. Sammle, as an unimportant supernumerary, was allowed to be present, but had no privileges, either deliberative or catechistical. He was, however, graciously permitted to exclaim 'Guidness gracious!' at intervals, under his breath, but that was felt to be his limit.

I had great difficulty in restraining Davie on the way up to the house of Rathan, so as to keep my promise in letter and spirit.

'Oh, Maister Maxle,' he called out, as soon as ever he came within shouting distance, 'sic a tirrivee as there has been in the auld burgh toon!'

'Hold your tongue just now! Jump out, and help me with the boat.'

'But I maun tell ye! Sic a thing will never be heard tell o' atween noo and doomsday!'

'Not a word till we get to the house, Davie Veitch, or ye'll get Eppie's stick across your shoulders with a vengeance.'

'Will I so? Lord!' cried Davie, contemplating this painful close to a day of delights. 'Weel, Maister Maxle, lend me your napkin to ram intil my mooth as I gang up, or I declare I'll burst!'

At last, however, Davie was ready to tell his tale. He was seated in the fine old house-place of Rathan, with the fire dimpling on the hearth, and throwing a thousand dancing reflections on the brass and copper vessels, preserving-pans, and candlesticks, which, even more than the consolations of religion, were the delight of Eppie's reasonable soul.

Conscious of all our eyes upon him, Davie took his final sup of porridge-and-milk in some haste, and, with a long sigh of manifest repletion, stretched out his legs to begin the tale. For Eppie had insisted on this reading of the old saw, 'There is nae talk between a full man and a fasting.'

'Na, na, tak' your parritch first, laddie!' she had said. 'A hungry man's tale is no worth the hearin'. He aye wants to say 'Amen,' and be at his bicker.'

'Had the puir lad a sair way-gaun?' said Sammle, who could not understand all this pomp of preparation for what would have been a small matter with him. But Eppie hushed him, for, like the Athenians, she took great delight in telling, and even more in hearing, a new thing.

'Let the boy tell his tale, Sammle Tamson, and haud ye your wheesht!' she commanded. 'Ye haena shown yoursel' sae fu' o' wisdom thae last sax months that ye canna wait five minutes to increase your stock!'

'That's the very reason I hae need to be in a hurry,' began Sammle but, chancing to look up, the mere terror of Eppie's countenance struck him suddenly dumb.

And, being thus assured of an attentive auditory, Davie opened his budget.

'It was a brave day, and a pour o' folk a' the road to Kirkcudbrie,' he said, settling himself comfortably to a lengthy recital. 'I declare it was like a holy fair, only instead o' Testaments and Psalm-buiks in white napkins, ilka body carried flasks and wee bottles o' brandy made flat for the pocket—very serviceable and commodious. I had some.'

'Davie,' cried Eppie, 'gin ye hae been led into ony sinful excesses—I'll hear o't, mind ye, and as sure

279

as my name is—'

'Let the boy gang on!' said Sammle. 'He's sittin' there aneath your nose, talkin' like a Christian, and what mair wad ye want? Smell his breath an' hae dune wi' it!'

'A bonny Christian!' said Eppie, scornfully, 'wi' his brandy bottles afore nine o'clock o' the day, and him no yet oot o' his teens!'

Davie waited for this little marital dispute to be settled, and then philosophically continued his story. He alone knew. The others only wanted to know. It was a fine position.

'Weel,' said Davie, 'we gat to Kirkcudbrie in coorse o' time, and I declare the street were fair black wi' fowk. There were booths and tents and drinkin' wickers, a' wattled wi' sauch wands as if it had been a Stanykirk sacramental occasion, or maybes Borgue Fast Day. And the singin' and dancin' in the square, afore the puir laddie that was to be hangit cam' oot, was fair sickenin' to behold. For me, I juist couldna hae tholed the sicht o't if I hadna gotten' (here he caught Eppie's eye)—'a wee drap milk!

'Sae awa' I gaed roond the big bulk o' Maclellan's Wark, and there at the back, awa' frae the feck o' the crowds I gets my e'en on a score or twa o' muckle swank fellows, and though the mornin' was braw and fine, wi' a kindly sun and nae wind, every man o' them was wrappit up in his plaid cloak, as if it had been blawin' snaw in the month o' December.'

(At this point Eppie stole a glance at Sammle Tamson, as if to convict him of an interest in these plaided men; but Sammle was gazing meditatively at the firestone, and drawing figures of eight in the air with the red end of a stick which he had lifted from the hearth.)

'So I keeped as near them as I could, and faith! when I gat a glimpse of their faces, I kenned mair nor half o' them—'

'I think ye were mistaken, mair likely,' said Sammle, with a sly kick at Davie, still gazing, however, at the stick. The red end had gone out, and he began to rub the newly washed hearth with the blackened end.

'Wha's interferin' wi' the tale-tellin' noo?' cried Eppie to her husband, at the same time reaching forward and taking the stick out of his hands.

'And if I were a man,' she said, 'and had been catched frequentin' sic company, as ought not to be so much as named afore my married wife, I wad at least hae mair sense than to fyle her clean hearthstane wi' dirty scrabbles!'

Sammle sighed, but made no reply. When, however, Eppie bent forward to throw the stick to the back of the fire, he got an opportunity of treading heavily on Davie's toes, which caused that youth to emit a sharp 'Ouch!'

'What's that?' said Eppie, looking up suspiciously at the pair of them.

'Oh, it was juist a spark frae the fire!' averred Davie, promptly. 'Green birk is the deil an' a' for spelkin'!'

'Weel, drive on, then!' cried Eppie. 'We want to our beds afore the cock craws in the morn.'

'Sae I left the lads wi' the plaids at the back o' the gaol, for I didna like their looks, and comes roond again, elbow-in' my way through the tents and booths. And then there gaed up a great cry frae the folk, for the marshal men began to drive them this way and that. The tents and sweetie-stands were cowpit and whammelt here and there, as if there had been a sudden and maist violent hurricane had descended out o' the lift o' heeven—'

Davie was proud of this touch, and paused a moment to observe its effect upon his circle of hearers. Greater orators and tale-tellers than Davie do the same. But, alas! there is no Eppie Tamson to keep them in check.

'If ye dinna tell what ye hae to say straightforrit,' cried Eppie, with a significant motion of her thumb over her shoulder, 'mind ye, the hazel-stick hangs ahint yon door. It has garred ye speak the truth, and that richt hastily, before noo!'

'Weel,' said Davie, proceeding more humbly as to style, 'hurricane or no hurricane, at ony rate the booths were knockit heels ower heid in a minute, and a' the aipples an' brandy-balls disappeared in the tuilzie. I gat some!

'Then oot frae the barracks where the sodjers had been musterin' (it was just a wheen hooses they turned the puir folk oot o') we hear the soond o' the trump and kettledrum. Fegs! they gied me pin-and-needles doon my back, to think o' the puir blind wretch in there that wad be hearin' them, too. And then a muckle sheet that they had coverin' a kind o' black platform afore the Castle fell to the grund wi' a whush! And there, in front o' oor e'en was the awesome gallows, and the hangman, Saunders Lennox, and anither lad, frae I kenna where, standin' waitin'. And as I am a leevin' man, though when the folk first saw the black 'wuddy' and the ' drap,' they gied a kind o' soond like 'A-A-A-Ah!'—in ten minutes they were busy at the drinkin' again, and some o' the ill-set burgh loons were playin' 'tig' between the blacky grewsome legs oh! Faith, and I do not wonder, for there on the platform itsel' stood Saunders, the hangman, crackin' jokes to his mate and testin' the slip-knot o' the hempen rape wi' his teeth! Heard ye ever the like o' that, Sunday or Saturday?'

None of us ever had, and, as we all wanted to hear the immediate sequel, Eppie motioned imperiously to Davie Veiteh to proceed.

'Then, wi' a brisk rataplan, rataplan, and a muckle jingle o' braw-glancin' swords and a shakin' o' bridle-bits, the dragooners marched into the square, dividin' here and formin' there, drivin' the folk afore them like sae mony sheep.

'And the wonder o' it was that they appeared to care nae mair than if they had been on the side o' Ben Gairn, wi' no a soul near them forbye the whaups and the black-faced sheep! Oh, it maun be a graund thing to be a dra-gooner, better than-'

Here Eppie half rose from her seat, with a glance at the hazel-wand and a kind of compression of the lips which were quite enough, for thereafter Davie proceeded with increased speed.

'But there was nae mair daffin' amang the

282

crowd, nae knockin' doon o' auld wives' stalls, but a queer dinnelin' kind o' silence as the sodjers arrayed themselves in a muckle square afore the scaffold. And the strange thing was that they turned the heids o' their horses to the platform and the beasts' hurdles to the crowd. And whenever the folk began to be ower pressing, yin o' the sergeant loons wad say a word, and syne half a dizen of the muckle black chargers wad begin to back in amang the folk and mak' play wi' their heels. Levellers, indeed! My certes! gin ever it comes to a fecht wi' the Levellers, the dragooners has only to turn their horses and chairge hinderlands on, and—weel, Davie Veiteh will no be there! Na, na!

Davie will be 'ower the hills an' far away as the auld sang says.

'But this wasna for lang. A' the folk began to look at a window i' the side o' the keep. The frame, if ever it had yin, was gane, and noo it lookit juist like a door, and was hung wi' black on ilka side. Then for a lang minute a' was quiet as pussy, and the queer dinnelin' in my inside gat aye the queerer. I didna appear to myself to hae a single article in my wame aneath my heart, and that gaed thump-thump, heavy and slow, as if it wad burst my verra ribs.

'And fegs, as the sweat brak' cauld on me, I wasna sae sure that after a' it micht na be Davie Veitch that was gaun to be hangit that day.'

'And a' the while there was a muckle drum somewhere that had been duntin' muffled-like and steady—no yin o' thae wee skirr-r-rin' yins, but a muckle slow, solate, Day-o'-Judgment kind o' drum that it made me fair meeserable to hear. And a' in a minute it stoppit, and there—there at the black window was a minister comin' through wi' an open buik in his hand. He was dressed in his gown and bands, like an Episcopian, and ahint, wi' a sodjer richt and left o' him, his hands pinioned to his sides, but for a' that straight as the fir-tree in the clints o' Screel, cam forth the man they were there to hang—Hairry Polwart.

'Ay, and though the folk had cursed him afore, ye ken, and caaed him 'bluidy murderer' and ither siclike ill names, as soon as they saw him, and his sichtless e'en as white as bane, there grew up a kind o' peety for him, too. For the folk began to mind that, after a', it was nocht but a couple of gangers that had been made awa' wi'!

'And Guid kens,' said the man at my elbow, 'there's nae lack o' them that I ken o' in this country-side, that they should make siccan a to-do aboot a odd couple!'

'Sae instead o' cryin' to the hangman to 'gie him a short drap and a lang kick,' as is the custom, there fell sic a silence amang the folk that we could hear the minister busy at his prayin', though the words that he spak' we couldna hear.

'Then cam' the sheriff, and dooms grand he lookit wi' the sword o' justice carried in state afore him; and he had something to read frae a paper, I ken na what. But last o' a' he askit Hairry Polwart if he had onything to say before he was Maunchit into eternity.' That was what he caaed being hangit, but I jaloose it was a' the same thing.

'Howsomever, the gypsy was a fine-pluckt lad, and answered sae that everybody could hear that he had nocht to say, and that if they were ready, he was.'

'Then the folk gied a bit cheer that died oot maist afore it could be caaed a cheer. But the sodjers looked sideways at yin anither, and says here and there atween the ranks, 'We are hanging a man this day!'

'And though I had been watchin' the scaffold wi' a' my e'en, yet I hadna missed to tak' a glance by whiles at the wee cloud o' lads wi' the plaidies that keepit sae close thegither. I could see them workin' in and workin' in till they were close to the horses' heels o' the dragooners. And syne, when I lookit closer, plague on it I if they hadna in the midst o' them twa men grippit. I couldna think what their purpose micht be, but I wasna keepit lang in suspense. For the sheriff ended his speechification and stood back. Then Saunders Lennox began to bustle and mak' himsel' great, stampin' on the platform o' the scaffold, tuggin' at the rope, and arrangin' it careful-like roond

284

the puir lad's neck like a 'gravat'—syne aff wi' it again, as if he couldna get the fashion o' it to his mind.

'Stand a wee this way, ma man,' we heard him say, 'an' ye will swing some easier.' And faith—there got up a 'Booh!' amang the crowd at this, and a voice cried oot:

'Be quick, Saunders, or we'll gie ye a bit swing yoursel', and never chairge hangman's dues for it neither!'

'Then a' at yince, when every e'e was on the platform and waitin' for the faain' o' the drap there cam' a sudden disturbance at the far side o' the square. The dragooners' horses were pushed aside like sae many collie dogs, and the score o' plaided lads rushed into the clear plot o' grund afore the scaffold. The sodjers drew their swords and plunged after them, but afore a blade had time to faa some yin amang them cried oot:

'Up wi' them, lads!'

'And there on the scaffold, maist touchin' Hairry Polwart, him wi' the death-bonnet drawn ower his sichtless e'en and the hangman's cord round his neck, stood the twa deid excisemen. Supervisor Craig and Robin Trevor, that he had been condemned for murderin'!

'Oh, it was graundly dune, and sic a yell gaed up as never was heard aboot the auld waa's o' Maclellan's Wark.

'Craig!' they cried, and syne, 'Trevor!' 'To the wuddy wi' them!' 'What business had they cheatin' us like this, and us come to see a hangin'!'

'For, ye see, bein' excisemen, everybody within ten mile kenned them by headmark—if it were only to keep oot o' their gate, and lee to them when they cam' speerin' quastions. And, faith o' my body, mistress, the Kirkcudbrie folk was fair wild to be cheatit, and were for hangin' the gangers there and then, Craig and Trevor baith. Ay, and they micht hae dune it, too, had the sodjers no been there!

'But the sheriff gaed up and talkit to the excisemen, and a wee, ill-lukin', hurkled body, like a dwarf or brownie, hirpled up after him, for a' the world like a puddock crossin' the road afore rain.'

'But the plaided lads had ta'en themsel's aff withoot ever a Guid-day or a Fare-ye-weel! There wasna yin o' them to be seen. And aye the folk raged and cried oot, some yae thing and some anither. And some were for gangin' on wi' the hangin' o' Hairry Polwart on general grunds, as it were—because he was a gypsy, and if he hadna killed thae twa he had dootless slain plenty o' ithers—or at least stealed sheep whilk in the e'e of the law is the same thing.'

'Some, again, were keen for hangin' up the excisemen and some the sheriff. Yin or twa even thocht that the minister was at the bottom o' the hale affair, so as to hae something to preach aboot for the next sax months—him being dooms fond o' 'improvin' the occasion, as it is caaed. And sae a score or twa, but maistly Dissenters, cried for the minister to be thrown doon to them in his goon and bands. But, indeed, for the maist pairt the fowk didna ken what they wantit, save and except that they had comed there to see somebody hangit, and hangit somebody behoved to be! Sae they were catchin' a messan yellow dog that belanged to naebody, but was a kenned and notable thief, to swing the puir beast in Saunders Lennoxes rope, when presently comes the sheriff to the front, and the bearer o' the sword o' justice cries for silence. Then the sheriff speaks again, and he says how that was a maist happy and unlooked-for termination to a solemn occasion, and how it appeared that these two gentlemen of his Majesty's excise had, by order of a certain noted outlaw named Hector Faa—

('Here,' said Davie, breaking off, 'there were loud yells of execration. 'Hang Hector! Hang the yella dowg!' and mony siclike speeches.')

Then the narrator continued the speech of the sheriff, in quite another voice:

'These gentlemen have by order, as I say, of this noted outlaw, been secreted and sequestered (in the common tongue, hidden away), though treated with no indignity, till delivered by the good offices of Mr.

Thomas Ankers, vintner and change-house keeper at Tarkirra!'

'Weel dune. Grisly Tam,' cried a voice at this from the crowd. 'Hang him—he's ower ugly to leeve!' cried others.

'So,' continued the sheriff, 'though I cannot anticipate judicial procedure, there is no manner of doubt that the prisoner Polwart has been wrongly condemned, and that he will, in the ordinary course of justice, shortly be set at liberty. Furthermore, it is the duty of all good burgesses and lieges forthwith to disperse to their homes, and the captain of the soldiers has our commands to see that this is done in the King's name.'

'And that,' said Davie Veitch, 'is a' that I ken about the hangin' that was nae hangin', and aboot the comin' to life of twa men that were never deid!'

'And was there no more?' I asked him.

'Ay,' he said, rubbing his shins tenderly, 'the yella dowg bit me in the leg when I was tryin' to rescue it frae a violent death!'

Davie was silent a moment, and then added, 'But the puir thing meaned nae ill. Ye see it belanged to Mick McGormick, the sweep, and maybes had na been accustomed to kindness, as yin micht say!'

We sat for some time silent about the dying fire. The marvel of Davie's tale was still upon us, and we knew not what to say or do, when, turning at a slight noise in the transe, I saw a figure I knew well in the dusk by the wall. It was Joyce Faa, and behind her, as it were, laying a restraining hand on her arm, stood Marion of the Isle.

'Then he is not dead,' said Joyce. 'He was condemned to death, and you never told me, not one of you —you whom I thought my friends—not even you, Marion, whom I have trusted with more than my life!'

'Nay!' cried Marion; 'I knew nothing whatever about it. I heard not a word till this moment!'

Joyce went on without heeding her.

'But now that he is alive and free, my way is clear! It is my duty to seek him—to be his wife, if he

287

still cares to claim me. I will go this very night. I will bide no more min this place where I have been deceived and kept in the dark!'

'Joyce, Joyce! Not tonight!' said Marion, trying to calm her. 'Let the night pass first! Tomorrow, if you will. But tonight he will be still in the prison. You could not see him. Wait this one night, and I will go with you. For, in spite of all the kindness and the love of my good kinsfolk, I have not been a whit happier here than you! Wait till tomorrow, Joyce, and. Heaven be my judge, I will accompany you and see you through your trial, whatever it may be and however it may come!'

And, though it be accounted a shame to me, I must record that I was so stricken dumb by the outcome of the tale that I sat silent and found not a word to say, either to Marion of the Isle or to Joyce Faa, whom I loved. I ought furiously to have combated their resolutions. I knew this well, but my weakness had again come upon me, and, as God knows my heart, I could not.

Instead I took my hat and staff and went out to walk all night on the sands of the Isle, with the westerly wind blowing chill in my face, and the waves of Solway lashing up about my feet in foam.

CHAPTER FORTY ONE
ONE HOUR OF LOVE

Yet I was not to have at least one chance of an interview with Joyce Faa taken from me, here in mine own tower and with my father's servants about me. That had been altogether too hard a fate.

I know that it does not say much for mine own contrivance or initiative, that I had not devised the matter before. But for some reason or another that I could not fathom at the time, Marion would not consent to favour me in the matter, perchance considering me too slack and fashionless in my wooing, as was perhaps the truth.

Nevertheless, I was learning, and when Eppie, according to her own kind thought for me, managed to send Marion on an errand with Grisel to the house of Orraland, I went boldly in by the secret way, and knocked upon the inner portal of the Aumry of Isle Rathan.

The voice of Joyce Faa bade me come in, and as I opened the door I saw her draw a shawl about her shoulders hastily, for she thought, mayhap, that Eppie had been her visitor.

Moreover, when she saw me, she looked this way and that, even going a step towards the door of the outer room which overlooked the sea, as if hoping to find a way of retreat thereby.

But instead she beckoned me without into the sunshine, with the feeling, doubtless, that it was more fitting for me to speak and for her to hear out there, with the gulls and terns making a wild melody about our heads, and the sea water jabbling with a pleasant sound beneath the rock.

Further than this Joyce Faa used no courtesy, neither did she invite me to take one of the wooden benches or stone seats upon the outer balcony. She simply waited for me to speak, to say my say, and be gone. And there is no attitude of a woman (if they only knew it and were able to practise it) so hard to combat as this.

Of old, in the Dungeon of Buchan, at the

pleasant Shieling, she had never seen me enter without a smiling welcome, but now no ordinary courtesy of life or kindly greeting seemed possible between us any more.

Since the previous night Joyce had taken off the dress which Marion had given her and put on again the old black gown in which she had accompanied me across the Silver Flowe of Buchan, endured the terrible thunder-storm on the heights of Bennanbrack, and stood up to be married to Harry Polwart in the Manse garden of Minnigaff.

I went over close to her, and all I can say is that she did not move or in any way shrink from me. She only seemed dead at heart, without any answering consciousness of eye or voice or gesture.

'Joyce,' I said, 'I do not mean this for an intrusion upon you, but I think I have some right to be heard. Do you refuse me that? It is the right of every prisoner at the bar.'

Still she did not speak, but only moved her hands, and, more slightly, her shoulders, in the French manner, as much as to say, 'Do I refuse you? Can I refuse you?'

Then, knowing that my time was short, I began to speak clearly and to the purpose.

'Joyce, I love you! I have always loved you from the first, and I always shall love you! Let us take that for our starting-place.'

I watched carefully the effect of these words upon her. I did not take her hand. I felt instinctively that she would resent that. But I stood close enough to note the changes upon her cheek, and though she turned her head so far away that I could see little more than the tip of her ear and a part of her neck, I could see that these grew slowly of a rosy red. It was almost like a young maid's first conscious yielding, but I knew too well that a maiden's rose-blush shame at hearing love spoken in her ear was very far indeed from being Joyce Faa's mood.

'I cannot see why my love has not its rights as well as your word passed to Harry Polwart,' I said. 'I love you, Joyce! I am young, and have all my life to

290

offer you. I have other things to offer also, that I will not shame either of us by naming. For I know that in a cot-house or in a stable-loft I should be happy with you—ay, if I had not a penny in the world—even if I had to carry the meal-poke for you and beg our bread!'

It was when I thus spoke of poverty together that for the first time I saw some of the old feeling come back into her eye, some of that graciousness and sweetness which had drawn all my heart from selfish folly in the long summer days on the hills of the Dungeon.

Joyce had her hands clasped before her, and she lifted them up with a kind of wringing movement, the exceeding pain of which I cannot express in words.

'Maxwell,' she said, in a moaning voice that had yet something I was glad to hear in it, 'if you had truly loved me you would have spared me this!'

I was instantly at her side, but before I could reach her she had sunk down upon one of the stone seats from which there was at all times a view of the sea. I bent down also, half kneeling by her side, and, taking one of her hands in mine, looked into her face.

'Joyce,' I said, 'listen to me. I think it would be best for Harry Polwart that you should not marry him—'

Here she turned and gazed eagerly into my eyes, as if to read my thoughts.

'Ay,' she said, with a certain bitter hardness, 'show me that, if you can! How can it be best for the woman on whom a man depends for his very being to break her word to him?'

This speech set me on my mettle.

'Well, first then,' I said, 'you do not love him. You love me—I know you do. In promising yourself to him you promised what was not your own—but mine. For you are mine! By the right of love I claim you, Joyce, and I will not let you go away again!'

She smiled now, sweetly, most sweetly, yet wistfully withal. She said no word of denial. Nay, she lifted my hand half-way to her lips, as if she were about to kiss it, and then slowly let it drop again.

'You speak well, Maxwell,' she said, not turning away from me any more, but keeping my hand in both of hers, and even pressing it a little between her palms, 'nor will I say a word of reproach to you. Part of what you say is true. I deny it not. But I see my duty to be with this poor, blind Harry Polwart, whom I do not love, and not with—with those whom I do love.'

I think she was going to say 'with you,' but at the singular pronoun her courage failed her.

'He would die in a ditch without me; you—even if you love me as you say (and I think you do), would yet, after a time, love another. No! do not deny it, Maxwell! I know you are not of my degree. You despise my people. You have your lands, your duties, your riches, your learning and books. And I—I am only poor Joyce Faa, the daughter of the outlaw of the Dungeon, whom in a few months you would forget. And as for that other—whom I do not love—in the hour when the hand of God struck him down, it was laid on my heart to live only for him, who, in trying to serve us two, had been shut out at once from the light of the sun and the faces of men and women!'

'But, dear Joyce' I said, 'consider that it is in my power to place Harry Polwart beyond reach of want—a good home on my father's lands, security and comfort all his life. It shall be no sad lot, I warrant you that. He shall play reels and strathspeys at all the weddings and christenings. He shall build the haycoles and thresh the corn. He shall be first at the harvest-home and last at the kirns when the granary is cleared for dancings and the good Scots ale goes round.'

But even when my tongue was drawing the picture I knew how futile were my words. It was sadly, yet a little scornfully, that she answered this time.

'Ah, Maxwell, it is little you know of the hill-gypsy, or you would never speak of Harry Polwart being a pensioner at any man's gate—least of all at yours. For, hear ye. Maxwell, I have been plain with him, and he biows that which—I have never told even to you.'

'That you love me, Joyce.'

I was on both my knees now before her as she sat on the stone seat. How I came there I know not, unless it were for conveniency of putting my arms about her, which I certainly had somehow accomplished.

'That—I — love — you! Yes! I do love you!'

She spoke the words slowly, as if each one had to pass a barrier ere it was permitted to reach the outer air. But she turned to me as she spoke also, and, with a quick sob, threw her arms about my neck and sank her face against mine, pressing it close and closer.

I remember little definitely or consecutively about the time that followed, and I would not write about it if I could. I recall, though, the warm wetness of her cheek, the salt tears on my lips as I kissed her and she kissed me. Perhaps I wept also. I cannot tell. I only know that never can I see a bright October day, with the wind from the north making the sea sapphire blue and sparkling, but I think of that cave of the Aumry, and Joyce Faa for a thousand moments all too swift giving herself np to love and me.

God forgive me! Before that day I might have done as she said, and been content without her—yes, even when I entered through the passage and tapped at that inner door. But after that breaking down of the barriers I was hers forever. Nor have I to this present altered in jot or tittle of all that I vowed to her then.

After a while, how long I knew not nor cared, quite suddenly she withdrew herself from me and stood up, putting up her hair that had fallen down, and looking out to sea with wet, delicious eyes.

I watched her with a new pride and joy. For it was now for the first time that I knew certainly how that glorious creature loved me. And that she was indeed a glorious creature all might see. The troubles of these later days had, if possible, developed still more fully the superb outlines of her form. Ever erect as a hill-pine, she had grown more gracious and rounded in outline, without losing in the least the old lissom alertness of her carriage, as of some wild thing unaccustomed to restraints and the dwellings of men. Now, when she had heaped her hair together in its usual dark and tempestuous masses, and tied the silken snood about it—a broad scarlet ribbon which I had given her—she turned again to me, very calm and pale.

'Dear,' she said, 'this is noways worthy of you and me. We forgot ourselves. The blame is mine wholly, for the sacrifice and the compulsion must be mine. But now. Maxwell, you and I will be strong from this time forth. And God, who knows all, will not visit the weakness of one upon us both!'

I did not speak, for I read the unswerving purpose in her face, and, though my heart was black and heavy, I could not help being thankful, too, that He in whose hands arc the hearts of men and women, had given me to know the greatness of this woman's heart, greater, to my thinking, in its weakness even than in its strength.

She reached me both her hands, and stood regarding me, eye to eye.

'No,' she added, 'this is no wrong to any that we have done. For God knew before how I loved you, and that other knew also when he and I first made the bargain together to save your life. But the moment was ours and the love. It shall abide with me in many a darksome night and horrible place. For now I must take up the burden that has been laid upon me. I go to Harry Polwart, that I may be his so long as he has need of me. Do not come with me. As you love me do not follow me. Let us part here, where for a moment I forgot, where for one hour I was happy without thought. Surely God is not angry when the happiness of a life had to be put into a day?'

She drew me towards her with both hands, kissed me gently on either cheek in her foreign fashion, and then, with a sweet and tender solemnity, lifted up her lips for me to kiss them.

I did so. There was the rustle of a dress, the shutting of a door, and Joyce Faa was gone. I was left alone in the Aumry, under the wide useless brightness of the sky, with the sunlit Solway clattering emptily without upon the rocks beneath the place of our first and last love-tryst.

That 'the blood of the martyrs is the seed of the church' is true also of smaller causes, and humble folk who would never aspire to the honourable designation of the Faithful Slain.

And of this the camp in the Duchrae Bank Wood was a proof. The rough-riding squadrons of Colonel Tereggles, the domiciliary visitations of his fellow-colonel the Galloway laird, the erratic descents and perquisitions of General Fitzgeorge (who dragged at his heels a very reluctant aide, in the person of Captain Austin Tredennis), had issued in this—that the forces of the Levellers had collected at last and intrenched themselves behind ordered lines of trenches and bastion, scarp and counterscarp.

Thrice had detachments of Colonel Collinson's force been put to complete rout by surprise parties descending upon them unexpectedly—once from the rough hill-sides of the Bennan, as the troopers straggled through the marshy narrows on their way up to the valley of the Ken; again at the fords of the Dee, where out of a wood arose suddenly a hundred men, armed with pike and musket, and with surprising suddenness sent to the rightabout two companies of a marching militia regiment hastily called up from the neighboring shire of Dumfries. Lastly, and from General Fitzgeorge's point of view most alarming of all, the sacred person of the commander-in-chief had been in manifest danger. Indeed, he had only been saved by the reckless gallantry or his aide-de-camp, Captain Tredennis, of Ligonier's Horse, who, at the risk of his life, rode within a few paces of the rebel lines and dared them to fire upon him. For some reason not clearly understood at the moment, they did not fire, but stood with grounded arms till the captain had brought his general off the ground without a scratch upon his semi-royal body.

Naturally after these occurrents many were the criticisms and observes made upon the weakness of the government. Frantic were the appeals for additional forces, met by the usual polite indifference and unbelief in high quarters, while at the local headquarters reigned a completeness of disorganization which ought to have filled with joyful gratification the heart of the late Special Commissioner, Captain Tredennis.

But as this is a private, not a public, history, we can take little and brief account with these petty 'ruffles' and 'rencontres' as they are slightingly described in the despatches of the commander-in-chief.

But to his royal relative (putative) General Fitzgeorge wrote in other fashion, entirely abjuring the classic turn of phrase which distinguish the official communications passing under the unenthusiastic eye of his aide.

'Dr. Cozin George, Yr note to hand with the orders. This is a damnble country and verry poore. No wimmen to speak of, and these either pert minkses or blowzie dames. If you do not recall me soon, I must rezine and go to Bath to drink the waters. I heer Lady Bettie Trippit is there. Ther is a felow heer, Capt. Austane Tredenis, of Liegonr's Hoars, mutch in my way. Have him made a Col. or Depty.-Governr., or something els, and sent to amerika or some Islande, very desolate. My humble service to yr. Royl. Highnss. I hope the Dutchss and her Majty are better Friends. My respect to the former—as this is a private letter.

'Yr. lovg. humble Servt. and Cozin,

'G. FITZGEORGE.'

'P.S.—Dr. George,—I am verry poor, or shall be when I reach anny place wher I can spend Monny, as Bath, where Lady Bettie is.—G. F.'

That this kindly though unofficial mention in despatches did not bear immediate fruit is owing to the fact that the august personage to whom it was addressed was temporarily absent on a visit to his Continental dominions —so that, in the meanwhile, and pending his return, Austin Tredennis still remained 'mutch in the way' of the relative of kings.

Nevertheless, it could not be denied that he had

greatly distinguished himself. His courage had been proved on the occasion of his bringing his superior officer out of imminent peril (as mentioned in General Fitzgeorge's public despatches). He it was who held the candle straight between the Gallic slackness of the commander-in-chief, who cared only for Bath, 'where Lady Bettie is,' and the domineering landlordism of Colonels Gunter and Collinson.

But what the motives were which caused him to offer his services as a spy in the enemy's country remained a secret to all save Captain Tredennis himself. He found himself at last on the high road to promotion—and, indeed, nearer to it than he had any conception of, not having seen a certain letter to 'Dr. Cozin George' which we have had the advantage of perusing. Yet, in spite of his very eligible position as officer in personal attendance upon the commander, forgetful of the excellent dinners at headquarters (which were always fixed where the best game and wine were to be had)—in spite of these and other advantages too numerous to mention, Austin Tredennis offered himself as a volunteer spy, to adventure into the rough country about the embouchure of the Dee and the Ken, where the camp of the rebels was situated.

'I cannot spare you,' said the general, at first. 'Blood me I but I decline to be left alone with a pack of Galloway lairds, who eat with their knives like ploughboys, or deuced old moneygrubbers and land-thieves like Kirkham and Gunter! You are a rough fellow, Tredennis, but George Fitzgeorge owes no grudges. In fact, you were perfectly right. But, indeed, I cannot afford to let you go, for you play a devilish good hand at piquet. So don't ask me, my dear sir. I pray you don't ask me again!'

But Austin Tredennis did ask again, pointing out with much cogent argument the advantage of ending this foolish strife expeditiously and, if possible, without shedding of blood.

'There is no honour to be gained—that is, for a general of your world-wide reputation' (Oh, Captain Austin!) 'by riding down these poor ploughmen and shepherds. No honour, save in getting the whole thing settled out of hand, and that these landlords will put off as long as possible, so as to have as many as possible sent out of the country.'

'D—n them!' exclaimed General Fitzgeorge, quite in the Hanoverian manner of his august relative.

'Well, consider,' the Macchiavellian aide went on with his subtlest smile, 'it must be dull enough here for you a man of your fine tastes, when you ought to be at-'

'Bath! ah, yes—yes, so it is, so it is—deuced dull!' murmured the general, half-closing his eyes, and seeing, doubtless, a vision of the Pump Room and other things yet more pleasant in the City of the Waters.

'You will have all the credit if I succeed,' continued Austin, 'I, and I only, will be blamed in case of failure—'

'Very proper—very proper!' said the son of kings, quite audibly.

'And you will permit me to say, sir,' said Austin, 'that with your success here will doubtless come also your rank as a Royal Duke, which has been shamefully delayed, and a more desirable post than the command of his Majesty's forces in these barren and remote parts of his dominions.'

'Yes, yes I good fellow, wise man!' murmured General Fitzgeorge, nodding approvingly, and helping himself to a sixth glass of wine, without remembering to offer any to Austin. 'Admirable way of putting things! Wish I had it I Never could—blood me! None of our family can!'

So, leaving his commander-in-chief to discuss the remainder of the second bottle of claret, Austin departed, much elated by the permission to run his neck into the most absolute and terrible danger. The distinguished field-officer lay back in his chair, and as he slowly tilted the silver goblet, from which he always drank when on service (a baptismal present from his late royal godfather, and father), he cast up his eyes to the ceiling and meditated.

'Ah!' he said, 'it will do no harm, in any case. It

299

is a quicker way than promotion, if the fellow fail. I shall be able to console myself in this dull dog-hole without any more of his Puritanic interference, blood him! And if he should happen to succeed—why, then I shall get away to Bath. Ha! I stand to win either way. Never thought of that before—never thought of that—clever fellow, George, deucedly clever fellow!'

Austin Tredennis had been a spy before. In the Netherlands he had passed from army to army more than once, and knew that intoxication of excitement when a single false step may bring you before a firing-party, or a word too much or too little deliver you to the provost-marshal with his rope.

It cannot, therefore, be any derogation from the courage of the captain of horse if we confess at once (from information received) that other thoughts were stirring in his heart than desire to taste danger in full draught undiluted, or even the hope of immediate promotion.

The brain of the soldier lay within its casement—large, collected, and cool—working out problems, and choosing the best means of attaining ends as unimpassionedly as it played his hands at piquet with his superior officer—when he won or lost, not according to the cards, but according as he wished to influence the mood of his opponent.

So far the head; but the heart—ah! that was another matter. The heart of Austin Tredennis was a seething turmoil, of which no fleck or spray was suffered to reach the calm, rather grim features, or to twitch the mouth set so sternly under the great mustache. For, to be brief, the captain of horse was in love! More, he was piqued, or rather, angered—with a feeling as much stronger than pique as eau-de-vie is stronger than water. But the word 'pique' must be used, because it alone expresses the line of his feeling, though by no means the distance he had travelled along that line.

Since the night when Marion had first flouted him, and tossed him aside like a finger-worn gauntlet, while yet utterly in his power within the prison at Kirkcudbright, he had never slept soundly, save with the sleep of supreme fatigue. He did professionally the work of an entire staff, and earned his reward by sleeping for three or four hours a deep and dreamless sleep. From this he woke to the angry torture of the man who falls deeply in love late in life, yet who is baffled, angered, flouted, crossed at once by circumstances and by the object of his love.

'Now I will show her!' said Austin, twisting the broad flank of his mustache into his mouth, and biting savagely upon it. 'Now—at last.'

He strode away to his solitary quarters and summoned his soldier-servant, a wiry fellow who had been with him for many years and in various climes.

'Beech,' he said, 'I am on the old game again. Get me the Yorkshire toggeries—the drover suit with the big buttons.'

Beech—a tall, spare middle-aged man with a marvellously lined countenance and a huge nose down the side of which he looked at his master as if along a levelled musket—stood still in astonishment forgetting even to salute.

'The old game, sir?' he said. 'Surely that's for younger men, and, if you will excuse me, sir, for men of lighter build and figure than you be!'

'General's orders. Beech,' said Austin, curtly. 'Button me on the leggings.'

The white moleskin leggings aforesaid, rough and weather-beaten, were worn over an old pair of cavalry boots. To these were added blue pilot-cloth small-clothes, roomy as a house even for Austin's honourable girth, a buff waistcoat of a twilled material, with immense pockets flapped and ornamented with immense steel buttons, a short coat of the same stuff as the small-clothes, splashed and frayed, a flapped black hat caught up in the front with one of the steel waistcoat buttons. A weather-worn grey cloak of a material like frieze to lay across his pony's back completed the equipment of Mr. Job Brown, Yorkshire drover and cattle-dealer, who stood in front of the camp mirror of the late Captain Austin Tredennis, of Ligonier's Horse, disappeared. Austin groaned as he ordered Beech with a pair of scissors to sheer away the solid magnificence of his mustaches as close to the skin as steel would cut. But at that moment Austin was in a mood for the greatest sacrifices.

'Any orders, sir?' Beech whispered in the dark of the archway of Austin's lodgings, when, having settled his cloak and seen to his pistols, he held the stirrup for his master to moimt the stout little pony which was to carry the fortunes of the spy-lover.

'None,' said Tredennis, 'except to keep your mouth shut.'

And so, with a heart quieter and more satisfied than it had been for many months, Austin Tredennis went out into the outer dark, and rode away northward with the good-night bugle call of his troopers ringing in his ears as an unconscious godspeed to their commander.

CHAPTER FORTY THREE
CATTLE-DEALER AND SPY

There is a ford across the Lane of Grenoch, near where the clear brown stream detaches itself from the narrows of the loch, and a full mile before it unites its slow-moving lily-fringed stream with the Black Water o' Dee rushing from its granite moorlands. The Lane of Grenoch seemed to that comfortable English drover, Mr. Job Brown, like a bit of Warwickshire let into the moory, hoggish desolations of Galloway. But even as he lifted his eyes from the lily-pools where the broad leaves were already browning and turning up at the edges, lo! there above him, peeping through the russet heather of a Scots October, was a boulder of the native rock of the province, lichened and water-worn, of which the poet sings—

'Auld Granny Granite girnin' wi' her grey teeth.'

He made a tall, handsome cattle-dealer, this Yorkshire-man; none so hearty or willing at a bargain had been seen among the farmers of the straths for many a day. Wherever he went Mr. Job Brown left behind him a trail of smiling faces and drained dram-glasses. It is true that when Lorimer of the Boreland, came to think it over afterwards, he could not remember that much actual business had been done. But, on the other hand, Mr. Brown had looked at everything, and 'When I return from Ireland,' he had said— 'ha, ha! then we will see if you Galloway lads can beat the Paddies at a drink or a bargain.'

Good-wifely smiles acknowledged Mr. Brown's judicious praise of the dropped scones or the poultry. Mutton-hams like those of Mistress Lorimer had never been seen in Yorkshire. Yes, he was a bachelor. It was his misfortune, but he would settle in Galloway gladly if only Mistress Hislop, of Barnboard, would look out a suitable partner in life for him. He was a shy man. She was doubtless a better judge of good wives than he.

Sentiment such as this in the mouth of a well-looking, well-to-do, unmarried man, spoken, moreover, to the mother of six, all untochered and marriageable lasses, creates an impression something more than favourable.

At the little moorland public-house of Clachanpluck Mr. Job Brown left his beast, to be sent back that same night to Kirkcudbright, duly consigned to the care of one Daniel Beech, at Mistress Davert's, in the Back Row. Mr. Job was going into the hill-districts of Kells and Minnigaff to buy black-faced sheep for Carlisle Tryst, and the roads, or rather, the broad heathery breast of the fell extending mile after mile, and varied only by bottomless loch, green, treacherous, shaking bog, and deep, purple-black moss-hag, was not exactly the country most suitable for an English-bred beast.

In fine, alone and on foot, Mr. Job Brown crossed the Crae stepping-stones just where you will find them to this day, as I tell you, at the shallow place a furlong or two northward along the road from the Duchrae Loaning.

What Mr. Brown was doing there was not at first very clear. For the road to the brig-end of Dee Watcr (where the great fight of other days had been fought) did not then pass by the water-side as now it does, but over the moor by Parkhill to the Folds— where, indeed, you may yet trace it with pleasure to yourself any idle summer afternoon by its velvety tuft, greener at the sides, along which the bairns, with their bare feet, trotted to school, and rougher with corn-cockle and hard-head in the grooved mid-track, where from generation to generation the pack-horses followed each other in a long swaying line.

But without obvious cause Job Brown had forsaken the main road when it left the loch side, and continued his journey by the rough foot-path, now soft, now perilous, by which the country-folk were wont to pass up the glen to the ford and thence to the hill-farms of Slogarie, Airie, and the two Craes— Upper and Nether.

But at this point we may as well drop Mr. Job Brown, drover and cattle-dealer from Yorkshire, and say that with eyes keen and trained to the closest observation. Captain Austin Tredennis, in the disguise which has been already described, strode circumspectly across the stepping-stones, paused a moment on the huge central block, and then made his way up the hill by a path-way distinctly marked through a tangle of heath and bog-myrtle to the farm-town of Upper Crae, on the brow of the hill which looks out towards the north.

The night of late October was closing rapidly in. The sun was already behind the Airie Hill. The country was unknown, destitute of passable roads—perilous, too, for the rebel lines were now very near. The scouts of the Levellers were everywhere, and each moment as he strode forward, his bundle swung over his shoulder on the crook of his staff, Austin Tredennis expected to find himself challenged.

He had waited two days at Clachanpluck, entertaining all and sundry at the village inn, knowing well that this was the safest introduction he could have when he betook himself to the more dangerous neighborhood of the Levellers—or, greatest peril of all, endeavoured to penetrate their camp on the strongly fortified peninsula opposite the Hollan Isle.

It was, in a manner of speaking, by simple instinct that Austin sought for Marion in the camp of the Levellers. She was not at her home; of that he was confident though had he known of the existence of the Aumry, on Isle Rathan, he might not have been so well assured. He was certain that so bold and determined a leader would go back to her followers, when at last they were making a stand in the open against the forces brought against them.

The premises of the captain of horse were not quite correct. Nevertheless, he argued with judgment, and his conclusion that Marion must be looked for in the camp of the Levellers had much more probability than most purely speculative conclusions.

At that very moment when Austin Tredennis was taking the Grenoch stepping-stones in his stride, and driving the dew from the bog-myrtle with his riding-boots, one Captain Dick of the Isle was visiting posts and arranging defences not more than a scant

Scots mile to the northward.

It was Austin Tredennis's plan to introduce himself at the farm of Crae, if possible, get a night's lodging there, and on the morrow, on pretext of seeing the owner's flocks and herds, obtain a bird's-eye prospect of the fortified camp in the Duchrae Wood, and, if possible, hear some tidings of his sometime prisoner in Maclellan's Wark.

Tredennis strode up to the door of the little thatched farm-house on the hill. His arrival was, of course, heralded by half a dozen clamorous collie dogs, which mounted themselves upon cairns of stones gathered off the fields, and appeared from barn and stable open-mouthed and voluble of warnings.

He had hardly time to knock when Mistress MacCormick, wife of Anton, fanner and indweller in Crae, opened the door, and, with an air of remarkable heartiness, bade him enter.

'Ye'll be the Englishman frae the Clachan, nae doot?' said the lady, a tall, middle-aged, capable-looking person, with heavy black eyebrows, and a habit of swooping about the house from side to side as if she had been unexpectedly shut up there by accident, as a swallow might in a church.

Austin intimated that he was indeed the person referred to, whereupon the lady of the house ushered him in without further catechism to a comfortable house-place, where a couple of men were sitting. One was a little, grey-haired man, with bent back and a rosy face—Anton MacCormick himself—a shrewd man at a bargain at kirk yett or town market-place, but, for all his chirpy good-humour, held in the direst servitude by his wife. Among other peculiarities this lady had an inordinate passion for cleanliness, and was perpetually scrubbing and polishing some portion of her domain. Sometimes the kitchen would be in the act of receiving attention, in which case worthy Anton was known to take his dinner frugally upon the doorstep, eating out of a platter that was handed to him from within, like a beggar at a rich man's gate.

At other times the bedroom of the pair would be

under vows of purification, when the lady slept alone on a shakedown in front of the kitchen fire, while poor Anton (on the plea that he would most likely set either himself or the house on fire) was sent to make what shift he could in the stable-loft with the serving-man.

On this occasion, however, it happened that the lady was in high good-humour, and save that she invited Tredennis's attention rather abruptly to a wet rag which she kept behind the door for foot-cleansing purposes, she made no objection to his staying the night in her house.

The master of the house, however, was profuse of hospitalities.

'Ye mind me,' he said, rising from his seat, and holding out his hand. 'I was wi' (Geordie Moatt and Andrew Lowden, frae Drumlane, at the change-house o' Clachanpluck the nicht before yestreen. And little did I think when ye sang us your braw English sangs, that ye wad be sittin' at my ain fireside before the mune was twa days aulder!'

'It's no muckle ye shall get to pour doon your thrapples here,' said Mistress MacCormick, making a swoop upon the dresser, and locking the lower compartment. 'Anton cam' singing up the loan, and even answered me back when I reproved him—answered back to his married wife! What think ye o' that, Silver Sand?'

The second man at the table had never taken his dark, twinkling eyes off the new-comer, but now he turned courteously towards his hostess.

'I think,' said Silver Sand, smiling, 'that your husband's conduct was most unseemly, and altogether inexcusable.'

'Ah! but, Silver Sand,' cried the master of the house, 'it is easy for you to speak, wi' nae wife to say ' Where goest thou?' or 'Whither comest thou?' Weel may ye side wi' the weemen folk! But gin ye were as tichtly wedded as me, ye wad sing a very different tune. But what says to that Maister Job Broon, frae Yorkshire?'

Austin, having immediately understood who

buttered the bread in the house of Crae, of course answered with every reasonable promptitude that, being also unmarried, he looked upon all women as angels, and married women in especial as archangels.

This obliging reply put Mistress MacCormick in high good-humour, and while a more substantial supper was preparing, she opened the cupboard she had so abruptly locked, drew from thence a square-faced green bottle of Hollands, and arranged glasses upon a silver tray on the table.

'We will be able to keep the guidman in order this nicht,' she cried, smiling in great good-humour. 'Anton, ye lazy sumph, get the stranger a chair, and, sir, tell us the best o' your news. What think ye o' the lamentable state o' this distractit country?'

Austin answered cautiously that he had as yet thought little about it that it was his business to inspect cattle and sheep with a view to purchase; but that by the time he returned from Ireland he hoped that the trouble would be over, as he found it almost impossible to get men to drive his beasts to market.

At this announcement the little, red-cheeked man visibly brightened, and said that he had threescore sheep in prime condition, besides a dozen Highland cattle out on the hill, all which he would be pleased to show Maister Broon the next day as early as he liked.

'But the best o' them are gane, sir!' cried the lady. 'Thae Levellers! vaigabonds that they are.'

'Wheesh, wheesh! cannily and smoothly, guidwife! Mind whaur ye are speakin'!' said Anton, with a glance across at Silver Sand, who sat steadily regarding the fire on the hearth.

'Deed, an' I'll wheesht nane,' cried the angry matron, who, like most women, became strongly partisan as soon as politics touched her personally. 'To think o' the bonny wethers that hae gane aff the hill, and never a penny to pay for them! And two bullocks that had no their match between Merrick and the sea, a' boiled in a pot to pamper the stammocks o' a wheen blackyards, the scum o' the earth! Oh, that I had married a man, and no a bundle o' sauch-wands that the wind blaws through and through!'

As she spoke she looked at the sturdy form and square shoulders of the English drover with a directness of admiration which made that modest gentleman most uncomfortable.

'Sure am I,' she continued, raising her voice for the third time, 'that rather than lose the sheep oot o' his parks and the nowt aff his hill, Maister Brown wad hae ta'en his musket and whinger and ga'en to the heather to hae satisfaction o' a wheen thieves an' catherans that caa' themsel's Levellers, and wad a' be the better o' a guid bangin' by the neck, ilka yin o' them!'

'I fear if he had done so. Mistress MaeCormick, that yon might this night have been a widow,' said Silver Sand, smiling qnietly.

Mistress MaeCormick of Crae was filling Austin's glass with a second supply of Hollands when she heard these words, and as soon as she had finished she cast a wide circuit about the speaker's chair, ostentatiously leaving him out of my further distribution of good things, and merely adding a little to the contents of her own and her husband's glasses. Silver Sand watched her with a look of quiet amusement.

'Widow or no,' she replied, tossing her head, 'at least I wad hae been free to mairry a man, and that's better than bein' the wife o' a craitur wi' nae mair backbane in him than the dishclout!'

To heal the little disturbance, Anton had risen from his seat by the fireside, and set on the table a plateful of oatcakes and a segment of very solid-looking skim-milk cheese.

'Hae, lads!' he cried, with an attempt at merriment very obviously forced, 'sit in, an' try some o' my wife's cheese. It's her ain makin', and I'se warrant ye there's neither dirt nor butter in't!'

But Silver Sand, observing that his presence was not to the mind of the lady of the house, presently lifted his hat, and amid the loud lamentations of his host and the dour silence of

Mistress MacCormick, courteously took his leave. He shook hands with Austin Tredennis, and said as he did so, with an emphasis which the soldier could not fathom, 'Till our next meeting, sir.'

As soon as Silver Sand was well out of the kitchen and safe down the little loaning, the storm which had been gathering within the farm kitchen suddenly and over-whelmingly broke.

Austin sat silent and even a little intimidated, in spite of his amusement, while the tornado lasted. With great solemnity the lady of the house took the rolling-pin from a shelf in the corner where it reposed in company with the potato-beetle and a wide earthenware 'byne' of blue skim milk. Then, with haughty tread and menacing air, she stalked across to her husband, who sat holding on with both hands to the arms of his chair, apparently stricken dumb by these warlike preparations. He had been sitting with his hat on his head, as is the honourable right and custom of the master of the house when presiding in his own house at a meal of any kind.

War was formally declared by the belligerent dame knocking her husband's hat from his head with her left hand. It went spinning into the corner, while its owner looked ruefully after it, well knowing that if it fell in the water pail he alone would be blamed. After that, however, for some time other matters claimed his attention. But it says something for the excellence of his training that, so soon as he was again at liberty, he went meekly into the corner after his head covering, and carefully dusted it with his sleeve, whirling it meanwhile round upon the points of the fingers of the other hand.

Then, still silent with the awful silence of an approaching thunder-cloud. Mistress MacCormick proceeded to shake the rolling pin fiercely in her husband's face, so close that if he had moved in the least it would not have needed the Levellers to make a widow of the mistress of Crae. The rolling-pin would have done it for her.

'I daur ye, Anton MacCormick!' she cried, 'as ye value your worthless life, to bring that craitur Silver

Sand into this hoose again! If ever—frae Yule-tide to Yule-tide, in winter or spring, frae morn to midnicht, or at ony ither season—ye let the craitur set foot in this hoose, I, Jacobina MacCormick, will break every bane in your body wi' the beetle, and syne set ye to the loanin' fit, never again to show your face within sax guid Scots miles o' the Upper Crae. Wha brocht ye your gear and plenishin'? Jacobina MacCormick! Wha stockit the farm wi' Ayrshire and shorthorn nowt-beast and Hielant kyloe? Jacobina MacCormick! Wha's sheep are bein' robbit aff the hill, and wha's bullocks are slaughtered to mak' broth for your friends the Levellers, doon in the Duchrae Wood? Wha's but Jacobina MacCormick's? And that Silver Sand, wi' his saft tongue, and 'By your leave, madam!' steppin' in and oot like Baudrons, oor pussy cat, at a mouse-hole, doesna tak' me in! Na, Anton MacCormick, frae this day forth, never let me see you or hear tell o' you in that gypsy's company! He comes here for nocht but to spy oot the land for his friends doon there. Noo, there's nocht o' the spy aboot this gentleman. He comes steppin' muckle and braw and gawcy up to the door, chaps at it like a man, and fills the chair he sits on when he set him doon, as featly as parritch fits a bicker.'

'Noo mind, Anton MacCormick, I hae warned ye for the last time! And faith, my man, if I find ye takin' up wi' ony spies or ill-contrivin' Levellers, to the loanin' yett ye gang, you and a' your guid-for-naething crew! Dod, and it wadna tak' Jacobina MacCormick lang to get a better man than you—aye, if she had to mak him hersel' oot o' a hank o' whipcord and a wheen peasticks.'

It was after this, as the history has already recorded, that the master of the house went into the comer and picked up his hat.

While she was preparing supper, Mistress MacCormick was very willing to give Austin Tredennis any information in her power, and as soon as she imderstood that he had small sympathy with the Levellers she spoke freely.

'Ay, ye will see all-and-hale o' them the morn's

morn-in,' she said. 'I will tak' ye mysel' after I hae lockit up yon in the milk-hoose.'

(She indicated her lord with her elbow as he still stood by the transe humbly wiping the whitewash off his hat)

'There's twa hunder o' them, or maybes three, and their trenches and warks are a sicht to see. Maist o' them are raw young lads, ploughmen and cotmen's sons. But there's a score o' smugglers and hill-gypsies, and they say (but I kenna for the truth o't) that Hector Faa himsel' is there amang them, and his dochter, her that brak oot o' the gaol o' Kirkcudbright'

'What!' cried Austin Tredennis, in apparent amazement. 'Surely there are no women with them—in such a place, and without tents?'

'Oh, as to that,' cried the mistress of the Crae, 'they allow nae women as a general thing! Only this Joyce Faa is wi' her faither, and they say (but mind, I'm no forcin' ye to believe it) that their head captain is a young lass frae the shore-side—a terrible clever hizzie she is. They ca' her Dick o' the Isle. I met the jaud ae day, a' wrappit up in a great blue coat, and a bauld-lookin' besom she was, wi' petticoats kilted half-way to her knee and a pair o' pistolets at her belt. For me, that am a decent woman, I want nae comin's or gangin's wi' the likes o' her, whether she be man, woman, or deil!'

And as Austin Tredennis laid himself on the comfortable bed in the 'prophet's chaumer' of the Higher Crae, he shut his eyes upon a vision of a young girl in a great cloak of blue with a silver tache and neck-chain, setting sentries and visiting posts in the autumnal rains, and sleeping at night under these late and unkindly northern heavens. And in spite of the condemnation of Mistress MacCormick, he resolved that if he had not considerable 'comings and gangin's' in the days that were to come with the young Captain of Levellers, the fault would not be his.

On the morrow Austin Tredennis spent most of the morning visiting the flocks and herds secured to the farmer of Tipper Crae by his wife's dower (a fact kept in the good man's recollection very constantly by the lady herself) and as he went he kept an open eye for all that was to be seen of the Levellers' encampment in the Duchrae Wood.

He could discern a line of sentinels drawn from a point a little below the stepping-stones by which he had crossed up to Mount Pleasant, a wooded hill bare at the top overlooking the Cave and the head of the Loch of Grenoch. His guide pointed out the outpost on the hill-top, and remarked, with much acerbity, that they were engaged in cooking.

'And verra likely yin o' my ain yowes,' she exclaimed, 'and the guidman in the milk-hoose no carin' jot nor tittle.'

Austin thought that if he had been locked in the milk-house, he would have shown himself equally indifferent as to the fate of his gaoler's dowry.

But it was, of course, the camp in the wood that occupied most of his attention. The situation was naturally a strong one, that is, if, as was most likely, it had to be attacked solely by cavalry or by an irregular force without artillery.

In front the Grenoch Lane was still and deep, with a bottom of treacherous mud. Swamps encircled it to the north, while behind there was a good mile of broken ground, with frequent marshes and moss-hags. Save where the top of the camp mound was cleared to admit of the scanty brushwood huts and patchwork tents of the Levellers, the whole position was further covered and defended by a perfect jungle of bramble, whin, thorn, sloe, and hazel, through which paths had been opened in all directions to the best positions of defence.

Here and there, out on the opener country towards the east where the camp was not defended by the river and marshes, Austin could see that trenches

313

had been made and earthworks raised, with loopholes regularly constructed of wood and stone for the defenders to fire upon any assailant. The main camp itself was encircled with a fosse very wide and deep, but even from his elevated station on the side of the opposite hill Austin Tredennis could see nothing of the immediate defences of the position. Nevertheless, he marvelled greatly where Marion of the Isle had gotten her military skill.

A bugle sounded presently, not ill-blown, though the call was not one used by his Majesty's forces. And it was with considerable amusement that Austin, from his elevated post on the Hill of Crae, could see the Levellers moving in fair order over the open ground, their formation, however, being presently broken up as they reached the glacis and shelter trenches of their rude fortification.

But that there was good discipline among them of a rough and ready sort Austin could see. In his eagerness to make out more he would have approached nearer, but the mistress of Crae motioned him away, even taking his arm to pull him further up the hill.

'They are no chancy!' she said, earnestly. 'There are some that wad as soon put a shot intil a man as a knife in a sheep's throat. It's sair—sair on decent folk that pay rent honestly to a guid laird to be harried and harassed wi' a pack o' scoundrels, the gather-up o' a' the riff-raff i' the countryside!'

But the sound of the bugle in his ears, and the knowledge that a certain blue cloak was within a clear mile of him, prevented Austin from paying that undivided attention to the nowt and wethers, the ewes and lambs of Mistress MacCormick's flocks and herds which that lady considered their due. Nevertheless, she brought him back to the house of Crae, and liberated her husband from his ignominious position in the milk-house, with the comfortable conviction that she had paved the way to several excellent bargains when the 'Muckle Englishman' should be upon his return from Ireland.

Then, after a comfortable muirland dinner of

'braxie' ham and such bits of meat as had been boiled in the broth, Austin prepared to set out. He had given his entertainers to understand that it was his intention to proceed farther up the strath of Ken. And his host, making secret and anxious signals to Austin to support him, observed to his wife that he should show the stranger a road by which he could avoid the armed bands of the Levellers, but his wife promptly forbade.

'Na, na, Anton,' she said; 'brawly do I ken ye, my auld man. A' that ye want is juist to hae a chance at the public-hoose up by at the Newtown o' Gallowa'! But that ye are nane gaun to get! Sit ye doon on your decent hinder-end, guidman, and read Naphthali, or the Sufferings o' the Saints, or, by my certes, back ye gang into the milk-house again!'

It thus happened that after a brief convoy from the goodwife of the Crae, and a farewell which almost verged upon the tender, Austin Tredennis was left to his resources on the brow of the hill overlooking the tangled depths of the Hollan Isle. Twilight was yet a good hour off, so there was plenty of time for thought before it would be safe to take any steps in the direction of the camp in the Duchrae Wood.

Mistress MacCormick's last gift had been a handsome mutton ham which Austin had admired that morning, when she took it down from the 'baulks' to cut a 'whang' for breakfast. She also bestowed on him on unopened bottle of Hollands. Consequently he was somewhat at a loss to know how to acknowledge in kind this exceeding courtesy, as his plain equipage of travel was not of the sort to please a lady. But remembering a mother-of-pearl snuff-box which he had long carried for his friends' use, he presented it to Mistress MacCormick with a low bow, at the same time apologizing for its lack of value.

'Certes!' cried Mistress MacCormick, almost pouncing upon it in her eagerness, 'gin ye gie me the precious rappee that's in it, that will be payment mair than sufficient for ony little I hae dune. But the braw, braw boxie, na, na, keep it for a younger an' bonnier lass, and yin no taigled wi' an auld dune man, that

may yet hoast and hirple on for a score o' years yet—
Guid kens hoo lang, mair's the peety!'

However, upon Austin gallantly affirming that
the snuffbox could not have a fairer or in any respect
more eligible owner, and insisting on the lady
retaining both box and contents, her objections were
overruled. So, in the hood of his cloak of frieze, the
disguised soldier carried away, as in a saddle-bag, not
only the mutton ham and the square-faced green
bottle, but also a dozen stout scones newly baked for
his especial behoof, and as many smaller articles of
diet as he could be induced to accept for his arduous
journey into the wilds of Kells. It was, indeed, well in
some respects, considering the weight of his pack,
that his journey was destined to be a shorter one.

The more Austin turned over the subject in his
mind, the more determined he became that he would
not permit himself to be braved and thwarted by a girl
like Marion. He had allowed her to depart
unquestioned from the prison of Kirkcudbright
because he thought she would go home and abide
quiet in her father's house as was, indeed, her duty.
But here was she back again in the ranks of the
Levellers, and, according to report, in the company of
men who were little better than thieves and reivers.

It did not, however, occur to him that he, Austin
Tredennis, was not his brother's keeper, far less that
of an adult member of the opposite sex in no way
related to him—a girl, too, not of his degree, tainted
with rebellion, and mixed up with all sorts of doings,
not to be condoned, much less approved, by an officer
of the King's regular army.

But Tredennis was far too logical to be at any
time without a reason. He had, indeed, twenty
explanations of his feelings and actions, each more
complete and convincing than the last. Beyond all
doubt he was surely treading the obvious path of duty
in thus endeavouring to obtain such information as
would put a stop to this foolish and fratricidal little
war. If he could remove the leader from the affair, the
rebellion, such as it was, would collapse. It was
ridiculous, at any rate, that a woman should be

mixed up with the affair. Suppose his Majesty's troops should be ordered to take the camp, how would it appear if a woman were among the killed and wounded? His Majesty's cavalry did not make war on women.

Nevertheless, it did not occur to the young man that he was in love. In his own view, he had no selfish motives whatever. He would carry off Marion in order to give her up to her parents, or in some other way prevent her from having more to do with this foolishness. On such occasions there are wont to be whole Golcondas of unselfish devotion to duty in young men's hearts.

It did not strike Austin as ludicrous that though he had been credibly informed that a maiden by the name of Joyce Faa was also present in the camp of the rebels, he made absolutely no plans for her behoof. Joyce Faa might take her chance. Captain Tredennis's charity began and ended with Marion of the Isle.

When the twilight was sufficiently advanced to render his progress down the hillside safe from any observation from the opposite bank, Austin Tredennis slowly made his way towards the fords of the Black Water. It was not his intention, indeed, to cross directly into the camp, or to make any decided move till mature observation had shown him the best way and time of action. He knew that on all the rugged hills behind their main position the Levellers would have outposts, but he judged that, their water front being protected by the deep and impassable Lane of Grenoch, it would be more slightly guarded.

It was his plan, therefore, to begin operations by getting upon the little wooded triangle of island, opposite the camp, called Hollan Isle. This place was perfectly suited to his twin purposes of concealment and observation, being surrounded on both sides by the deep Lane, which bifurcates almost immediately in front of the camp, and on the other side is closed in by the Black Water of Dee itself.

Austin had observed this woody fastness in the morning. It promised abundance of cover of all kinds.

It was immediately in front of the enemy's main position, within earshot almost, yet perfectly safe. For the black lily-pools were here at their widest and deepest, and, swimming being an unknown art among the farm folk of Galloway, it was unlikely that he would be discovered or disturbed.

Following the branch of the Lane farthest from the camp, Tredennis came before long to the Black Water, which runs here in a rapid, shallowish, brawling course. This he crossed without difficulty, the water not coming to the top of his military boots. But it was a different matter when, a few hundred yards lower down, he had to re-cross again to the Hollan Isle. This time he had perforce to take off his boots and stockings, and in a brief and airy costume to make his way over into the recesses of the isle. During the transit he had cause to remember that the month was October.

Very cautiously he made his way through the dense undergrowth to the edge of the water opposite the camp. He could hear the cheerful voices of the Levellers, and, as the darkness grew deeper, discern in the sky the reflection of their evening cooking-fires.

Tredennis dried himself as well as he could, and put on his boots and leggings. Then in order to guard against possible chill, he took a short pull at the bottle of Hollands for which he had paid with politeness and the mother-of-pearl snuff-box. Though the night was cold, he felt not altogether uncomfortable. For Austin Tredennis, being an old campaigner, knew well how to attend to the prov-end as well as how to make the best of any situation, however unpromising.

He made it, therefore, his first care to seek out and arrange a place where he might pass the night with some degree of comfort. Of course, the making of a fire was out of the question on any part of the Isle. He was much too near the camp of the enemy (which was yet not the camp of his enemy). But broom and furze abounded on the Hollan Isle, as well as heather so long and tangled that he waded in it to the waist like a bather in the sea. The long drought of summer and early autumn had made the ground (which is here sometimes moist) dry as a bone, and Austin had no difficulty in selecting a spot near the centre of the island, sheltered from every wind, under a dry, gravelly bank, and with whin and broom rising on every side like a green fortalice. He pulled sufficient heather from different places to form a couch light and elastic. Then, carefully marking the spot by observing the forms of the trees against the sky, he glided away towards the nearest point from which he could obtain a view of the camp of the Levellers.

His curiosity was strongly excited and it was with a beating hearty more like that of a recruit than that of so old an adventurer, that he parted the last bushes with a slow and careful hand, and gazed across at the camp on the opposite shore.

The eminence on which the main defences had been erected rose high above his head and he could only look up the steep slope and observe that it had been carefully levelled to form a glacis, and furnished with earthen bastions at the comer to provide stances for cross-fire in case of direct assault.

Down on a little, smooth piece of meadow within the outer lines, yet convenient to the water-edge, several great fires were burning. Sometimes Austin could feel the warmth of the blaze as great quantities of fresh brushwood were continually thrown on. It was, after all, a kind of play to many of these lads, and scores of them laboured incessantly, joking and laughing as they did so, at bringing dried wood, branches, heather roots, and other light fuel to add to the flames—oftentimes even embarrassing the cooks by their endeavours, and in one case actually setting fire to the tripod upon which the evening stew-pot was swinging.

More than once, so strong was the light that Austin involuntarily drew back into the deeper shade, fearful that his presence so near at hand might be accidentally revealed. But really he was in no danger, for since from a lighted room one cannot see out into the dark, so those within the circle of the camp-fires could see only the dim blur of blackness which represented the isle of Austin's observatory.

Upon a felled tree which formed part of the defences on the land side a group of older men were seated, talking soberly together, evidently discussing plans and, in the intervals of speech, cleaning such arms as they possessed.

Tredennis was astonished to see how many of excellent pieces there were in the hands of the Levellers. He did not know that the folk of Scotland, like the Spaniards, are an armed people, security having only of late come into these southern straths. In addition to the guns, there were smugglers' jocktelegs, now made longer than had been intended by the original Jacques de Liege, whose name was still stamped on the blades. Every man possessed one of these. Some wore also whingers, or short swords like cutlasses, and pistols of all kinds were common, from the miniature article made to swing at a horseman's wrist so as not to interfere with his reins or break his sword-stroke in a charge, up to the mighty horse-pistol with its bell mouth and a charge of powder like a blunderbuss. He noted, also, the pitchforks and Irish pikes affected by a few of the Wigtonshire men, while as an additional weapon of offence many of the lads had mounted the prongs of a pitchfork upon the muzzles of their guns, in such a way as not to interfere with the firing of the piece, forming a rude but highly effective sort of bayonet.

Presently there came again the bugle signal from the Levellers' headquarters upon the summit of the main camp, and therefore out of sight of Tredennis. At the sound there ensued a great running to and fro, and crying of names and numbers, all which diverted him exceedingly. Then, in a trice, and with an alacrity which the old soldier could not but admire, the men fell into messes of about ten, and rations were served out.

A hot word or two was bandied occasionally among the younger men, evidently having relation to charges of unfair division, which could hardly fail to occur when so large a portion of the provender consisted of the rabbits which abound all about the

Duchrae Bank and scurry and patter within the limits of the camp itself.

Presently, however, Austin saw a sight which thrilled him, and he started forward automatically, forgetting alike the danger of his position and the deep, still Lane which separated him from the camp in the Duchrae Wood.

As the men were finishing their portion of food a tall figure, closely wrapped in a dark cloak, came down from the main camp and moved with youthful alertness of gait from group to group. He knew that cloak. His hard-won, belated pay had settled the score for it. He knew the figure also. It was his sometime prisoner of Maclellan's Wark. His lover's instinct had not played him false. She was there, her life every day in danger, the girl whom for a moment he had held weeping in his arms. It did not seem possible now; but so it was, and so, Tredennis told himself, with a certain dour, masculine pride, it would be again.

As the meal ended there ensued a solemn interlude. Grey-clad men, with blue bonnets, came pouring down the sides of the earthworks. They sprang like pixies out of the covering trenches. They appeared unexpectedly, like grave fairies out of the wood, and before Tredennis could make out what they intended, the whole force of the Levellers was gathered on the greensward before the camp-fires, and the notes of their solemn even-song were wafted far on the light wind. These were the words they sang:

'O God of Bethel, by whose hand Thy people still are fed, Who through this weary pilgrimage Hast all our fathers led.'

'Our Vows, our prayers we now present Before Thy throne of grace, God of our prayers, he the God of our succeeding race!'

And, all unconsciously, Austin uncovered also, standing up reverently behind the shelter of a thick-leaved hazel, while these poor, unlearned, often misguided men sang their evening song of praise to the God of Battles, to whom once more they committed their griefs and wrongs and injuries.

CHAPTER FORTY FIVE
THE OLDEST WAY OF WOOING IN THE WORLD

Accustomed to the watches of the camp and the wakefulness which becomes second nature to a man much employed upon dangerous services, Austin Tredennis often left his lair among the gorse and heather to steal down to the water-side, in order to see what he could of the order and discipline maintained during the night in the camp of the Levellers.

He had managed to construct for himself, of somewhat impromising materials, a not altogether uncomfortable nest, and by dint of turning round two or three times, like a couching dog, so as to mix the ingredients well together, Tredennis snatched enough sleep to satisfy a frame well indurated to war's alarms and a mind which habitually worked best in the midst of dangers. A pretty girl who, after showing the bravery of a Paladin, suddenly dissolved into tears, might, indeed, upset the mind of this captain of horse; but to lie all night within a few hundred yards of an enemy who would undoubtedly shoot him at sight, to wrap himself in a frieze cloak, and couch among heather and bracken for all covering upon an October night, arrived to Tredennis merely as part of the day's work.

The Levellers watch was well kept, and more than once Tredennis saw the tall, slim figure in the blue military cloak passing from post to post, as if to be assured of the sentry's watchfulness. And it was with curiously mingled feelings that Austin remembered that the device on the silver tache was that of Ligonier's Horse. Once the watcher thought that he was certainly discovered. The sentinel who had the beat immediately along the opposite bank of the Lane halted directly opposite the place of his concealment. It chanced that Austin had laid himself out at full length upon the trunk of a willow, which was inclined almost at right angles over the pool. He had been hoping to see the figure in the cloak again pass by, and perhaps the dying firelight glisten on the

322

clasp of silver. Late at night and alone, men watch long for such things as these, or, when they cannot see them, they think upon them.

The sentry passed on his beat directly opposite to Tredennis, and within fifty yards of where he lay prone on his gnarled willow-trunk. He stood so long motionless that Austin slid his hand back to grasp the hilt of his ready pistol; but the next sentinel reaching the extremity of the beat, and after a turn or two observing his comrade still intent upon something, cried to him, 'Rab, do ye see onything?'

'Ay,' said the stolid Leveller, shouldering his piece and resuming his march, 'I saw a trout loup.'

Morning came chill and grey about six of the clock, and it was with a start of surprise that Austin found himself awakened by a strange bugle-call. He felt for a moment an instinct to spring to his feet and give the alarm. He could have sworn that he was once more in the Low Country wars, and that the enemy was attacking the sleeping camp. But his eyes rested on the green gorse bush out of which he had hollowed a nest, and upon an ancient thorn-tree, now turning russet and covering itself with scarlet berries. A sparrow and a chaffinch were quarrelling over their breakfast of haws, and as Austin raised his head a squirrel ran down to the fork of a branch and chattered angrily at the intruder.

And again the bugle-call sounded from the brow of the Duchrae Bank.

In a moment Austin was on his feet and stealing with tenfold care through the underbrush. Upon the margin of the water he opened the reeds carefully with his hand and peered across.

Parties of Levellers—mostly of the younger and more reckless sort—were pouring into the camp, some driving cattle and sheep before them, others with pigs and poultry secured in various ways about their persons. A porker with a curly tail escaped and ran squealing across the camp, bounding through a recently lighted fire, scattering the dried twigs, and squealing out all the while its objection to die a violent death. Austin, from his lair among the reeds, could hear the loud boastings of some of the members of these expeditions, how this one had accounted for so many roods of Colonel Gunter's new stone wall, how that other had uprooted a plantation of young firs that had been planted upon his father's croft, and how yet another had driven off a dozen cattle belonging to an ardent 'Encloser.'

It was obvious that the Levellers, in spite of their morning and evening song of praise, had a truly Old Testament conception that the Egyptians were given them to be spoiled, and that war ought still to be conducted upon the ancient principle of living as much as possible at the enemy's expense.

The sight of all this preparation for eating reminded Tredennis that he had not partaken of anything since he left the hospitable house of Crae and his friend Mistress Jacobina MacCormick. Marion did not again show herself, and so, after waiting twenty minutes, Austin withdrew himself noiselessly through the reeds and brushwood till he had reached his night's shelter, where in the lee of a bieldy hazel he cut and ate alternate slices of wheaten loaf and mutton ham.

Water is never scarce on the Hollan Isle at any season of the year. A score of ripe hazel-nuts also made no contemptible dessert. Indeed, the name means the Island of Hazel Bushes, and the fame of the Hollan Isle as a Golconda of nuts is great in all the countryside, and it was, indeed, Austin's chief danger that half a dozen Levellers, having nothing better to do, might adventure over to the island in search of a bagful to crack by the camp-fires in the evening.

As against this, however, Austin could see that hazel bushes grew in abundance all about the camp. Indeed, the men went about cracking nuts as they marched hither and thither on their errands. The sentinels cracked as they stood by the river-bank, and threw the shells into the water, and even Marion, musing apart from the hurrying throng of hinds and shepherd lads, put up her fingers and pulled a cluster abstractedly, like one deeply immersed in thought.

The bands of raiders who went forth from the camp were composed mostly of the younger and more active men, but these were in charge of officers elected by themselves, mostly sedate and soldierlike men, who had seen service in Morton's or the Cameronian regiment.

And all the while there ran in Austin Tredennis's heart a stream of anger, hot as lava and fierce as a stormy sea. The feeling for law, order, obedience, was strong within him. He had never thought much about the relations of men and women in the abstract, contenting himself with a simple soldierly solution of such concrete problems of sex as chance brought in his way. To be faithful in dealings, to comfort one's self honourably in all things, to speak the whole truth to a man, and as much as possible of it to a woman; these were his simple, but in the main not incompetent, standards.

But that the woman was created to obey the man was really, in the inmost recesses of Austin Tredennis's heart, a fundamental dogma. And that a girl should flout and disregard his will, a girl for whom he had risked so much, stung him inexpressibly.

For myself, I have found everything quite otherwise. The masculine standpoint is one I take with difficulty. I can understand women (I may say, without self-gratulation) like one of themselves. But no woman has ever loved me, because I have set out to master her, and succeeded in doing so.

There are several reasons why women love men, and, thank God, I have no reason to complain. But Austin Tredennis's simple code admitted only of one. So he set himself to master Marion, as a man might bite on his nether lip and promise himself either to break in a restive, high-spirited colt or to break his own neck.

But Tredennis made the mistake of showing his hand too soon. The girl divined and resented his too obvious intent. Pride and self-will rose insurgent in her breast, and the affair resolved itself into a battle for the mastery.

The curious thing was that this temper of obstinacy, this rivalry of determinations goes on quite distinct from the operations of the heart. I am not exactly informed what was the state of the affections of either Marion or Tredennis at this period, but I am quite sure that their external attitude to each other had nothing to do with that inward feeling.

Just as last year, when I was in France, that great kingdom was engaged in foreign war over-seas with half the world, yet within her own bounds everything was quiet as an English rural parish. Dreamy oxen swayed and tinkled through the streets; labourers joyously brought in the vintage; maidens went singing to the well. All the heart of the country was sound and quiet and at peace, while from over-seas came nought but wars and rumors of wars.

This, when you come to think of it, was much the estate of Marion and Tredennis as they fronted one another across the narrow, deep lily-pools of the Grenoch Lane.

The afternoon wore swiftly away, and Tredennis had not again moved. He lay with his head settled low among the reeds, tirelessly watching the camp, and calculating what were his chances of being able to carry off Marion from the midst of her Leveller army.

It was a wild scheme. He did not deny this, even to himself. But he had the limitless confidence of the man who succeeds. And very grimly was the mouth shut—all mustacheless now—as he registered the mental oath that the woman did not live who could afford to flout him, Captain Austin Tredennis, of Ligonier's Horse. If Marion would go with him, good. If not, also good. He would take her yes, like a sack of corn across his shoulders, if in no other way. He would have her, with her will or against it—all one now, when it had come to this.

And after a while (here the smile was pleasanter) after a while she would like it. She would be glad, this without a shade of coxcombry, for of that there was not a trace in the man's nature.

This Austin Tredennis was the true savage, the man with original instincts but little overlaid, and that overlaying mostly worn off by the rough straits of many campaigns, so that not only did the method of obtaining a wife by capture seem a perfectly natural one to him, but also he expected the lady to like it!

It was in this mood—simple and elemental in itself, but owing to our polite education and conventions requiring considerable explanation, that Tredennis made his preparations upon the Hollan Isle.

He noted that at one point of the defences, which Marion visited every few hours, the distance between the posts was much greater than elsewhere. This was owing to the fact that the enemy's main advance was expected from the south, and also because the northern side of the camp was protected both by the Hollan Isle and by the swamps which reached across to where the old Raiders' Brig spans the Black Water of Dee.

Austin Tredennis resolved to make the attempt when the posts were set for the night, after supper and the singing of the Psalm—that is, supposing that the routine should be the same as before.

Bodily, Tredennis was a very strong man. His father had been a famous wrestler, and he himself had laid many grown men on their backs while still a boy at school. It was, therefore, with a determined squaring of massive shoulders that he prepared to make his attempt. He would compel the girl to leave this rabble. She should accompany him, gagged if necessary, to the nearest farm where he could obtain horses, and from thence to Kirkcudbright. He was resolved to go all lengths; to carry off the girl by brute strength if necessary, to shoot any man who stood in his way, to steal any man's horses, and in general to risk all penalties of the law and all vengeances of enemies, but, as a result, to remove Marion out of the rebel camp, or to leave his bones to bleach on the Duchrae Bank.

That was Austin Tredennis's way when in love, and a very good way it is. Only every man is not an Austin Tredennis, and even for him, but stay, the historian must not anticipate.

At that higher portion of the Leveller's camp most remote from the greensward in front of the Hollan Isle where the fires were earliest lit and the dinners mostly cooked, a small shelter of hewn boards had been erected. Here, almost at any time during the day which Tredennis spent on the Isle, two persons might have been seen in consultation, seated on stools at the door of the hut, or standing with elbows resting amicably on the trunk of the same tree. It was Marion of the Isle talking to her friend Silver Sand. Within the shelter sat a second girl busily plying needle or knitting-pins, a maid whose thoughts seemed very far away indeed from the low-toned conversation of her companions without.

'I have told you from the first, Marion,' Silver Sand was saying, 'that it will come to nothing! It is bound to come to nothing. You cannot thus put back the wheels of time. All the old landmarks will be broken down. All the ancient standards ended; gypsies and gypsy Earls of Little Egypt, cottiers' bit gardens, and the wide, free hills where any man's feet may tread, and any man's beasts may graze! 'Tis done with, Marion, that old world, and you and I may just make up our minds to submit with what of grace we can muster It depends not on our say-yea or say-nay! It is the will of God!'

'The will of the lairds, more like!' cried Marion, bitterly. 'But they shall not! No, they shall not, while I can keep these brave lads together.'

'That is just it, though' said Silver Sand. 'Ye are a clever lass, Marion. During seventy years of earth I never yet saw your like. But hark ye! Ye may drive off a company or two of the King's redcoats; ye may plunder the lairds and weary the tenants. But there is one thing ye cannot contend with—the winter weather that will soon be upon the land.'

'We are prepared to suffer hardships,' said Marion firmly.

'Doubtless, doubtless!' returned Silver Sand;

'you and some few, most part of them outed cotters, and (here, he smiled knowingly) an odd rascal or two who are here for what he can pick up. Ye will keep them; but the rest —ah! they will melt away like snow off a dyke in the front of May.'

'They are brave lads,' said Marion, with an affectionate glance down the hill, 'and I will not believe it of them.'

'Then,' continued Silver Sand, 'there is another thing. When I left Kirkcudbright they were speaking of releasing Harry Polwart. He may be here at the Duchrae Bank any day. Have you thought what that will mean?'

'Why, that if he gets his way, he will marry Joyce,' said Marion, turning half round as if to include the girl in the conversation. Silver Sand smiled indulgently.

'Marion,' he answered, 'though you have worn the trews, ye think as a woman still. It will indeed be an ill day when (if ever) Harry Polwart marries Joyce Faa. But it will be a worse for the Levellers of Galloway when he sets foot among them in the Duchrae Wood!'

'And why?' queried Marion, hard to be convinced. 'It was to Harry Polwart I first owed my position here. He it was who vouched for me to the Levellers in their council in the Caldron of Ben Tudor.'

'Ay, because he knew that he would never be accepted as a leader himself; therefore he hoped to rule through you. But now—I have seen him since his blindness and imprisonment. His speech is all of blood and revenge. Either you must join with him or he will carry away from you all the more vehement spirits, and leave you only the men who are willing to come to terms with the authorities.'

'We shall see! We shall see' said Marion, biting her nether lip, 'whether these lads will follow Harry Polwart or me!'

Silver Sand smiled, and looked with undisguised admiration at the girl's beautiful head thrown haughtily back, her finely cut nostrils dilated by the anger which sparkled in her eye and quivered in her voice.

'On the face of it, indeed,' he said, 'the choice is easily made. If I were a young man—as I am an old—it would not have taken me long to decide. But remember that Harry Polwart has a tongue like devouring fire. He will stick at nothing. Robbery is his trade, murder his pastime. Before he comes among you to sow disorder, I advise you to get the better-disposed of your followers to agree to a compromise. Stop this useless pulling down of boundary walls, this rooting up of young plantations. The lairds are sick-hearted with your present success, though it be only for a time. My friend Mr. Patrick Heron will conduct negotiations on the best footing. He tells me that this Captain Tredennis, who at present has the ear of the commander-in-chief, is an honest man and no partisan.'

'With him I will have no dealings, direct or indirect!' exclaimed Marion, mighty stiffly.

(And it was at this moment that Austin Tredennis was crossing the Black Water on his way to the position he had chosen for himself.)

Silver Sand glanced keenly at the girl as she spoke.

'You know this man?' he asked, softly, with a certain silken intonation which was a danger signal to those who knew him best.

'It was he who captured me at Minnigaff, and thrust me into the prison of Maclellan's Wark, at Kirkcudbright.'

'I do not see,' said Silver Sand, mildly, 'how in the face of the accusations made against you he could well have done less. Remember, a soldier has his notions of duty very clearly defined.'

'Those of Captain Tredennis are certainly peculiar,' commented Marion, acidly.

Noting the tone, Silver Sand thought he understood. Yet for once that old diplomat was wrong. His idea was that the captain of horse had been upon occasion somewhat overgallant in respect of Joyce Faa, his other prisoner, and that Marion, in spite of her military attire, had chosen to be jealous. His premises, therefore, were entirely wrong; but the conclusion he drew was irreproachable, and in its outcome equally fatal to the plans of the officer in question.

'You have a crow to pick with this Captain Tredennis, then?' said Silver Sand, bending towards Marion and lowering his voice.

'The crow is part plucked, but there are a few feathers yet remaining,' said Marion, smiling.

'Then,' said Silver Sand, 'I have something to say which may be of interest to you.'

And he bent down and whispered for some minutes in her ear.

At first the commander of the Levellers listened a trifle listlessly; but presently vivid colour flooded to her face, her breath came fast, and her fingers twitched nervously and pulled at the braid on the blue military cloak.

'Where?' she asked, almost under her breath. And, when Silver Sand had answered her, 'Very well!' she said, and, turning on her heel, she walked abruptly away.

Which is why Captain Austin Tredennis, alias Mr. Job Brown, cattle-dealer and spy, fording the water to reach the clump of willows where he had resolved to make his attempt to carry off the leader of the rebels, walked right into the arms of half a dozen stalwart Levellers, and, after a most valiant resistance, found himself overpowered by numbers, and was presently transported, helpless and blindfolded, into the presence of Captain Dick of the Isle.

CHAPTER FORTY SEVEN
A NOISE IN THE CAMP

It was a curious and unique situation for Marion and Tredennis, but they both faced it with that piqued doumess of temper which was at once their bond of similarity and the spur of their clinched antagonism.

'Remove the napkin!' commanded Marion. 'Loose the bonds about his legs that the man may stand on his feet.'

And there, in front of a lighted camp-fire Austin Tredennis, in his drover's habit, found himself face to face with the late prisoner of Maclellan's Wark. He had expected to meet her in another fashion, but the heart within him was stout and undaunted. And as he looked over the slender figure, the small head, the clear-cut spare outlines, he remarked to himself with satisfaction, 'I could have carried her!' It was not his plan that had broken down, but the unforeseeable that had happened.

Then after a moment he added, half aloud this time, 'And I will yet!'

Marion had removed her military cloak of blue, and stood erect in her plain boy's blouse and the kilted skirt and boots, which met half-way to the knee. She wore no slightest attempt at adornment. Her hair, worn short as a youth's, curled naturally from under her blue bonnet. She held a hazel switch lightly in her hand.

They were alone, for Marion had bidden Austin's captors to stand back. Silver Sand was nowhere to be seen. He had vanished completely after launching his whisper in the girl's ear.

'So, captain!' she said, scorn in her eyes and voice, 'your interest in the poor Levellers has induced you to visit them, and me?'

Austin Tredennis bowed, but said nothing.

'I suppose you will admit that you are here as a spy?' she said.

'I do not deny it,' said the young man, calmly.

'And you know the treatment that spies have to expect when caught in disguise?' she continued. And then in a moment blushed crimson, for she saw how she had laid herself open to the crushing retort—that he knew well how a certain person caught in disguise had been treated in the prison of Maclellan's Wark. But his actual reply astonished her.

'If I were in your place, and conducting this war on ladylike principles, I should have them shot, with popguns!' he said.

The flush faded, and left the girl pale with anger.

'He flouts me still!' she thought. 'He scorns to remind me of the obligations under which I lie to him for twice giving me the opportunity to escape from prison.'

And aloud she said: 'Strange that one so wise and powerful should yet be worsted by a girl, and that the troops he commands should thrice have turned tail rather than face a fire of popguns!'

'Not the troops I have the honour to command,' corrected Austin, with a bow.

'And such a brilliant scout!' continued Marion; 'so secret, so daring, so full of excellent devices and clever bargainings! But yet, the poor fellows with the popguns had one among them who could trace your whole course; yes, Captain Tredennis, from your first riding out of Kirkcudbright all the way to the inn of Clachanpluck, and from the kitchen of the farm up there on the hill to your lair on the Hollan Isle! I wonder that a veteran soldier should do his work no better. In shorty this paragon has turned out a bungler—and now where is he?'

'Where he wishes to be' said the soldier, succinctly, looking the girl straight in the face.

For the fraction of a second Marion caught her breath, and a pang traversed her heart. Tredennis remained silent, but keenly vigilant.

'You have nothing to remind me of, nothing to ask,' she said, at last.

'Nothing,' said the soldier. 'Do with me what you will. I shall be content. A log to sit down upon, a platter of the stew I smell simmering in your pots, and permission to roll a cigarette; perhaps you will grant me these while awaiting your gracious pleasure?'

And, without stopping to receive that permission, he coolly seated himself on the stump of a tree, and continued: 'Captain Marion, if your goodness of heart be equal to your beauty of face, order one of your men to halter me securely about the feet and loose my hands, so that I may roll me the little article in question, the art of which I learned from a Spanish friend in whose plight I am at present. You may even put me on parole not to attempt to escape. I do not break my word!'

The accent on the pronoun brought the red back to Marion's face.

'You mean that I break mine!' she said, fiercely. 'You insult me, sir!'

He shrugged his shoulders with a hopeless gesture.

'I suppose you cannot help it,' he said, gently, and as it were with considerable compassion. 'Women will make a personal application of everything, even when they rise to be captains of rebels.'

'I will not stay to argue with you!' she said. 'You shall remain in the camp tonight. I will have you safely guarded and in the morning I will let you know my pleasure!'

She moved away with no inconsiderable dignity, which Austin Tredennis from his tree-stump appeared to regard with a quiet but unfeigned amusement. When she was twenty yards away he called after her.

'Captain Dick!' he said aloud, as one soldier might address another of equal rank.

Marion turned round, thinking that he was about to ask a favour, perhaps that she would treat him as a certain young officer of Fencibles had been treated in Maclellan's Wark.

'Well,' she said, the tears almost in her eyes, ready to melt into kindness at a word.

'Do not forget about the cigarettes!' he said.

When she reached her wattled booth Marion fairly stamped her foot with anger, and snapped out such fierce monosyllables at Joyce, who asked her for news, that the poor girl, with her thoughts full of Harry Polwart and the fear of his coming, opened her great, dark eyes and sat silently wondering. Indeed, at this time Joyce was frequently silent, for during these days of suspense and waiting she was fighting the hardest part of her battle.

It is comparatively easy, as it seems to me, to will a great renunciation, a little more difficult to make it irrevocable, but hardest of all to fill in the dreary waste of days that follow inevitably—days of which every several hour is like an eternity, when the morning cry of the tortured heart is still, 'O God, would that it were evening!' and its evening petition, 'O God, that it were morning!'

But Joyce Faa had not much longer to wait when Marion came in, angry and baffled, from her first interview with the prisoner.

Marion had pulled off one of her top-boots, and was thoughtfully engaged in the unromantic occupation of greasing it to keep out the wet of the Duchrae Swamp and October dews when a noise to the northward of the camp attracted the attention of the two girls. Joyce stopped her knitting and listened. Marion palled on her boot again hastily, and, rising up, thrust a pistol into her belt.

'Has the attack come at last?' she thought, and was not sorry, for she, too, had grown a little nervous with waiting.

But the ear of Joyce was truer, and the fear in her heart led her to hear in the tumult that which was inaudible to Marion.

She stood with her hand pressed against her side, pale as ashes.

'He has come!' she said. 'They are crying aloud the name of 'Harry Polwart'! Aid me, Mother of God.'

It meant much to both the women, most immediately to Joyce, of course; but Marion had also reason to be anxious, remembering the warnings of Silver Sand.

Looking out, a scene of wildest and most turbulent rejoicing lay immediately beneath their eyes. The blind gypsy, mounted on the back of a plundered nag, was being brought into the camp with wild shoutings and the reek of multitudinous hasty torches. Strange and sinister he looked, his face unshorn, his matted locks hanging down to his shoulders, his feet bare and encased in great wooden stirrups half-filled with straw, above all, his blind eyes shining with strange, ruddy gleams in the reflection of the torchlight.

But his face turned every way as he came, as if his ear was listening for one voice that he did not hear. He called aloud, but for the first time or two the words were drowned in the jubilation of his followers. Then, seeing his lips moving and his hands imploring silence, they desisted suddenly, and the voice of the blind man was heard.

'Joyce Faa! Where is she? I want Joyce Faa!'

And Joyce, with her features ashen pale even under the red glow of the pine-root torches, moved forward to meet Tiim. She put her hand in his, saying, simply, 'I am here, Harry.'

Then there came a great and sudden illumination of joy upon the face of the stricken man.

'I knew it!' he cried. 'Joyce Faa speaks no lie! She promised, and she will perform—yes, even to Harry Polwart, the blind gypsy, she will not break her word!'

And Joyce, with her hand still in his, helped the man to dismount, as a servant may help a master. For that is the custom of the folk of Egypt, and, when she could speak, she said, gently, 'I will keep my promise.'

CHAPTER FORTY EIGHT
THE MINISTER OF BALMAGHIE

Then, while they gave him to eat, after Joyce Faa had washed his face like the face of an infant, Harry Polwart told them the story of his journeying.

'Three cruel days have I been on the road,' he said, 'and the first day and night I thought within me that I would never win through, but fall over some linn or precipice. I heard the river rush and roar beside me, and the wind sough among the trees. But the folk of Kirkcudbright and the parts adjoining are dogs and accursed!'

(And here he spat with vehemence upon the ground.)

'Though I was blind and hungry, and craved like one asking alms, none would lend me a hand or put me on my way. The very bairns (may fiends rive their throats!) set the dogs at me and threw stones as I passed by, crying, 'Go on, blind Egyptian! Go on, half-hanged man!'

'And I laid me down somewhere, and for an hour slept like the dead. Then, because the night was the same to me now as the day, I rose and stumbled on. Thrice I fell and bruised myself. Nay, Joyce, do not look! It is not good to look. But, by the dread God, I will have vengeance for all—ay, and more—many vengeances!

'A day and a night I found none to pity. But in the morning—I knew it was morning, because I felt the sun strike warm on my face and dry the dew on my bare breast, a lout at a farm loaning cried at me, giving me the name of a beast. And, with my face held down, I gat slowly near him, as if I stumbled stupidly upon my way. And I listened when he laughed loudest, so very hard I listened. He was a great oaf, eating at a piece of rye-bread and laughing as he ate. Then, when I knew by the smell of the stable that I was within striking distance of him, I drew my gully-knife and rushed upon him! The yell he gave, I declare, could have been heard at Kirkcudbright! And in his haste to run he let the loaf fall. In a moment I was on it, like a famished dog. Then, fearing that he might raise the country-folk with their pitchforks upon me, I ran for it up the road, keeping the sounding of the river ever on my left hand, for that was all the guide I had. For, by good luck, I was at the time upon a piece of pleasant turf, without rocks, green, and kindly to the feet.

'Then, as I sat by the side of a little burn, and dabbled my sore feet in the caller water, I ate of the yokels bread. It was good bread and sweet in a famished man's mouth.'

'And as I bode there, wishing for some one to pass by that I might rob or put a knife in, I heard the sound of a horse's feet, not cantering or trotting, but only going at a dainty siccar priest's pace, as the saying is.

'Good day to you, honest man,' said a voice. 'You are eating. Have you given God thanks?'

'Priest,' answered I, for I knew the lilt of these cattle, 'if there be a God of Thieves, then I have given God thanks. For I stole this loaf.'

'In saying this I thought to have him at an advantage, and if he had been one of the ordinary priests; faith, he might, in addition, have gotten my knife in his throat. For what with the stoning and the dogs, I own that I was scarce fit to be spoken to.

'Well, my friend,' says he, riding nearer, as I could hear by the horse's hooves on the turf, 'ye look as if you had need o' a sheaf of loaf-bread, however ye might come by it. But if you will come with me to the manse of Balmaghie, Mary Gordon, my wife, will give you a better loaf than that, without the fash and danger of stealing it.'

'Then I told him the tale of the yokel on the fence, whereat he laughed, and for the life of me I could not think what sort of priest or parson this might be.

'Why,' says he, 'your feet are sore, poor man. Mount ye up on Donald, my daidling pony here. He is a lazy beast, and needs somewhat to wake him up. As for me, I grow fat, and it will do me good to walk by the beast's side some part of the way to Glenlochar.

We will make Donald carry double at the crossing, I wot. And for the rest, I shall be glad o' company.'

'So, as it was to Balmaghie that I wanted to go, I thanked him kindly, and said no word, but mounted on the beast. And as he trudged by the pony's side he spoke to me of the weather and the crops, and then, at long and last, of the state of my soul's health. Of that I had no good to report, but at last I was as faithful as he, and told him no lies. Then he warned me of the fate of the ungodly, the wrath to come, and suchlike things, and I hearkened him without ever so muckle as laying my hand upon the hilt of my dirk. This is what it is to be in the company of a good man! 'Tis a pity! One is apt to waste opportunities for conscience sake!'

'Now we came to a place called the Rhone House, not far from Kelton Hill, where the great fair is, and were riding caigily along when all at once there comes a cavalcade of riders down the brae.

'Good-day, dominie,' cries one. 'Ye are in very pretty company this day. That man is a kenned thief, and was half-hanged besides. What think ye of that?'

'I think but little of it. Colonel Gunter,' says my friend, who was keen of tongue, as if it had been sharpened with scythe-sand. 'If thief he be why, my Master companied with publicans and sinners, and at the last they whole-hanged Him between two of them!'

'Your tongue is witty, minister,'said Gunter, 'but let me tell you, sir, he is an outlaw, and there are pains and penalties for entertaining such. Take care that you do not subject yourself to them.'

'I snap my fingers at you and your penalties,' says the minister, cracking them merrily at the word. 'Twenty year I have been an outlaw myself. For I was cast out by my brethren and familiar friends. You sent your soldiers to oust me at their bidding! You yourself. Colonel Gunter, came riding with the sheriff that braw August day ye may yet mind off. But did ye stir the outlaw? By the faith delivered to the saints, not by so much as an inch. John MacMillan was minister of Balmaghie then. He is minister of Balmaghie still, and sets whoso he will on his beast—

thief or sodjer, red-coat or black-coat, rag or tatter, saint or sinner, outlaw or inlaw, barbarian Scythian, bond or free! Awa' wi' ye! Take that word hame to the Erastian master that sent ye!'

'And with that he fairly turned on his heel, cried, 'Gee-up, Donald, lazy beast!' and so left them standing there in the middle of the road, without a word wherewith to answer him.

'Then as we went I told him the thing that had been in my heart; to fall upon him unawares with my dirk, and to steal his beast; but that after he had spoken so I could not for very shame. And he said, 'Poor man, poor man! Give thanks to the God that withheld your hand from the shedding of blood.'

'So I told him that I had lived long and served my master faithfully. But that now, being blind, I was in a manner handicapped and disabled for the outlaw's mode of life.

'Poor man, poor mam,' he says again; 'there is muckle to be said for you. And I would be the last man to deny that blood-letting is not very necessary upon occasion. A little lively persecution,' says he, would set the spur in the flanks of a wheen time-serving ministers that I ken o'!' Though what he meant by that I know not.

'And the short and the long of it is that I told him where I desired to journey, though not my purpose in doing so, and, says he, 'I cannot go with you today, for I have a burying over by at Camp Douglas, and this is the day of my week-day discourse upon that most comforting text in the Prophet Ezekiel, the thirtieth chapter and the fourteenth verse: 'I will make Pathros desolate and will set fire to Zion, and will execute judgments in No!' But I will send my brother with you. You shall ride on Donald here, and the morn's mornin' I will come to the camp in the Duchrae Wood. It is in my parish; therefore it is my bounden duty to rebuke the ungodly and call the sinners to repentance. And, by what I hear, they are in some need of the Gospel preached in the camp of the Levellers o' Galloway.'

While he was speaking Harry Polwart had held

Joyce's hand, and now he leaned across and whispered a word in her ear that made all her face suddenly flame.

'No, no,' she faltered; 'not so soon! I could not be ready—indeed I could not!'

'You were ready once before, Joyce,' said Polwart, 'in your old gown and kirtle, the last that I saw or shall ever see you wearing! What need have you now of more preparation than in the garden of the Manse of Minnigaff?'

But before she had time to reply one of the younger men, perhaps desirous to be officious, told how they had taken a spy on the outskirts of the camp—a soldier, most likely an officer. In an instant there passed a most terrible and terrifying change over the countenance of Harry Polwart. While he had been telling the tale of his escape his expression had softened as he spoke of the minister's kindness, but now all that was in an instant smitten away. His face became like to the cruel countenance of a fiend in some antique print, like those my father brought back with him from Germany. He swore a dreadful oath, which thrilled even the more hardened of his hearers, and caused Joyce to withdraw her hand with a quick thrill of apprehension.

'Let me see him!' he cried, forgetting for a moment his condition. 'If none of you dare touch him—I, Harry Polwart, with my own hand, will cut the liver out of the sneaking hound! Ah I if only it should prove to be the scoundrel who arrested me and caused us all this trouble! But that is too good to be hoped for.'

At this point Marion struck in.

'I would bid you remember,' she cried, 'that I command here, and have taken the case of this man into my own hands. I am Captain of the Levellers, by free election, and so long as I am in charge there shall be no divided authority here!'

The dark face of the gypsy took on a look of savage malevolence at this interference.

'Very well, captain,' he said, 'I will say no more of this in the mean time! But tonight I claim that your prisoner be well guarded, and that tomorrow he be brought before the Council of the Levellers, when I may have a word or two to say. If, as you say, you command, it was I who gave you your authority. And those who gave may also take away!'

'Possibly!' said Marion, peremptorily. 'But in the meanwhile, and while the authority is mine, be good enough to obey promptly! Go to the quarters provided for you with the men! Joyce shall remain here with me!'

And as he rose to retire the gypsy turned his bone-white eyes upon the two girls, and his shattered countenance smiled with a ghastly semblance of mirth.

'Good-night, ladies,' he said, with mock courtesy. 'Tomorrow, at this hour, by the help of the minister of Balmaghie, Joyce shall obey me—and, by the help of the Council of Levellers, so may you, my brave Dick of the Isle!'

I have kept myself out of the story for some time, conscious alike of the poverty of my equipments for the part of hero, and also to give my readers some rest from my predilection for making excuses concerning my conduct, of which they have already had more than enough in the course of this narrative.

On the last occasion I started out with some flourish of trumpets to perform a heroic action, which, however, resolved itself into riding to Kirkcudbright in order to watch another man do one. But now I come in earnest to my own share in the affair, which I shall endeavour to trace with precision, and yet, I trust, without prolixity.

And first, upon Joyce going away, I did a second wise action. The first of these I count that of telling her my love frankly and freely, the second that I took into my councils my father. I have mentioned him often, but never with that loving particularity which he deserves. For, first he hath told his own story in such a fashion that I, with my stiffer scholastic manner, may not hope to equal. All his life my father hath had his own strokes of humour, his own quiet tastes, his own particular method of letting other persons' business alone—this last my father's speciality, and a most admirable one, as I see it.

On the day that I took my last farewell of Joyce (as I thought) in the outer cave-chamber of the Aumry, and as soon as Davie Veitch had returned from ferrying over the maids Joyce and Marion, I betook me to Orraland. I found my father in his library, busy with his Latin, which he had retaught himself during these last years, in order, as he said, to take the taste of county business out of his mouth. He loved the historians especially, his favourite being Livy, who, as he said, gave you most for your money. And he wrote and printed a little fragment in the style of that admired author, descriptive of a conference upon roads and bridges, in which, in the finest Livian Latin, Colonel Gunter, my Lord Kirkham, with several

343

others, were taken off to the life. This trifle so pleased the late Principal Carstaires that he inquired for an additional copy to send to a very exalted person indeed, with whom he was on terms of intimacy.

And this, it is said, had no small effect in bringing about the making of my father a baronet, over the heads, as it were, of so many richer and more important people.

In the library of Orraland, therefore, I opened my mind to my father, and asked his advice.

His first words were these: 'Have you said aught of this to your mother?'

I told him no.

'Then do not,' he answered.

I did not venture to ask his reason for this prohibition, but took it to be that, as on the former occasion when she attempted to interfere on my behalf, the generous and daring nature of my dear mother was liable to lead her into difficulties even greater than those which she took it upon her to solve.

In person my father was a little beyond the middle height, his hair abundantly sprinkled with grey, when, as in his study, he was without his powdered wig. Humour lurked in his quiet grey eyes. Being brought constantly into comparison with my sprightly mother, he passed in most companies for rather a silent man. Advancing years had made him a little disinclined for exercise, and love of reading kept him perhaps too much in his library. But when he could be aroused to exertion no man was more active and, as the present occasion proved, more daring.

I spoke to him of Joyce, and he encouraged me to speak my mind freely, keeping up a running comment of kindly nods and elicitory questions.

'Educated abroad, was she? The mother of good family; yes, your own mother told me of these! Beautiful as the morn—well, your mother used other words, but I took the idea well enough!' (By which I understood that my mother had told him that she was somewhat disappointed in my poor Joyce's looks, as might well be the case, considering where and after what she had first set eyes on her.)

When I had told my father everything, down to my last interview with Joyce in the Aumry—though upon the details of that I did not condescend or particularize—he sat a long while silent, murmuring words and phrases to himself, as his way was when turning anything over in his mind.'

'Bless the boy—foolish lad—foolish lad! Hum—hum! Well, I pleased myself, why should not he? I have it— no, that will not do!'

Then he whistled a bar or two of 'The Cameronian Cat,' which, being a religious man and no Jacobite, I had never heard him do before. But in the midst he checked himself and looked across at me.

'I suppose you are set on this lass?' he said. 'You have considered all the difficulties of the situation?'

'I think I have, father,' I made answer. 'Indeed, most of these last come from my having considered too much, as Silver Sand will tell you. He said I had but a poor appearance, and that you in your young days would have done quite otherwise.'

'I do not doubt it—I do not at all doubt it!' quoth my father. 'I did a great many rash and foolish things when I was a young man.'

'Such as marrying my mother,' I suggested, jesting with him.

'No, Maxwell, no!' he said, more moved than I could have imagined. 'I never did a wiser thing than that. It was just the hypocrisy of old age which made me speak so just now. If I were twenty, and had it all to do over again —why, I should do just as I have done. God forgive us old men! We calmly propose physic and plasters for the cure of young bodies and souls, which we ourselves would have thrown to the dogs when we were their age. Marry the lass, if you can get her, say I! Your mother was a farmer's daughter—nay, more, she was Will Maxwell's sister— and where is there a lady in the county this day to compare with her?'

And my father looked so glad and so proud that

I could have taken him in my arms for it.

'And so may your Joyce, if she is all you say,' he went on, 'and of that I would not attempt to unconvince you if I could. The question is how to get her out of the hands of that rascal Polwart. 'Tis a devil's pity they could not hang him when they had him safe in Kirkcudbright gaol!'

Then he mused a little, again falling into the seductive drone of the 'Cameronian Cat.'

'Ah, Maxwell!' he said, presently, sighing a little, 'thirty years ago we would just have taken down a musket and sword, mounted a good grey mare, and—' Here he stopped suddenly.

'What, father?' I asked him.

'Well, I am an elder in the Kirk of Scotland, and it doth not become me to say what we might have done. But times change—yea, the very heavens over us, though not, as sayeth the Latin author, the mind of man. The rendering is not, I know, allowable, but the truth of the apothegm is indisputable.

'If we give this half-hanged fellow enough rope he will soon do the deed wholly,' he went on. 'The mischief is that we have not the time. You may desire to marry Hector Faa's daughter, but it were a different matter to wed Harry Polwart's widow.'

I did not wholly grant that, but very naturally my feelings were with him. We must prevent that consummation by every means within the power of man.

'I think,' he said at last, drumming on the table with his fingers, 'that before we decide anything you should allow me to put some part of this before Silver Sand. I have done few things in my life without consulting him, and these few I have generally regretted.'

I could do no other than agree, but I warned my father that I did not think Silver Sand had any good impression of me. But he only smiled, and answered, 'What Silver Sand seems to think, is very seldom what Silver Sand does think. You may depend upon it that if he used any harshness of look or speech to the lad he received into his arms an hour after he was born, and has cherished ever since as a son, he had the excellentest of reasons for his severity.'

Now this saying of my father's greatly surprised me. For though I bore his name, I never knew that Silver Sand had any particular regard for me. Indeed, since he had taught me how to fish with the angle, to shoot straight, and to ride a kicking beast, he had secured to take little further notice of me.

When my father came back from his interview with Silver Sand, with whose uncertain whereabouts he was generally acquainted, I could see at a glance, even before he dismounted from his horse at the lych-gate of Orraland, that he was wondrously heartened. And from whatsoever cause, from that very hour my father was as eager in the matter of Joyce Faa as I was myself—that is, considering that his interest in the matter was of a somewhat less personal sort.

It fell out by chance that my mother was gone to Craig Darroch with Grisel for a few days, thinking doubtless that, with the two maidens Marion and Joyce safe at the Aumry, it was not likely that aught of importance would take place. So that my father and I were left more liberty and freedom of preparation at Orraland and Isle Rathan than if my mother had been there. For, as by this time all may see, she ever loved to be the head and forefront, the fount and origin of all incoming and outgoing, equipage and provend.

The next morning my father took me to see Silver Sand. His ways had ever been a mystery to me—as, indeed, they were to most people. He would sit by the fire at Orraland habited as well as any gentleman, and good company for the best, as late as ever any would sit with him. But he did not sleep beneath our roof, nor yet in any of the office-houses. Since my father and mother removed to their new mansion he was hardly ever seen at Isle Rathan. Yet when we youngsters were all saying good-night, or after a talk with my father over a parting tass of eau-de vie Silver Sand would wrap his great shepherd's plaid about him in such a fashion as completely to hide the manner of man he was, and step out into the

347

empty fields, the driving rain, or biting sleet, for all the world like a gentleman going to his bedchamber.

This habit of his, though I had observed it from my earliest infancy, yet I had never grown accustomed to. And, to make the matter more mysterious, several times when at Craigdarroch with my Uncle Will, after partaking of the roisterous cheer of that establishment. Silver Sand would take down his plaid from the ceiling-bars above the kitchen fire, where it had been drying, wrap it about him, and let himself out serenely into the black night, no man regarding him, and none offering to accompany him.

As a child I had often pictured him in winter with feelings of peculiar content, as I lay in my little cot and heard the wind drive the snow hard against the window-panes. I would hug myself with a warm comfort, to think of him battling on and on through the storm, and then at his journey's end entering a palace of snow and ice, like a picture I had once seen in Mynheer Vanderspuye's Travels into Russia and Tariary, of which my father had a tall copy in the French language, with many delightful gravures done on copper.

It was, therefore, with exceeding pleasure that I gat me on my pony to accompany my father on his visit to Silver Sand in his own dwelling-place. For even when a young man's mind is full of his own love troubles, he does not object to a few little adventures by the way. Or at least so it was with me, though perhaps I am as little normal in this as in everything else.

My father wasted no time in speech, but mounted and rode furiously, as was his custom when on business, mostly for eagerness to be done therewith and to get back to his books but now, as I thought within me, with pure desire to serve me, his son. Ah, there were few fathers like mine!

I should like well to enter into the particularity of that ride, but suffice it to say that we clattered over the hard sand and shingle of the Orraland shore, went more slowly over the rugged foothills of Screel, and presently bore away to the east across the lairy

Kirkmirren flats. After a long, breathing gallop through lands covered with short sea-grass, and bloomed over even now by the stone crop and blue maritime holly, my father dismounted in a little wood, and tied his beast to a tree in a place very retired and secret.

'Let them bite their nose-bags for a little here, while we go forward,' he said. 'Our good Silver Sand does not love overly many horse-tracks about his abode.'

Then, having thus arranged matters with satisfaction to himself and the beasts, my father took along the first of the broken-down dykes (for we were now off his lands), and, making a detour to the right, emerged suddenly upon an old grey tower, apparently ruinous and wholly desolate. On three sides it was surrounded by hills, for the most part thickly wooded with natural scrub, but on the other, towards the east, the ground was more open. The tower looked upon a green valley, through which a little lane ran, or rather, as it were, loitered and lingered with a temperate gladness. Beyond that, again, a high hill rose up abruptly and sheltered the tower from the sea. There were the ruins of a considerable farm town near by; but all was now deserted—only in the midst was an ancient tower standing up, called, as my father now told me, the Bound Tower of Appleyard. I remembered that I had seen it on a boyish ramble many years ago, but that, being alone, I had taken to my heels and run home at some fancied noise which I heard—a sound as of a hollow knocking upon wood high up in the tower—the pixies making some one's coffin, as I then believed. So I ran home at full speed, lest the coffin should prove to be mine, and the little pechts should catch me and fit me into it forthwith.

My father and I went up to the outer door, a rude and apparently frail construction of boards nailed together, as it had been to keep out cattle, but yet resisting my utmost strength, and, as my father showed me afterwards, that of a dozen stronger than I.

After waiting awhile and seeing nothing moving

far or near, my father removed a square stone at the apex of a little arrow-slit, and a stout cord was revealed. This he pulled vigorously, and the door immediately swung back on large hinges. I saw then that it was strengthened with iron within, and that the rude railings outside had simply been added to deceive the eye of any curious traveller who might pass that way.

Then, having secured the door, in an uncanny kind of silence we clambered perilously upward. The stairs were in no very excellent repair and, of course by being shut within such narrow bounds, they twisted every few steps, so that I never saw more than my father's feet as he went upward with admirable agility.

At the top we came to another door, or, rather, our progress seemed to be blocked entirely. But on my father giving a peculiar knock with his foot a trapdoor opened overhead. Whereupon, setting his foot on a step at his right hand in a well-accustomed manner, he hoisted himself into a quaint little circular room, doubtless in part a legacy from that period of hiding and riding when there was scarcely a family in all Galloway, highland and lowland, unprovided with some such shelter.

But this mansion of Silver Sand's had been greatly improved by himself, and certainly, even in this crisis of my affairs, deserves a brief description, for I bestowed a somewhat close attention upon it.

As a swallow's nest is made in a chimney, so Silver Sand's chamber of shelter on the Solway shore was constructed in the topmost story of the ancient round tower of Appleyard. The roof was of wood, of recent construction, but strongly jointed and well pitched to keep out the winds and rains, both of which were wont to put some pith into their work up there.

After Silver Sand had taken me by the hand in token of amity, I had time to look about me. At one side was a little bricked fireplace, where on a fire of sticks Silver Sand did his simple culinary needs. A low bed set deep into the wall occupied the eastern wall, with a narrow window opening above. For Silver Sand, like a true son of the Orient, loved to turn his head in that direction when he slept, and, rising to look his first waking look towards the sunrise.

I need not detail the conversation which followed. In brief, the substance of my tale and my hopes were put before Silver Sand. I feared at first that he might make some allusion to my intolerable stupidity and tardy-footedness at the Shiel of the Dungeon. But, with his usual admirable courtesy Silver Sand spared me all reference to that most shameful episode. And for this I thanked him in my heart.

Now it was this interview which sent Silver Sand into the hill-country of Galloway, and brought him in good time to the farm-kitchen of the Upper Crae, and afterwards to the camp of the Levellers in the Duchrae Wood.

CHAPTER FIFTY

THE WIFE OF BOANERGES

Every day after our visit to the Round Tower of Appleyard, my father and I sent Davie Veitch to Kirkcudbright to bring us word if Harry Polwart were yet set at liberty. Each night he came back with the news that he was still detained on this pretext or that, remanded for examination, investigation, authentication. But at last the time came when he must be set free. No real reason for keeping him in prison had presented itself, and as the blind gypsy would speak no word, good or bad, he could not be condemned out of his own mouth.

At last one night in the final week of October word came to us at our House of Orraland that the devil was loose. Harry Polwart had been released that morning at ten o'clock, and, as we anticipated, he had at once turned his face northwards in the direction of the Levellers' camp. Davie had even seen him stoned out of the burgh gates by a score or two of the idle loons who hang about the port.

So that it behooved us to be brisk, and fortunate it was for us that my mother was so far from home as at her brother's house of Craigdarroch, or I doubt not she would either have tried to prevent our going at all, or, if worsted in that, she would have made no bones about accompanying us; I fear me to the utter undoing of our expedition.

But, as it was, we rode very quietly away, leaving Eppie in tears at the great gate of Orraland and Sammle tying his shoe-strings to hide his emotion down by the stables.

We were both well armed and equipped for the journey, and my father had filled his purse with good gold and silver, for, as he said, 'Some things are better paid for than fought for.'

By a curious chance it was to the Manse of Balmaghie that my father was now directing our steps, or, rather, the hoofs of our good beasts. I will not again risk being tedious by inserting any details of our journeyings. Suffice it that my father told me how he and John Macmillan had been good friends at the College of Edinburgh, where a certain young Pat Heron had had the good fortune to be of service to the raw lad from the moorland-farm town, and that on more than one occasion.

'And though,' said my father, meditatively, as he ambled along on his beast at a pace more befitting his feelings than mine, 'there are some things in his later proceedings that I cannot approve, I understand well the buckram-stiff righteousness that drove him to these devisive courses. And, by heavens, sir, if I had been in his place, and a man given to disturbing myself about kirk rights, covenanted heads, and so forth—I dare say I should have done pretty much as he has done. For John Macmillan was, indeed, very hardly served by his brethren. But mind you. Maxwell, do not for the life of you begin to argue with him. For a dourer, more opinionated limb of Geneva than this same John Macmillan of Balmaghie is not to be found through the length and breadth of Scotland.'

'And why, then,' I asked him, 'did they cast him out of the kirk?'

My father lifted up his hand with a kind of alarmed hopelessness.

'Before we enter into that question,' he cried, 'I think we had best see to the saving of your lass out o' the hawk's claws!'

The welcome that we met with from the minister of Balmaghie left nothing to be desired in the way of heartiness. The manse, which (though long deposed) he still occupied, was a little two-storied house of five rooms or so, cowering in a hollow surrounded by trees, while the kirk itself sat high upon a little hill above the Dee Water, looking pleasantly down the vale and out across the gentle flood like a benediction done in whitewash.

Yet, as I well knew, it had seen troublous days yea, and that very manse also in which we were so kindly received had stood its sieges, and played its part in the life-story of John Macmillan and Mary Gordon of Earlstoun, his noble and beautiful wife. For though the minister had gone forth (as has elsewhere been related of him, under the thin disguise of another name,' expecting never to return, yet his folk, ill-satisfied therewith, compelled him ere long to bring his young wife back to the manse of Balmaghie. There children were born to them, and from this small, white house in the bield of the Kirk Hill, the minister of Balmaghie, a true standard-bearer of the Blue Banner, rallied for the last time the folk of the covenant beneath the flag which had taken the breeze so gallantly at Drumclog and gone down in blood at weary Bothwell Brig.

But at that time I knew nothing of these things and cared less. For my father, though willing enough to tell us stories of the martyr days of Peden and Renwick, of Cameron, Cargill, and the hill-folk, yet showed clearly that there was something to be said for the government as well. And after he had done with his tale he would say: 'Now this is what happened; you can make up your minds for yourselves.'

But I do not know that either Grisel or I did make up our minds to anything, save perhaps that we wanted our father to tell us yet another tale, which, indeed he could do incomparably well.

We found Mary Gordon, the wife of John Macmillan and the daughter of the notable Sir Alexander Gordon— the Bull of Earlstoun, as he was called—to be a most gracious and beautiful lady, as, indeed, rumour had ever most truly reported of her.

But we found nothing of that pride in her lineage with which she hath been not unfrequently attainted. Certainly she did the modest honours of the manse of Balmaghie with such dignity that her manners would not have shamed a prince's palace. But I see nought out of place in that. For she was gracious to the beggar at the door and to my father— the laird of Orraland and Isle Rathan—ay, and not more so to the one than to the other, save only in this that Patrick Heron had been her husband's friend. But I am sure that if it had been the beggar who had done the kindness, she would have bidden him into the parlor and done to him even as to us.

'And what, Patrick,' cried the minister, heartsomely, 'brings you and your lad thus far from your cosey down-sitting and new-built mansion so late in the year?'

My father looked across to me for permission, and began to tell Mr. Macmillan of my imprisonment and all that had flowed from it. And seeing me blush and put my head upon my palm like a girl, the gracious woman, who had retired to the farther end of the apartment that the gentlemen might talk more freely, laid down her broidery and came and sat beside me. Nay, when my father spoke of Joyce Faa, of our love and her promise (gently shading away all blame from me, and showing me merely as a true lover in danger of losing his beloved), Mary Gordon bent over and kissed me gently and motherly on the brow, as one woman might kiss another for comfort in trouble,whispering, 'I understand. Do not be cast down. All will yet be well.'

And so have women done to me ever, when I was in any distress; all of them, that is, save one, but she only after I had made love to her as a man ought to do to the woman he adores.

But as my father told his tale a strange expression, a kind of expectant dread, stole over the features of the minister of Balmaghie, usually so kind in expression, and yet so eagerly belligerent. Presently he held up his hand to my father to stop.

'Patrick,' he said, 'I know something of this. God guide me aright into what I ought to do! Listen! Before you go further I must tell you what I know.'

And he told the tale, with me sitting there in the manse parlour, and with the hand of his wife lying on my wrist in a kind of caress—all the story of his going to Kirkcudbright upon his necessities, and of his meeting with the blind gypsy Harry Polwart.

'And the mischief of it is,' he cried, striking the palm of his hand upon his brow with an orator's gesture of despair, but quite natural to him, 'I have promised to marry the fellow to Joyce Faa tomorrow in the camp of the Levellers down there by the Duchrae Wood.'

For a long minute we simply stared at each other dumbly. I would have risen to my feet, but the pressure of Mary Gordon's hand on my arm held me gently in my place, as one who would say, 'Hush! let me regulate this matter!'

'But now, of course, you will not?' said his wife, looking over at the minister with a steady appeal in her dark eyes.

John Macmillan, as it seemed to me at the time, rather avoided his wife's regard, and it was my father to whom he replied.

'Patrick,' he said, 'there is nothing in the world I would not do for you—except break my word!'

'John,' interposed his wife, before my father had time to reply, 'I have often heard you break out upon the sort of person who is always ready to do everything in the world for his friends except the thing those friends happen to want.'

'Ah, Mary!' said the minister, looking at her more gently than one would have expected of so vehement and Boanergian a man, 'you do me an injustice. I said not that in this case I should refuse to help my friends to the limit of my powers. But let me think what these are.'

'Has the intention of marriage been proclaimed in the parish kirk in due form?' said my father, hoping, I think, to furnish him with an excuse.

'I fear me much that I cannot found upon that,' said Macmillan, a little ruefully. 'In my journeyings throughout Scotland it has been my custom to dispense with such proclamation among the scattered peoples to whom I have been called to minister.'

'But,' said his wife, 'surely this case is very different. The man is a malefactor, and you are delivering the girl, who, as we hear, loves another, to a life of shame and misery.'

'The objection might delay, but cannot prevent, the marriage so long as the woman declares herself to be willing,' said the minister.

He thought a little, knitting his brows and frowning upon the ground, as was his custom, while the rest of us sat silent and expectant, Mary Gordon's fingers pressing the back of my hand with a kind of unspoken but hopeful pity.

At last the minister voiced his resolve.

'This will do,' he said. 'Hitherto, I have heard but one story. Now I have also heard the other. I will accordingly make it my duty to go to the camp of the turbulent and there make further inquiry. Thereafter, according to the satisfaction of my conscience, I will act.'

'But not tomorrow? You will not do anything hastily?' said his wife, watching him narrowly.

'No,' he answered, after a pause, 'I think enough has been brought before me to render at least delay necessary.'

'And no other minister can be got? You are sure?' I cried the words out eagerly.

The stately woman looked at me with a kind of indulgent pity for my ignorance.

'None dare go near the rebel camp except my— except Mr. Macmillan,' she said.

'But, sir,' said my father, with obviously increased respect, 'you must consider. You place your life in danger. You have a wife and family!'

'Trouble not yourself about that matter,' said Macmillan. 'Not a hair of my head shall fall to the ground without my Father. And as to wife and family, sayeth it not in David, in a certain place, "I have been young and am now old, yet have I never seen the righteous forsaken nor his seed begging bread"?'

It was a wonder and a pleasure to me to see a man so clear upon his call and mission, that he could apply the words of Scripture to his own case with such sincerity and confidence.

Then, as he uttered these words, his wife rose from the chair where she had been sitting by me and went over beside her husband, by whom she continued to stand for the rest of the conference, her hand resting upon his shoulder. And I do not wonder. For, though I am a man that has had the good or bad fortune to have had most of his heroisms done for him, I can yet admire the naked article in another all the more for that.

After this the talk fell mostly on the dead state of religion in Scotland, of the indifference of ministers comfortable in their kirks, of professors at ease in Zion, with other pregnant matters which I scarcely cared to follow for the fear of the morrow lay heavy on my heart. I felt myself in the grasp of circumstance, and powerless to do anything. Tredennis in my shoes might have been in reality equally impotent; but then, at least he would have attempted to carry off his sweetheart upon his shoulders, as the Romans did the Sabine virgins or Samson the gates of Gaza. And till the very moment when his failure was apparent he would have been lifted above evil chance by the belief that he would succeed. But I, born with far less strength of body and power of will than he, yet saw the more clearly, and knew that we both imagined a vain thing. It was this instinct and overkeen perception which oftentimes took from me the power to act with vigour —whereby I lost not only the credit of being a man of forlorn hopes, but also that ninety-ninth chance by which the forlornest of hopes sometimes succeeds.

But to return. In a kind of daze I remember taking part in the function of family worship; also, with a curious clearness, that the tune was Coleshill, and that my father, in the effort to do his best, sang most villanously out of tune.

Then, as we were bidding good-night, I mind that the minister put his hand upon my father's shoulder.

'Patrick,' he said,' as a guest in my house and a friend of many years, I would pray the favour of a word with you as to the state of your soul.'

My father nodded, for he was ever a man that took the bitter with the sweet. And I saw the minister look at me also, but his wife shook her head. 'No,' I heard her say, 'not tonight, John.'

And for that courtesy of excuse I thanked her in my heart.

But, marvel of marvels, when my father came to bed, entering to find me sitting looking out at the tombstones in the graveyard, their flat table-tops glistening white in the moonlight—lo! there were tears in his eyes. And these he did not try to conceal, as I would have expected of him.

'Do not be repelled by a rough seeming. Maxwell,' he said; 'ye lie down in a good man's house this night. And, verily, the effectual fervent prayer of a righteous man availeth much. I own myself greatly cheered.'

And with that he laid him down to sleep.

Whether he did indeed sleep or no I cannot tell. But as for me, I sat up on my window-seat, not even removing my clothes, and thought on the great mystery of conscience, and how sternly it is held by some, how lightly by others. Here were two as far apart as Joyce Faa, the outlaw's daughter, gypsy-born and Papist-bred, and John Macmillan, the Cameronian saint—each ready to spend their lives that they might keep their charge. While as for me; well, I will not dishonour a faithful man's house by telling what I would have done in either of their places.

That this business of conscience was not a matter of religious denomination or profession, I could see very well, nor of upbringing, or even of good and godly counsel. Finally, I decided that few men (and hardly any women at all) have Effectual Consciences, but that those thus troubled possess several rolled in one.

And, having arrived at this sapient conclusion, I threw off my coat and stretched myself on the bed beside my father.

CHAPTER FIFTY ONE
HIGH CONTRACTING PARTIES

The light was coming redly from the east when I woke. I got up hastily, and, putting on my travelling-cloak, for the air was shrewd even in the little thatched guest-chamber, I let myself out of the never-locked door of the manse. The grip of late October was in the air. There were heavy clouds all over the sky, which grew rippled and irregular towards the east, across which lay a great, solemn bar of blood-red sky. There was no hoar-frost, the clouds having, as it were, held it up. I stood a moment shivering in the cold-drawing air from off the water, the wind that comes before the sun.

The little kirk of Balmaghie is, as I have already mentioned, set on a hill, and from where I stood its roof and low tower were clear cut against the crimson dawn. So red was the sky that, by contrast, the very tombstones took on a kind of unearthly green, and as the shadowing trees waved their dead leaves—or, shaking them off, sent them balancing down—what with the flaming light above and pale efforescence beneath, it seemed as if the spirits of the dead went wavering upward from their tombs, gibbering with filmy hands and moaning as they went.

There are, indeed, moods of morning far more terrible than those of the blankest midnight; perhaps premonitory of the shuddering rigors which shall take us when the pall of the future is removed and That Day dawns upon us; remote, awful, glimmering with those infinite possibilities that are only revealed to us in moments of mortal sickness.

As I thus watched the dawn, and my soul was mysteriously disturbed within me, my feet turned of their own accord in the direction of the little hill-set kirk of Balmaghie. I turned its eastern side that I might find the gravestones of the two martyr Hallidays, of which the mistress of the manse had told me the night before.

By this time the red colour in the sky had mounted full to the zenith. The sun was transmuting the lower cloud-bars to fantastic islands of purest gold. The whole pageant of the dawn stood upon tiptoe, and there, all of a sudden, calming my harassed and fearful soul, I was aware of the broad Dee Water slipping along, a sea of glass mingled with fire, as it seemed, straight from the throne of God itself.

As I looked past the gable-end of the little kirk my heart stood still, for I saw a man kneeling, like Daniel, with his face to the east. It was Macmillan himself, and there in the dawning he was praying to his Master. I will not set down his prayer, though I can recall much of it at this moment. It is sufficient that he prayed for clear light and guidance to do the will of God that day as became a good soldier. Moreover, he prayed for my father, for me, for Joyce, and most of all, I think for poor Harry Polwart

I slunk away, ashamed, yet somehow better in my soul that I had thus spied on a good man's devotions, and, as it were, intercepted the words that were meant for no ear of flesh, save One.

I expected to see the minister at breakfast; but when I asked for him his wife replied that he had gone out early, having broken his own fast from the cupboard, as was his constant custom.

Nor did Mary Gordon seem anxious or harassed about her husband for so much of that day as we spent with her, but went about her household cares, called the bairns and handmaids in to religious exercise, which she courteously asked my father to conduct. This he did in few words, but with a fitting solemnity that made me prouder than ever of him.

Having risen from our knees, we went out, after having taken leave of our hostess, promising to come back for news that night about eight of the clock.

'Do so,' replied that gracious and Christian lady. 'My husband will doubtless be returned by that time.'

Then my father murmured a text or quotation, of which I only heard the words, 'All things work together for good.' I could not at the instant remember the rest, but resolved to look it out on the first occasion when I should find myself alone with a

Bible.

As soon as we had crossed the road which extends along the river-side going north, my father set his face towards certain heathery mountains of a dark purple colour which stretched immediately in front, not high, but very rugged and steep.

'These,' he said, 'are called the Black Domels, and our road lies over them. Now, Maxwell, if you desire to save your lass, I have but one word to say to you—leg it!'

And though Patrick Heron of Rathan, was none so young as he had been when he courted my mother, I soon found that I had all I could do to keep up with him. As we breasted the hill the weather grew ever tiie gloomier, and though it was but the end of October, it seemed almost cold enough to snow. We were soon up among rocks and heather, and more than once a fox started out at our very feet and coursed away over the hill, with an occasional disdainful look backwards over his shoulder, and a curl of red and insolent brush.

We soon gained the summit of the ridge we had been ascending (for we had not crossed the highest point, but somewhat to the left), and there the clouds seemed close above us, and in colour and texture not unlike unbleached linen cloth. Still, it was clear enough down below, and we could discern under the level cloud canopy, as under a tent, all that troubled and turbulent square of country popularly known as the Headend of Balmaghie, girt by waters on three sides, the long lochs of Ken and Grenoch parallel on either hand, the Black Water of Dee joining these two together to the north, and, as it were, penning this centre of disaffection and rebellion within severe and natural confines.

And though there was spread out before us as on a map a marvellous prospect, yet we halted not for that, but with a speed hardly to be expected from a leader who took exercise so moderately as my father, we plunged down a series of rocky screes and scaurs to the little farm of Craig, which sits on its green shelf with a few scanty fields about it, a house of constant kindliness and the home of kind hearts ever since I have known it as indeed it remains to this day.

My father walked straight up to the low-thatched dwelling-house, and, opening the door without ceremony, he walked into the flagged kitchen. Three men were sitting about the fire with their toes turned to the blaze. The first of these was Silver Sand; the second a tall, heart-some, grave, heather-mixture sort of a man, James Cameron by name, the farmer of Craig, as I rightly judged. There was shy but evident pleasure in his eye as he rose to welcome my father. I had known that look well ever since I was old enough to go about with Patrick Heron.

'Proud am I to see ye Laird Rathan,' said the honest farmer. 'You and me are both somewhat more bowed in the shoulder since the time when—but maybe it's better giein' that bit maitter the go-by for the present.'

I think he meant the great raising of the country against the raiders, and for the moment I saw not the necessity for silence. I was standing with my back to the third man of the company, who had leaned so far within the chimney seat that his face was completely hidden from view. Silver Sand was already on his feet, and as I turned me about to greet him I saw that the third, sitting there as calm and collected as an elder in the kirk, was no other than Hector Faa himself!

For a moment I was dumfounded. I had no more use or backbone in me than a bundle of rushes.

But the next moment Hector Faa had risen, and was bowing to my father with dignity and as became a gentleman of an ancient, if somewhat irregular, house, as indeed he was.

My father also bowed with grave, severe dignity, and looked from one brother to the other, as if he had not expected to meet his ancient enemy there.

'This is the man who alone can help us,' said Silver Sand, turning to my father, upon seeing that neither made any attempt to shake hands.

However, I had no such qualms or niceties. For I remembered the much kindness he and his had shown me —that is, after the first rude carrying of me to the Shiel of the Dungeon. So I stepped up and offered Hector my hand, the which, after a moment's hesitation, he accepted. This being done, my father and he only looked at each other again, and bowed simultaneously, like opponents about to fight a duel. It was a pretty thing to see; two men most courteous to each other, without prejudice to their private enmities, past and future.

And watching them, I knew in a moment how men look at each other to their dying day, who in early life have quarrelled about a woman.

'Sir, I have come here at my brother's request,' began Hector Faa, who comported himself with a certain black and haughty pride that sat very well upon him. 'He informs me that I alone can right certain things that are wrong. 'Tis not much in my line, gentlemen, to preach or, you will say, to practise either. But if here and now we can come to a clear understanding, I am at your service. You, Mr. Patrick Heron, wish for something which you cannot obtain without me. I, on my part, desire to set right an ancient wrong. And it appears to me that I can best do it through you and your son. Let us, therefore, draw the matter to a head, and that as swiftly as possible, for, as I understand it, Harry Polwart is like myself in this, that he does not stick at trifles.'

It was to a young man very instructive to see these three men draw in their chairs about the table which our host, James Cameron, had pushed forward. He had also, as a matter of course, opened a cupboard and set glasses and a decanter in the midst, that being the rule of the ancient hospitality of the Free Province.

Then he beckoned me out of the room with a crook of his finger.

'I think you and me, Maister Maxle,' he said, 'will hae a quiet hour amang the nowt, and leave the gentlemen to their talk.'

At which I was not best pleased, being, as I thought, so deeply concerned in the matter. But as my father nodded an affirmative, I had no option but to obey. So for an hour or so we two wandered about, while douce James Cameron discoursed to deaf ears of Clydesdale horses and brood-mares, of the black cattle which need winter feeding, and the new sort which can be left out in the fields most part of the year, and so on and so forth, till at a cry from the house-door we turned us homeward again.

As I entered the little kitchen place I saw that the table was strewn with papers and parchments. My father was sitting with one of the latter in his hands, and as I came in alone he called me forward, and said, 'Maxwell, this gentleman (nodding across to Hector Faa) wishes your assurance that you are willing to marry the lady whom you have hitherto known under the name of Joyce Faa.'

'Known under the name of?' I interrupted. 'Is that not her name?'

'For the present the name does not matter,' said my father, waving his hand. 'If you are willing to marry the maid as Joyce Faa, surely the rose by any other name will smell as sweet?'

'As to that,' I said, 'I do indeed love her with all my heart, and have always done so. I ask no better than to marry her, now or at any other time, so being that she will have me.'

I could see the pleasure light up Hector's dark face as I spoke, but nevertheless he had a question to ask of me.

'And why, this being so, did you refuse when this marriage was proposed to you by my brother at the Shiel of the Dungeon?' he said.

'Because,' I answered, as boldly as I could, 'then I was a prisoner, she your daughter. I understood that neither of us were to be allowed any choice in the matter, and I would not have any maid's will coerced into marrying me.'

'Well,' said my father, dryly, to cut short dangerous argument with a man like Hector, 'since there is now no question of that, you will be wise to sign this agreement —which, I may say, I have read, and which you, if you choose, may also read. It is meant solely to give effect to the desires which you have just expressed.'

I felt that it was not a time to be over-nice, so I seized a pen without further words and signed as he directed me.

'Now, gentlemen,' said Hector, accepting the papers which my father handed to him, and exchanging them for another packet he had in the pocket of his coat, 'it is time for us to take a little promenade in the direction of the Duchrae Bank Wood. There are some few lads without who will be proud to accompany us.'

'Pray pardon me one moment' I said to him, 'but how do you know that your daughter is not already wedded? The minister of Balmaghie went there this morning very early. Harry Polwart may have compelled him to marry them by this time.'

Hector Faa tossed his head in a slighting way, and smiled his gloomy and sardonic smile.

'Bide,' he said; 'wedded Joyce Faa, indeed, may have been. But by my faith, if she be, this hand will make her a widow long before the hour arrives for marriage supper or bridegroom's posset. Among other settlements this day, I have one with Harry Polwart that shall be made without counted siller or scrape of lawyer's pen!'

As he went out upon the green a fine snow began to fall; rare flakes disentangling themselves languidly from the unbleached linen of the sky; what was my surprise to see a full score of men standing about upon the open space before the barn, comprising both the immediate followers and the occasional reserves of Hector Faa's company. Several of them had already been some time in the camp of the Levellers, but had one by one stolen away to join their ancient chief. In the foreground my old acquaintance of the Dungeon, Grice Baillie, pulled a rusty forelock. Mort Faa gave one swift glance at me, and then looked away with an elfish grin, as who would say, 'We will see what mettle you are made of ere we are a day older!' I felt a touch on my arm. 'Look to your accoutrement,' said the voice of the ex-dominie Orr MacCaterick, at my elbow. 'He is carrying his priming powder in his waistcoat-pocket!'

And he pointed to Hector Faa as he spoke.

Then Mort Faa, who had been running back and forth to the corner of the barn continually, to look up the green slopes towards the Ullioch Cairn, cried out suddenly, 'Here he comes!' Whereupon we all went about the house. And there, bent low like a coursing dog, came one of Hector Faa's scouts, hot-foot from the camp of the Levellers.

I would have given much to know what he said to his chief as he whispered into his ear, his hands pressed hard on his heaving sides, where a stitch evidently gripped him, for every moment or two his body was doubled up with pain, and his breath whistled in his throat like wind in a broken pair of smiddy bellows.

As soon as the messenger had stopped speaking I walked across to Hector and asked him plainly if there were any news of Joyce. But the outlaw's face was like a wall, and he answered me fiercely, 'None to delay us for a moment in our march! Keep your weapons ready, young man, and, if need be, fight like the devil! Rest assured—maid, wife, or widow, you shall marry her. Let that content you!'

It had perforce to content me, and yet I desired very much to say that, if it was all the same to him, I preferred that it should be as the first.

CHAPTER FIFTY TWO
TWO SOLDIERS OF TWO KINGDOMS

In the camp of the Levellers on the Duchrae Bank Harry Polwart certainly carried out Silver Sands prophecy to the letter. Marion found that not only was Tredennis in a very critical position but that her own authority was seriously threatened. Indeed, had it not been for the gypsies preoccupation about Joyce, and a curious desire on his part that their marriage should be carried out with a certain ostentation, she could not have postponed the outbreak that was fast approaching.

The wilder and more youthful spirits of the camp, though they had at first been pleased with the notion of a handsome and clever girl as their captain (and Marion's genius for leadership was unquestioned among them), now began to realize the hopelessness of their position, and to crave for change and excitement.

It was this party which acclaimed Harry Polwart so vociferously on his arrival. They drank in eagerly his wild counsels of blood and vengeance, and sat far into the night with him drinking and applauding till they felt themselves able to undertake the most desperate enterprises. They would burn every mansion house in the three shires, take a booty of prodigious value, carry by sudden assault a ship in Loch Ryan or the Port of Kirkcudbright, and sail away to a life of riches and ease on another continent. All wild talk, doubtless—but at that hour of night, and to the heated imaginations of these ignorant lads, such feats seemed easy and simple of accomplishment.

Thus hour after hour they sat open-mouthed, listening to the desperate and bloody adventures of the gypsy smuggler, who in his youth had added to his other experiences a spice of piracy on the high seas.

'This is no life you live here,' he was saying once when Marion passed by. 'These wretched shelters on the wet ground, nothing better than rabbits and half-starved sheep to eat, when you might be dressed in the best, jingling money in your pockets, and, if you cared for that kind of thing, with a lass and a home of your own!'

'But the risk!' objected a Leveller, one not so bleared with raw country spirit as the rest. 'Why, we should all be hanged, hanged, drawn, and quartered long before we got half-way to your wonderful new world!'

But Harry Polwart overbore his objection on the instant, and the others, too eager for this new Elysium to listen to a word of cavil, angrily shouted him down.

'Risk!' cried the gypsy, scornfully echoing his first word, 'of course there is risk! But nothing to the risk of remaining here with winter coming on. Your captain is a clever lass, but (here he lowered his voice) women are well enough till it comes to be a question of a little blood-letting, then they are as much out of place as at a pig-killing.'

'Speaking of pigs, Harry,' said one Peter Kelly, a Wigtonshire man of a lowering aspect and a long upper-lip, 'have you seen the spy we gat hold of this afternoon?'

He had not heard what had already passed on that subject between Marion and Harry Polwart. The face of the blind man lit up with a ghastly joy at the remembrance. He had an idea. He called the men nearer to him, till their heads were bent together in a circle.

'Look you,' he said, 'I will tell you a secret. Your captain is either in love with this fellow or wants to keep him as a hostage to save her own life. She would not let me have a word of speech with the man tonight. '

'I believe' said Peter Kelly, suddenly, 'that the officer is the same who rode at the head of the dragoons when they brought you down from Minnigaff to be hanged. I was at the Brig End of Cree as you passed.'

'Ah,' cried the gypsy, 'if only I were sure of that! But we will wait till the morning and make certain!'

'Yes,' said Kelly, 'but tonight the old gang are

about, thick as herring in barrel. Old Bob Galtway and Young Bob, Will Grey and his brother Adam—all the grey-beards of the council.'

'Wait,' said Harry Polwart. 'We will settle that and many other things, as you say, in the morning. If this be the man I suppose we will blow out his brains as a little moral lesson! It needs only that to strike terror. You have played at this sugar-water business too long!'

The drink continued to circle more quickly about the fire. Wilder and wilder grew the talk; vaster swelled the spoil, till each of these poor, ignorant lads saw himself rich as ten kings. They would take St. Mary's Isle, the town of Kirdcudbright, Drumlanrig Castle. Every day they would add to their numbers and their power. Dumfries itself might fall. The government had no troops to oppose them nearer than London—so Harry Polwart averred, with many oaths, and by the time these could arrive every man Jack of them would be safe over-seas.

And Marion, going on her rounds sadly, left behind her these sounds of revelry, drunken shoutings, and horrid threatenings, new in the douce camp of the Levellers, with their worship at morn and even, and their sober motto written across the blue flag of St Andrew, ' A free land and a free folk.'

Yet for the moment she dared not interfere; not that she feared for her own life, but that she knew well that that of Austin Tredennis hung upon a hair. If she could not keep a majority of the saner and more open-minded men on her side to show a strong front on the morrow to Harry Polwart and his gang, the blood of the man who had risked so much to save her would be on her hands!

Now she would have given all she possessed that Tredennis might go free. But, alas! she herself had made that impossible by committing his custody to the most responsible members of the Levellers' Council, so she had perforce to await the event of the morrow with what equanimity she could compass.

And Joyce! What of her? I warrant it was little that she slept that night. For from across the camp platform came songs and drunken merriment in which she could distinguish the voice of the man who tomorrow was to be her husband.

Never had the path of duty seemed so hard, and more than once she rose and, from the edge of the camp platform, looked down at the black pools of the Grenoch Lane, sleeping deep in the shadow of its woods. But a hope of something—she knew not what—awaiting her in the future withheld her from self-destruction.

Here also the morning came red and glorious, even as I saw it from the fair Kirkhill of Balmaghie. Only through the reddening leaves of the wood the flaming lift seemed more completely arched with fire, and the pale, emerald reflection made the bodies of the sleeping men appear like unburied corpses on a field of slaughter.

Of the four whose fates intermingled and interdepended in the camp of the Duchrae Wood, only one remained unconscious. Marion, Joyce, and Tredennis were all awake; but Harry Polwart slept long, the fumes of the spirits he had drunk on the previous night uniting with the terrible fatigues of his journey to prevent him from waking betimes.

And so it chanced that, quite unknown to any there, a tall, strongly built, determined man was striding rapidly over hill and dale towards the camp, and when Harry Polwart awakened it was to find the minister of Balmaghie standing over him and asking him how he did. The gypsy did not return to consciousness in any favourable mood. His yesterday's gratitude to his benefactor had passed, and now that his debauch was dying out of him its usual consequents of fierce headache and villanous temper became apparent.

'When you have made you ready,' said Mr. Macmillan to Harry Polwart, 'I desire some conversation with you. I have made a long travel for that purpose.'

'Say what you have to say here and now!' growled the gjrpsy. 'Though this is my wedding-day, I have no great toilet to make.'

371

And, bidding one of his tail of obsequious followers to bring him a basin of water and a towel from Joyce Faa's tent, he sat down with his fingers laid across his aching brow.

'I fear,' said the minister, looking at him observantly, 'that your recent marvellous deliverance has not brought you to repentance.'

'Now, sir parson!' cried the gypsy, leaping up fiercely, 'listen to me once for all! I desire no preaching! You did very well yesterday in bringing me here, but you must remember that I also did my part in sparing you the knife in your ribs that I had intended for you! So consider us as quits, and keep the sermons for Sundays and fast-days!'

'If ye like my introduction so little, friend,' returned John Macmillan, who was not a man to be so daunted, 'I fear me ye will like the 'pirliecue' (summing-up and conclusion) even less.'

To this the blind gypsy did not reply, and the minister went on.

'I have been informed,' he said, 'that you are intending to marry this girl without her father's consent. Is that a true word which I have heard?'

A fierce and blood-thirsty expression leaped into the man's scarred features.

'I know the white-livered hound who told you that!' he cried. 'I have had his blood once on this knife-back. I shall send it deeper in ere long! It was Maxwell Heron —that fine ladys puppet whom I will break across my knee like an ash-twig!'

'It matters little who told me,' said the minister. 'I ask you is the word a true word?'

'As little it matters to you or me whether it be true or not!' cried the gypsy, rising, and laying his hand fiercely on Macmillan's shoulder. 'Hearken, minister! you shall marry me to Joyce Faa this day, or I take all hell to witness that I will send this knife to your heart—or, if you prefer it, a bullet through your brain! Do your work, minister, and do not cross a desperate man. The girl is' willing. That is sufficient for the law of the land. Let it be enough for you. As for God Almighty and Hector Faa, I will be responsible to them!'

It was a grasp wellnigh as strong as his own that removed the blind gypsy's hand from the minister's shoulder, for as to his thews Macmillan was no weakling.

'Man!' he said, still holding the gypsy's wrist, 'I wonder you have no more sense, after what you heard yesterday, than to threat John Macmillan with your swords and pistols, as if he were a fearful bairn. Sir, I value neither you nor your boasts one oat-straw! Answer my question, and the others which I will put to you. If I am satisfied, I will marry you to this maid freely and gladly. If not, you may sheathe your knife in my heart, an' it please you, but you will not shake my determination!'

'Ay, and he will stand to it, be sure,' said one of his followers, who knew the repute of the minister of Balmaghie. 'He did you a good turn, Harry. Besides, he is a godly man. Speak him fair. They say he has the second sight.'

'A good turn!' cried the gypsy. 'Did I ask him for his good turn? Did ever Harry Polwart ask a good turn from any man save the hangman that he might kill him quickly? And now he asks only that this braying ass might as expeditiously do his task. And so we shall see, ere this day be done, or some whose heads are high shall bite the dust! Hallo! What is this noise? Whom have we here?'

The minister turned round, and saw half a dozen men, some of whom he knew as cottiers and parishioners of his own, rather shamefacedly guarding a prisoner towards the main camp.

'John Cannon! Allan Dempster! What do you here? You had been better employed wearing the sheep off the hill, than with that decent man tied up between yon like a common thief!'

'Bring the fellow hither!' cried Harry Polwart, in a tone of fierce command, instantly recognizing his opportunity.

The men were about to proceed, for the presence of the minister in the gypsy's company encouraged them.

'Do you hear?' shouted Polwart. 'Hither instantly with the sneaking hound!' And, when they still hesitated to obey, he broke into low and brutal oaths and revilings.

'Sir,' said John Macmillan, with great dignity and elevation, 'I am a minister of God in my own parish and though it has been my hap to be deposed by the Presbytery, His arm has sustained me among this people. I do not love to war with the weapons of flesh, but I tell you plainly that I will listen to no such words, either from you or from any other man!'

Polwart laughed harshly and defiantly.

'You will hear a good deal more that you have never yet heard before if you dare to cross Harry Polwart,' he retorted. 'Listen well with your ears and look well with your eyes while I deal with this spy. And if he be the man I think him, be warned, minister, or you may chance to accompany him on a longer journey than that from Kirkcudbright to the Manse of Balmaghie.'

Tredennis was now brought close to the gypsy, who remained sitting on the trunk of a felled tree on the edge of the outer fortifications.

'Your name?' cried the gypsy, with savage truculence. 'Do not lie to me! I know ways of making you speak, remember. I have dealt with gentlemen of your kidney before.'

'I do not recognize any right that you have to ask it,' said the soldier, with quiet decision. 'But my name, at any honest man's service, is Austin Tredennis, captain in Ligonier's Horse.'

The gypsy rose hastily to his feet.

'And you prate of honesty, who passed yourself off as one Job Brown, a cattle-dealer!' he cried. 'You came here spying within these intrenchments! You were captured in disguise on the outskirts of the camp!'

'I am a soldier of the King's!' said Tredennis, boldly. 'I have obeyed my general's instructions in this, as I did when I took a certain outlaw and murderer suspect, Harry Polwart, prisoner at the Manse of Minnigaff.'

374

The face of the blind gypsy became livid with rage, and his features were distorted almost out of any semblance to humanity.

'Then you are the dog who arrested me, and you glory in it!—who took Joyce from me, who thrust me into prison, who has kept me in this accursed land? If it had not been for you, she and I would have been clear of everything, and in another country! Curse your black, sneaking heart! Now I will have your life! I swore it in prison, yes, on the scaffold, with the rope round my neck, I yet hoped that I might be spared to kill you with this hand!'

The blind man took a step forward in the direction of the prisoner and as soon as he touched him with the palm of his open right hand he smote him once, twice, and thrice across the face.

'Take that for an earnest of what I will presently do for you, Captain Spy!' he cried. 'But first you shall be best man and dance at my wedding. Then we will take you out to the dyke-side, and my lads here will give a certain skulking dog a little dose of lead that will prevent him forever from apprehending innocent men and women and shutting them up in his dog-kennels !'

He would have struck Tredennis again, but the minister of Balmaghie thrust himself in between, and cried aloud, 'Harry Polwart, once has the vengeance of God touched you! Beware how you provoke Him to wrath the second time! If this man be your prisoner, and you are waging a warfare against the crowned King of this realm, remember that he but obeyed his orders and did his duty!'

Then, at this interference, the rage of the blind gypsy passed all bounds. He drew his dagger, and sprang forward to strike the minister to the earth.

But Macmillan drew himself up to his full height and folded his arms.

'Let us see, sirs,' he said, addressing the bystanders, 'how far God will allow him to go! Strike, sir, strike! Aha, you cannot! It is not permitted to you! I thought not. You cannot touch the Lord's servant before the time!'

And true it is that though the gypsy foamed at the mouth with fury, though the muscles of his arm twitched convulsively with desire to strike, though his left hand clawed at the empty air within an inch or two of the minister's shoulder, his right, in which the knife had been uplifted to strike, fell powerless to his side!

Something between a temporary paralysis and the rigor of death fell upon him for a moment. He trembled from head to foot and muttered words in a strange tongue.

But the minister's words came clear and distinct, even defiantly: 'I praise the Lord, Who hath strength to deliver my soul from the sword; my darling from the power of the dog.'

CHAPTER FIFTY THREE
THE STORMING OF THE CAMP

When Austin Tredennis was first smitten on the face he had turned a ghastly white, and for a moment his bound hands strained at his bonds. But in a moment he had controlled himself, and for all the feeling that was expressed on his countenance, the gypsy might as well have struck a marble statue.

It was at this moment that Marion came upon the scene. She found Austin standing with his guards by his side. The minister of Balmaghie, with his arms folded, was looking straight at the gypsy, and Polwart still clutched the knife in his impotent fingers.

'Why have you not brought the prisoner directly to me?' she cried, sharply, ignoring the blind gypsy and his retinue.

The guards did not speak; but Polwart, instantly collecting himself at the sound of the new voice, answered, 'Because I bade them bring him to me!'

'And by what right?' cried Marion, indignantly.

'By the same right by which you had him arrested— because I had men to do my bidding!' retorted the gypsy, who, baffled momentarily by Macmillan, now began to feel the strength of his position in the camp.

'The Council shall decide between us,' said Marion. 'Men, bring him to my tent!'

With a sudden rush forward, Harry Polwart caught Tredennis by the arm, scattering the guards this way and that. These were elderly men, and had an almost superstitions fear of the blind gypsy.

'To me,' cried the latter, 'all who wish to see justice done! This precious captain of yours is keeping this officer as a hostage for her own life! She is selling you to insure her own safety! Why else has she kept you here doing nothing for weeks and weeks, while the enemy gathered strength? It was a bargain, I tell you; and this spy was her go-between—perhaps her paramour! Make an example of him! Shoot him on the spot, and so perish all red-coat spies and all traitors to the cause.'

And while Marion still stood rooted to the spot by the very shock of her surprise, Harry Polwart's words drew fifty or sixty men about him, and in a moment the main camp was in his hands.

True, she had a nominal majority still. But it consisted chiefly of older men, averse from blood and unwilling to come to blows. With Polwart, on the other hand, were most of the younger men, together with those who had gone on the raiding and destroying expeditions. So that, as Silver Sand had foretold, by permitting and encouraging these, Marion had been forging a weapon for her own destruction.

The Polwart party did not attempt any actual violence against herself, but they took entire possession of all the principal works and of the headquarters hut, in which Joyce Faa remained. Around this they settled themselves, with the minister and Tredennis guarded in the midst.

Presently Polwart, being guided by one of his followers, knocked at the door of the little, roughly built shelter, and, entering, presently came out again leading Joyce by the hand.

'This,' he said, addressing the minister and the men who stood about, 'is the daughter of Hector Faa, to whom I was in the act of being married at the manse of Minnigaffy when I was arrested on a false charge by this spy and his troopers. It is fitting that before he dies he should help to repair the wrong he has done. Joyce, is it your will that we be married here and now?'

'I gave my promise, and I am ready to redeem it,' Joyce answered, with her eyes upon the ground.

'You hear, minister?' said the gypsy. 'She is of full age, and, father or no father, she is quite able to decide for herself whom she shall marry. Do your duty, sir, or take the consequences.'

'Sir,' said Mr. Macmillan, 'I will not be coerced into doing my duty, nor do I need any to tell me what my duty is! As I said before, I am not satisfied, and I decline to marry you to this woman!'

'Oh, do not cross him, sir!' cried Joyce, lifting up her hands in appeal.

'Do I gather that you also wish this marriage to take place?' said the minister, astonished in his turn. 'I was informed—I was given to understand that—that—'

'I have passed my word to marry this man,' answered Joyce, 'and if you will not do what he asks you he will kill you! I know he will! I would have no more blood shed on my account!'

The minister paused a moment, and then addressed Harry Polwart again. 'If I do this thing will you promise to save this soldier's life?'

'By heavens, no!' cried the gyipsy. 'His life is forfeit, in spite of a thousand marriages! Be thankful, parson, that you save your own! That is enough for you!'

'Then,' said the minister, raising his voice so that all might hear, 'let your father the devil couple you, if he can! I will have nothing to do with the matter. And I solemnly adjure and command this misguided maid to flee from such a servant of Satan and such a monster of iniquity as you!'

And as he spoke Austin Tredennis, who had been looking steadfastly upon the ground, suddenly turned and gazed fixedly at the bold minister of Balmaghie with the unmistakable look which says, 'You also are a man!'

'To the water-side with them both!' commanded the blind gypsy. 'Six of you who are the best shots bring your muskets! Oh, that I had my eyes! These fellows should not flout us! But give me a hand, Peter Kelly. I can still set a pistol to their heads and blow out their brains.'

So, all in a hasty turmoil of words, shoutings, and confused noise, Tredennis and the minister were hustled away. But some part even of Polwart's immediate followers was ashamed and hung back; not so much from the killing of the soldier, but from laying hands upon a minister.

Knowing well what it was that stuck in their throats, Polwart cried out, 'They are spies both of them! They came to find out the nakedness of the land! If we let them go they will tell all to the enemy.

They have seen your defences. They will identify you when the hellhounds of an unjust government are trying to hang you as they tried to hang me! Kill them, I tell you, and be done with them! That is your only safety!'

'But the minister, Harry!' cried some. 'It is not well to slay a minister! It brings a curse! Think of Grier of Lag, and how he died—in cold water to the waist, and crying out that he was already in hell-fire!'

'Lies! lies!' cried the gypsy; 'old wives' tales to fright bairns! Besides, this man is no minister! The true ministers cast him out long ago on account of his wickedness.'

'Nay, not for his wickedness!' denied another. 'You are wrong there, Harry.'

'For what, then, did they cast him out?' vociferated the gypsy.

'Nay, that I know not,' replied the other, 'but I do know well that it was for no ill. I did not neighbour him for thirty year at the Clachan of Shankfoot without finding that out.'

The minister of Balmaghie turned upon the speaker quickly. He had not spoken for some time but the sound of the man's voice seemed to rouse him.

'Ah, Gabriel Dobie!' he said, 'is it you? I will mind this when you come up for your token next communion season. I will debar you, sir, from sealing ordinances for your company with such unbelievers, and for being a partaker of their iniquities! On the stool of repentance shall you sit, as sure as my name is John Macmillan! Also, Gabriel, I will commune with you for your soul's health. I will correct you with rods and chasten you with scorpions!'

But in the very midst of these threats of ecclesiastical discipline Gabriel Dobie was pushed to the side, and a wave of angry men, shouting 'Kill the spies!' 'Shoot the traitors!' 'He is no true minister!' carried Tredennis and Macmillan to the corner of the intrenchments overlooking the Lane, and nearest to the Hollan Isle, at the last of which Austin (though he judged that his time was come) looked across not without interest. But his thoughts were mostly busy

380

with Marion. He would have liked to bid her farewell, if only in a word. Then he shrugged his shoulders, and muttered to himself, 'What matter? She would not care!'

All the while the blind gypsy was busy stirring up anger and jealousy, crying blood and vengeance on all traitors. They would at last show their persecutors that they were not to be trifled with.

'One dead dragoon sent in a cart to Kirkcudbright,' so he told them, 'will be a better proof that you are in earnest than a score of petitions and claims of right. Stell them up and shoot them down, say I!'

But the men, with the exception of a few of the most deeply committed, still hung back, whereupon Harry Polwart, with angry vows of vengeance, laid hold on them, and with Peter Kelly to aid him and a pistol cocked in his hand, marched them one by one to the place where Austin and Macmillan stood waiting their doom.

'Let any man dare to cross my vengeance!' he cried. 'I swear I will scatter his brains on the sod, if one who has joined with me refuses now to obey! Charge your pieces, men!'

Meanwhile Tredennis was speaking in a low voice to the minister.

'They mean business this time!' he whispered. 'Your legs are free. Over with you, and take to the water! My feet are fettered, so I have no chance; but I can hold them long enough to give you a start. The Hollan Isle is within a hundred yards, and if these fellows shoot, ten to one they will miss! I can see they are new to the trade.'

The soldier and the minister stood six yards or so from the firing-party, quite close to the water, and Macmillan really had a fair chance of escaping across to the Hollan Isle, especially from such indifferent and unwilling marksmen. But he only shook his head.

'You and I will go the one road, friend,' he said; 'at least, so far. But what of your soul? Are you prepared? Have you an interest in the kingdom that is above, not made with hands, eternal in the heavens?'

'That I do not know,' said Austin, gently. 'I am but a plain soldier, and have done my duty poorly either to King George or to That Other of whom you speak. Yet I have done the best I could.'

'Good!' said the minister, nodding his head, 'yet I fear there is Arminianism in the reply. I should like to argue the question of faith and works with you, if we have not time here, well, up above!'

Many of the Levellers stood round watching the event, with uncertainty and terror manifest on their faces. They could not bring themgelves to come to blows with that fierce and desperate clique now controlled by the blind gypsy. Yet in a few moments it would be too late. Marion, to the northward of the main camp, was trying to get together a sufficient number of the older men to attempt a rescue. But Harry Polwart, suspecting her purpose, hastened to bring the matter to an issue.

'Now, minister!' he cried, 'I put it to you for the last time; will you do your duty, and perform your promise of yesterday? I give you this one chance. You have a wife and children. Think of them. I need not remind you that you are wholly in my hands, and that I am not a man to say one thing and do another. For the last time, will you keep your promise and depart in peace, or be shot for a traitor and a spy? Take your choice!'

'Poor worm!' said the minister, 'and you, yet poorer deluded lads! I am heart-wae for you, so sadly are ye left to yourselves! You may indeed lay me dead by the side of this honest soldier, but what will that profit you? How will ye answer for your deed in That Day?'

'Hold your prating tongue!' cried Polwart, afraid that he might even then influence them. 'We do not want your preaching! Once more, will you do your office, ay or no?'

'Then on my conscience, No!' cried the minister, lifting up his right hand to heaven, 'and I leave my testimony that I have warned all these poor lads of their danger. Go to your own homes, and take your punishment like men. And for me, I take these woods and fields to witness my solemn, dying warning, these distant hills and clear-running streams, that this day I have preached to you repentance and forgiveness of sin! Scatter! leave the sinner to perish in his sin! Flee from the wrath to come —from the judgment that shall surely fall on the ungodly! While yet there is time, turn to Him and live! The harvest is past, the summer ended, and ye are not saved! Why will ye die, O House of Israel?'

'Make ready there, lads!' cried the gypsy. 'Are ye charged? Present your pieces!'

Austin Tredennis said nothing. No change passed over the immovable calm of his countenance. Not a quiver of the eyelid betrayed that he felt the position in which he was placed. A slight drawing up of the tall figure perhaps there was, a squaring of the shoulders which alone showed preparation to meet the death volley. Nevertheless, deep within his heart he said the Lord's prayer. But the minister of Balmaghie, though, as we know, not afraid of the martyr's death, yet conserved cheerfully the martyr's right of testification. He had another word yet to add.

'I die,' he cried, 'adhering to the declarations and testimonies put in by me before the Presbytery of Kirkcudbright, and to the covenants, national and solemn league! Bide a moment, lads; let me say out my say! Ye will not? Then into God's hand I deliver you all, and especially Harry Polwart; unjust, bloody-minded, and ungrateful. And may He who feeds the ravens take care of Mary and my poor young bairns!'

At this crisis of affairs there was heard a noise of guns on the upper side of the camp, the confused crying of many fierce voices. The men of the firing-party turned irresolutely, and looked behind them.

'Shoot the spies! shoot, I bid you!' cried the gypsy, fiercely. 'Cowards that ye are, fire upon them! Dogs and sons of dogs! Kill them first, and then we will settle the other matters after!'

But from the upper camp swelled a tumultuous shout: 'Upon them! Down with them! They run! The place is ours!'

'Tush!' cried the blind man, 'it is but that

383

woman with her following of fools and greybeards! What can they do against us? Stand by Harry Polwart, and we will make minced collops of them. Oh, you cowards! Lend me a hand there, Peter Kelly! Joyce, come hither to me! Great God! if I only had some one to help me I could kill a score of such curs and brutes!'

But down the sides of the undefended trenches, and up from the depths of the hazelwood, swept a wave of compact fighting-men, before whom the Polwart faction fell back amazed, or turned and fled after firing a few hasty shots. Something about the newcomers, something darker, grimmer, more determined, in a moment reduced the Levellers to mere herdsmen and country ploughmen. Tredennis noted the difference in a moment.

'If Fitzgeorge and Collinson have to face these fellows,' he thought, 'they will know a difference.'

More fortunate than the soldier, or perhaps favoured by those who had tied him, the minister had succeeded in twisting his hands loose. And just as Harry Polwart, foaming with impotent fury, drew his knife and was groping for Tredennis to plunge it into his breast, crying, 'You, at least, shall not escape!' the minister of Balmaghie, who had been a wrestler in his youth, tripped him up, and sent him flying headlong down the slope.

'The Lord forgive me for using the arm of flesh!' he said, as the gypsy disappeared among the water-side bushes with a crash.

'I owe you my thanks, sir,' said Tredennis, 'you saved my life! I think your arm of flesh was indeed the very arm of Providence to me.'

'Well taken, but disputable, sir,' returned the minister. 'I should like a more convenient season to argue the matter at length. But here are others, who, I fear, have also been using the arm of flesh!'

It was Silver Sand who came up, putting back a discharged pistol in his belt, while his brother Hector as carefully wiped his sword before resheathing it, and Marion sank down on a fallen tree, and, covering her face with her hands burst into a passion of tears.

All was over!

The camp was in the hands of the attacking party within five minutes of firing the first shot. This was owing to the fact that the assailants found the first defences and outworks in the hands of Marion and her followers and it did not take long for my father and Silver Sand to convince her that we were there as friends. During the negotiations Hector Faa, of course, kept in the background. But when the attack was made on Polwart's faction Marion charged by his side, and, to do myself justice, I do not think that I was more than three paces behind them, not from lack of will, but because of the halt in my gait, which was the result of Harry Polwart's knife thrust at the Shiel of Buchan. However, in spite of this, I arrived at the top of the mound in time to see the blind gypsy emerge dripping from the water and disappear into the coverts of the Hollan Isle.

Then I turned and ran at full speed back to the hut in front of which the blue flag of the Levellers hung limp on its staff.

Joyce stood within the doorway with both her hands pressed upon her heart. I caught her in my arms.

'You are not married?' I gasped out. For that fear was ever before my mind.

'Are they dead, are they dead? Has Harry killed them?' she cried, not answering my question.

'Whom do you mean?' I said, much surprised, for, of course, at that time I knew nothing of what had taken place in the camp after the arrival of Mr. Macmillan.

'Captain Tredennis and the minister!' she said. 'Harry Polwart took them out to kill them by the waterside.'

'They are both safe and unhurt,' I answered her, a little piqued that at such a moment she could think of anything but my coming to rescue her.

At this moment Hector Faa came in and Joyce ran gladly to him.

'My father,' she cried, and threw her arms about the gypsy, dropping her head on his breast.

He looked over her shoulder at me with a sad and even wistful expression on his face.

'You see,' he said, a little more bitterly than I thought the circumstances called for, 'this is a good deal to give up, even to a lover of your quality!'

'Sir,' I answered him, 'I have told you already that I love your daughter with all my heart, and have done so ever since I first looked upon her. If you give her to me as my wife, she will not be the less your daughter for that.'

'Tis all you know!' he observed, and went out abruptly.

Then, forgetting Hector Faa's bitterness, and disregarding all the noise and turmoil without, I clasped my love again in my arms.

'You have not answered my question,' I said. 'Surely I am in time, you are not married to Harry Polwart?'

'Would I be here if I were?' she answered, simply, looking at me.

And I thought it was strange that she never asked of the gypsy, whether he was dead or alive, nor said one word about the promise she had made, but only clung to me and trembled.

'I knew you would come,' she said, 'only I feared you might come too late.'

'That I should have found you married?' I asked her, to see what she would say.

'That you would have found me dead!' she whispered.

And out of her pocket she drew the one of my father's pistols that I had given her when she rode away to Rathan with Davie Veitch, from the Loch Fergus brae-face, where we had met her on the morning of her escape from Maclellan's Wark.

'But I should have kept my promise,' she said, glancing significantly at the pistol.

386

CHAPTER FIFTY FOUR
THE BURSTING OF A SHELL

So great was the scene of excitement and disorder in the camp of the Levellers after the unexpected incursion of Hector Faa and his men, that Austin Tredennis, still shackled at ankle and wrist, grimly remarked to himself that if Gunter and Collinson had followed up his footsteps, as had been arranged, now was their time.

But it was remarkable within how short a space Hector Faa had all into order again, his men at their posts, the trenches manned, a lookout set on the Duchrae Crags to the south, and another perched on the woody summit of little Mount Pleasant to scan the open country to the north. Yet, with a certain nobility which has more than once peeped through during this history, Hector continued to issue his orders as if he had been subordinate in authority to Marion.

Yet Captain Dick o' the Isle rather tacitly permitted him to do this, than take any further share in the arrangements. The burden of affairs had grown too heavy for her. The brave, and even gay, confidence with which she had taken up her task had vanished. Even her enthusiasm for the oppressed no longer sustained her.

'I am not sufficient for these things,' she mourned. 'He was right. I had better go back to Isle Rathan, and get my mother to teach me how to bake scones, or share Joyce's knitting and embroidery.'

She was determined to call a council of the Levellers and lay her resignation before them. Twice she had been displaced, once openly defied by Harry Polwart. The two parties seemed irreconcilable; one ready to submit on almost any terms, the other eager for measures of blood and vengeance which she could not countenance. Then, to make impossible what had been difficult enough before, there was this new element, the wild gypsy company from the outmost hills, outlaws to a man, fierce and insubordinate to the control of any council, yet united and determined so far as their own leader was concerned.

Last of all, there was Captain Austin Tredennis!

As she thought on these things, there were not many more puzzled young women in the land of the Picts that dark October noontide than Marion of the Isle. To add to the perplexities of the situation, the snow, which had been threatening so long, began to fall all over the Duchrae Wood in a lawny sift of finest flakes. So it came about that there were two councils sitting at one time in solemn deliberation—or, rather, three; but with that third we have at present nothing to do. The first was the solemn and regular convocation of the Levellers summoned by Marion. The second, of a more private and informal nature, consisted of my father, Silver Sand, Hector Faa, Joyce, the minister, and myself. Tredennis, unbound and on parole, was seated some distance off, his great frieze cloak wrapped about him, rolling cigarettes in the Spanish manner as calmly as if he had been watching his troopers watering their horses.

As to the third—far down the valley, dripping wet and furiously angry, the blind gypsy and his henchman Peter Kelly held a yet more informal conference.

The weighty consultations of the Levellers may escape with brief notice. Marion laid her resignation before them and gave an account of her stewardship. She advised them that, after making certain conditions, they should disband and return to their own homes. She offered to be their envoy to the authorities in Kirkcudbright, and she declared my father's willingness to accompany her and to be her sponsor on such a mission. These and many other emergent matters were discussed, wisely, no doubt, and certainly with much heat. They were duly voted upon, and the negative or affirmative adopted. But as subsequent circumstances rendered inoperative and nugatory the whole of them, I need not take up my now scanty space with an account of them.

On the other hand, anything more brief, more instinct with life and surprise than the deliberations of the informal council round the headquarters staff and the blue St. Andrews cross, it has never fallen to

388

my lot to chronicle.

It was Hector Faa who, after nodding to his brother and making a bow to my father, opened the negotiations.

'We have a little time,' he said, 'and I will say what I have to say briefly. I came here with my good fellows in obedience to the summons of my brother, who, whatever difference may have arisen between us in the past, I shall ever acknowledge as the chief of the clan and only Lord and Earl of Little Egypt.'

I looked for Silver Sand to acknowledge this courtesy, but he took it simply as the statement of a right unquestionable.

'But I came also because I had two private matters to rectify—one connected with the maid Joyce, who has hitherto passed as my daughter.'

Then, with a quick cry, Joyce threw her arms about his neck, crying, 'Oh, father! am I not then your daughter?'

He shook his head sadly and kindly.

'No, Joyce,' he said, holding her a little way from him and looking into her face, 'that is what I have to tell.'

'Then,' she cried, 'you have always been a father to me! I will not leave you! I love you as much as if you were!'

I could see the gypsy flush with a certain pleasure through his swarthy colour and deep, sunburnt tan.

'You have indeed been the best of daughters,' he said. 'But I have come to undo as best I can an ancient wrong. Joyce, you are not my daughter! I took you out of your dead father's arms on board a sinking ship. I went with you to Paris, where, in the same convent in which my poor wife had been brought up, the good nuns received and educated you. At this distance of time it might have been somewhat difficult to prove your real identity, save that your father, being on his way to Scotland on legal business connected with his wish that you should succeed to his title, had an unusually complete series of documents in his possession when he died. I have taken care, in conjunction with an excellent French lawyer, that at no stage should your identity be in danger of being lost or questioned. I have placed these papers in the hands of Mr. Patrick Heron, of Isle Rathan and Orraland, who will produce them upon occasion.'

'A title!' thought I, with some consternation. 'Joyce Faa with a title; property also, doubtless! Perhaps in that case she will not think of me!'

But Joyce sat unmoved, watching Hector Faa's face, and at intervals laying her hand sympathetically upon his arm.

'For some time,' he continued, 'I have seen that it would be impossible much longer to maintain myself among my native mountains. I have a presentiment also that the end will not be long delayed. I wished, therefore, that Joyce might find herself a mate suitable to the rank in which she would be placed. For this purpose, therefore, I carried off a young man of property and position who fell accidentally in my way. I let the young couple be much together. All seemed to be going well for some months, when I sent my brother Silver Sand with certain proposals to this young gentleman which, if they had been accepted at the time, would have saved a vast deal of trouble to all concerned.'

Here, as may well be believed, I blushed hotly with shame; but Joyce broke in with all her kind heart in her voice, eager to clear me of any blame:

'It was not Maxwell's fault, father, it was I who refused!'

And at that I was fairly drowned in shame, as, indeed, I had good reason to be, remembering the long look with which, by the shores of Enoch, she had appealed to me, and how I had let that mute question fall to the ground unanswered in her hour of need. How these women shame us when our love is set fairly against theirs!

Hector Faa let his hand rest caressingly on Joyce's hair, but a slightly sardonic smile still flickered across his countenance.

'Well, it may be so,' he said, grimly, 'at all

events, my offer was refused. And though severity is always painful to me in dealing with young people, I was compelled to try other measures. But my hand was forced, for Joyce here, taking too seriously some random words of mine, obtained Maxwell Heron's escape by means of a foolish bargain with a false and perjured clansman of mine with whom, when I meet him, I will yet reckon once for all, as very well he knows !'

'Hush, father!' said Joyce; 'let him go. He was always kind and good to me!'

'I shall not forget—I shall not forget!' said Hector. 'He shall go the easier for that!'

But the grim determination on his face did not relax, and though I felt the implied scorn in his tone when he spoke of me, I was glad that I had not come under the major ban which he had laid upon Harry Polwart. The countenance of the blind gypsy was terrible enough in anger, but there was something infinitely more daunting in the steely glitter of Hector Faa's eyes as he spoke of his enemy. I would rather have faced Harry Polwart a thousand times.

'I have little more to say,' said Hector Faa, slowly dropping his words as if with an effort to choose Ihem aright. 'Let the young man to whom I confide this maiden, whom I—love as a daughter— stand forward.'

But here Joyce, at last evading his restraining hand, rose and threw her arms about his neck. And as she hid her face in his breast, he continued, looking at me, 'I can trust this young man. I think he loves her truly.'

He paused a moment with a bitter smile, gently disengaging her arms. Then he took her hand and put it in mine. It was chill and trembled.

'Though, had the thing been possible, I know not but I would have preferred to confide her to the lad's father, my most ancient enemy!'

It was a doubtful conclusion enough, though in full accordance with the character of the man.

So there I stood, with Joyce's hand in mine, striving for speech; yet speech would not come to me till Joyce herself, the wiser and braver of us two, pressed my hand and spoke out before them all:

'None of you know Maxwell Heron as I know him! Not one of you can know him; no, not his own father! It is easy for men to ride here and there killing and cutting and shooting; but to treat an outlaw's daughter as if she were a great lady.'

'So she is,' smiled my father.

'But he did not know it—even if it be true! No! I will not be stopped, even by you, sir. To be thoughtful and tender as a woman, brave as any man, to be as ready to dare all for me as to give up his most cherished purposes to please me, few women find these things. And I have found them!'

'Thank you, Joyce,' I said; 'from my heart I thank you! I do not deserve these words, gentlemen, but from this day I will try.'

'No, of course you do not deserve them, you rascal !' cried my father, who for some reason was in high good humour; 'an angel from heaven would not deserve all that. But (here he advanced towards Joyce with a thick roll of papers between his fingers) I am permitted by your guardian to have the honour of first saluting you as the Lady Joyce, in your own right Viscountess Tredennis !'

'Thank Heaven!' I murmured in her ear. 'I feared you would be a duchess at least!'

'With regard to the estates,' he continued, 'I understand that they are administered by the Court of Chancery pending the establishment of your claims. As to the title, we are likely to have trouble with the next of kin.'

As my father spoke, the tall, drover-like man, with the six-days beard bristling black all over his face, who had been sitting on a stump in profound abstraction, threw away his cigarette, and, advancing with much deliberation, saluted the company in the military manner.

'I have not been able to avoid overhearing parts of your conversation, owing to the fact that you have chosen the limit of my parole for your conference. But let me introduce myself as Captain Austin Tredennis,

392

of Ligonier's Horse. My dear cousin, I salute and congratulate you! I shall claim cousinly privileges later, when—ah!—when I have the good fortune to encounter a razor. Meantime, I can assure you, madam, as your sole relative on this side of Hades, that you will have no opposition from me, but on the contrary every assistance in the establishment of your claims.'

He looked round him with hearty kindness on his face, but even as he spoke his countenance changed. His quick ear, accustomed to military sounds, had caught something we could not distinguish, and the next moment the ground was shaken with a tremendous report. Fragments of boughs and shivered wood were dashed everywhere, and the black, mossy earth was splashed in our faces.

'Great God!' he cried, 'where is Marion? Pull down that flag! The troops have arrived and they are shelling the camp!'

CHAPTER FIFTY FIVE
TREDENNIS WAY OF MARRIAGE

It was true. The end had come upon us, and at a most unpropitious moment. How his Majesty's troops had arrived near without being seen by the watchers was a thing inexplicable, and seemed clearly to point to treachery somewhere.

The first shell had fallen down among the ashes of the watch-fires on the green in front of the Hollan Isle, scattering the turf and wounding two or three men who were preparing dinner, though, perhaps owing to the fact that the shell buried itself deeply before exploding, not very seriously in any case.

Then the scouts and messengers came pouring in. The enemy, it seemed, were advancing in two columns from opposite directions. The first, with more than one piece of considerable caliber, had evidently crossed at the shallows above the stepping-stones; while the other, taking up a strong position to the south, had occupied the long ridge of the Folds, driving in the little outpost on the Duchrae Craigs.

'There!' cried Tredennis, giving orders as if to his men, 'yonder comes another! Get into the trenches and lie down! Marion, do as I bid you!'

And, indeed, all of us except Silver Sand and his brother immediately took refuge in the deep trench which surrounded the main camp. I fairly dragged Joyce after me. The next projectile passed overhead with a hiss, and fell with a shattering crash on the poor little hut that had been Marion's headquarters, knocking it to pieces, and laying bare the pitiable makeshifts which Joyce had added from her experience of shielings and other temporary abodes among the hills.

Tredennis had taken refuge with the others; but with soldierly readiness he was out again, pointing to where the little puff of smoke still hung high above the rocky side of the Crae Hill.

'There they are—regular artillery, too,' he said. 'Now down with that flag! It is your only safety!'

And as he spoke he advanced to loosen the

halyards; but Hector Faa stepped in front with a sneer upon his dark face.

'You are, as I understand, a prisoner on parole,' he said. 'Be good enough to remember your position, and let the flag alone.'

'Is it the flag you fight under?' said Tredennis, as fiercely glancing aloft at the blue St. Andrew's cross, with the Levellers motto, 'A Free Land and a Free Folk,' embroidered across its folds. 'I think the skull and cross-bones would suit you better!' He muttered this below his breath. For he had all the soldier's hatred for the lurking outlaw who is likely to cost him more trouble than a dozen campaigns, without any equivalent honour attaching either to his killing or capture.

Nevertheless Tredennis restrained his temper, and pointed out to Hector Faa that it was impossible to hold out for a single day in the camp, which was, indeed, obviously at the mercy of a force with artillery planted on the heights of the Crae.

Meanwhile Silver Sand also whispered almost incessantly in his brother's ear. Marion strode to and fro, seeing that the men were in the best places for protection. But her heart was black and bitter within her.

'These are the men whom I have buoyed up with false hopes!' she thought. 'Their forfeited lives will lie at my door—all honest lads, simple and easily led! Oh, if I could save them how gladly would I give my life!'

More than once Tredennis warned her to get to cover. But she broke from him, crying, 'Let me die, I have been the ruin of all these! Why should I live?'

Then the soldier, his eye ever on the opposite slopes of the hill, from which, through the chill, thin-dropping snow-veil came ever and anon the red tongue of fire, saw the little white cloud of smoke, and heard then the answering roar, hiss, and explosion as the shell buried itaelf in the earthworks of the camp wood.

Though the thing was now quite feasible, escape did not once cross Tredennis's mind. He must get

395

Marion out of this wolf-trap first, and then; well, he would see.

Then, observing my father and Silver Sand in deep consultation, Tredennis stepped over to them and saluted.

'Gentlemen, this is going to be a mere butchery!' he began, abruptly. 'These men cannot resist either artillery or a bayonet charge any more than a flock of sheep in a pen. I know well what his Majesty's soldiers will do. Whatever his faults may be, Collinson is a soldier, and he will move round to the right and gradually shut you in. Then he will attack the camp with the bayonet under cover of his artillery from the opposite heights. Now I see the northward road is still open. If there is a vigorous resistance to the south and east for half an hour Collinson will be delayed. More than that, it is probable that the firing of the cannon will bring down the snow. In either case, the troops may wait till morning, or at least give sofficient time to draw the men off. That is their only chance. Let the poor fellows slip away to the north and scatter each to his own hiding-place. I do not think there would be any very eager pursuit, and certainly no killing unless they are taken with arms in their hands.'

'And the women?' said my father. 'We cannot have two girls out all night in a snow-storm, or left to the mercy of some hundreds of victorious soldiers!'

The minister of Balmaghie had come up during this colloquy.

'There is a good boat at the Rhone Foot,' he suggested, 'the ferryboat, good for a dozen, at a pinch. And I never saw the night so dark that I could not undertake to conduct them there—ay, and steer you down the river, too! Then, when we arrive at the manse, the ladies can wait till the morning. Or your two horses are there, and those in the chiefest danger can ride on without loss of time out of reach of any pursuit.'

'I will speak to my brother,' said Silver Sand, going over to Hector, who remained by the flag-staff, to all appearance entirely immoved. They whispered awhile together.

'I will do it,' he said, nodding gravely, after a pause for consideration. And instantly summoning his men with the silver call, he made his way towards the rapidly approaching enemy through the thick brush which sheltered the camp upon the south and east

It was not long before the rattle of musketry was heard, and Austin Tredennis heaved a sigh.

'If old Fitzgeorge is there, that should be enough to stop him for the night; that is, if he has a farm kitchen to use as headquarters. The mischief is that, after all, it may be Collinson. In that case I stand a chance of finding my back to a wall and a firing party six paces to my front.'

In a few seconds Silver Sand, passing from group to group, had communicated the intelligence to the Levellers that further resistance was hopeless. Indeed, from the moment when the first puff of smoke upon the Crae Hill had told that the troops had artillery with them, the end had been self-evident.

But just then the long-threatening snow-cloud, whether brought down by the heavy firing or no, at last descended, and in five minutes all the Duchrae Wood was filled with the scattering white particles, eddying and chasing each other like kittens at play. There was no wind, and the fall was so steady that soon the Crae Hill waa blotted out. The shaggy, heathnry summits, along which in the greenish gloom the red flashing of the assailants' muskets could be clearly seen, were also lost in the storm. Then nearer at hand the lithe defenders, darting from clump to clump and from copse to copse, were also diut out of view. And the heart of Austin Tredennis grew lighter and lighter with each successive disappearance, and as the firing waxed fainter the Spanish tobacco of his cigarette seemed appreciably to improve in quality.

By this time those of us whose duty it was to accompany Joyce and Marion were ready to make our first attempt. The men of the Levellers who were not actively employed with Hector's men in repelling the fury of the enemy's attack were already stealing away

397

through the hazels along the water-side towards the Raider's Bridge, from this place it was easy for them to scatter over the wild and trackless moor which extends for thirty miles in almost every direction from the Flowe of Mossdale. All was going well for the successful evacuation of the camp.

But there was yet Marion to be reckoned with.

Tredennis went up to her, as she stood with a kind of angry desperation on her face. The soldier looked so alert, so strong and purposeful, that a quick, jealous anger was kindled within her. It came easily in these days.

'I suppose you are glad,' she lashed the words upon him like a weapon, 'glad that your soldiers will butcher these poor fellows, who have done no wrong to you or any mortal!'

'If the poor fellows only do as I advise them,' he answered, calmly, 'I do not think that one of them will be killed, except by accident.'

And he pointed out to the girl the groups of ten and a dozen already white from head to foot with the falling snow, stealing away towards the Hollan Isle and the bridgehead.

Then, as they stood and watched, there came clear from the north the rattle of musketry, and a crying of huzzas which did not come from the lips of the defenders. There was something disciplined even in the sound. Tredennis's face flamed. The combat was certainly coming nearer.

'I fear Hector Faa's men are falling back. It may be Collinson, after all. You must leave immediately!'

The girl shook her head.

'No!' she said, decidedly, 'I will stay! It has been all my fault! I brought them to this, and I will not run from the consequences!'

Tredennis bit his lip to repress a desire to shake her.

'Will you not go if I tell you it is best both for you and for all these that you should not be taken?'

Marion still shook her head.

'Listen!' he cried, impetuously. 'Once for all I promise you that I will see all your Levellers safe out of this trap before I go! I know what the soldiers will do, and the plans that have been formed. I have nothing to do with these gypsies and outlaws, or they with me. But if you will do as I say I promise you lie lives of your Levellers—every man of them! You know you can trust me to keep my word. Now will you go?'

'I cannot!' she said, sadly and fixedly.

The angry blood flamed in Tredennis's face. He caught her fiercely by the arm.

'But I bid you! You shall go!'

'Indeed!' she said, looking up at him with something strange in her eyes. 'And pray what do you propose to do? To come with me?'

'I shall wait till every Leveller is clear out of this slaughter-pea,' he said, 'then I shall go straight out yonder to my comrades!'

'Ah, to your friends!' sneered Marion. 'And pray what will happen then? Perhaps you will set them on our track?'

'I shall tell the truth to the general,' he said. The girl never once took her eyes off his face.

'In every particalar?' she inquired, in a low voice that was almost a whisper. 'About, about me?'

'Yes, about you,' he said, strongly and firmly, 'you and myself!'

'And what will happen then?' Now her voice came fast and faltering.

'I shall probably be tried by court-martial and shot for treason!' he said, looking at her full in the eyes.

Marion gasped. A little, sharp cry rose in her throat

'No!' she exclaimed, catching him swiftly and fiercely in her anas, 'you shall not! Come with us, with me! We will go away somewhere! I will obey you! I love you! I never meant to tell yon, but I love you!'

Tredennis canght her in his arms for a moment. A kindly swirl of the snow shielded them.

'If I come safely through this, you will marry me?' he questioned.

'I will do anything, anything you wish, only come!'

Tredennis then took the girl by the arm, and led her over to the party who were waiting to set out for the Rhone Foot of Dee, under the guidance of the minister.

'Marion has promised to marry me,' he said. 'I have only a moment, but I want to make certain. I understand that it is the law of this country that we can be married by making a simple declaration. We have here a justice of the peace and a minister of the gospel. Is it not so?'

'For myself I decline, without proper cause shown, to be a party to any irregular and hasty marriage!' said the minister, firmly.

'I would not ask it, sir, for myself,' said Tredennis. 'But slip-knots do not hold this young lady, as perhaps you know. Marion, are you willing to be my wife?'

'I am,' said Marion, simply. Her hand was still in the strong, imperious grasp of the captain of horse.

'And I, Austin Cavendish Tredennis, declare myself your husband before these witnesses,' said the soldier. 'I understand that that is sufficient?' he added, addressing the minister.

'It is certainly binding!' assented Mr. Macmillan, reluctantly, 'but if either of you were a member of my denomination I would introduce you to the stool of repentance!'

'Then, by Heaven, you shall obey me now!' Tredennis exclaimed, swiftly stooping and kissing the girl. Marion of the Isle stood silent and apparently incapable of speech.

'Go with them,' he commanded, 'and if I win through with life and credit I will come and claim you. But I will not have you own a man as your husband who has dishonoured his name among his fellows. Good-bye, Marion.'

And Marion went with us without a word.

CHAPTER FIFTY SIX
THE CHIEF SAVES THE CLAN

After the way-going of the party for the Rhone Foot under the charge of Mr. Macmillan, nothing could have been more melancholy than the aspect of the camp in the Duchrae Wood. It was not dark with the darkness of night, but a heavy oppression of yellow frost fog weighed down everything. The combat to the north had died away in random splutterings of musketry. The snow sifted down thicker and thicker over all the face of the hill country. The dead leaves fell with a melancholy rustle as the flakes accumulated and bore them down.

The officer in charge of the troops on the eastern side retired his men; but from the hidden breast of the Crae Hill a random shell still came at intervals, not wholly inaccurately, for, in spite of the mist, the gun still preserved its general direction. But, owing probably to some deflection in recoil, most of the shells, falling short, plumped into the darker waters of the Grenoch Lane, or exploded harmlessly among the whins and brambles of the Hollan Isle. Hector Faa stood gloomily by the staff from which the Levellers' flag still drooped, now scarce visible in the slow, downward sift of the snow. Silver Sand busied himself in going to and fro, overseeing the escape of the last remnant of the Levellers in the direction of the bridge.

As before, Tredennis sat on a stump and smoked placidly. He said nothing, but wondered how far Marion and the others had proceeded on their journey, and who was the idiot in charge of that gun on the Crae Hill. He ought to be cashiered, Tredennis thought. Then he looked at his watch. It was little past one o'clock of the day, though the temporary snow-darkness had made it seem like the approach of night.

Hector Faa strode towards him as he sat rolling his cigarette.

'Your friends are over there,' he said, with bitter quiet; 'you had better go to them!'

'I have not been released from my parole,' said Tredennis, curtly.

'Then I release you!' said Hector Faa, abruptly. 'I command here! Go! and quickly! We do not want you here!'

'If I do go,' said Tredennis, suddenly exasperated at the outlaw's tone, 'it shall be to my comrades over there!'

He indicated the direction of the Crae Hill, from which still came the dull roar and plunge of the random shell. 'And if I go,' he added, boldly, 'I promise you I shall do better for you than that!'

'Go to the devil, if you like!' cried Hector, fiercely. 'Do anything you choose, tell anything you know! But rid us of your presence, and at once! Do you hear?'

There was hatred, instinctive and overpowering, between the two men.

Tredennis rose to his feet.

'I will go!' he said. 'But remember, I take you at your word! I go without conditions! If what you say is true, I am under no obligations to you. You have kept my cousin out of her name and rights for twenty years!'

'Ah!' said Hector, with a cold sneer, 'you were the next of kin, I am informed! I can understand your disappointment! I dare say you would have had no objections if I had kept her out of her inheritance altogether!'

Tredennis looked the outlaw full in the face. He was, of course, wholly unarmed

'You lie, and know it!' he said, curtly.

Hector Faa laughed a short laugh, in which, however, there was more of respect than he had yet shown for Tredennis.

'I can trust you,' he said. 'You may go to your friends when you will, you will tell them nothing. I understand such men as you!'

'You mistake,' said the other. 'I may indeed tell nothing, but I shall do as I am bidden! And I warn you that I shall use my own best endeavours to rid the country of such a gang of desperadoes as you and

402

your friends!'

Hector Faa pointed over the trenches, which were now held in force by his own following.

'There lies your way,' he said; 'you have five minutes' law! For that space none shall harm you. But if we come across you in an hour at the head of your redcoats; why, then, you may be reminded that you have given the lie direct to Hector Faa!'

'You can never be so mad as to propose holding such a place as this against King's troops?' cried Tredennis, in amazement.

'That, sir, is for you to'find out!' retorted Hector, coolly. 'I came here for my own pleasure, and I do not leave it for yours. Meantime, yonder lies your way! Make use of your five minutes!'

And he turned his back upon Tredennis, and walked again to the flag-staff, against which he leaned in thought, wrapped in his cloak, while the snow drifted ever the deeper over camp and trenches, and on the rugged back country where his Majesty's troops, with infinite bad language, torn hands, and small clothes, bivouacked, as they waited for orders, among patches of bramble and stunted thorn.

Tredennis stepped coolly down the glacis of the camp, he scrambled up out of the ditch and stood a moment on the opposite slope.

'You have given me my liberty and five minutes' he said; 'in return I give you two hours. That is ample time to have every man out of the camp and in safe hiding beyond Dee Bridge. After that, if I find you here; well, look to yourself, Hector Faa!'

But the outlaw, leaning against the pole of the Levellers' flag, his watch in one hand, did not even deign to reply. He simply motioned Tredennis contemptuously away with the other.

Left to himself Hector Faa stood a long while moodily musing, revolving what dark thoughts we may imagine, but cannot know, till from the riverside his brother came up in haste, and with more agitation manifest on his countenance than was customary with one naturally so sedate and reticent of emotion as Silver Sand.

403

'These poor Leveller lads have won through,' he said, 'but it was narrow indeed. The last of them had to hide while a patrol passed by. The dragoons are riding all across the country. The infantry on the Folds ridge may attack at any moment. If you want to escape, or get the clan clear off, it must be at once. Their ceasing fire was only a ruse. Keep such men by you as you can rely on to the death, and let the others go. With half a dozen you could hold the soldiers back long enough to let the rest reach the bridge. Unless you do that, not a soul will escape.'

Hector laughed a low and scornful laugh.

'And you, my elder brother, so full of excellent advice, what will you do?'

'I will stay with you.'

'What?' cried Hector Faa, suddenly, 'you would not leave me like the others?'

'No,' said Silver Sand, calmly, 'you and I have brought the clan here to do our business. It is your business and mine to get them away in safety—with our lives if need be!'

Hector Faa went over and took his brother's right hand in both of his.

'After all, you are the chief!' he said.

And the outlaw kissed the thick ring of ancient workmanship which Silver Sand wore.

'Now bid the clan go,' said Silver Sand, assuming the command; 'we have not many minutes.'

Hector Faa blew his silver call once more, and at the summons the men came tumbling up out of the trenches and in from the outer posts.

'Lads,' said Hector, 'this is the end, for the present, at least. Make your way up the waterside towards the Dungeon. Do not attempt to keep together. If I do not follow in three days, lift the hearth-stone of the Shiel, and divide fair and equally all you find there. It is yours. Hector Faa will be dead, for he will not be taken alive. Then let each man shift for himself. Then make for different seaport towns and get abroad at once. Do not tarry by the way, or you are lost Good-bye, my brother! I, and I alone, will keep them back, till such time as you shall have crossed the bridge. You have been brave lads, and true to the blood of Egypt. Farewell!'

Then Grice Baille fell down before him, and caught Hector Faa by the knees.

'Let me stay, master,' he pleaded, in his thick utterance. 'Send the others away, but let me stay!'

But Hector, having set his hand a moment kindly on the surly man's shoulder, bade him join his companions, in a tone that brooked no questioning. But as they went down the road Grice looked ever back over his shoulder, and the tears ran down his cheeks.

'They are coming!' said Silver Sand, in a low voice, peering over the parapet of the camp. 'I can hear them fixing bayonets!'

And for the first time in nearly thirty years the brothers shook hands, as it seemed, almost fiercely.

When Austin Tredennis went down the glacis of the camp in the Duchrae bank, he never thought of being in that hated and hateful spot again. But fate ruled otherwise. Before the final darkness of that long October night closed in he had come back. And this is how it happened:

He marched straight to the top of the little hill called Mount Pleasant, and, crying his name and holding up his hands, he surrendered there to the sergeant and half a dozen men who held it. But these, having no knowledge of Tredennis's mission, scoffed at the idea of an officer in his Majesty's service masquerading in the guise of a cattle-drover. That is, among themselves, for there was that upon Tredennis's face which prevented the bravest man of them from choosing that day to take a liberty with him.

'Who commands here?' he demanded of the sergeant.

'General Fitzgeorge, sir, in person.'

'I thought so' said Tredennis. 'Well, send a man with me. I must go to him at once. I have information which he must hear.'

The sergeant was on the point of making some objection, but gave way before Austin's imperious manner.

The general's headquarters were in the little farmhouse of Duchrae, where, while his staff made itself as little uncomfortable as possible about the outhouses, the general had already succeeded in making himself agreeable to the pretty housewife. Mistress Dickie, wife of Richard, a rank Leveller, presently safe in hiding among the moss hags of the Orchar.

'Good Lord! what have we here?' cried the general, looking up in astonishment when the drover presented himself. 'Tredennis, by gad! ha, ha! Hey, captain, you are certainly not tricked out to take the eye of the ladies!'

And the illustrious general indulged in a burst of hearty laughter at the appearance of his former aide-de-camp.

'Well, what news do you bring? Out with it!' said the general. 'They are in strongish force, I hear. And the dogs fight rather well. I have not heard from Collinson up on the heights. But we can hear his old bundles of scrap-iron thundering away, so I suppose the earth is flying somewhere. Where do you come from, Tredennis?'

Captain Austin looked with a doubtful air at little Mistress Dickie, who was busy about the fireplace, thinking of her husband, and making ready the general's supper.

'I come from the Levellers' camp, sir. May I speak with you a moment alone?' said Tredennis, gravely.

'Tut, tut, no necessity, no necessity that I see!' said the general, getting on his legs, however, and leading the way into the lower room, where several young officers were playing at cards. These they shuffled hastily together and thrust out of sight as the general entered.

'Get out, young men!' said General Fitzgeorge, courteously. And in a moment Austin and he were alone together.

'Well, quick with it!' said the general. 'What have you discovered?'

'I have a communication to make to you, General Fitzgeorge,' said Austin, 'which will probably cause you to put me under arrest, and possibly have me shot against the nearest wall. I have broken my oath as an officer, and do not deserve to be a moment longer a soldier of the King!'

'Gad!' said the general, 'this is curious. Most of us might have said as much in our time. But hang me if we would run to our general with the news; no, blood me if we would! Well, who's the woman? What? What? Out with it?'

Then, as concisely as possible, Tredennis recounted the whole story of his love for Marion, his double breach of duty in liberating her and Joyce Faa, and his true motives for going as a spy to the camp. He told him how through his own folly he had been trapped, and, finally, that before returning he had arranged and carried out the escape of Marion, and most of the Levellers from the camp.

The general whistled thoughtfully while Tredennis was speaking.

'And so you wish to be put into irons, or had out against a wall and shot, do you?' he chuckled, his little grey eyes twinkling from an acreage of red face as he spoke.

'I am quite willing to undergo any punishment you may think necessary, general,' answered the captain of horse.

'Much good that would do the young woman; a pretty one, too, as ever I saw, by gad! reminds me of Lady Betty Trippet a friend of mine, ha! Tredennis. That was what I was trying to tell her when you were so confoundedly hot that night in prison. Well, after all, I like to see a man ready to go to the devil for a woman—yes, blood me if I don't! Didn't think you had it in you, Tredennis, I didn't, indeed! What's that—oh, come in, will you?'

It was Ensign Gunter, who stood in the doorway of the little room.

'Oh, general,' he'cried, breathlessly, 'two deserters who have just come in say that they can lead us right into the heart of the camp without firing

407

a shot, but that the last defences will be a hot push. They are held not by Levellers, as we supposed, but by the wild gypsies from the hills. Hector Faa and his gang, outlaws every man, who will fight to the death! What are we to do, sir?'

'Ham—bam!' said the general, considering. 'Now there is your chance, Tredennis! Take that camp. These fellows will show you the way. And when you have done it, if you get oat alive; why, come to me. I shall have something in my pocket for you, and we will say nothing more about the little affairs of the heart you have mentioned to me.'

For in certain elements of generous forgetfulness. General George Fitzgeorge could be entirely regal.

Hector Faa and Silver Sand stood together and looked over their armament. They had six or seven muskets, besides nearly as many pistols, while each of them wore a cutlass and sheath-knife. Of ammunition there was enough and to spare.

'Do you take the right, Hector, with the three best guns. You were ever the marksman!' said Silver Sand, as calmly as though he had been arranging the field for a day's shooting on the moors. 'I will guard the waterside with two muskets and the pistols. The range will be shorter there.'

And the younger brother, whose word had been law in the clan for thirty years, obeyed his senior without a murmur.

There was an uncanny quietness all along the outer lines, now mostly untenanted. Over the long, snowy ridges to the south not a gun was fired from the enemy. Even the field-piece from the hill-side opposite had become dumb.

Suddenly, as they waited in a tense silence, there was heard a sound as of some one thrusting his way through the thick underbrush. Hector stood up in an attitude of supreme determination, his gun to his shoulder. His eye was already glancing along the barrel, and in another moment he would have fired, when Silver Sand, from his lower post, called him imperatively to stop. It was Grice Baillie, wild-eyed and panting, who stood before the two last defenders of the camp of the Levellers.

'The Bridge-head of Dee is held,' he stammered. 'I came back to tell you. The clan is turned. A full score of them cannot swim, and the Black Water is in flood. It will take half an hour to make floats of drift and rushes, can the enemy be kept back so long?'

'They must be kept back!' said Silver Sand, grimly, 'at any cost, they must be held. The chief must save the clan. It is our family law and gospel! Happily, neither you nor I are married men. Hector.'

Grice stood a moment uncertain, licking his lips and lingering uncertainly. His eye watched furtively for that of his master, like a dog that has done wrong and expects a kick.

At last he seized a musket, and plumped down behind the earthworks, midway between Hector and Silver Sand.

The former raised himself angrily, and ordered Grice Baillie back to the others who were making their escape.

'They can mak' their floats withoot me,' said Grice, sullenly, 'and mair nor that, I tell you plainly now that I am here, here I bide!'

Hector turned upon him with his gun pointed at the man's head.

'Grice!' he thundered, 'go, or I will shoot you like a dog!'

'Shoot awa'!' said Grice, and never budged. Yet he cowered, nevertheless, from his master's angry eye.

'Are you married, Grice?' asked Silver Sand, quickly.

'Na,' answered Grice, 'I never yet saw the woman I wad mairry!'

'Then, if you bide, you are little likely to see her now, Grice,' replied Silver Sand. 'We three are all bound for the other world—Hell, Purgatory, or Paradise, within the next half-hour, as our case may be!'

'Whilk ever ane your honours please!' said Grice Baillie, indifferently, and tested the loading of his

409

piece, listening carefully to the thud of the ramrod, and observing how far it descended in the barrel.

'I have not found so great faith; no, not in Israel!' quoted Silver Sand, with much solemnity. 'Let him stay. Hector!'

As Silver Sand said, they had not long to wait. From two sides the soldiers attacked sharply, and, so far as musketry was concerned, the besieged responded with vigour. The bullets buzzed overhead like bumblebees, clipping the snow-laden branches or burying themselves in die ground with vicious whisks. The light had grown somewhat clearer again, and the assailants were often quite distinct on the white ground as they scudded from cover to cover, coming ever nearer to the final defences.

Between every, half-dozen shots, Silver Sand looked at his watch.

'Will they be over the ford by now, think you, Grice?'

And Grice, intent upon his musket and pistol, would shake his head. He thought not yet. It was cumbersome getting so many across a river in flood.

At last the assailants came so near that all the outer trenches on both sides were in their hands. From the camp itself there was no escape possible now, but they might delay the rush till they had saved the fugitives.

'We cannot keep it up very much longer!' said Hector. 'They are on our flank—on our rear— everywhere!'

'Grice knows how long it will take,' said Silver Sand. 'Load away!'

And with fresh energy the besieged kept up their end of as warm an engagement as ever the attacking veterans of King George had experienced in Flanders.

'Surely they are over by now?' cried Hector, charging pieces that were hot to the muzzle.

'There's nae mair than time yet!' responded the inexorable Grice, taking aim at an officer who had incautiously exposed himself.

Hotter and hotter grew the fire of the enemy.

410

Presently the besieged experienced their first casualty. A bullet, striking first on a stone, hit Silver Sand on the left side, momentarily stunning him. But in a minute he was back at his post again.

'Surely another five minutes will do it now, Grice?' he asked, suppressing a groan.

The sullen man nodded.

'They will be clear by that; ay, every man o' them,' he acknowledged.

'Then let us hold the place for five minutes more,' said Silver Sand, 'for the sake of the women and bairns that are waiting for them.'

Suddenly Hector Faa cried out sharply.

'Here they come! Stand fast! I see their bayonets at the charge! Good-bye, John!'

'Good-bye, brother, good-bye, Hector.'

It was the first time the outlaw had called his brother by his first name for thirty years. There was no one to bid Grice Baillie farewell; but that silent man did not expect it. He only hugged his piece to his shoulder, and hoped he could, as he expressed it, 'Get yin first.'

They were coming; yes, coming in two divisions, overwhelming in numbers, in courage, in energy. On, on; over the wide-cleared space, crashing through the brush, down into the deep trench, up the face of the slope, men dropping singly in the ranks as the muskets of the defenders cracked. Then these were discarded, and they fell to with the pistols at short range.

'Come on,' cried Austin Tredennis, fiercely. 'There were only sixty of them in all,'

There were, however, somewhat fewer than this estimate. For Grice, the dour and faithful, had dropped forward in the act of discharging his last musket, a bullet through his forehead.

Hector Faa fired his final shot at Peter Kelly as he came up the glacis with Harry Polwart by his side. The blind gypsy felt his guide drop, but fell on his old chief, sword in hand, with a fierce shout of triumph.

'Ah, Hector, I am revenged! I have you at last!' he cried, as he clutched him by the neck.

'Ah! have you?' said Hector, grimly, driving a knife deep into his breast, one instant before he himself went down under the charge of a dozen bayonets.

Silver Sand fronted Tredennis full as, sword in hand, he sprang up the slope and over the last defence of earth and felled trees. His pistol was at the breast of his assailant before he could strike.

But he checked himself in the very pulling of the trigger, recognizing his opponent.

'Pass,' he said, smiling, 'for your wife's sake! I have none!'

And he fell forward upon his face.

The chief had saved the clan.

ADDEND AND COMPLEMENT

Letter from the Lady Marion Tredennis, wife of Major-General Sir Austin Tredennis, Governor of Prince Edward's Island, Nova Scotia, New Brunswick, and the various English Settlements on the River Saint Lawrence, to Mr. Maxwell Heron, younger, of Orraland and Isle Rathan, in the County of Galloway:

'My Honoured Friend, Indeed it will be a disappointment to you to receive no more than this from me in answer to your detailed and very accurate history. Austin has read it, but I do not think that his criticisms and objections can be considered either pertinent or particularly valuable. They consist chiefly of desires, I vigorously expressed in the military manner, that you should excise all references to himself or his doings. He also is of opinion that it is not dignified to represent a governor's lady as going about clad—in fact, he objects to the 'breeches parts'—moreover, he thinks that since I was fortunate enough to be included in the general amnesty and pardon proclaimed by government, all these things had better be forgotten. However, as you are not his wife, you are able to please yourself in these matters.'

'I think, however, that you ought to mention that General Fitzgeorge was most kind in obtaining a free pardon for the poor fellows, as he was also instrumental (through his personal connection with the King) in promoting Austin to his present lucrative post. You will be glad to know that we have been able to settle the families sent out (one hundred and seventy in all) on the newly annexed lands, and that most of them appear to be on the high road to comfort and a moderate fortune. The sole exceptions have been the gypsies of Hector Faa's band, who have mostly wandered off south into the New England settlements, where they have taken once more to their natural pursuits of cattle-dealing (in a fairly legitimate way), tinkering, fortune-telling, and horseshoeing.

'My dear love to Joyce and you all. I am very happy here, and the old ill time seems very far away

413

indeed. I send you a money-draft of a hundred pounds for my father and mother, though I know how comfortable and happy they are with you. If possible, buy them a strong, quiet beast that will carry them cantily to the kirk on fine Sundays, and my father to the market whether the day is fine or no.

'At present, farewell. I have promised to meet my husband, who is out shooting. The post-rider goes immediately—and, at any rate, I would not for the world disappoint Austin.

'Your friend and servant, 'Marion Tredennis.'

When this letter arrived, it wrought some considerable commotion in our little family in the old Tower of Rathan. Joyce had to take boat, and go over immediately to the cottage of Eppie and Sammle Tamson to tell them about their daughter's present, as well as to show the epistle of the governor's wife to my father and mother at Orraland.

Left alone with my contemned manuscript, I did not find the drastic excisions proposed by the eminent governor of Prince Edward's Island to be feasible. So Marion's part must remain intact, as I have written it, breeches and all. But presently my sister Grisel, wandering in and looking over the last chapters in her usual superior and off-hand manner, offered a criticism which seemed to me far more to the point.

'It is easy to be seen that you are a man,' she remarked, tossing down the heavy roll of paper that had been so far-travelled. 'You never say a word of your bringing Joyce and Marion home to Rathan, or how everything came to be as it is!'

Having delivered herself of this dictum, Grisel went out to render Jasper Jamie's life a burden to him. They are to be married as soon as Jasper enters upon his appointment under his Majesty's Board of Customs, where (entirely through influence) he will presently find himself the senior and official chief of Mr. Inspector (late Superintendent) Craig, who has only spent his entire lifetime in the service.

Now I cannot take Grisel's very offhand advice;

414

for this, among other weighty reasons, that the book is too long already.

Moreover, after I have written of the end of the oldest and most faithful friend of our house. Silver Sand, I do not feel that I can speak much of things light and comfortable. The grass is green again on the Duchrae bank, and over the graves which hide the reunited brothers and the stubborn faithfulness of Grice Baillie.

Beneath the Grenoch Lane is deep and silent and mysterious as ever, and the nuts have many times formed and ripened and been gathered upon the Hollan Isle. It is a place where, in life Silver Sand loved to set up his encampment, and now that he is dead, I cannot think that he is wholly unconscious of the fitness of his resting-place.

I spoke to my father about some monument to him, but he did not encourage the idea.

'He would not have liked it, I know,' he replied, very thoughtfully, 'and Maxwell, what end would it serve? His monument is here! I shall never be the same man again.'

And as he spoke he laid his hand upon his heart.

And neither, I think, has he ever been, for Silver Sand was his one friend. But my mother is bright and sprightly as ever, and all, save the sour-natured and the ill-hearted (two classes not wholly unknown in Galloway) speak well of her.

And Joyce, I write of her last. For I know she will not permit me to say much. But this I will set down, that she has stood the greatest tests of character, prosperity and happiness together.

Fair she is still as she was by the window of the Dungeon Shieling. Perhaps the dark curls lie a trifle smoother on her head. There is a more matronly graciousness and housewifeliness; which, indeed, seems to enter a room along with her. But as of old, in the deeps of her glorious eyes lie hid yet greater and more passionate possibilities of love, unselfishness, and sacrifice.

Samuel Rutherford Crockett (author)

Born in Balmaghie on September 24th 1859, Samuel Crocket was the illegitimate son of dairy maid Annie Crocket. He was brought up on the farm of Little Duchrae by his strict Cameronian maternal grandparents, and the family moved to Castle Douglas in 1867. He gained a Galloway bursary to Edinburgh University in 1876. His writing career began as a way to support himself through his studies. He had articles and short stories/sketches published in a wide range of contemporary magazines. He travelled abroad extensively and became a Free Church minister in 1886. He married Ruth Milner in 1887 and they had four children. His writing became successful following the publication in 1893 of 'The Stickit Minister' and he gave up the ministry to concentrate on his writing in 1895. His popular, episodic and serialised style of writing ensured him bestseller status in his day and despite prolonged ill health he published on average 2 novels a year throughout his long career. He died on April 16th 1914 in France.

Cally Phillips (editor)

Brought up and educated in Dundee and Edinburgh, Cally is a graduate of St Andrews University and worked professionally as a screenwriter and playwright for twenty years before shifting focus towards creative advocacy. Cally was first introduced to the work of S.R.Crockett when she moved to Galloway in 1995, where she was Writer in Residence for three years (2002-2004). Over the past decade she has set up and run a variety of innovative creative projects. She now lives in North East Scotland where as well as being series editor for Ayton Publishing, she also reviews, edits and writes fiction and non fiction.

Ayton Publishing Limited

The 32 Volumes in this collection represent those of Crockett's published fictional work for adults which feature Galloway as a central component of the narrative. There are more works by Crockett for children and also for adults with a variety of settings. We hope to publish these in separate collections in the years to come

If you are interested in finding out more about S.R.Crockett and Galloway as portrayed in his works you can join The Galloway Raiders for free. There is a website with a host of interesting and informative material and special offers on publications for members.

Join now at www.gallowayraiders.co.uk

For more information about Ayton Publishing please visit our website www.aytonpublishin.co.uk

The Galloway Collection

Republished to commemorate the 100th Anniversary of the Death of S.R.Crockett on April 16th 1914 and available in paperback and ebook format, The Collection is listed below with dates of first novel publication.

Volume 1 The Black Douglas (1899)
Volume 2 Maid Margaret (1905)
Volume 3 Men of the Moss Hags (1895)
Volume 4 Lochinvar (1897)
Volume 5 The Standard Bearer (1898)
Volume 6 The Cherry Ribband (1905)
Volume 7 The Raiders (1894)
Volume 8 The Dark o' the Moon (1902)
Volume 9 Silver Sand (1914)
Volume 10 The Moss Troopers (1912)
Volume 11 The Smugglers (1911)
Volume 12 The Banner of Blue (1903)
Volume 13 The Stickit Minister (1893)
Volume 14 Lilac Sunbonnet (1894)
Volume 15 Bog Myrtle (1895)
Volume 16 A Galloway Herd (1895)
Volume 17 Lad's Loves (1897)
Volume 18 The Stickit Ministers Wooing (1900)
Volume 19 Love Idylls (1901)
Volume 20 Cleg Kelly (1896)
Volume 21 Kid McGhie (1906)
Volume 22 Kit Kennedy (1899)
Volume 23 Strong Mac (1904)
Volume 24 The Dew of Their Youth (1909)Volume 25 Cinderella (1901)
Volume 26 The Loves of Miss Anne (1904)
Volume 27 Vida (1907)
Volume 28 Rose of the Wilderness (1909)
Volume 29 Sandy's Love (1913)
Volume 30 Mad Sir Uchtred of the Hills (1894)
            And The Play Actress (1894)
Volume 31 The Bloom o' the Heather (1908)
Volume 32 Raiderland (1904)